## "You're pregnant!"

Her face turned bright red. "Yes," she said through gritted teeth.

Lexie had slept with someone else. The room tilted. Lexie had slept with another man.

"I'm sorry you had to learn about it this way," Lexie said. "I wasn't sure how to tell you."

"How could you do this to me?" He'd be the laughingstock of his Hot Shot crew, of every crew and support group from Montana to Arizona—if he wasn't already. Had Lexie left him for this guy?

"I didn't mean for this to happen, but it doesn't change anything between us."

"You've been walking around like...like...*that* for months, haven't you? And everyone in town knows you're pregnant."

"Probably."

Jackson rubbed his sleep-deprived eyes. "Who is he, Lex? Who did this to us?"

Lexie's mouth dropped open, then she narrowed her eyes at him and said, "You did, you idiot."

Dear Reader,

This year I will celebrate twenty years of marriage to the same man. But don't look to me for marital advice. Sometimes I wonder how we made it, given several cross-country moves, job changes, financial challenges, kids, kittens and puppies. One thing I do know—we're not the same two people who held hands and recited vows so long ago. We've grown and we've changed.

Lexie and Jackson Garrett are high school sweethearts who marry young. Jackson chases his dream of becoming a Hot Shot fireman—fighting wildland fires from Alaska to Florida. Holding down the home front alone for months at a time, Lexie faces a different set of challenges. It's not life or death, but it's still survival. Despite loving Jackson deeply, Lexie can't handle facing another family crisis alone. Unwilling to settle for a relationship that is less than what she deserves, Lexie asks for a divorce.

When Jackson realizes he's not immortal, when he understands what he's lost, when he finally starts to *change*, he heads straight home to Lexie with one goal in mind…getting married again.

I hope you like Lexie and Jackson's story. I'd love to hear from you. You can contact me at P.O. Box 150, Denair, CA 95316 or through my Web site at www.MelindaCurtis.com. Enjoy!

*Melinda Curtis*

# Getting Married Again
## Melinda Curtis

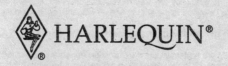

HARLEQUIN®

TORONTO • NEW YORK • LONDON
AMSTERDAM • PARIS • SYDNEY • HAMBURG
STOCKHOLM • ATHENS • TOKYO • MILAN • MADRID
PRAGUE • WARSAW • BUDAPEST • AUCKLAND

ISBN 0-373-71187-5

GETTING MARRIED AGAIN

Copyright © 2004 by Melinda Wooten.

This edition published by arrangement with Harlequin Books S.A.

® and TM are trademarks of the publisher. Trademarks indicated with ® are registered in the United States Patent and Trademark Office, the Canadian Trade Marks Office and in other countries.

Visit us at www.eHarlequin.com

**Printed in U.S.A.**

With much love and thanks to…

My husband and kids,
who have learned this year—through trial and error—
how to work the toaster, microwave and iron.

Michael Rhodes, Nicki Amburn and Rick Priest, for sharing
Hot Shot and base camp stories, maps, nicknames and
information. Any mistakes are mine alone.

Those who keep the home fires burning
while their loved ones are away putting out fires—
whether out on a fire line or away at the office.

And finally,
to the brave men and women who fight wildland fires,
who risk their lives to "face the dragon"
without much more in return than personal satisfaction
and a paycheck as they protect our homes and
national treasures. You are an inspiration.

Those who have fallen will not be forgotten.

**Books by Melinda Curtis**

**HARLEQUIN SUPERROMANCE**
1109—MICHAEL'S FATHER

Don't miss any of our special offers. Write to us at the
following address for information on our newest releases.

Harlequin Reader Service
U.S.: 3010 Walden Ave., P.O. Box 1325, Buffalo, NY 14269
Canadian: P.O. Box 609, Fort Erie, Ont. L2A 5X3

## PROLOGUE

DRIVEN BY THE WHIPPING WIND, roaring flames made torches of the drought-dry trees on the ridge. Jackson Garrett could feel the heat increase as a wall of fire advanced toward him. Embers shot into the air like Fourth of July rockets, blossoming into flame as they hit the earth.

Ignoring the sweat trickling down his face, Jackson turned to watch the progress of the ground fire, which crept slowly up the steep slope in the direction of him and his crew. The panicked voices on the hand-held radio crackled in his ear over the building snarl of the fire. The words were in Russian and, although he'd been in Russia for nearly half a year, they were speaking too fast for Jackson to understand. Except he did understand.

They were dead.

Not yet, but it was only a matter of time. Ivan, Levka, Potenka, Breniv and Alek. Men he'd trained these past few months to fight forest fires the American way. Men he'd become fond of despite the language barrier and their reluctance to learn a method some bureaucrat figured would help the Russians stem their annual forest fire devastation.

What a joke. You needed equipment to fight fires—reliable equipment that wasn't salvaged from some war fought fifty or more years ago—and well-trained, well-conditioned men. His Russian team was shaping up, but they had little experience. The men worked sluggishly on the mountainside in the one-hundred-and-ten-degree heat of the fire. They fought without the fire-resistant protective gear that Jackson had taken for granted in the States. As for equipment, in this area of Siberia it included garden-variety shovels, a relic of an airplane that was supposed to be used to drop retardant on the fire—except that after months of fighting wildland fires there was no fire retardant left—and an antique fire truck with only two working gears, reverse and first—not much use in the mountains.

When Jackson had arrived in Russia and realized the limited experience and resources of the men he'd been assigned to, he'd laughed. A smart man would have filed a report with the government agency that sent him over and taken the first plane back to the States.

But then, most smart men didn't have a freshly signed divorce agreement tucked in their passport.

Jackson had nearly ten years' experience as a Hot Shot, one of an elite group of government firefighters trained to battle the hottest part of wildland fires. Hell, Jackson figured, he'd be able to teach his ragtag crew a thing or two about fighting forest fires. They had shovels, didn't they?

So he'd stayed, not yet ready to return home and smile at his Hot Shot buddies and hide the fact that his wife had blindsided him with a divorce, or fess up that he hadn't been able to sweet-talk his way back into their bed. That last night he spent in Silver Bend, Idaho, he'd told his best friend, Logan McCall, that he wouldn't have to sleep on Logan's couch again because his wife, Lexie, had called and wanted to meet him for dinner.

When Jackson met Lexie at that Boise restaurant more than six months ago, he'd been stupidly sure of himself—even after he'd signed the divorce papers and finessed Lexie into a motel room in Boise, convinced they'd rip the papers to shreds come morning. He was so confident they'd reconcile, he'd been thinking about how he'd brag to his buddies about Lexie's hot temper and how that made making up that much hotter—while she was putting her clothes back on and walking out on him for good.

"This was breakup sex. Nothing more," Lexie had pronounced, her eyes brimming with tears, the divorce papers clutched in one hand and the motel room door handle gripped in the other. "I didn't believe those empty promises of yours at dinner. I just had to…" Lexie paused, swallowed, blinked rapidly. "It was breakup sex," she reaffirmed before disappearing out of his life.

Now, Jackson wondered why Lexie had slept with him that night and why she'd been so upset about it afterwards. He remembered the first time he'd asked her out in high school. He'd given her some smooth line. He couldn't even remember now what it'd been. She'd laughed at him—after he'd spent weeks working up the nerve to ask her out—and told him he was full of hot air. She'd gone out with him anyway…after he'd asked her out three more times.

There was a joke. Soon, he'd be nothing but hot air, his body incinerated and smoldering. Lexie would cry for him when she found out, because she had a heart that was big enough to mourn an idiot like Jackson, even after she'd kicked him out of her life. It'd be harder on his little girl, Heidi. But Heidi had Lexie, and Lexie would support their daughter and love her no matter what. Heidi could count on Lexie.

According to Lex, Heidi couldn't count on him.

The idea that his family would go on without him held no comfort. Jackson swayed on the mountainside, suddenly feeling every ounce of the forty-plus pounds of gear he carried, as he realized how dispensable he was to Lexie and Heidi. He'd become just a voice on the other end of the telephone line, a house payment, medical coverage. He wanted his family back. Not that he was in a position to get them back now, caught between two fires halfway around the world. He didn't even have a way to call them and hear their voices one last time, to tell them how much they meant to him.

He'd been in tough spots before, but he'd always made it out. His Hot Shot crew back home nicknamed him Golden because they could always rely on him to get them out of sticky situations. Now he realized the reason he believed he'd make it was that Lexie had always been waiting for him.

She wasn't waiting for him anymore.

With his right hand, Jackson reached into his pocket and fingered the small medal Lexie had given him years ago. It was his good luck charm. No. That was wrong. Lexie was his good luck charm. Things just weren't the same without her in his life.

"Damn it," Jackson muttered, as the fire above him roared a challenge—*fight or die.* Time for him to stop moping and realize he needed to battle for the only woman he'd ever loved. He couldn't die now. Somehow, he'd screwed up his life, but he wouldn't go like this. He wouldn't leave Lexie and Heidi without trying to be a good husband and dad one more time. He'd figure out where he went wrong later, after he found a way out of the firestorm closing in on them.

Scowling, Jackson watched his team of trainees futilely attempt to complete the fire line he'd abandoned the moment he'd seen the fire peak the ridge. But with no chopper rescue possible, and no planes to drop a load of water to form an escape route, they were as good as crispy.

They needed a miracle.

Or a man who had to make it back home.

# CHAPTER ONE

"WELCOME TO SILVER BEND, Idaho, Population 770."

"Off by one," Jackson mumbled to himself from the driver's seat of his idling truck. Nobody had subtracted him from the sign when Lexie divorced him seven months ago and he'd gone to Russia to join a humanitarian aid party. Facing death there had made him realize he had a lot to live for.

Strike that. He had a lot to do over. Jackson just hoped that he'd be able to figure out where he went wrong, hoped Lexie would give him a second chance.

He recalled Lexie's face when she'd handed him the divorce papers that last night he'd spent in the States. Her shuttered, pale features so different from those of the vibrant, smiling girl he'd fallen in love with in high school. All those years ago, he'd won her heart and she'd followed Jackson everywhere, from one party to the next. Twelve years later, she didn't want to do any of the things they used to enjoy together. Toward the end, she wouldn't even go with him to hang out at the Painted Pony, the restaurant his mother owned. Not for the first time, Jackson wondered when Lex had changed.

How was he going to win her back when she didn't want anything to do with him?

If he turned left here, on Lone Pine Road, he'd be at his house in minutes. It was Lexie's now. He hadn't contested any of her requests. Why would he have? He hadn't thought she was serious about splitting up.

Since he'd fought his way out of the Russian fire, Jackson had wanted to come home to reclaim his family. As soon as he'd been able, he'd said goodbye to his comrades and hopped on the first plane back. He should just charge up the mountain, fall on his knees, promise her anything and beg her to take his sorry ass back.

Yet, he hesitated.

Trouble was, a severe case of groveling might not be enough for Lex. He needed something meaningful to say, something to sway her. He doubted "I had the crap scared out of me in Siberia and realized I can't live without you" would cut it.

And that's what held him back.

Jackson reached for the paper-wrapped bundle sitting on the seat beside him and fingered the handmade wool shawl—a gift for Lexie. Breniv, one of his Siberian fire-fighting trainees, had taken Jackson aside the day before he left for home. They had stood alone on a muggy, empty side street outside of the fire station, the laundry waving from windows high above the street.

"You bring gift for woman?" the burly Russian had asked in his broken English, dark bushy brows drawn low.

Jackson, who had said nothing about Lexie to anyone, had given Breniv a cool look and a curt "No." One of Jackson's reasons for hanging around his Russian counterparts rather than the other Americans was to avoid personal conversation, particularly about his marital status—about the plain gold wedding band he still wore.

Breniv ignored Jackson's off-limits demeanor. "Woman know you love, no?"

"No." Jackson shook his head and looked out on the sturdy brick buildings along the street, reminded of the ache in his heart.

"Here, we have way of showing love," Breniv persisted patiently, as if Jackson were a child. "You face death, you show love."

His words caught Jackson's attention, because that was exactly how he felt. Life was more fragile to him now. Love more precious. He wanted to be with the ones he loved.

"Yes." Breniv spoke as if reading Jackson's thoughts. He pressed a small packet into Jackson's hands. "Keep woman warm, she love you back."

Jackson carefully lifted the ends of plain folded paper, revealing a beautiful black shawl with pink roses that was made of the finest wool. Jackson had seen shawls like these in the market, had heard other American firefighters talk about the high prices of the handmade, hand-blocked shawls.

"Breniv, this is too expensive. I can't accept it."

But Breniv was already backing away, his expression solemn. "You save life."

"Not all of them." He couldn't accept the gift. Didn't Breniv realize Jackson had almost killed them all by taking them out to fight a forest fire when they were so ill-equipped? Fighting a fire without benefit of weather reports to predict the impact of strong winds or air support to monitor the progress of two converging fires was foolhardy at best. Fighting a fire without an escape route was plain-ass stupid.

They called Jackson a hero.

He was no hero.

While the flames had roared toward them, he'd made his team shore up two sides of a crevice carved naturally into the mountainside, not an easy task given the hard-packed forest soil. Only as the fire leapt closer did he see the look of terror in Alek's eyes. It was the young man's first summer fighting fire. Jackson doubted the rookie had ever seen a fire's rage mere yards away.

They'd crammed themselves like sardines into the grave they'd made and covered themselves with Jackson's fire shelter—a one-man tent made of silica, fiberglass and aluminum foil that reflected heat. Everyone jumped in, except Alek. The fire had passed over the men with heat so intense it blistered exposed skin.

Alek had not been so lucky.

By the time the vivid memories of crackling wood, unbearable heat and failure receded, and Jackson returned his attention to the humid street in Russia, Breniv was gone.

Now the shawl sat on the passenger seat next to Jackson as if holding a place for Lexie. The rest of the gifts he'd brought back were tucked into his backpack on the floorboard of his truck.

Who was he kidding? Gifts and groveling weren't enough to get her back. She wanted the one thing he'd been unable to give her—another child.

Jackson pulled onto the highway and headed into Silver Bend. He needed a beer before he decided what to say to Lex. Since it wasn't noon yet, a strong cup of coffee would have to do, and if that cup came with a bit of advice from his mom, so much the better. He could use all the help he could get.

As Jackson drove by the gas station, the attendant nodded in greeting while pumping gas into Marguerite's shiny new Cadillac. Marguerite Sterling, his mother's friend, craned her neck far enough in the direction of his passing truck that Jackson feared she'd knock her spine out of alignment again.

Jackson waved, somewhat comforted by the familiarity of it all.

Smiley Peterson tottered out of his client chair in the barbershop and pressed his bulbous nose to the glass when Jackson parked his truck on Main Street in front of his shop. The old man shuffled to the front door, opening it with a clang of the bell that Jackson had helped him install.

"Hey, Jackson, that you?" he called.

Jackson climbed out of his truck, working the kinks out of his body after sitting for so long. It took him a bit to answer, but Silver Bend was a quiet town where slow wasn't necessarily considered stupid.

"Yeah, Smiley. It's me." Jackson slung his backpack over one shoulder.

"Seen Lexie?" Smiley asked, not smiling. Jackson couldn't remember when he'd seen Smiley without his trademark toothless grin.

Ignoring the feeling of emptiness that hearing Lexie's name gave him, Jackson shook his head, pushing off his unease. Lexie was fine, he was sure.

Jackson gestured to Smiley's candy-striped barbershop pole listing dangerously to one side of the door. "How long has that sign been broken? Some fool will smack into it if they aren't watching where they're going."

"Blew loose in a summer storm a week or so ago."

"Got a screwdriver handy?" It wouldn't take but a few minutes to fix it.

Now Smiley grinned. "'Course I do."

The old barber leaned against the door frame while Jackson tightened the pole back into place. "Wanna shave that beard?"

"Naw." Jackson stroked the thick growth covering his cheeks and jaw. He hadn't shaved since he left home, hadn't had a haircut in months either. Besides, no one let Smiley near their hair anymore. He'd nearly taken off a little kid's ear a couple of years back because his eyesight was atrocious and his hands were too shaky. Now, he employed younger hairstylists in the afternoons and on weekends, but he still hung out all day in the shop.

"Shame. Goin' back soon?"

"I start back in two weeks." The Department of Forestry hadn't expected him to return for another five months, so there weren't any immediate job openings for a Hot Shot leader. His slot as superintendent of the Silver

Bend Hot Shots had been filled for the year by Logan. He'd been assured they'd find something for him in two weeks. In the meantime, they had granted his vacation request.

Bureaucrats may talk about budget cuts and downsizing, but when push came to shove, the Department of Forestry found the approvals and moneys necessary to keep valuable assets like Jackson on the ground where he could make the most difference.

An asset. That's how his boss at the Department of Forestry in Boise had referred to him this morning when Jackson explained that he was thinking about giving up firefighting.

There were fewer than one hundred Hot Shot superintendents in the United States, employed by various government agencies including the Department of Forestry. There were less than fifty with Jackson's tenure of service, and fewer than twenty who had served overseas. The Department of Forestry wanted Jackson back on the first line of defense against wildland fires—not exactly the ideal situation for a guy who broke into a sweat just remembering the feel of heat on his skin.

Jackson hadn't wanted to listen to his boss's protests, but he couldn't help himself. He was a second-generation Hot Shot. Fighting fires was in his blood. The last thing he wanted to do was quit. But what choice did a coward like him have?

Despite his boss's protests, he'd applied for two different desk jobs, one as a fire specialist—to predict the path of destruction a fire might take—and one as a member of the Incident Command team—an on-site group that managed the various crews and support personnel needed to combat a fire. Both jobs were with the National Interagency Fire Center, which monitored fires in the nation, processed requests for assistance with fires burning on government land and recommended deployment of resources, which included everything from fire engines to portable showers to fire fighters. The DOF and NIFC were both located within the Boise airport.

Jackson handed the screwdriver back to Smiley and accepted the old man's "Welcome home" before continuing on his way.

Jackson walked down the empty sidewalk to the Painted Pony, noticing the vast number of cars and trucks parked in the lot beside the life-size plastic horse that was the restaurant's icon. He recognized many of the vehicles as being owned by his Hot Shots. In this part of Idaho, forestry and firefighting jobs were a big part of the community. A few tourists came for the rafting on the Payette River, but Silver Bend, with its ranger station and Hot Shot base, was considered by locals to be a fire town.

He entered the town's lone restaurant and local hangout, then paused to allow his eyes to adjust to the darkness, letting the familiar smells and sounds envelop him.

Almost immediately, the door opened behind him and another of his mother's friends, Birdie Lowell, local busybody and grocery store owner, came in on his heels. Jackson had thought Birdie was old and cranky when he was a kid. Today, she looked ancient and cranky. The last time he'd seen the old woman, she'd told him the one way to get Lexie back was to take her camping. As if roasting marshmallows over an open fire would win her back.

Jackson stepped aside to let Birdie pass. He wasn't in the mood for her brand of advice today, but Birdie stopped in front of him anyway.

"Have you seen Lexie yet?" Birdie asked, forehead crinkling as she craned her neck to look him in the eye.

Jackson's jaw tensed. It was clear that everyone knew about the divorce, which was damn irritating when Jackson was trying to figure out how not to be divorced. "Not yet, Birdie. How're you?"

Birdie pursed her pale, thin lips while she studied his

face. After about thirty seconds, she huffed "Fine," and then strutted out with an ungainly, jolting gait similar to a pigeon's.

Obviously, something funny had been added to the water in Silver Bend, because everyone was acting as if Jackson needed to run straight to Lexie. Sure, he'd just returned from Russia, but it wasn't as if Lexie was anxiously awaiting his return.

That was the problem—she was too damn good at taking care of herself.

Jackson took a moment to reacquaint himself with his mother's restaurant. He'd grown up cooking, bussing tables and doing dishes at the Pony, idolizing the Hot Shots that treated the place as a second home. There was nothing like the combined aromas of yeasty beer and seasoned curly fries to make him feel like he was back where he belonged.

Nothing had changed here, thank you very much—from the retro blue-green and chrome chairs to the faux white marble countertops to the mural of a rearing black-and-white pony. The scarred pool table still stood to his right, a small video game section to his left. Three rows of oblong tables cascaded back to the bar.

One of the tables near the kitchen was overflowing with familiar faces. Most of his Silver Bend Hot Shots were congregated for a late breakfast. In their fire-resistant Nomex green pants and yellow shirts, they looked ready for battle. The group glanced at him curiously, at first not recognizing him behind his beard.

"Well, look what the cat dragged in." Logan McCall, who had been the best man at Jackson's wedding, kicked his chair back and strode across the room "Slummin', Golden? Or did they kick your lazy butt out of Russia?"

Jackson grinned and took two steps before receiving a bone-crunching hug with much backslapping. "I heard the fires were raging back home, so I took the first plane out,

Tin Man.'' Jackson used Logan's nickname, bestowed after one particularly disappointed woman publicly proclaimed Logan to be lacking a heart. Logan was a confirmed bachelor who enjoyed women as long as they didn't expect more from him than a night or two of his company.

"Just in time,'' Logan said. "We're shipping out today. Got us a nice runaway in Wyoming over at Bighorn.''

Like most Hot Shot teams, Silver Bend fought fires anywhere they were needed, from Alaska to Florida. It was dirty, exhausting, dangerous work fighting fires from the ground with little more than a shovel and a Pulaski—a combination ax and hoe. The physical job requirements were so tough, only the strongest passed the arduous work-capacity test. And only the most courageous lasted more than a few seasons.

His gut clenching at the thought of facing flames again, Jackson concentrated on holding on to his smile.

"Have you eaten? The guys would love to hear some stories.'' Logan pointed to the table and walked back as if assuming Jackson wanted nothing more than to join them.

Jackson recognized many of the faces there, had trained most of these men. Those who he didn't know watched him with the eager expressions of novices. Jackson quickly looked away from their curious stares.

Logan introduced Jackson to the newest Hot Shot members, and slid him into a chair facing the kitchen. "Best view in the house,'' Logan said with a private grin, as if he, and he alone, were privy to some inside joke.

Someone poured Jackson a cup of coffee.

"Did you teach the Russians how we fight fires...Golden...sir?'' This from a fresh-faced boy, introduced as Rookie, who didn't look old enough to drive, much less shave, although he had the broad shoulders and beefy arms of a seasoned firefighter.

Most Hot Shots kept in shape, but the Silver Bend Hot

Shots trained like fiends—lifting weights and running miles across the mountainous ranges in the area to increase their strength and endurance. They had a reputation for the ability to build more fire lines than any other crew, and generally considered themselves the best of the best. Up until last year, Jackson had believed leading the Silver Bend Hot Shots was a job he'd been born for.

"I did teach my Russian crew something." Jackson only half smiled, trying to ignore the hero worship in Rookie's eyes as he remembered another eager, young recruit. Unwilling to elaborate, he felt his easy grin slip away as his mind flashed upon that face, filled with terror.

*Why did you run, Alek?*

The table was oddly silent as everyone waited for Jackson to say more. He took another sip of coffee, unable to talk about what had happened over there. The goofy grin on Logan's face was starting to wear on his nerves.

He could hear his mother in the kitchen, banging pans and talking to herself. Now would be a good time to excuse himself, greet his mom and ask her what she thought he should do about Lexie.

"They spoke English, did they?" Chainsaw Hudson asked after a bit. Chainsaw carried his namesake into battle. One of the shorter crew members at only six feet tall, Chainsaw was a burly man who was a terror to trees standing in the way of a firebreak.

"Some. I had an interpreter most of the time."

"A blond-haired, blue-eyed beauty?" Chainsaw waggled his brows suggestively.

Jackson chuckled, thinking of Levka, the pudgy, wrinkled firefighter that had been assigned to the team of U.S. firemen. "Something like that."

That was just what the crew wanted to hear. Chainsaw slapped Jackson on the back as other crew members pulled their chairs closer. "Gentleman, our boy is definitely back in the dating game. Anyone want to offer him some tips?"

Everyone started talking at once.

Jackson brought his coffee cup to his lips, letting the table's enthusiasm roll over him unacknowledged. He didn't want his team to know he was still devastated over his divorce. He'd never live something like that down.

If only he could hide his cowardice as easily.

"I suppose you'll have lots of stories to tell. Knowing you, they'll be good ones." This from Spider, who had a love of scary movies and wore only black when he was off duty.

Jackson didn't answer. He didn't plan to tell many stories, especially stories about that last fire. The heat. The smell of fear so pungent you could taste it.

He took another sip of his coffee, trying to drown the gnawing monster of doubt eating away at his gut. The same demon had been his constant companion since the fire. Nothing seemed to keep the demon at bay—not coffee, not alcohol, not exhaustion.

"Seen Lexie yet?" Spider asked, stretching his wiry frame and tipping the chair back on two legs.

His control—already worn down from exhaustion and longing—at its end, Jackson leaned forward. Appearances be damned. "Hell, no, I haven't seen my *wife* yet. Why do you ask?"

"But…but," Spider sputtered. "You're divorced."

Jackson stared real hard at Spider.

Spider let his chair fall forward with a solid thunk on the hardwood floor, averting his gaze. "I'm just gonna keep my mouth shut," he mumbled.

"Jackson!" Mary Garrett gasped before running around the ancient wooden bar of the Painted Pony.

He'd shot up out of his chair upon seeing her, and was ready when she threw herself into his arms.

"I wasn't expecting you until tomorrow." His mother squeezed him tight.

"We finished up a little early," Jackson replied gruffly,

holding his mom close and trying not to remember that he almost hadn't made it home. He wanted to tell her that he loved her, but he rarely uttered those words, even to Lex—and there was his reputation to consider, with half a team of Hot Shots watching his every move. Instead, Jackson put some distance between them and reached down into his backpack for the gift he'd brought back for her. Awkwardly he thrust a book of Russian fairy tales her way.

His mother ran her fingers over the brightly colored cover, then flipped through the pages. "What fun this will be to read with Heidi," she said, her eyes bright. With a sigh, she laid the book carefully on the bar.

"Let me look at you and make sure those Russians took good care of you." His mother studied him. "You were always such a picky eater, and I worried you wouldn't have anything to eat over there."

"Mom." He scuffed his boots against the wood floor as if he were thirteen, not thirty, hearing Logan's chuckle behind him. His mother often treated him as if he were still in the seventh grade. The only saving grace was that she treated every one of the Silver Bend Hot Shots as if they were in the seventh grade. The Painted Pony was the last place the Hot Shots stopped before leaving to fight a wildland fire, and the first place they gathered when they returned.

His mom gave him the once-over, then peered at his face. "Have you slept at all?"

"Not much." Jackson still had frequent nightmares about the fire's advance and continued to carry the emotional scars from his brush with death. It was tough enough for him to fall asleep when he was alone, even harder when he'd been worried that he might wake up screaming or in a cold sweat on an airplane full of strangers.

"It's a good thing I'm working, then. You can go get some sleep and then take me to dinner tonight."

"Dinner? I suppose you'll want to go somewhere nice

in Boise and spend all my hard-earned money," Jackson teased.

His mother's eyes widened. "Oh, I forgot. I can't go to dinner with you tonight. Bridge night. Where are you staying? I'll call you later."

"Uh…" The question was so unexpected that Jackson stroked his beard as he searched for a tactful reply. "I thought I was staying with you. I don't have a room at the barracks." Unless they had a family, Silver Bend Hot Shots bunked down together at a large ranger station up the road.

"Me? Oh, honey, I'm sorry, but you'll cramp my style." She glanced over her shoulder toward the kitchen as if concerned something might catch on fire.

"Your style?" He wasn't welcome in his mother's house because she was exercising between the sheets? His father died eighteen years ago and his mother hadn't dated since. In her late fifties, Mary Garrett sported a lined face and the brown mottled complexion of one who enjoyed the outdoor life. Neither slender nor overweight, with short hair turned completely gray, his mother was a bundle of energy, but there was nothing Jackson saw in his mother that someone of the opposite sex would find…well, sexy.

"That's right." Her voice was firm and her chin lifted.

What had gotten into his mother? Then she changed the subject on him again.

"Have you seen Lexie?"

Jackson gritted his teeth as he shook his head. "No. Is she working today?" Lexie worked at the Painted Pony during the breakfast shift, as both a cook and a waitress.

"Working?" His mother seemed incredulous. Then she reached up to pat his cheek. "No, honey, not really."

"Dad?" Heidi appeared at the counter, carrying two mountainous platters of pancakes that wavered when she saw him. She stood frozen in place for a moment, blue eyes filling with tears.

Mary came to the rescue and took the plates from Heidi before she dropped them.

Jackson couldn't breathe past the sudden lump in his throat at seeing his baby girl, who looked a good inch taller and more like an adult than ever before. At eleven, Heidi was the spitting image of her mother—thick brown hair, bright blue eyes and dimples. Her long ponytail bounced as she ran into his arms. Unable to contain his excitement, he spun her around, then plunked her back on her feet and planted a kiss on her crown.

"I can't believe you're back." Heidi squeezed him again as if reassuring herself that he was real. "It's been, like, forever."

Not trusting himself to speak, Jackson just grinned. Heidi was the reason Jackson and Lexie had married before their high school graduation. Lexie had planned on going to college, but the baby had pretty much made that dream impossible. Yet, she'd never once told Jackson she regretted getting married, raising their daughter and abandoning her dreams. They'd wanted to have more children, but the doctors said that Lexie wasn't able to carry any more babies. That news had broken Lexie's heart, and eventually, Jackson believed, his marriage as well.

"I almost didn't recognize you with that beard." Heidi reached up and tugged gently on his whiskers. "Are beards popular over there?"

"It's the poor-man's nose ring," Logan said, grinning as he loaded up a plate with pancakes.

"Uncle Logan!" Heidi rolled her eyes, then hugged Jackson close. "Wait until I tell Mom you're home."

LEXIE IRRITABLY SCRATCHED OUT the figures on the tablet in front of her until the pencil lead snapped. No matter which way she looked at it, she wasn't going to have enough money this month to pay every bill. She crumpled up the yellow sheet and tossed it in the trash. The money

Jackson transferred automatically to her account covered the mortgage and house insurance plus the majority of the grocery bills. It didn't cover the rest, including the vet bill, and new school clothes for Heidi, who'd grown over the summer.

Lexie shifted in Mary's chair, trying to ease the pain in her lower back. She'd come over this morning to help Mary feed the departing firefighters and she'd overdone it just a bit. Lexie didn't regret a few aches. She was just as fond of the Hot Shot crew Jackson used to lead as Mary was. They deserved a little pampering before they risked their lives on a mountain where raging fires sent temperatures soaring above one hundred degrees.

Besides, she needed something to keep her mind off the ticking clock and her mounting bills. When she'd drawn up the divorce settlement, Lexie had been too proud to ask for much money. She'd had a steady paycheck and had thought she could make her own way. That was before she'd had to give up her job at the Painted Pony.

Lexie unfurled herself from behind Mary's desk and rubbed her back as she headed into the Pony's kitchen. Not for the first time since the divorce, Lexie wondered if she'd done the right thing. It wasn't just the money. There was Heidi to consider. Was it fair for Lexie to raise their daughter alone?

Lexie snorted. As if she hadn't been raising Heidi alone her entire life. Jackson was never home. He was either in another state fighting fires, out somewhere training, or off with his never-ending list of friends. She'd always love Jackson, but their marriage was past the point of salvation. She'd been his housekeeper, his cook and his mistress, but somewhere down the line they'd stopped being friends, stopped being lovers, stopped talking about anything other than his schedule and how he wasn't going to be around. Finally, Lexie told him not to bother coming home.

Absently, Lexie rubbed her stomach, fighting the

slightest twinge of guilt. A year ago, Lexie had discovered she was pregnant. At first, she'd thought the doctors had made a huge mistake; they had told her long ago that she couldn't get pregnant again. But a miracle had happened—and she had begun to believe that this was the sign she'd been looking for. Her love with Jackson was worth saving.

She'd asked him to meet her for lunch in Boise in a swank little café on the outskirts of the city. Jackson had told her he'd be there after he was done helping a neighbor clear away brush from their house. Lexie had waited an hour before she started to cry.

And then the bleeding started.

Lexie had driven herself to the hospital—alone. Checked herself in—alone. Held herself together throughout the miscarriage when she couldn't reach Jackson. Then she'd driven herself back to Silver Bend. During the trip home, Lexie had come to realize that she was no longer important to Jackson. This wasn't the first time Jackson had stood her up, or Heidi, for that matter. How could anyone treat those closest to him—his wife and daughter—so callously? If this wasn't a sign that their love was unsalvageable, Lexie didn't know what was.

When Jackson showed up after having missed dinner, with some excuse about a friend's car not starting, Lexie made her decision. She asked him to move out that night without ever telling him of the child they'd lost.

Lexie sighed, pushing back the guilt. She needed to focus on her current problems, not her past. She'd make it somehow. Just a few more months and things were bound to get better.

The Hot Shot crew in the dining room of the Pony roared with laughter, the raucous sound carrying over the noisy fans in the kitchen. Lexie glanced up from the steaming bowl full of scrambled eggs she'd left on the counter for Mary and Heidi to carry into the dining room minutes before. Something was going on out there. The

Silver Bend Hot Shots were such a boisterous, upbeat group that their mood was infectious. Lexie needed some of those positive vibes right now.

She carried the bowl of eggs over to the kitchen window where she could look out on to the dining room. A bearded man with hair touching his shoulders stood with his arms looped around Heidi and Mary, their backs to Lexie. He wasn't dressed in Hot Shot gear, but the way he stood reminded her of someone. Lexie stretched to put the big, heavy bowl of scrambled eggs up on the shoulder-high countertop, feeling its weight all the way down in her belly. And then he laughed.

*It can't be.*

The heavy crock slipped out of her fingers onto the countertop with a sickening *crack,* splitting the bowl in two and cascading eggs across the counter and onto the floor. Everyone's head swiveled in her direction, including that of the bearded stranger. Only he wasn't a stranger. He was the man who still held the key to her heart.

Light-headed, Lexie gripped the counter, grateful that it stood between her and Jackson so that he couldn't see all of her, couldn't see that she carried his child.

A child she hadn't told him about. The child they'd created the night Jackson signed the divorce papers.

Their eyes met and held, making it hard for her to breathe. Having been a firefighter's wife for so long, she couldn't resist taking inventory, making sure he was all right. His tall frame was still sturdy. Blue jeans covered his powerful thighs, and his broad shoulders filled a forest-green T-shirt. His sable hair fell uncharacteristically below his ears and brushed his T-shirt collar in the back. A thick, dark beard covered his square jaw, making him look less like the young man she'd married and more like a weary man of the world.

Jackson was safe. She couldn't think beyond that fact. Firefighters who came home early from assignments weren't always unscathed. Broken bones. Singed body parts. Eyes so red from bitter smoke that they couldn't see. But Jackson stood solidly in front of her. Unharmed.

The desire to touch him overwhelmed her. She wanted to run her fingers through his hair, feel the strength of his chest beneath her palms, reassure herself that he was, indeed, home in one piece.

"Are you all right?" Mary darted into the kitchen, gave Lexie the once-over, and then started cleaning up, effectively distracting Lexie from the spell Jackson had put her under.

He may look oh-so-right, but he wasn't able to love them as a father and husband should. Yet, she couldn't resist looking at him again.

Jackson's smile was tentative, his green eyes guarded. It was the first time in a long time that she'd seen him unsure of himself. Oh, he had his weak moments, but Lexie also knew that Jackson hid behind his charm. Few knew he didn't have the hidden reserves of confidence he'd prefer everyone believed. He certainly had never been anything but upbeat and positive with Lexie through their entire divorce.

"How're you doing, Lex?" His voice coasted over her like warm honey from across the room.

Lexie licked suddenly dry lips. She should have told him months ago about this baby. He'd know how she was "doing" the minute she stepped out from behind the counter.

The baby thumped against her ribs, trying to capture her father's attention from deep within the womb.

Heidi hugged Jackson, her joy in seeing her father apparent in her radiant smile. "He's home, Mom, for good. Just like before. Isn't it great?"

Jackson's smile broadened. The Hot Shots at the table were nudging each other and grinning as if this was the best show in town. She supposed it ranked right up there with the time old Marguerite slurped one too many strawberry daiquiris, shimmied into the lap of a highly embarrassed and uninterested Sirus Socrath, the former superintendent of Silver Bend's Hot Shot crew, and sang "Like a Virgin."

"Your father is back from Russia, but I'm sure he's off to fight fires somewhere," Lexie said, hastening to correct the impression that Jackson was home to stay. It was the height of the fire season and there were several forest fires rampant across the western states. She pasted a smile on her face and looked at Jackson hopefully.

Jackson tugged Heidi's ponytail, grin firmly in place. "Nope. I've taken two weeks off."

"In the middle of the fire season?" Lexie's voice cracked on the last word. Any hope she had of keeping her pregnancy a secret from Jackson faded fast. Would he be angry with her? Would he even care?

"Yep. I decided I needed a break, needed to reconnect with my family." His eyes, dark rimmed as if from lack of sleep, seemed to glow warmly at her, but Lexie was anything but reassured.

"Wow. That's…" Lexie's head bobbed as she floundered for something to say, some way to break the news to Jackson gently. She used to be known for her witty comebacks. Now, all she could manage was "That's… Wow."

"Aren't you gonna hug Mom?" Heidi asked, looking innocently up at her father.

One of the Hot Shots chuckled.

"Oh dear," Mary said, and disappeared into the back room.

Lexie's eyes narrowed even as her chest heaved. She was being set up by her own daughter, in front of an audience, no less. Emotions warred within her—indignation at being caught off guard and outmaneuvered by an eleven-year-old, anxiety that Jackson might find out how close she was to needing his help, a feeling of relief that Jackson was home safe, the sour guilt of her secret.

The baby slugged her bladder.

Jackson walked closer, his footsteps a slow herald of the moment of truth. Everyone was looking at her now, probably hoping she'd fall back into his arms as if he'd never broken her heart and shattered her dreams of family. Each step Jackson took made Lexie want to shrink back into the kitchen, but she still had enough pride to stand and face him.

## CHAPTER TWO

JACKSON FELT about as nervous as the first time he'd asked
Lexie out. She looked great. At least the part of her he
could see looked great behind the counter. Thick lashes
framed wide blue eyes unadorned by makeup. He could
gaze into those eyes forever. Her hair, begging to be
touched, fell in soft brown waves about her shoulders. Her
cheeks were flushed, and there'd been a few moments
there when their eyes first connected that he'd been glad
he came because of the way she was looking at him, as if
she were happy to see him.

Heidi was pushing his luck a little, but heck, if he could
get a hug from Lex on day one, that was something, right?

He gave Lex his best "hey, trust me" smile, planning
to take this as slowly as she wanted, and entered the
kitchen. The sight of her full, lush body made him stop in
his tracks.

"You're pregnant!"

Her face turned bright red. "Yes," she said through
gritted teeth.

Lexie had slept with someone else. The room tilted.

"When did this happen?" Jackson's eyes bounced
around the room from Heidi—*argh, don't ask Heidi*—to
his Hot Shot buddies—*he'd never live this down*—to his
wife. "How could this happen?"

Lexie ran her hands over the blue T-shirt—*his T-shirt*—
covering her very pregnant belly.

"Why didn't anyone tell me?"

"I tried to tell you the last time you called, Dad, but I don't think you heard me." Heidi leaned over the counter and smiled sweetly as if she hadn't been in on this secret for months.

Jackson tried to remember the conversation Heidi referred to. It took a few seconds for something to click. He dropped his head and shook it slowly from side to side. "You said she was *perfect*."

"No, Dad, I said she was pregnant," Heidi corrected, then had the nerve to look back at the Hot Shot crew and grin.

The men, of course, heard their exchange and roared with laughter. Oh, this was one for the record books, all right.

Jackson struggled to control his emotions. He wanted to throttle whoever had gotten his wife pregnant, or at the very least, punch a wall.

Lexie had slept with another man.

"The ink wasn't even dry on our divorce." Jackson's gaze returned to the floor. He couldn't bear to look at her. How could she do this to him?

"Heidi, go get yourself something to eat." Lexie's voice brooked no argument and Heidi scooted over to the table with the firemen. She was always more inclined to obey Lexie than to listen to him.

Jackson lifted his suddenly heavy head and stared at Lexie, barely able to contain his sorrow. He'd never get her back now. How could he, with this child between them? "You were the only thing…" Jackson let his voice trail off, swallowing thickly. She was the reason he'd found a way out of that fire. She and Heidi had been his reason for living. Lexie was his talisman, for heaven's sake.

A cold emptiness settled inside of him. He leaned against the kitchen wall, needing support for knees suddenly as limp as spaghetti.

"I'm sorry you had to learn about it this way," Lexie said, her voice barely above a whisper. "I wasn't sure how to tell you."

"How could you do this to me?" He'd be the laughingstock of his Hot Shot crew, of every crew and support group from Montana to Arizona—if he wasn't already. Had Lexie left him for this guy? And what about her infertility problem? Maybe it wasn't her problem, after all. Maybe all those doctors were wrong. Maybe all his sperm weren't accounted for.

"I didn't mean for this to happen, but it doesn't change anything between us."

And then the reality of the situation hit him. He pulled Lexie deeper into the kitchen and lowered his voice. "You've been walking around like…like…*that* for months, haven't you." He pointed to her swollen belly.

She arched her brows at him as if he'd lost his mind. "That's right."

"And everyone in town knows you're pregnant."

"Probably." Lexie crossed her arms just underneath her very full breasts, resting her arms over her round stomach.

Jackson pinched the bridge of his nose. "That's why everyone I saw today asked if I'd seen you. They're salivating out there right now." This time he pointed toward the dining room. "Just waiting to hear how I react to…to…you!"

"Probably."

He forced himself to lower his voice. "Smiley. Birdie. Spider. And who knows how many others."

"It is a situation that people appear to be curious about."

Jackson slapped the wall with his palm. "Well, I'm curious, too, damn it."

"Really?"

Jackson tilted his head to the ceiling as if the cracked stucco held the answer to his problems. This other guy was going to move in, sleep in his bed, and kiss his wife good-morning, not to mention good-night.

Lexie was lost to him. And Heidi…

Oh, hell.

Jackson rubbed his dry, sleep-deprived eyes. "Who is he, Lex? Who did this to us?"

Lexie's mouth dropped open, then she narrowed her eyes at him and said, "You did, you idiot."


"SAY AGAIN?" Jackson squinted at her.

Keeping her arms crossed, Lexie tapped her forefinger impatiently on one arm, unable to believe Jackson thought she'd slept with another man. And here she'd assumed he'd been upset that she was pregnant. "I'm seven months along." Three months ago, she'd been told not to be out of bed for more than a few hours at a time or she'd lose the baby because of an incompetent cervix. She'd spent three months being unable to do things with Heidi the way she wanted. Months spent teetering on the edge of failure. Months of—

"And?" Jackson prompted.

Maybe the breakup sex hadn't been as memorable for him as it had been for her, or maybe he couldn't add. Lexie wasn't sure why this wasn't sinking in. Finally, when she couldn't stand the fact that he didn't comprehend her, Lexie tossed her hands in his direction. "*And* it's yours."

Her outburst was loud enough to carry to the dining room. Somebody mumbled at the Hot Shot table and was promptly shushed. The Hot Shots weren't this quiet and attentive at the movie theater. She and Jackson were putting on quite a show.

It took a moment for Jackson to process this information, in which time Lexie wondered, as she had for months, how Jackson would react to the idea of becoming a father once again.

Then Jackson smiled at her. Even with half his face covered by a beard, his grin was still powerful. Jackson's smile could charm the birds out of the trees, convince a teacher that his dog had indeed eaten his homework or reassure a lonely teenage girl who'd never felt loved before that she was the most important thing in the world to him. When Jackson wore that smile, people believed everything he said.

"This is fantastic, Lex. I wish you'd told me sooner."

Before Lexie knew what was happening, Jackson had his arms around her. His warmth enveloped her. Jackson's fingers began making circles around the small of her back in just the right spot to relieve the soreness. For the first time in months, Lexie felt a little of the pressure inside her ease.

*Wow.*

Instinctively, she melted against him. They'd dreamed of a large family, tried as many fertility treatments as they could afford, all to no avail. A part of Lexie had died with the baby she'd miscarried last year, but still, she'd told no one, denying herself the comfort of Jackson's arms because she wouldn't settle for anything less than a strong, loving relationship.

Jackson nuzzled her hair and she felt his breath waft across her cheek. Then he pressed a gentle kiss on her temple as if they were still a couple very much in love.

Heidi whooped, spying from her position at the kitchen window and the Hot Shot crew broke into applause at her cue.

*Uh-oh.*

Dumbfounded at finding herself in the one place she longed to be, the one place she couldn't be without risking her heart again, it took several heartbeats for the alarm to register in Lexie's head. She knew Jackson cared for her, but if he were to make a list of his priorities, she'd come out somewhere near the bottom. Lexie would be a fool to let him back into her life, even if he was the father of the little one growing inside of her.

The baby poked her.

Lexie began to pull back. "Jackson, you shouldn't be touching me like that."

"Another baby, Lex. This is perfect."

His fingers were magic, but Lexie needed to fight against his touch. They were divorced. She couldn't go through the disappointment and heartache of having Jackson in her life again, seeing him leave to risk his life to fight a fire, gluing herself to the television screen in the hopes that she'd see him, praying she wouldn't recognize him on screen because then the danger would become all too real. And when he was home, he found dozens of reasons to stay away, to help others, leaving Lexie and Heidi on their own.

"Jackson, I'm asking you to stop."

"Why?" He gazed down at her with such tenderness, Lexie found it hard to find the words she had to say, found it hard to move away. She forced herself to dredge up all the unpleasant memories—Jackson missing from the dinner table, Jackson forgetting to pick up Heidi's Christmas present from the store in Boise, Jackson unreachable when she'd miscarried. For Lexie, love meant putting a priority on someone and being there through the good times, the bad times, even the boring times. She and Heidi deserved that much.

The baby stretched, pushing on Lexie's bladder and her lungs simultaneously, and holding the position. This kid was definitely into yoga.

Lexie managed to step back. "We're divorced."

Jackson's brow puckered. "It's my baby."

"So? You weren't around to raise the first one." Shocked at the harshness of her own words, she retreated another step as she struggled to catch her breath.

"I work in a job that takes me away for weeks at a

time.'' His words were clipped and his green eyes flashed a warning.

Here was the anger Lexie had expected when she'd asked him to leave a year ago, the anger that she'd thought would prove he still loved her.

Too late. Why was Jackson always too late?

''I know that.'' When it seemed he'd argue further, Lexie held up a hand, willing it not to tremble. With her other hand, she tenderly pushed on her stomach, encouraging the baby to give her breathing room. ''I'm not going to talk about this now. You've just found out about this baby, and you're upset.'' And Lexie hadn't had any time to prepare for this meeting.

''I'm not upset, I'm ecstatic.'' He wasn't smiling. In fact, when he spoke, it was with a clenched jaw. ''I'm coming home. I'm moving back in. We'll get married.''

''No,'' she protested weakly, wanting to protect her fragile heart. Except, a little voice deep inside whispered that this was meant to be.

The air suddenly seemed too thick, the kitchen too hot. Lexie sank down to her knees, barely aware of Heidi shrieking her joy that Jackson was moving back in.

Jackson eased Lexie into his lap. ''Head between your knees, darlin'. Breathe deep. That's excellent.''

Jackson was elbowing his way back into her life. Nothing was going to be excellent again.

''WE'RE NOT GETTING MARRIED,'' Lexie whispered at him.

Jackson sat across the table from Lex, having helped her to a chair while she scolded Heidi and the Hot Shots for fussing over her. All the while, Jackson couldn't help but think that this baby was the reason he'd made it home safely, the reason he and Lexie would get back together. She was his good luck charm.

But she didn't seem to see it that way. ''We're going to be friends.''

"Like hell we are. Show's over, boys," Jackson growled at the firefighters hovering over his wife. "Don't you have a bus to catch?"

"Sure thing." Logan slapped Jackson on the shoulder. "Welcome home." It took the acting superintendent less than two minutes to drive his crew outside.

"Heidi, come help with the dishes," Mary singsonged, as if the world hadn't just come crashing down around her son's ears.

Jackson waited until the door closed behind the last fireman and Heidi followed his mother into the kitchen before confronting Lexie. "Give me one good reason why I shouldn't move back home." He stared pointedly at Lexie's belly.

"We're not married," she said wearily, shifting in her chair in a way that had Jackson recalling how Lexie's back bothered her when she was pregnant all those years ago. Her eyes kept skittering away from his, as if she couldn't stand to look at him.

Smiles generally came easily to Jackson, but when he tried to smile at Lexie, he felt as if he were a wolf baring his teeth at her. "We can fix that. Marry me."

Her eyes widened and she looked at him dead-on. "Please don't suggest that. We had our chance."

Jackson opened his mouth to contradict her, then closed it. He couldn't have said for sure, but there seemed to be panic in her big blue eyes. Why did the thought of his moving back in scare her? Unless there was someone else.

Jackson's heart sank to his toes. He clasped and unclasped his hands, studying the face of the woman he loved. Everything had seemed clear and simple in Russia. Here at home, the reality of winning Lexie back was daunting, perhaps impossible.

What would he do if she'd fallen in love with someone else?

Jackson swallowed hard as the silence stretched between them. Lexie was back to squirming in her chair, trying to get comfortable. But what if she wasn't squirming to ease an aching back? What if she was squirming because she didn't want to tell him about another man in her life? She'd had plenty of time to fall in love again. Pregnant or not, she was a beautiful woman that turned heads. How did you ask a woman if there was someone else more important than you in their life? Words bumbled through his head, quickly discarded. Anything he said would just distance them further and wound his pride.

"This shouldn't be so hard," Jackson blurted, inwardly cursing himself as the coward he was. If there was another man, he didn't want to hear it from Lexie. The way Silver Bend talked, he'd hear about it soon enough.

"It shouldn't be anything," Lexie replied, her expression distant, almost aloof. "All we have to do is add the baby's name to the visitation papers. End of problem."

"Problem," Jackson murmured, shocked by how callous his wife had become. His softhearted Lexie was also an incredibly capable woman, who'd demonstrated on several occasions over the years that she didn't need him. Just once, he'd like Lexie to want him for something other than an errand or a chore around the house.

Old wounds reopened, smarting more than they had the first time she'd sent him away. That night, he'd attributed her rejection to moodiness, assuming it was temporary. So, he'd been calm. Reasonable. This time, her dismissive words drove his anger uncharacteristically to the surface.

"Is that all I am to you? A problem?" He leaned across the table. "There was a time when you begged to have me as your problem."

Lexie stared toward the kitchen, one hand rubbing the curve of her stomach.

"In fact, I remember our wedding night when you said you couldn't imagine life without me."

Her face seemed to pale; her lips tightened into a thin

line. The saner part of his brain, the one that had paid
attention to hours and hours of medical training, told him
that now was the time to back off. But his brain didn't
seem in control of his rampant emotions.

"Or was that just a lie?"

Her hand stilled. She seemed to barely take a breath.

Jackson pushed on. "Do you remember the day you
asked me to leave?"

She nodded almost imperceptibly, her profile to him.

Jackson lowered his voice, but his words were still cru-
elly edged. "You told me you loved me that morning, then
you told me to get out that night. And what about my last
day in the States? You asked for my signature on the divorce papers, then came with me…willingly…to a motel
where we spent hours…" He couldn't stop himself from
looking at her stomach. "…Apparently making that baby
you're carrying."

Lexie's head dropped. Her eyes closed.

"Tell me, Lex. What's true between us and what's a
lie?" He wanted her to say she still loved him.

After a moment, she blinked and lifted her soft, watery
gaze to him. She always cried right before they made up,
but still Lexie said nothing, gave him no explanation for
her actions, nor did her tears well over and fall.

"I don't want to be a problem to you or *our* baby."
Jackson extended his hand, palm up, across the table toward her. "I'm here for you, Lex, just like I've always
been."

Lexie's features stiffened. She rose awkwardly from the
chair and stared down her slender nose at him. "I'm not
taking you back."


"THANKS FOR THE VODKA. Hopefully I won't have to use
it to bribe some tight-ass supply manager for some of
Chainsaw's gasoline." Logan stroked the Russian bottle

of spirits almost reverently before tucking it into his backpack. "The bus is late, as usual."

The Forest Service arranged for ground transportation to and from fires outside the area on vans and buses, sometimes as spartan as school buses. They stood outside the ranger station in Silver Bend, along with twenty other men checking their packs and shooting the bull. Most of the crew kept their distance from the two leaders.

Logan had just finished telling Jackson about a fire that the Silver Bend Hot Shots had worked in Oregon. The fire had been a tricky one to control, requiring several crews, smoke jumpers and air support. Jackson could barely contain his envy or his anxiety. He would have loved to fight such a fire. In the past, he'd reveled in the challenges of leading a team against something so incredibly powerful.

A nervous sweat broke out on his upper lip as the cowardly demon danced a tango across his bowels. Self-consciously, Jackson wiped at his mustache.

He was done fighting fires on the line. He'd made his choice. Why hadn't the demon left him?

"You're too quiet. You're never quiet," Logan remarked when Jackson couldn't bring himself to talk about the fire. "It's depressing."

Jackson blew out a breath. He was the first to admit he was upbeat, but no one was up one hundred percent of the time. After all these years, he would have thought that his closest friend wouldn't require him to be "on" every second. That's what he'd loved about Lexie. From the first time they'd met in high school, she'd seemed to understand that he needed to be quiet sometimes, that his perpetual optimism and outgoing nature wasn't everything he was. She didn't ask him ad nauseam what was wrong if he was quiet or contemplative. She didn't try to joke him back into an "up" mood.

God, he missed her. When she'd kicked him out, he'd gone out of his way to be nice, solicitous, the perfect gentleman. He could win anyone over with a smile. But his smile hadn't worked. Maybe he should have let her know how hurt he was, how lost he was without her. Instead, he'd thrown himself into his work to avoid the pain of her rejection and he'd rarely seen her, hoping that she'd miss him as much as he missed her—and take him back.

Jackson slouched against the green wall of the ranger station. His neck was stiff and his body sluggish, unused as it was to this time zone and abused by a fitful night of horror-chased dreams on the airplane. He needed to see Heidi again soon. He'd forgotten to give her the souvenir he'd brought home, so distracted was he by seeing Lexie pregnant.

"Why didn't you tell me about Lex?" No one had wanted to tell Jackson about this baby, this gift. Lexie most of all. Wasn't that a kick in the head? Jackson still loved her, and she couldn't even tell him they were pregnant again.

As the silence lingered, Jackson experienced a moment of doubt. Was Logan seeing Lex? It was always the best friend, wasn't it?

"Lexie isn't any of my business," Logan said finally, giving Jackson a level look. "Never has been."

Jackson released the breath he'd been holding, turning his attention to his other burning question. Painful as it was, Jackson had to ask. "She's not…seeing anyone, is she?"

After looking around the lot at the men assembled there, Logan shook his head.

"The baby is mine," Jackson said with more force than he had intended.

"Everyone in town knows who knocked her up," Logan admitted with an easy grin.

"Yeah, I'm going to have another baby." Jackson grinned, too. He thought he'd given up on that dream a long time ago. Part of him was overjoyed, yet frustration seethed just beneath the surface. Another baby wasn't enough. He needed Lexie back.

His smile faded.

"What's up with you?" Logan asked, scrutinizing Jackson's expression.

Jackson tried to smile, but his cheeks felt heavy. Finally, he spoke, drawing his words out slowly. "Do you remember that fire a couple of years ago in Hell's Canyon?"

Logan nodded, casting his gaze out toward two men whose voices were raised, bodies angled toward each other in anger.

Seeing Logan glaring at them, the two men went to separate corners of the station. Although not nearly as broad as Jackson, Logan was a couple of inches taller and didn't take crap from anyone. The team knew better than to mess around with Logan when it came to discipline.

"Bitch of a fire," Logan noted.

"That fire kicked our butts and singed our whiskers," Jackson agreed.

"Everybody made it out alive," Logan pointed out. "What with the steep slopes, erratic winds, and Incident Command telling us to pull back and regroup three different times, I wasn't sure we'd all make it out safely. Not that you ever doubted it."

Jackson made a noncommittal sound. He'd thought at the time that the brass had pulled them back too soon, but now he wasn't so sure. When he thought about it, he was surprised that more firefighters weren't lost to the powerful devastation of fire every year.

He didn't used to feel that way. Hot Shots lived for the exhilaration of a fire. They didn't fight fires with bulky protective jackets as city firemen did. Fire trucks? Hell, no. Hot Shots fought fire in fire-resistant clothing and hand tools. *Mano a mano.* Battling such a powerful force was addictive. Some guys never wanted to give up the rush.

Most Hot Shots were forced out when they could no longer meet the physical demands of the job.

Or when they lost their nerve.

Jackson swallowed the bitter thought. In his wildest dreams, he'd never imagined he'd be one of the washouts. *Loser was more like it.*

Jackson sighed. "I thought we were invincible after we got that fire under control." In his mind, he relived the flames licking at the tent above his shoulders, heard its mocking crackle as it moved past him and the other men, eating up the oxygen.

"Nobody's invincible, Golden."

There seemed to be an undercurrent of sadness in Logan's reply. Could it be that Logan battled the fire demon, too?

"Do you ever wonder if we've had more than our share of luck? I mean, look at us, Tin Man. We've been fighting wildland fires for, what? Ten years now?"

"What are we talking about this for? You're the *golden* one. You've got a never-ending supply of luck." Logan searched Jackson's face for a minute, then looked away and added in a more serious tone. "Some civilians never live to see their thirty-first birthday. Car wrecks, suicides, cancer." He shrugged. "So we've got our share of scars. But we're still here, still in one piece."

"Yeah, but for how long?" Jackson's heart sank. It would have been easier to deal with his cowardice if Logan felt the same way. And wasn't that exactly the way a coward was supposed to think? Afraid to do anything alone.

Up until a few weeks ago, Jackson lived to fight fires, keeping his body in top condition because he loved the physical demands and mental challenge of the job. In Jackson's opinion, there was no other work that made him feel so alive. And yet, his stomach now roiled at the thought of facing a fire again. Because for the first time, he'd allowed fire to bring death to someone under his command.

"Jackson, are you quitting?"

Jackson's chin lifted, but his eyes felt gritty and his vision blurred, as if he'd been out on the line under heavy smoke too long. "I'm thinking about it."

"What the hell for?" Logan pushed off the wall.

Jackson shrugged. "You're the sup now. It's time for me to move on."

"Hey, I was happy as a clam being your right-hand man." Logan lowered his voice. "These guys look up to you. They'd follow you anywhere."

"Don't sell yourself short. They'd do the same for you. It's just…" Jackson ran a hand through his shaggy hair. When he continued, he hoped it was with the truth. "I can't get Lex back if I go back to the line."

"So, you're cashing it in just to make up with her?"

Jackson didn't answer, letting his friend believe Lexie was the only reason he was giving in.

"Man, I hope you know what you're doing," Logan said, shaking his head.

A ranger stepped out of the station and scanned the crowd of Hot Shots until he found Logan. "You guys got lucky. They're using a local crew for Bighorn. They say you can stand down."

Curses and groans filled the air. The Hot Shots were clearly disappointed. The men began picking up their belongings and lugging them back to their barracks.

Rookie grinned at Jackson as he walked by. "Maybe we'll get one tomorrow," he said.

"That kid's too young to be out here," Jackson grumbled to Logan.

Logan didn't look up from gathering his gear. "He's twenty, as old as you and I were when we started."

"You make sure you watch out for him."

"He's been out here for months. He'll be okay." Logan

stared at Jackson. "Maybe it's you I should be watching out for."

Jackson frowned and glanced at his boots. He could feel Logan waiting to hear what was bugging him. Logan could wait all day; Jackson wasn't going to say a word. He clamped his lips tighter together, willing his mind to see the green vibrant trees before him and not the burning giants of Siberia.

"You know, you and Lex are something else." Logan sighed. "Stubborn as a pair of mules. Can't you just tell me a joke or something? I could use a little levity about now."

"Why? Are you that bummed out about missing the Bighorn fire? Because that rookie is right. There probably will be another one tomorrow."

"No." Logan chewed on the inside of his cheek. "It's Deb. She's not…she's…she's dying." These last words came out and lay between them in a strangled, raw heap.

Deb. Logan's twin sister. To say they were close was an understatement. An abusive, drunken father had driven the siblings to a near-psychic connection. Without Deb, Logan would be left with no one.

"How? Why?" Jackson put a hand on Logan's shoulder when it seemed his questions might crack Logan's composure. "I'm sorry. Don't answer that."

Logan bowed his head.

Crap. *Tell him something amusing, anything.*

"Uh…hey, did I tell you that Russian customs confiscated my stash of toilet paper?"

Eyes still cast to the ground, Logan rubbed his nose, so he missed Jackson rolling his eyes. Jackson couldn't believe he was going to tell Logan about this.

"Yeah, they swiped my twelve double rolls of Charmin. They claimed it was contraband."

Logan drew a labored breath. The guy must be going through hell.

"You never go anywhere without your Charmin."

Jackson patted Logan none too gently on the back, hoping it would help him regain his equilibrium. "T.P. has many uses beyond what it's sold for. Remember that time I bandaged Whitey's blistered hands with it? Or when I used it to start a fire when we were back-burning in Wyoming?"

"I find it hard to believe—" Logan looked up with a weak grin "—that you only brought twelve rolls when you were scheduled to be there a year. What did the mighty Golden do without his handy-dandy Charmin?"

"I bought six copies of the newspaper every week."

Logan's grin broadened. "Russia was quite an experience for you, man."

"It's good to be back in the States." It would be better to be home with Lexie.

JACKSON'S TRUCK BOUNCED over ruts in the dirt and gravel road that wound between tall pines on what had been his and Lex's property. Tossed about as if in white water, Jackson was reminded of how much Lexie hated the ruts. It was the first thing she fixed outside after the spring runoff. Only, she hadn't gotten around to fixing them this year.

He could offer one big guess as to why she hadn't. Their baby.

Jackson drove out of the grove and onto the main property. There was nothing like the sight of home—a red barn that had seen better days and, up on the hill, a small ranch house painted bright green. A dog barked somewhere and Heidi ran toward his truck, ponytail flying out behind her as she raced through the knee-high grass.

"Dad!" she cried, waving. The smile cracking her face was as broad as his.

Jackson parked in the middle of the drive and jumped

out of the truck to catch her hurtling herself at him. He didn't think he'd ever tire of hugging his little girl.

"I have so much to tell you." Heidi looped an arm around his waist, tugging him up toward the house.

"You have all the time in the world, Runt. I'm home." Jackson's throat tightened on the words. How he wished that were true. He held his daughter close. He could just picture himself walking up the hill and having Lexie run down to meet him halfway, throwing herself into his arms with the same enthusiasm Heidi had shown.

Jackson glanced up toward the house and took a deep breath. Heidi still loved him. He would make things right with Lex.

"We've been so busy." Ever the drama queen, Heidi hopped a few steps ahead of Jackson to command his complete attention. She held up her forefinger. "First, the most major of bummers. Our VCR is broken, so no movies all summer."

Heidi popped up a second finger. "Then there's Rufus the Re-pro-bate, as Mom calls him."

Rufus was the chocolate Lab that Jackson had bought Heidi the week before he left for Russia. The scrappy puppy had been all belly, with big soulful eyes and soft fur. Jackson had picked the pup out of the litter because he admired his spunk.

"Rufus is a *bad* dog," Heidi proclaimed in an ominous tone. "He chases gophers, which is good. But he doesn't catch them, which is bad. He leaves lots of gigantic holes in the yard."

Jackson reached over, rubbed Heidi's shoulder, and tried not to think about Lexie's reaction to a dog demolishing her precious backyard. Lexie had worked her fingers to the bone making that forty-by-sixty-foot plot resemble a well-groomed yard like most of their friends in Boise had. Jackson didn't understand it. They lived in the middle of the National Forest, not a suburb. Who needed tamed, trim grass and shrubs?

Heidi held up a third finger. "And who could forget Marmy."

"Who?"

"The orange-and-white kitten you gave us with Rufus. Mom called her Marmalade, but now we just call her Marmy. She doesn't poop in the corners anymore when she comes inside, but she still brings Mom field mice. And they're not always dead." Heidi was almost squealing with excitement. Her dimples deepened. "Mom screams loud enough to be in the movies."

Heidi dissolved into giggles, eliciting a smile from Jackson. He could appreciate the humor of it all. But did two pets that were nothing but trouble bode well for his case with Lex?

"Mom's resting. She has to do that a lot. I wouldn't want to be her for anything."

"Is something wrong?" Jackson tried to keep his voice steady.

"She's just tired." Heidi tugged on Jackson's arm, pulling him up the hill and closer to the house. "So smile and make nice. If she's still in one of her moods, I'll offer to bake her some cookies and you can take out the trash."

"She's in one of her moods?" Jackson wasn't so sure that he wanted to be rejected twice in the same day. In fact, he couldn't face Lex without arming himself with the proper defenses. More gifts. That's what he needed.

Jackson resisted Heidi's tugging. "Hey, what do you say we do a little shopping while your mom rests?"

"Shopping? Clothes shopping?" Heidi clasped her hands to her chest and leaned against Jackson. "Need you ask?"

"Go ask your mom and hustle back out." Maybe if he gave Lexie a little time to get used to him being home, she'd come around to his way of thinking. Getting married again was the logical move.

Jackson glanced over at the house, longing to go inside. If Lexie acknowledged him when Heidi came back out, he'd talk to her—calmly, patiently and with a reassuring smile that would cover the fact that he was feeling anything but calm or patient.

He braced himself with a smile when Heidi pushed open the screen door and came back outside, but the door banged closed behind his little girl as firmly as if Lexie had shut him out herself.

"What did she say?"

"Mom said it was okay. She asked how you were doing and said to make sure I got some low-rise jeans."

All Jackson heard was that Lex had asked about him. For a moment, hope flared.

Then a silent Heidi blinked up at him innocently.

Too innocently.

Jackson's eyes narrowed. "She didn't ask about me, did she?"

"Well, she wanted to," Heidi hedged.

Tilting his head back, Jackson stared at the clouds gathering in the blue sky above him. "And the low-rise jeans?"

"That was a definite no."

# CHAPTER THREE

"LOOK OUT!"

The screen door banged open, jerking Lexie awake just in time to see a large, brown streak bounding toward her. Rufus leaped at Lexie's feet, narrowly missing Marmy, who scampered away down the hallway with the brown pursuer hot on her heels.

"Rufus, no!" Jackson yelled, as he and Heidi followed the Lab into the living room. "Sorry, Lex. Are you okay?"

"I'm fine." Lexie took a deep breath and rubbed her tummy, which had clenched tight at the prospect of forty-five pounds of dog landing in her lap. Her heart was racing. The baby kicked her ribs once. And again. Then started a drumroll.

Jackson gave Lexie a once-over, which did nothing to slow her pulse.

"Sorry about that, Lex. He wormed his way past us."

"I'm fine, really." She'd feel better once he quit looking at her. Lexie rubbed the numb spot that the baby was pounding.

"Mom, look at all this stuff we bought." Heidi sank to the floor near Lexie, sharing her treasures, the drama of their entrance already fading. "I promised Dad I wouldn't wear any of it until school."

Heidi shook out three blouses in rapid succession. Lexie barely had time to look at them before her daughter brought out another shopping bag.

"And new jeans."

"Blue jeans," Lexie said wistfully, almost able to feel the thick denim on her legs. What she wouldn't give to be able to pull on a pair of pants that didn't have an elastic waistband. "Did you spend all of your father's money?"

"Almost. We spent what was in my wallet, anyway." Jackson shouldered open the door, carrying an oblong box that looked suspiciously like stereo equipment. The box effectively distracted Lexie from gazing too long at Jackson's muscular arms.

Rufus returned, shoving his nose repeatedly under Lexie's arm until she petted him. He gave her a pink-tongued grin.

"Who's that for?" Lexie asked, keeping her eyes on the box as Jackson set it on the floor. Her pulse had finally decided to return to something close to normal and the baby was peaceful once more.

Heidi folded her loot. "Dad bought a DVD player and he got five free movies, too. Isn't it great? Now we can watch movies again."

"All our movies are on video," Lexie said, trying to catch Jackson's eye. Between the electronics and the clothes, Jackson easily could have spent three hundred dollars or more.

That was just like Jackson. He never approached a problem head-on. He always worked his way in the back door. If he thought she was taking him back and returning to the same lifestyle—worrying about him nine months out of the year, sleeping solo in their king-size bed—he had another thing coming.

"Birdie rents DVDs at her grocery store," Heidi pointed out. "Oh, and I forgot we picked up a pizza on the way back into town." She shot out the door.

Jackson continued unpacking the box. "Heidi mentioned the VCR was broken, and you know it costs just as much to fix one as to buy one."

"A VCR, sure. But not a DVD. Those are more expensive."

"It'll last a long time." He began pulling out cords from behind the television as if he had every right to be rearranging her wires.

Heidi returned with the pizza and placed the box on the coffee table. "I'll get you some milk, Mom, and napkins. Then can we watch a movie?"

Lexie sighed, giving in. "I suppose." Eventually, she was going to have to learn to be in the same room as Jackson without letting herself long for his touch. For Heidi's sake.

But eventually seemed a long time away.

"And you'll be leaving after the movie," Lexie added, when their daughter had disappeared into the kitchen.

"I can sleep on the couch," Jackson said from behind the television, his denim-clad buns in clear view, just as toned and tight as ever.

"No, you can't." It was a mere twenty feet from the couch to their—her—bedroom. They used to joke about that. Twenty paces was not nearly enough distance between Lexie and temptation. If it weren't for Heidi, she'd send him on his way right now.

"How've you been feeling?" Jackson turned his head and smiled at her.

She told herself it was the same smile he'd always had, but something about him seemed tired and drained.

"I've been better." The bleeding had been scary the first few times it happened several months ago, but she'd become used to it. And the nausea had returned a few weeks ago, which was unpleasant. Yet, all of this hardship was bearable when she compared it to shutting Jackson out of her life. That's how she measured this pregnancy—against the void in her heart. Asking her husband to leave and sticking to her decision had been the hardest thing she'd ever had to do. Everything else—even this difficult pregnancy—was easy by comparison.

"Are you getting all the rest you need?" he asked.

"What did Heidi tell you?" Lexie glanced back toward the kitchen, then sighed. Jackson needed to know about the health of this child. He deserved to know about the child they'd lost, too, but she wasn't ready to tell him that yet. "I've had to take it easy since my fourth month." It seemed like forever. But then, it seemed like forever since she'd sat with Jackson and talked.

"I'm sorry about the things I said earlier." He stood up straight and turned to face her, green eyes bright. "You caught me off guard."

He really knew how to work her. She could feel her resolve softening "I suppose anybody would be upset to come home and find this—" she pointed at her belly "—waiting for them."

His eyes bore into hers. "Are you sorry? About the baby, I mean."

Lexie shook her head.

"Me, neither. It's a gift, Lex."

Speechless, Lexie cradled her belly with both hands.

Jackson ran his fingers through his long hair before admitting, "No matter how much I loved you, I couldn't give you another baby. I knew that was hard on you."

This was the real Jackson, the man he rarely showed to anyone else—sincere, open—nothing like the man he'd become when she'd asked him to leave—annoyingly upbeat.

"Is Heidi happy about the baby?"

"She's excited." This was the man she'd fallen in love with. The man her heart longed for. The walls around her heart weakened. "You know, she always wanted a brother or a sister. Growing up, I did, too." Until she'd realized how messed up her life was. Welfare, social workers, humiliation, a father who hadn't loved her enough to hang around. She'd contented herself with the stingy, conditional love her mother offered. Until she found Jackson and realized there were other kinds of love.

Only later did Lexie learn that even Jackson's love was fragile and fleeting.

Heidi entered the living room, carrying a tray with three glasses. "I got everyone water. We're out of milk." This last was said somewhat testily, as if it was Lexie's fault that they'd drunk the last of the milk.

Lexie experienced a twinge of guilt that she hadn't been able to keep as much food in the house since she'd gone on public assistance.

"Start a movie, Dad," Heidi commanded, sinking to the floor.

"And then your dad needs to leave. I'm sure he has lots to do," Lexie said firmly.

Jackson stared at Lexie with such a haunted expression in his eyes that Lexie had to look away. She'd barred Jackson from her life for a reason. He'd buried the man she'd fallen in love with underneath a veneer of confidence and easygoing charm.

She just had to work harder to remember that what she was seeing now was only a rare glimpse of the man he'd once been.

THE TWITCHES CAUGHT LEXIE'S ATTENTION.

Propped against the couch at Lexie's feet, Jackson had fallen asleep soon after the movie started. The twitching had begun about twenty minutes later. Still, he seemed fine, until the movie's credits started to roll.

"Don't. No." Jackson muttered and turned his head from side to side. "Come back."

"Is he having a bad dream?" Heidi asked.

"Don't! Alek, no!" Sweat covered Jackson's brow. His leg bucked, as if fighting to move.

"Mom?" Heidi scooted closer to Lexie.

"It's just a dream." Lexie put her arm around Heidi's shoulders. She raised her voice. "Jackson, wake up. You're dreaming."

"The fire! Alek!" Jackson's face scrunched up as if he were in pain.

The hair rose on the back of Lexie's neck. Without thinking, she knelt next to Jackson, placing her hands on his shoulders. "Jackson." She shook him gently. "You're dreaming."

"Don't!" He sat bolt upright and gripped her arms above her elbows. Glazed eyes stared into hers.

"You're fine. Everything's fine. It was a bad dream," Lexie said soothingly.

A violent shudder rippled through Jackson. He drew a deep breath. Then he seemed to return to wakefulness. At least his eyes blinked. His grip was starting to numb Lexie's arms.

"Dad, you're scaring me," Heidi said in a small voice.

"Jackson." Lexie pulled back slowly until his hands fell away.

Jackson washed a hand over his face. As quickly as he had snapped to awareness, he was gone.

Before she realized what she was doing, Lexie had pushed herself up off the floor and was following Jackson out the door. If he left like this, he'd never get to sleep later.

Jackson was opening the door to his truck when she reached the porch.

"Wait."

The sun had gone down and the blue sky had given way to purple, casting Jackson's face in shadow when he turned to face her.

"Wait," she repeated, hurrying over to him.

Jackson stood outside his truck, watching her ungainly approach. "You shouldn't move so quickly."

"Then, don't run out like that." Lexie panted from the

exertion it took to make her body move that fast. "Who's Alek? What's wrong?"

"Nothing. No one." He wouldn't look at her.

Of course he'd say that. Lexie sighed. Why did she expect him to open up to her when he hadn't done so in years? "I don't know why I followed you out here. I guess I was worried. Never mind. Some things never change."

Jackson stepped after her and caught her hand when she would have returned to the house. Against her better judgment, Lexie found herself facing him in the deepening shadows.

He clasped her other hand.

"Jackson—" Lexie warned, even as she felt her heart beat faster at his touch.

"I've missed you, Lex."

Uh-oh. This was how she'd gotten into trouble the day they'd signed the divorce papers. "I should go inside."

"We're friends, right? Talk to me."

She could hear the smile in his voice. He was turning on the charm, turning the attention from his problems to something he wanted to talk about. For some unexplained reason, Lexie's voice and motor skills were conspicuously absent. She could only stand and listen.

"Two hearts destined to be together," Jackson lowered his voice, quoting a phrase that had been part of their wedding vows.

The intimacy of the night, the feel of his hands clasped around hers, standing facing each other as they had on their wedding day... Lexie's eyes filled with tears of regret. She wished the porch light were on so that she could break the spell between them.

She took a shuddering breath and tried to pull back, but Jackson held on to her.

Jackson searched the sky above them. "The first stars are beginning to shine, Lex. Tell me, what's your dream?"

Lexie's breath caught in her throat. It was a silly game they'd indulged in when they were younger—wishing on the first star of the evening. She'd wished for another baby, and later, when they learned a second child wasn't in their future...

"Do you still wish for a business of your own?" Jackson completed her thought.

"How can you remember my dreams and not remember the important stuff?" Like Heidi's birthday or their anniversary.

"I've always told you your dreams are important. Everyone says you should sell those marinades you make—"

"And call them Hot Shot Sauces. I haven't forgotten." She'd given up on making her people-pleasing spicy marinades a paying reality. His dream had always been to be a Hot Shot, like his father. His dream *was* a reality.

He cupped her cheek. "I don't want to argue."

"Me, neither." It felt too good standing here in the darkness with her hands in his. Lexie knew that tomorrow the sun would come up and he'd still be the man who wouldn't open up to her. She'd give herself sixty seconds more of the fantasy that Jackson was perfect for her, and then she'd gather her strength and return to the house.

As if sensing he'd pushed some limit, Jackson said, "You'll remind me tomorrow why we can't be together, won't you?" His words were tangled with bitterness. "Damn it, Lex."

"Don't." She placed her fingers over his lips. His warm breath wafted across her skin. She'd done her duty. She'd soothed whatever had unsettled him inside so that he had a better chance of getting some sleep. "I'm going inside now."

Lexie felt his lips tighten as if in a frown. She pulled her fingers back and rested her hand on her belly.

He released her other hand.

"Before you go, can you...can you tell me about Deb?"

Lexie had to close her eyes against the tears. Deb was Lexie's best friend, and had been since high school. "You heard she's dying." Leaving behind two beautiful, nine-year-old twin girls. Lexie stroked the baby in her tummy.

"Logan wouldn't tell me much."

"She's got an inoperable brain tumor. By the time they diagnosed her, it was too late for chemo." Lexie swallowed against the dryness in her throat, and tried to lighten her tone. "You should see her. She's so strong and brave about it, it makes you feel guilty when you feel like crying in front of her."

He leaned back against the truck. "And the girls?"

"They're scared, but I don't think they believe she's really going to die. They still believe their mom is invincible. Logan's the one who treats her like glass. I don't talk with him much about Deb."

He mulled that over for a bit. "Thanks for telling me."

"You're welcome." Lexie turned back to the house. She'd survived that encounter well. They hadn't hugged or kissed. She hadn't ended up in a motel room with him. They seemed to be almost on friendly terms. Lexie thought she could handle their relationship turning into friendship.

"Lex?"

She paused, looking over her shoulder.

"Will you marry me?"

"SHE'S NOT TAKING ME BACK." Jackson leaned against the door frame of his mother's office in the Painted Pony, arms crossed tightly over his chest. The Hot Shot in him felt as if he should act like he didn't care—be strong, be a man—while the rest of him felt bruised, spent and in need of a rest. Lexie and Heidi had just witnessed a display of his weakness.

He could still hear Heidi's voice. *"Dad, you're scaring me."*

And then to limit himself to holding Lexie's hands in the darkness, trying to draw her back emotionally into the past where their love had been strong, only to have her put a *friendly* distance between them. Reclaiming their love seemed hopeless.

He doubted his mother would be able to put a bandage on his heart, kiss his brow and make him feel better. She couldn't fix a broken heart or give him back his courage. He didn't care, as long as he could get some rest and perhaps a bit of her advice.

His mother looked at him over the top of her reading glasses. Bills, invoices and receipts were scattered across her desk. An old calculator was perched at her elbow. Jackson recognized the distracted look in her eyes. She was focused on something and didn't want to be disturbed.

"She told you she's not taking you back?" his mom asked.

"Several times." It was easier to talk about his failed marriage than his grim future. With a sigh, Jackson walked over to the kitchen cupboard and took out two fluorescent light bulbs. "The light isn't strong enough in here for you to be reading that fine print."

As he replaced the burned-out bulbs in the ceiling above her, Jackson felt his mother's scrutiny. Any time now, she'd tell him what she thought he should do. When he was finished, he stood next to her desk. Only, she'd returned her attention to her work.

"I was chugging along until you came in. I've got a bridge game tonight, you know." His mother focused on the stacks of paper in front of her.

Jackson sank into a chair next to the desk. Waiting. She'd start lecturing him any time now.

His mother added up a stack of invoices. She jotted the figure down on a yellow pad, then slipped the papers into a folder. Jackson drummed his fingers on the tabletop.

"I'm about to become a father for the second time. And I'm not sure what to do about it."

Without acknowledging him, his mother began to add up a pile of receipts.

Jackson leaned forward. "Aren't you going to say something?"

She stared at him over the top of her glasses again. "About what?"

"About me. About my life and how I screwed it up."

"We've had that discussion. More than once. We disagreed, as I recall." She straightened the pile of receipts and began to add them up a second time.

"Let's have it again."

"Jackson, I don't have time for this."

"She's not going to take me back." His voice sounded weak and pitiful. He pushed himself out of the chair, telling himself that at thirty a man shouldn't need his mother's advice. "Never mind."

"Jackson—"

"I know you said I couldn't stay with you, but I really need a place to bed down until I get back on my feet. I'll bring a sleeping bag out of the garage so you won't have to wash any sheets." He started down the hall.

"Of course you can stay with me. You're always welcome home. I was joking earlier."

"My *home* is on Lone Pine Road." There was that defeated tone of voice again. He walked quickly toward the back door, away from people he knew in the Pony's dining room, as if he could escape the fact that he'd lost his family for good. Never mind that he'd already lost the guts to fight fires.

"Jackson, you don't need a sleeping bag. You can sleep in your old room. How you'll fit into that single bed is beyond me. Although I know you and Lexie spent some time there in your youth.''

He hesitated, head hung at the reminder of the love he once had. His mom laid her hand on his shoulder.

"I didn't mean to ignore you." She chuckled once. "Well, maybe just a little. I do need to finish the monthly expenses before I go to Birdie's. And it was the only way I could stop myself from giving you advice."

The pressure that had built on Jackson's chest eased a bit. There had been two constants in his life after his father died—Lexie and his mother. "You know I always listen to what you say."

She chuckled again. "You may listen, but I know you don't hear me."

Jackson spun around, reached for his mom and squeezed her tight. She knew him too well—it was true, he hadn't listened to her advice in the past. If he had, he wouldn't have gotten Lexie pregnant, wouldn't have married her so young, and would have crawled back to her on his hands and knees when she asked for a divorce.

After a moment, Jackson released his mom. "Is your advice in abridged form or a long-winded version?"

"Need you ask?"

"We better sit down." Jackson led his mother back to the office.

"I need a cup of coffee first," she said, detouring into the kitchen. His mother was a coffee fanatic. "Want one?"

"Sure." If he could, he'd load up on caffeine and never sleep—or dream—again.

A few minutes later, when his mom was settled in her chair, Jackson raised one eyebrow. "Well?"

"I'm not sure where to begin."

That didn't sound encouraging. Needing something to do with his hands, Jackson sipped his coffee.

"Why on earth would Lexie take you back? I wouldn't take you back if I were her."

Jackson very nearly sprayed coffee all over his mother. "This is your advice?" he asked when he could manage to speak.

"I love you, dear, but sometimes I don't understand you."

With deliberate movements, he set the coffee cup on the desk. "So you think I should just give up?"

"Not at all."

Closing his eyes, Jackson sank back into the chair.

"I know that you love Lexie. She's wonderful. She did everything around the house. She cooked. She cleaned. She even mowed the lawn. You didn't have a care in the world."

It was the same argument Lexie always made. Jackson used his standard defense. "I bring home a steady paycheck. I don't drink too much, and I don't beat my wife. Why does it always comes back to how much she did around the house? My job takes me away." A job he was giving up. But Lexie still wasn't going to give him a second chance.

Jackson slumped farther into the chair. "Besides, you do everything around the Pony *and* the house."

"Yes, but I took on all those responsibilities *after* your father died because they wouldn't have got done if I hadn't. I see now that Theresa and I pampered you far too much." Jackson's father had died fighting a fire when Jackson was twelve, leaving Jackson as the man of a house where he was outnumbered by two females more than happy to take care of him.

"I'm lazy. Is that it? She left me because I'm lazy?" This was the last thing he wanted to hear from his mother. His mother was supposed to be his strongest supporter. Suddenly Jackson couldn't sit still any longer.

"Well—" she began.

"I'm a deadbeat Dad, like you see on those afternoon TV shows. That's what you mean."

"That's not—"

"I've had enough advice for one night, Mom. See you in the morning." Jackson ignored his mother's pleas to return and raced out to the parking lot.

"WE THOUGHT YOU WEREN'T COMING," Marguerite announced upon opening the door to Birdie's house, wearing a plunging, lacy dress Mary considered more appropriate for Madonna than for a plump, widowed retiree.

"It's not even eight-thirty." Mary tried to keep her tone even as she stepped inside, although she longed to snap at someone. It wasn't Marguerite's fault that Mary was late to the group's weekly bridge game.

Mary wasn't upset at Jackson for delaying her, although he hadn't wanted to listen to the rest of what she had to say about his relationship with Lexie. Mary's mood had more to do with her anxiety about her own love life. She had recently made a decision to return to dating.

For nearly twenty years, Mary had avoided thinking about men as anything other than friends. She'd warmed her toes at night with her grandmother's hot-water bottle while she kept her mind busy worrying about her kids and the business she'd started with Jeremy's life insurance money. She had the Painted Pony to run, gray hair she'd earned every right not to color and an occasional whisker she plucked off her chin. She thought men, romance and sex were a thing of the past.

That all changed a few months ago when Sirus Socrath, Jackson's former Hot Shot superintendent, stopped to help Mary change a flat tire alongside the road. She'd been driving into Boise to pick up supplies, when a tire blew. While she was struggling to loosen the last lug nut, Sirus had pulled up.

"Having trouble?"

"I think this one lug is rusted on." Mary gaped at Sirus's long, lanky frame. From that angle, he looked like the cock-of-the-walk, as her mother used to say. Mary blinked, unused to thinking of Sirus as anything other than a hardworking man of the community and her friend. In that moment, she saw him for the first time as M-A-N as if she were W-O-M-A-N. Mary shook her head and dismissed the odd feeling. She was a grandmother, for heaven's sake.

Sirus knelt next to her on the road's dirt shoulder and loosened the lug nut with ease. His hands were as long as the rest of him, his arms strong from years of fighting fires.

"Not rusted. It just needed a man's touch, you know?" Sirus's faded blue eyes gazed directly into Mary's and his lips turned up ever so slightly at the corners.

Was Sirus Socrath flirting with her? Mary reminded herself that she was fifty-five, and Sirus was sixty if he was a day, and twice divorced to boot. But that didn't stop her heart from pounding as it hadn't for years.

A few days after the flat tire incident, Sirus showed up at Birdie's on bridge night even though he'd never been there before. He claimed to have come to replace Smiley, who could barely see the cards anymore, although Mary imagined Sirus joined them to spend more time with her. Still, nothing changed between them. Sirus didn't seek Mary out or call her, try to hold her hand or kiss her. Sirus never gave Mary any reason to think he wanted her to be anything more than a friend. Yet, Mary was sure he did want more.

Either that or she was going insane.

Perhaps she'd swallowed too much river water, or maybe she was finally completing menopause. It didn't matter what the cause was. Once Sirus lit the dormant spark within her, Mary couldn't seem to put it out.

The seed had been planted—she'd been alone too long. Mary stepped inside Birdie's house, feet thumping on the hardwood floor as loudly as her heart pounded now in her ears. She could feel Sirus's eyes upon her. He had kind eyes. Patient eyes. Eyes that let her know he'd wait for Mary to decide when she was ready for him.

Ready for him? She'd been alone for nearly two decades. She could take care of the house, her car and her business. But she'd forgotten how to take care of a man.

Mary had promised herself she'd work up the courage to ask Sirus back to her house for coffee tonight, the same as she'd been promising herself every Sunday night for the past month. They'd sit on the couch and talk. She'd ask him how he'd come by that scar on his forehead. Later, when she'd drunk some coffee that she planned to lace with a little confidence-building whiskey, maybe she'd work up the courage to kiss Sirus.

Mary couldn't look at Sirus now, for fear she was suffering from an overactive imagination and Sirus would be looking at her as just a friend. If he'd awakened these longings accidentally, Mary wasn't sure what she'd do.

There were snacks on the green felt-covered card table and mints in a crystal bowl that Birdie insisted was from France, though Mary had seen bowls just like it at the dollar store in Boise. The television blared. Someone, probably Sirus, had scooted Birdie's brocade wing chair up close to the set and Smiley perched on it, leaning so close to the screen that Mary thought the old barber might fall into it.

Sirus and Smiley had been sharing Sirus's small cabin since Smiley drove off the road two years ago and nearly killed himself. They weren't related, although Smiley was old enough to be Sirus's father. But neither of them had any family close by. It was just the way of the community to take care of its own.

Sirus gazed up at Mary from his seat at the card table and sent her a smile that warmed her to her toes.

*Would you like to come over to my house later for coffee?*

The question remained unvoiced.

She was such a coward. She couldn't even risk a little rejection from an old friend.

Mary slid into a metal folding chair across from Sirus. She'd found true love once, over thirty years ago with Jeremy Garrett, a Hot Shot, and had been blessed with that love for more than a decade. Then, eighteen years ago, Jeremy died while fighting a wildland fire. It had very nearly broken her heart when Jackson followed in his father's footsteps. Every time Jackson went out on a fire, Mary smiled bravely and prayed for his safe return.

"How are you this evening, Mary?" Sirus asked, bringing her thoughts back to the present.

The blender whirred in the kitchen. Marguerite and Birdie were making the strawberry daiquiris they loved so much. A quick glance at Smiley showed him engrossed in a television reality show. This was about as private as the evening was going to get.

"Jackson came home today." Mary tried to send Sirus a smile, but smiling at Sirus had become a self-conscious act for Mary, as if she were a teenager with an unrequited crush.

"Yeah, he stopped at the office. I didn't get much of a chance to talk to him." No longer able to keep up with the younger firefighters, yet still a prime physical specimen, Sirus now worked at the National Interagency Fire Center as an incident commander. He coordinated fire attack crews in the field. That meant working nontraditional hours and days. It wasn't unusual for NIFC to be staffed round the clock during fire season.

Sirus kept his warm brown gaze on Mary, while his large hands shuffled the deck of cards. His face was as long and narrow as the rest of him, but not sharp. Nothing about Sirus was sharp, not even the faint scar along his temple. Carrying himself tall and proud, he was a hand-some man in his own way. Mary liked looking at him. He was a sturdy man, too, in both stature and personality. You could rely on a man like Sirus.

"Jackson's staying at my house." She'd known Sirus for years without so much as a stray spark of interest flaring between them. Why now? She was happy with her life the way it was. Wasn't she?

"How's he doing?"

"He's…" Mary frowned, struggling for the right word. Her son was still heartbroken over Lexie, but there was something else about his demeanor that didn't seem right, something she couldn't quite put her finger on. "I don't know. He's quiet. You know Jackson, he's always got something to say." She rolled her eyes. "I'm probably just imagining things."

Sirus considered her words for a moment. "Does he seem—"

"Look at this, Sirus," Smiley interrupted loudly, pointing at the television screen. "This fool's going to eat raw snake eggs."

Sirus shrugged apologetically and obliged Smiley by acknowledging the grossness of the stunt.

In the meantime, Mary's mind wandered. What if Mary kissed Sirus and liked it? Or worse, what if she were brave enough to take off her clothes and climb into bed with him someday? What if the sex was great? Her smile would give it away. Everyone in Silver Bend would know she was Sirus's love toy.

And if their lovemaking fell short of greatness…

Disaster.

Sirus was her bridge partner. If she began a relationship with him and it failed, she'd have to look across the table and see his disappointment on a weekly basis. Men were always dissatisfied when it came to sex. They didn't get it enough. They didn't get it with someone young enough.

They didn't get it wild enough. And Mary didn't even want to think about the extra pounds and wrinkles she'd accumulated since the last time she'd been with a man. Sirus was bound to be disappointed with her. She'd never be able to play bridge again.

The television segment finished and Sirus's eyes drifted down to Mary's hands and then back up to her face. "You must be happy that Jackson's home."

The temperature in the room rocketed up five degrees. "Words cannot describe how I'm feeling right now." Guilt. Disappointment. Lust.

*Lust?* Mary had to be imagining Sirus's interest, even if she wasn't imagining her own.

In the kitchen, the blender ground to a halt.

"Why don't you shuffle?" Sirus set the cards in the middle of the table. "Your hands move with such grace, it's a pleasure to watch."

Mary could picture her hands moving, all right. Her cheeks flushed with heat. She let her eyes follow the pearly snaps on Sirus's worn western shirt down to the edge of the table, wondering about Sirus's body. Long legs, long arms, long fingers...

She was depraved!

Mary's eyes snapped up to Sirus's. He chuckled, and it sent another tingle of awareness through her. Mary coughed, trying to break this spell he had over her.

"Here come the refreshments," Marguerite said as she brought in a tray full of the icy pink drinks.

"What's so funny?" Birdie asked, carrying a plate of cocktail wieners and cheese cubes, each speared with a toothpick.

"Jackson came home," Sirus said.

"Grew a decent beard in Russia," Smiley nearly shouted, not turning from the television.

"Smiley, turn that down. You're not deaf," Birdie instructed, holding her small frame as tight and precise as a bird.

Smiley did as he was told. Most everyone in Silver Bend did what Birdie wanted. She'd been married to the town mayor for years and then taken the position herself after his death.

"Never mind that. Did he see Lexie?" Marguerite sat down next to Mary and leaned her buxom qualities over the table.

"What did he say about the baby?" Birdie probed.

Mary blinked, then shook her head and made a weak attempt at a smile. "I don't know." Although Lexie didn't talk about it much, she had confirmed when asked that the baby was Jackson's. That knowledge had only made folks in Silver Bend more interested in Jackson's reaction.

Marguerite settled back in her chair. "He'll do the right thing."

"Should come in for a shave," Smiley added.

"She'll take him back, of course." Marguerite took the cards from the middle of the table and began to shuffle. The many rings she wore sparkled in the lamplight.

Mary looked away, not wanting to know if Sirus was fascinated with Marguerite's hands, too. She'd never noticed his interest in her before. What if she'd never noticed his interest in Marguerite, either?

"It's none of our business, anyway," Sirus said.

"Hogswaddle. We care about them. Besides, they were meant for each other. I'll tell Jackson tomorrow that he should send flowers." Birdie's words rang with authority.

"Flowers. That's so sweet," Marguerite crooned. "Maybe I'll stop by later in the week to see how they're doing."

"Let's just mind our own affairs and play cards." Sirus didn't sound happy.

It was all Mary could do not to look at Sirus. He was right, of course. But that wasn't the way it was in the tight-knit, small community of Silver Bend. If Mary wanted to explore these unsettling feelings Sirus had aroused in her, she'd receive just as much advice and meddling as Lexie and Jackson were about to get.

She was too old for this.

# CHAPTER FOUR

"YOU COULD HAVE CALLED to warn me he was coming home," Lexie gently chided Mary the next afternoon as she sat in a booth and rolled silverware in paper napkins. The baby she carried was oddly still.

Lexie and Heidi came by the Painted Pony on Monday mornings to help Mary put the place back in order after a hectic few days of weekend traffic. Mary's business was steady, but she, like everyone else in Silver Bend, ran lean in terms of crew. Although Lexie used to be a cook and waitress for Mary, the discovery of her pregnancy and the complications that made it high risk had forced Lexie to stop working altogether, swallow her pride and apply for assistance.

"Heidi, don't do that." Mary turned to Heidi, who had stacked glasses in a pyramid at the other end of Lexie's table without Lexie even noticing.

"I know what I'm doing." Heidi grinned. "Just a few more and I'll break my record."

"If any glasses break, I'd like them to be broken by paying customers," Mary chastised, but some of the sting had vanished from her tone.

Heidi's smile was nearly as powerful as her father's.

"Heidi, just because you started wearing a bra doesn't mean you can bend the rules." Lexie tried to tease Heidi into doing what her grandmother had asked.

"Mo-om." Heidi rolled her eyes. "Have I ever broken a glass?"

"Yes!" Mary and Lexie chimed in.

"That was a long time ago." Heidi delicately placed another glass on her pyramid.

"Two months," Lexie pointed out.

"Last June," Mary clarified. "Go put those in the dishwasher with the other dishes you're supposed to be washing."

"And if you break any, you'll be grounded until you're old enough to wear a girdle," Lexie added.

"I bet Dad would let me stack them." With a petulant pout only preteens could master, Heidi began loading her glasses into a plastic tub used to bus tables. "What do I have to do to get some respect around here?"

"Work your fingers to the bone." Mary waggled her fingers at Heidi. "Now scoot."

"Why didn't you tell me?" Lexie asked Mary again, when Heidi had retreated to the kitchen.

Mary reached a weathered hand across the counter to stroke Lexie's hair. "I couldn't warn you when I didn't know what he was going to do. Besides, what would you have done differently if you had known he was coming?"

Fainted on the floor as she almost did yesterday, then loaded Heidi in the truck and driven to Boise. That way, she wouldn't have had to face him at all. The memory of Jackson, eyes locked with hers, returned. She'd had a crush on Jackson Garrett since the ninth grade, when she and her mother had arrived in Silver Bend one hot August afternoon.

Lexie's mother had taken a job as a secretary for the Silver Bend school district, where her salary barely paid for a single-wide motor home in the middle of the forest. The first thing Lexie had seen that made her think the backwater town of Silver Bend was going to be tolerable was Jackson working outside of the Painted Pony, barechested as he pounded nails into a new board on the porch.

Later, Jackson's love had transformed Lexie's existence

from bearable to wondrous. Sometimes just the sight of Jackson could make her melt, just like yesterday when he'd held her in his arms again. He'd taught Lexie not to settle for less than what she dreamed or what she deserved. No one had ever believed in her before.

Funny thing was, all she wanted was his love, and when she felt she'd lost it, she refused to settle for less. His standards, his expectations were the reason she'd asked for a divorce.

"You can't postpone the inevitable." Mary's gaze was too knowing. "You had to face him sometime."

Embarrassed, Lexie ducked her head. "At least with fair warning I would've had time to figure out what to say."

Mary chuckled softly. "As if you haven't had seven months already?"

Lexie blushed and wrapped another set of silverware, wishing she hadn't started the conversation.

"I can't interfere, Lexie. He's my son and you've become as important to me as he is. Don't make me choose sides."

"I wouldn't make you do that," Lexie said, but she might wish it, just a little. She felt so alone. Her own mother was convinced Lexie was repeating her mistakes. How could Lexie argue with that? She'd gotten pregnant in high school, married instead of going to college, and now had no job skills and no husband to help with ever-mounting bills. She was reliving her mother's life.

If starry dreams did come true, a fairy godmother would have swooped down years ago, waved her magic wand and gifted Lexie with a college diploma and all the knowledge she needed to run a small business selling her Hot Shot Sauces.

"Can someone help me with the griddle? It's got a layer of grease so thick a kid could drown in it," Heidi called from the kitchen. "Mom, I'm definitely going to college.

Somewhere like Harvard. Because I'm not spending the rest of my life with greasy dishpan hands.''

"Thank you, Fairy Godmother," Lexie said under her breath. At least her daughter could dream big, even if Lexie no longer had the heart to.

"HE'LL MOVE BACK in. He wants to," Heidi said to Mary in the kitchen, using a soft voice so that Lexie couldn't hear them from her seat in the dining room.

"Not unless your mom bends." Or Jackson changes, Mary thought.

"We're doomed," Heidi moaned. "Mom's word is, like, law or something. I was hoping Dad would come back from Russia and sweep her off her feet. But she wouldn't even listen to him. It's so not fair."

Mary wasn't surprised that Lexie had turned down Jackson's marriage proposal, but she was disappointed. Until her son's return, Mary hadn't realized how much she'd been hoping he and Lexie would get back together.

"I bet if he kissed her she would have said yes. They always used to kiss a lot," Heidi noted.

"Maybe they've forgotten how," Mary said, trying to lighten the moment.

There was a pause, then Heidi mumbled, "Maybe Dad's been kissing someone else."

"No. Your dad is nuts for your mom. He always has been."

Mary had never believed her son's marriage would disintegrate. She'd seen the way Lexie made moon eyes at Jackson when he wasn't looking, as if she was waiting for him to come to his senses. Much to Mary's dismay, Jackson had chosen to handle things in his own way. But one look at the pain behind Jackson's eyes yesterday and Lexie should have known how much he needed her back.

"Heidi, it's time you learned what it means to live in Silver Bend. If two people aren't smart enough to realize they were meant to be together, we give them a helping hand." Mary was surprised at the conviction in her tone. After all, she wanted to avoid anyone intruding in her life. But this was different.

Jackson and Lexie were meant for each other.

LEXIE BLINKED sleepy eyes and yawned. Mary and Heidi were in the back of the restaurant. Lexie could hear their muffled voices and occasional laughter. It was good to hear Heidi laugh. Her daughter wasn't the carefree, smiling girl she'd been before Lexie had asked Jackson to leave last year. There was now more moping and outbursts of tears without warning. She preferred to believe this change in Heidi came from hormones rather than the divorce....

Sitting in a booth, Lexie arched her spine to ease the constant ache in her lower back, hoping it would quell the queasiness in her stomach as well.

It didn't.

She needed a distraction to keep her mind off of her body. It was a slow afternoon in the Pony. She shifted on the vinyl booth seat and propped her feet up on the seat across from her.

Lexie yawned again. She'd been unable to sleep for more than an hour at a time last night. The baby had been practicing nocturnal acrobatics, which meant Lexie had had little relief from thoughts of Jackson.

He wanted to marry her again.

Her heart couldn't help but beat faster at the thought. She'd never loved anyone else, couldn't imagine loving anyone else. Yet, his love for her had changed over the years and she'd made her decision to live her life without him.

On a practical level, her money problems would ease if she let Jackson into their lives again. But she'd still be alone. Marriage was supposed to be a partnership, not a management deal. No. It wouldn't work. The days of Lexie and Jackson cuddling on the couch and talking about anything and everything for hours were long gone. She was trying to channel the love she had for him toward friendship. Hopefully, he'd do the same so that they could share the parenting duties smoothly.

But even with friendship in mind, Lexie couldn't keep herself from worrying about Jackson.

*Did he suffer more nightmares now that he slept alone?*

Assuming he was sleeping alone.

The wooden screen door at the front of the Painted Pony creaked open. Lexie looked up, the customer a welcome distraction from her thoughts.

"Hey, Lex." Jackson shoved his hands into the front pockets of his jeans. His black T-shirt stretched snugly over every sculpted muscle in his chest. His eyes were ringed from lack of sleep and his smile could only be called attempted.

The sight of him combined with the sound of his voice shot through her like a jolt of strong coffee, chasing away her nausea and aches. Reflexively, Lexie's left hand smoothed her secondhand maternity blouse over her tummy in an effort to settle back down. As though in tune with Lexie's agitation, the baby kicked her.

Jackson watched her hand, and Lexie couldn't help but remember how he'd massaged her stomach when she was pregnant with Heidi and how that had led to sessions of slow lovemaking. His actions had made her feel special— even when he didn't express his love in words. That had set the tone for much of their intimacy. Later she'd come to believe his silence might mean something else entirely—that she only sated a physical need for him, not an emotional one.

He smiled at her. "How are you feeling?"

"Fine." Anything but fine. How could she be fine when he was in the room within touching distance? She was glad she was sitting down, otherwise Jackson might have made the world spin on her again. After the intimacy of last night, Lexie had to regain her distance and perspective.

"And you? Did you sleep well?"

Jackson drew back, his smile fading. "Why do you ask?"

"You had a nightmare yesterday at the house."

He shrugged but wouldn't meet her gaze. "Just one bad dream. That's to be expected after being up for two days and falling asleep sitting up."

She stared at Jackson, trying to read his expression. "It's not the first time you've had nightmares. You used to come home after weeks away and I'd know that the fire wasn't too bad if you slept peacefully."

Jackson grunted, shaking his head.

"It's true. You'd come home filled with all these stories that made light of the danger you'd faced. Then at night, I'd find out the truth." She'd cradled him in her arms and whispered soft words to ease his nightmares as if she could shelter him from whatever horrible event he'd faced while he was away. Away from her.

When Jackson still said nothing, she added, "Did you think I couldn't handle the danger? Do you know how much it hurt me that you shut me out all the time? Even last night?" She hadn't wanted to admit that. Things had gotten too close too fast, and it was all her fault. "Never mind. Why are you here?"

"I…I thought I'd take the Runt rafting." He looked a little shell-shocked.

"All right." The sooner he left, the better for Lexie's sanity.

"Maybe afterwards we could go into Boise for dinner."

Even better. That way she'd be guaranteed Jackson-free time. She'd just had another painful reminder of why they weren't meant to be married. They needed to be friends. Lexie forced herself to smile. "She'd like that."

"Would you?" He stepped closer.

She stopped smiling. Lexie held up her hand as if to make him keep his distance. "I don't plan on going."

Jackson frowned, his beard adding a harshness that his boyish expressions had lacked in the past, making him look older. His eyes, so bright green, seemed to dim.

"Friends, remember?" Lexie added before he could protest. Her stomach tightened. She told herself it was a practice contraction.

"How could I forget," he said quietly, staring at her so intently and with such an expression of loneliness on his face that she felt an uncomfortable blush creep up her neck. Finally, Jackson looked away. "I hadn't realized you knew I had nightmares."

Since he often returned from fighting fires sleep deprived and physically spent, she knew he wasn't aware of his sleeping habits. Still, it hurt to hear him say he hadn't known she'd offered solace all those times.

"Listen, I meant what I said yesterday, about being here for you."

Lexie dragged in a deep breath of relief, grateful for the change in subject. "Of course you did." As long as she'd known him, he'd always meant well. Jackson just wasn't the type to follow through.

"But that's not enough for you."

"It wasn't. Not at the end." She'd been so lonely in their marriage those last few years. She'd missed him.

"Maybe you should have married someone with a regular job."

Lexie was caught off guard by the raw anguish in Jackson's words, compounded by the fire in his eyes. They hadn't fought much and Jackson had rarely been the aggressor in their arguments. She'd mostly been the one to start things, until she began feeling like a shrew every time she opened her mouth to complain. Then she'd started to hold it all in, until she felt as if she were withering away, imagining the years passing her by until she was as cold inside as her empty bed each night of fire season.

"Maybe."

"Someone who'd be home every night by five-thirty."

Lexie couldn't speak, could only listen to the pain in Jackson's words, pain he hadn't shown during the months she'd pressed for a divorce. Why did he have to bare this side of himself now, when she was such an emotional and physical wreck?

"The sex wouldn't have been spectacular then, would it."

Lexie almost slid off the vinyl seat at the cruelty of his words. "You don't get this at all, do you."

"Maybe if you'd explain it to me, I would. Talk real slow so a guy like me who does manual labor for a living can understand."

Anger boiled in Lexie's stomach, bringing back the nauseated feeling. She pushed herself out of the booth and placed her fists on her padded hips, willing herself to hang in there a bit longer.

"All right. I could live with your having to be away at work for days or weeks at a time. I learned to cope with the fear that you might not come home. But at some point over the years, Jackson, you stopped being home when you weren't at work. Everyone was more important than your own family. Someone would come by or call and you'd be gone. I can't remember you being home for a family meal those last few months we were together. I was *lonely*. The only time I saw you was when you slipped into bed at night. And, yes, that was great, but fifteen minutes a day isn't enough to build a lifetime on. Not for me, anyway."

Jackson looked hurt, but Lexie hardened herself against the knowledge that she'd caused it. Maybe she'd sugarcoated things during their divorce because in one not-so-teeny corner of her mind she wanted him to fight for her.

But he hadn't, and now it was too late. Maybe a dose of reality was just what Jackson needed to accept their divorce.

When Jackson didn't respond, Lexie said, "I'll get Heidi." Before she could escape, the telephone rang and she answered it.

"Just like old times." She handed the telephone to Jackson, knowing she had been right to let him go. "It's for you."

JACKSON WATCHED LEXIE walk away from him. Then, remembering that he held a phone in his hand, he put it to his ear and said, "Jackson here."

"We've got several fires started by lightning above Garden Valley. You know how dry that area gets this time of year. I'm assigning you to a position and I need you to start ASAP."

Sirus Socrath, known as Socrates among the Hot Shots, had trained Jackson and just about every other wildland firefighter working in southern Idaho over the past twenty years. Jackson and legions of other firefighters looked upon Sirus with great respect. Many sent him Father's Day cards. That's the kind of impact Sirus had on the lives of his trainees.

"I just got back yesterday." With effort, Jackson kept his temper and fear in check. He needed time off to mend his broken marriage. He was owed this time, damn it. And he was far from ready to return to the fire line.

"I know, and I'm sorry about canceling your leave, but I need you."

Unfortunately, attempted reconciliation didn't qualify him for emergency leave. The only way Jackson would keep his vacation was if he confessed that he'd lost his nerve. They'd send him to counseling, ask him personal questions about his life, try to evaluate his relationship with his deceased father, which had been just fine, thank you. He might as well tattoo a big yellow *C* on his fore-head for *Coward*.

Request they honor his vacation? Nope. That wasn't going to happen.

"The Hot Shots?" Jackson asked, instead of rejecting Sirus's request outright. Sweat broke out on his upper lip.

"No, Silver Bend spots are filled. I want you on my staff."

"Incident Staff?" Jackson winced. It was one of the jobs he'd applied for at NIFC, far away from the danger and excitement of the fire itself. He'd applied just to ease his fears, not expecting to be given the position. Yet, relief flooded his veins. He wouldn't be fighting fires.

"One of my team just went out on maternity leave and another broke both ankles waterskiing."

Jackson mumbled something about as intelligent as "Oh."

Sirus's voice became less businesslike. "Give it a chance, son. It's only temporary."

Never mind the fact that the Hot Shots would give him hell for taking on a position that was—in their minds, at least—work meant for those who lacked the courage to hack the line. Jackson swallowed. "When do you need me?"

"Yesterday. There are thunderstorms brewing again this afternoon. The analysts at NIFC predict this one has all the right conditions on its side—wind, dry brush and steep slopes." Sirus pronounced the acronym for the National Interagency Fire Center as *nif-see*.

Sirus had taken an incident commander position at NIFC a few years ago when he couldn't cut the physical demands of active-duty Hot Shots anymore. "When you can't outrun and outlast the rookies, it's time to retire," he'd said at the time, a rueful smile on his face but pride in his voice. He'd gone out on his own terms.

Unlike Jackson.

In the present, Sirus said, "Garrett, all the crews know you from chow to laundry to firefighters, which is going to be a big help to me. I need you at the Command Center at Garden Valley in one hour."

"Are you sure you want *me?*" Despite the fact that he now fell apart at the mere thought of fighting a fire, his experience was as a firefighter, not an administrator.

Incident Command decided how to attack a fire. Some IC staff were almost psychic in their ability to allocate men and equipment to fires, while others were sadly lacking. Jackson had spent more than one day cooling his heels at the base of a fire predicted by some specialist at a desk to be a growing threat, only to have it burn out on its own. Sirus was one of the few commanders that had garnered the respect of firefighters. Jackson wouldn't be given so much as an inch of leeway to make a mistake.

This is how far he'd sunk. Fitting punishment for a coward to be assigned a desk job.

A coward who needed Lexie back. Some IC positions were eight to five. If he thought about it that way, maybe he could learn to stomach it.

As if sensing his reluctance, Sirus added, "It's not the end of the world, Garrett. Besides, it'll give you something to do on a real fire for a change."

As if the beasts he'd battled in Russia hadn't been real fires.

Jackson stared down the empty hallway, knowing that he'd have to leave for Garden Valley right now if he was going to accept this assignment. Any delay in sending assistance could mean loss of life or someone's home. That was a more immediate concern than getting his family back this minute. Even without an ounce of courage, Jackson knew he couldn't ignore the importance of his work. Jackson's head knew it. Yet, his heart didn't want to go along.

"I'll be there as soon as I can." Jackson placed the receiver carefully in its cradle.

"Dad!" Heidi ran down the hallway and wrapped her arms around Jackson's waist. "Are we rafting today?"

Jackson fingered Heidi's unruly brown ponytail, then looked up to see Lexie standing at the doorway to the kitchen staring at his hand. Jackson tried to smile. "Sorry, Runt. I've got to go to Garden Valley."

"I knew it." Heidi stepped back, her voice rising to a nearly hysterical pitch. "I knew you'd bail, just like you always do. There's always something more important than *me*." She glared at him.

Guilt over disappointing Heidi tightened Jackson's chest. Yet, the guilt couldn't outweigh the fact that the sooner he arrived in Garden Valley, the better the chance of getting the fires under control.

"This sucks," Heidi groused, running out the door. The screen door banged mercilessly behind her.

"We'll take that trip later in the week—" Jackson yelled the promise at the closed door, feeling his family and the life he'd known slip further and further from his grasp.

"What happened to that vacation of yours?" Lexie asked, walking forward with a soft sway of curves emphasized by a clinging pink maternity blouse. Jackson didn't think he'd ever seen a pregnant woman so beautiful. Her blue eyes may have been filled with disappointment, but everything else about the way she looked spelled home for him.

"Lightning's started fires above Garden Valley and, since every forest in the West is sparking, Sirus needs the extra bodies." He'd heard as much from Logan yesterday. He walked to the end of the bar and leaned against it.

She paused several feet in front of him, worry in her eyes. "You're going back with the Hot Shots?"

"No," he said, much too quickly, all too aware of how

she'd known about the nightmares he'd thought were secret. "I'll be working for Sirus on this one. Incident Command at base camp. Isn't that what you wanted? This fire's so close I could be home most nights."

Her gaze was indecipherable, occasionally flickering to his hand. It finally registered that she was checking out his wedding ring, the symbol of their vows to each other.

"We're still last on your list," Lexie said, somehow managing to step past Jackson at the bar without so much as a wayward curve touching him. She bent over slowly, reaching down into the bottom cupboard for her purse, exposing inches of creamy leg that had been covered by her simple black shorts.

Without thinking, Jackson moved into the middle of the space behind the bar. When Lexie straightened, he was blocking her path. She raised her dark eyebrows at him. In the past, a move like that would have been an open invitation for her to fall into his arms and steal a kiss or two without an audience.

"I'm making an effort, Lex." He desperately wanted the shelter of Lexie's embrace.

She looked away. "Mary's in the freezer. Can you stay a minute until she comes back up front?"

"Why don't you stay?" The impassiveness of her tone combined with the shuttered look in her eyes tested his patience. After all, Lexie worked for Jackson's mother and it was summer, so Heidi didn't have anywhere to go. Jackson had a drive ahead of him, and a huge portion of humble pie to eat in his role as management.

He'd rather nibble on something else, he thought as his gaze became fixed on Lexie's lips.

"I need to get home." Lexie's reply was cool. Her eyes drifted once more to his left hand. "Why are you wearing your wedding ring?"

"Because I still…" Jackson lowered his voice, trying not to choke on the words he so rarely said to anyone. "I still care, Lex. All the time I spent in Russia, I spent thinking about you."

Her eyes clouded with tears. The tip of her pert nose reddened.

"Can I see you later?" He spoke gently, continuing when she didn't immediately react. "We can talk this through. I know we can. I'll be back late tonight, but I'm sure I can get back earlier if you say the word. What we had was too precious to let go."

Lexie blinked. "No. I won't let you do this to me again." Lexie stepped closer, laid her hands on his chest and shoved. "Could you just…move!"

Although there wasn't enough power behind her effort to push him back, Jackson stepped aside and let her pass. Lexie scurried past him as fast as her legs could carry her, which, given her condition, wasn't all that fast.

"What about Mom?" he asked.

Lexie paused, then turned to face him. She looked defeated. "I don't work here anymore."

"What the… Where are you working?" Jackson strode to the door, but Lexie was gone.

"She's unemployed," his mother said, coming up behind him. "The doctor put her on bed rest months ago."

"I thought when she and Heidi mentioned she had to take it easy it meant taking an afternoon nap." Jackson looked out the door, then back at his mother. "I don't give her enough to pay all the bills. She wouldn't let me."

"I know."

"How is she making ends meet?"

Outside, an engine sputtered to life. Lexie's beat-up SUV. Jackson watched Lexie's wheels kick up dust as she sped out of the parking lot and onto the highway.

"She's Lexie," his mother replied with a shrug. "She gets by."

"She doesn't need me," Jackson admitted after a moment of awkward silence, still facing the highway.

"Nonsense." His mother made a derisive sound. "She loves you. She's loved you since the day she set eyes on you."

Jackson turned back to his mother and shook his head, trying to hold his sorrow at bay. "But she never needed me."

"I'll grant you that Lexie's independent. She's capable of taking care of herself and my grandbabies...."

"So? Where do I come in?"

"Let me finish, please. I wanted to tell you this last night." His mother frowned at him. "Love isn't about helping your partner with the chores...although that doesn't mean you shouldn't. Love is about feeling closer to your partner than to anyone else on the planet. Feeling so close that you know what it is they need. And needing to be with them more than you need to breathe air."

Jackson understood that. He'd huddled with four other men in the wilderness, barely breathing because the air under their aluminum shelter was so precious that breathing normally might have meant their deaths. He'd fought for his life because he had to return to Lexie and Heidi.

If what his mother said was true, if Lexie still loved him, there was hope. "All I have to do is figure out what she needs. Thanks, Mom. Gotta run." He gave her a quick kiss and raced out of the door.

"HEY, ANYONE HOME?" Lexie called as she opened the front door to Deb's house.

"Tess? Hannah?" Heidi slipped past Lexie and into the living room.

The two-story log house with its dark wood panels and dark hardwood floors would have been depressing if Deb didn't keep the windows wide open and colorful quilts and pillows tossed around.

Hannah, one of the twins, poked her head through the kitchen door. "We're in here."

Lexie waddled all the way into the kitchen. Her back was still hurting, making it hard to move. Heidi, of course, ran ahead.

"I'll do that, you sit down," Lexie said upon seeing Deb standing up at the kitchen counter chopping vegetables.

"Who needs to sit worse? You or me?" Deb asked with an impish grin. Everything about Deb was loaded with energy and enthusiasm for living. That's why seeing her smiling now as if she didn't have a care in the world—despite a cap on her shaved head where her long, blond tresses used to be and the bones of her frame sticking out—was that much harder for Lexie to take.

"You sit, Mom," urged Tess, the worrier of Deb's girls. "Heidi, let my mom sit in that chair."

Deb cocked a brow at them all. "I'll tell you when I need to sit." She returned her energy to the cutting board, hacking away at the broccoli with renewed vigor.

"I brought French bread and fresh peaches." Lexie moved to the counter with her contribution to dinner. She tried to share dinner with Deb a few times a week, helping her around the house and with the girls. Sometimes Lexie couldn't afford to bring much, so she just helped prepare dinner and then left.

"This vegetable casserole is going to be a big hit." Deb exchanged a wry smile with Lexie. All three girls tended to turn up their noses at vegetables. The two women often tried new recipes to entice them to eat the healthy stuff. "Lots of cheese and sour cream. Loaded with calories."

"We can both use the extra energy." Lexie patted her tummy. She glanced back at the girls sitting quietly at the table and staring at Deb as if death had already knocked on their mother's door. "Heidi, why don't you practice braiding the girls' hair?"

"I'm not a doll," Tess said, crossing her arms over her thin chest.

"I didn't say you were. I'm trying to teach Heidi how to keep her hair neat and it would help a lot if she could practice on someone besides herself." Lexie walked over and stroked Heidi's messy ponytail, not daring to look at the twins' wild blond manes. "Deb, you have some hair scrunchies somewhere, don't you?"

"In the downstairs bathroom. What do you say, girls? Sounds like it's either your hair or Barbie's."

"Sounds like fun." Heidi winked at Lexie.

Hannah shrugged. "Okay."

"Only if I get to braid Heidi's hair," Tess said mulishly.

Once the girls left, Deb asked, "How much did you pay Heidi to agree to the hair thing?"

"I had to promise her five bucks. Was I that obvious?"

"No, just to me." Deb sank into a kitchen chair with a sigh. She always seemed to keep up a bold front for her girls, but her illness was wearing her down.

Without a word, Lexie moved to the counter and began preparing the ingredients for the casserole.

"I hear Jackson's back in town."

"Yeah."

"And he found you at the Painted Pony."

"Yeah."

When Deb didn't say anything else, Lexie turned her head to look at her friend. "That can't be all you're going to ask me."

"You're going to make me cross-examine you? You think I can wait until you write a book about it? Tell me all. What was it like seeing him again? How did he look? What did he say about you-know-what?" Deb pointed at Lexie's belly.

Leaning against the counter, Lexie shrugged. "He came. He was surprised. And he left."

"Did I ask for the headline version? No. Give me details. I mean, this was the first time he'd seen you since the big night. He had to have something to say."

It took Lexie only a few seconds of hesitating before admitting, "He wants to marry me again."

"That's wonderful…" Deb paused, blue eyes widening upon seeing the expression on Lexie's face. "I take it you said no."

"Several times."

"You two so obviously love each other. Why are you putting yourself through this?"

Lexie rubbed her hands over her face as if she could smooth away the unpleasant events of the past year. "When I asked him to leave a year ago, he'd been busy fighting fires. And even though he knew something was wrong, he went to work on fires in Southern California and Arizona past the end of the regular fire season and into December." Lexie smoothed her blouse over the baby she carried. "Then he went to a few conferences, attended training in Boise, and when he finally managed to return to Silver Bend for more than one night, he told me that he was leaving for Russia the next day."

She'd never told Deb much more than that, but now she blurted the rest of it in a small, tight voice. "He never said much more than that he missed me or that he wanted to come home. Like an idiot, I kept waiting to hear him say he loved me and that things would change, but he never broached that topic."

"I'm sorry." Deb came to stand next to Lexie, putting her arm around Lexie's back.

Lexie sniffed, tossing her hands. "Come on. Russia? He hadn't even made the effort to talk things out with me before signing up to go to Russia. It was like he was begging for a divorce. I had no choice but to demand he sign the divorce papers if he was going to be leaving me again." Even though she'd realized later that she'd been hoping he'd talk her out of it. Instead, Jackson had turned on the smile, the charm and the sex appeal and taken her to bed, never even attempting to talk about their situation. She chalked her mistake up to the yearnings of her broken heart.

"You never had much willpower where Jackson was concerned," Deb observed.

"He's not going to talk his way back into my bed."

"What if he wants to talk his way back into your heart? A man doesn't ask a woman to marry him again if he hasn't learned his lesson."

"He's got a lot to prove before I say yes again." And the chances of him doing that based on his actions since he'd been back were nearly nonexistent.

# CHAPTER FIVE

*SO THIS IS WHERE THEY SEND WASHED-UP, useless Hot Shots.*

With feet of lead, Jackson stepped into the tent that had been set up as the Garden Valley Fire Command Center. Instead of facing fire, these people faced mounds of paperwork. Jackson couldn't imagine anything more tedious. He wished that he could join his brethren on the fire line, even as the thought sent needles of fear through him.

What would people say when they saw the mighty Golden shaking in his boots at the sight of a wall of fire? No. It was better to avoid the humiliation of returning to where he'd always thought he belonged, better still if he could win Lexie back by taking a job at base camp.

The twenty-by-forty canvas tent was wired with telephones and computers, packed with folding tables and chairs, and fully operational although the fires had started less than twenty-four hours ago. Computer screens showed the latest satellite maps of the weather system above them and the fire activity in the area. Men and women on telephones requested crews and supplies from other government agencies, NIFC and private vendors. A generator chugged in the background.

Near the center of the tent, Rob Hudson, a former smoke jumper, stood with his huge arms akimbo and a slim telephone headset on his crown. Smoke jumpers were similar to Hot Shots in that they fought the hottest part of the fire, the hardest section to reach. Only, smoke jumpers parachuted to the site, rather than hiking in. Smoke jumpers were probably the only group of wildland firefighters Hot Shots respected nearly as much as they respected other Hot Shots—although they would never admit it.

Rob was in his fifties, yet he was still in excellent physical shape. He was the ops chief in charge of deploying crews for fire suppression. He looked at Jackson over the top of his small glasses, then waved him over. All the while, he kept up a continuous stream of directions into his headset.

"Vicki, did Reno confirm the availability of a Hot Shot crew?" Rob asked over the noise of the generators, shaking Jackson's hand.

"Still waiting on final headcount," a woman with a beehive answered from a few positions away. She didn't glance up as her slender, age-spotted fingers tapped away at a computer keyboard.

"Did you hear that, Sirus?" Using his index finger, Rob pressed the earpiece against his ear. "Headcount hasn't been completed.... Well, they told me they've been training new crew.... I know it's the wrong time of year to be training, but apparently they needed to fill their roster midseason and we could use the bodies.... Hang on." Rob turned to Vicki. "What's the ETA on that headcount?"

"Twenty minutes," Vicki answered without breaking stride in her keystrokes.

"She said twenty. I'll call you back in twenty-five if you're not here." Rob pushed a button on the console in front of him and blew out a breath in frustration. "Thank God, you're here, Garrett. We have fires launching all over the place, crews rolling in as we speak, and I can't tear myself away from the phone long enough to send anybody out."

Jackson nodded his understanding. Often the wind died down after sunset and made fire attack easier. They needed to assign crews to a night shift and get them out to the field. "Sirus told me it was heating up here."

"No shit." Rob's dark stare was piercing as he assessed Jackson, no doubt looking for the streak that skunked his back.

Jackson withstood his scrutiny. He deserved no less.

"When did you get back from Russia?" the big man asked, picking up a green bag of vinegar chips.

Amazingly, Jackson felt as if he'd passed Rob's inspection.

"Yesterday."

"Hope you got enough sleep, because it's going to be crazy the next twenty-four hours."

Jackson shrugged. Although he was still jet-lagged, he'd make do.

"Here." Rob handed Jackson a small map. "You can see there are five different fires. With the meteorologist making more lightning predictions, we expect more spot fires by morning."

Jackson scanned the map, noting the five red circles with hatch marks indicating the point of origin. Each fire was circled by a solid line of red, showing the uncontrolled fire edge. None of the red lines overlapped. All five fires were bounded by a black dotted line signifying where the planned fire defenses would be. "Are you sending crews in to start fire breaks tonight?"

"Damn straight." Rob nodded approvingly. "Tractors, engine crews, Hot Shots, whatever I can get my hands on. You remember that fire up here a couple of years ago?"

Jackson remembered the previous Garden Valley fire. He and his crew had had to be airlifted out of harm's way as winds whipping up the river threatened to create a deadly firestorm in several ravines. After they were carried off to safety in a helicopter, he'd laughed off the danger. What a fool he'd been not to respect the power of the flame.

"They didn't have enough people to contain that sucker," Rob continued, his voice bitter. "Jumped a couple of roads, torched a few homes. This time it's on the other side of the mountain and it's not getting away from me.''

Jackson wasn't surprised that Rob took the threat of fire so personally. Lots of guys did.

"You're working as liaison officer. You'll be the main contact for every group working on the fire, from tactical to support, keeping in contact with crews here and their management back home. They'll want to know when to arrive, how long to be here, and how much overtime they'll get. They won't be shy about complaining about the assignments I give them or the laziness of the crew they work next to.''

"Sounds fun.'' Not.

"Great to have you on the team, Jackson. Might want to get a head start checking crew in. I know I saw the meteorologist earlier.'' Rob gestured to a large table with a computer and telephone. "Your box of paperwork is over on that table.''

"JACKSON, COME WITH US.'' Sirus had finished talking to Rob. Not waiting for his reply, Sirus and Rob headed out of the tent.

Jackson grabbed his fire helmet and followed. Sirus wove his way through the traffic jam that base camp had become—portable trailers with supplies for fighting the fire, modular units for preparing food and showering, vans carrying crews.

Jackson caught up to Sirus as he was nearing the heli-tack pad. The rotors of the helicopter started spinning. Sirus hopped into the open passenger bay, already nearly filled with other Incident Command personnel.

Jackson nodded to Wyatt Chappel, a pilot he'd worked with on several fires around western Idaho. About Jackson's age, Wyatt had a love of the adventure involved in firefighting that had rivaled Jackson's.

"We're going to take a tour of the fire," Sirus called over the ever-increasing roar of the helicopter.

Jackson's gut tensed. This would be the first time he'd seen fire since Russia. He barely had time to buckle his seat belt before the chopper lifted off and the bottom dropped out of his stomach. Immediately, wind whipped into the chopper's open door.

"Can't wait to see this mother." Rob elbowed Jackson in the ribs.

Jackson could wait. Perhaps a lifetime. He clenched his jaw and concentrated on looking calm. The rest of the helicopter passengers stared out the open door, hoping to catch a glimpse of the fire. Jackson focused on Sirus's face. The older man had never let him down. He'd be safe with Sirus.

As they neared the fire, smoke filled the air—first as light and wispy as summer clouds, then thicker and heavier. Nearly everyone was leaning forward now, eager for a first look at their enemy.

Everyone except Jackson.

"Look at that." Someone pointed.

"Flames must be fifty feet," someone else said.

Jackson could see bright orange out of the corner of his eye. He kept his gaze on Sirus as the chopper hit the turbulence created by the waves of heat coming off the fire. The air coming into the chopper became dry and hot. Jackson's skin felt warm and tight, as if he'd been sitting in the sun too long. He began sweating, only partly from the scorching fire below.

"This one's moving at a snail's pace, don't you think, Garrett?" Rob practically yelled in his ear.

Jackson turned his head slowly, looking down on a sea of flame devouring large trees and brush on a mountainside as far as he could see in either direction.

The dry air stole Jackson's breath.

This fire was a monster. No one could hope to contain it. He couldn't pull his eyes away from it.

"You okay?" Sirus asked loudly, his eyes assessing Jackson knowingly.

Jackson managed what felt like a grim smile, grateful that Sirus's question had managed to break the spell of the fire. "Just a little seasick."

After a moment's more scrutiny, Sirus accepted Jackson's half-joking reply.

"We can send a couple of Hot Shot crews over on the side ridges and try to slow it down," Rob suggested.

"No!" Jackson found himself disagreeing vehemently. The containment lines were miles away from this fire, allowing the men time to set up their defenses at a safe distance. Forcing himself to calm down, he explained. "These ridges are too deep and steep. It's too dangerous."

Rob scowled. "Firefighting is dangerous, Garrett. Or have you forgotten what it's like to fight real fires over here?"

Jackson ignored the barb. "Come on, Rob. Why do you think the entire slope is on fire at the same velocity? It's not dying down at the bottom or the top. This beast came hard and fast. There'd be no time for escape in terrain like this. I say stick with the original attack plan."

"We can use choppers as backup. Quick in, quick out," Rob countered.

The incident commander stared out at the flaming landscape beneath them as he considered the divergent plans of attack. "Let's not be risky right off the bat. If this fire isn't contained easily, we'll try more aggressive approaches."

Rob scowled at Jackson, clearly not pleased with Sirus's decision. Jackson bet that Rob wouldn't be doing him any favors after this.

Late that night, Jackson drove his truck out into the Garden Valley campground, looking for a place to sleep away from the noise and activity of base camp. He could have driven an hour to his mother's house, but that would just remind him that Lexie still didn't want him in her life.

He missed sleeping next to Lexie every night. Even when he was out in the field fighting fires, exhausted from working twelve, eighteen or twenty-four hour shifts, he found it hard to drift off when she wasn't pressed next to him, her breathing slow and steady as she slept. Other men fell onto the cots provided by NIFC and passed out from exhaustion despite the raucous sound of base camp—the constant chug of the generators providing electricity, trucks of all shapes and sizes rumbling past, tools for chopping trees and brush being ground incessantly.

Not Jackson. Lexie was everything to him.

Jackson climbed into the passenger seat of his truck and reclined it as far as it would go, which wasn't nearly horizontal enough. He wasn't optimistic about the night's sleep. The mountains were outlined by the orange glow of the fire—not exactly a reassuring night-light.

"SOMEONE'S COMING, Mom. Maybe it's Dad." Heidi ran out the front door before Lexie could stop her.

"It's only been a couple of days, Heidi," Lexie called after her. She didn't want Heidi to get her hopes up. From experience, Lexie knew fire camps lasted at least until the fire was under control. Based on news reports, the Garden Valley fire wasn't near containment. More lightning strikes had ignited fires in the area. Curious despite herself, Lexie found herself lumbering out onto the front porch. The one bright spot about this fire, she thought, was that Jackson wasn't out risking his life to fight it. He was shielded by a desk.

After a few minutes of standing around, nothing happened. No truck bounced up the driveway. Heidi looked up the hill at Lexie and shrugged. Lexie felt sorry for her daughter, pinning such high hopes on a man who was devoted to his job above all else.

"Maybe it was a truck on the main road, Heidi," Lexie suggested.

The baby elbowed her in the ribs as if to remind Lexie there would soon be three females in the house. Rufus whined behind Lexie. She turned and walked to the end of the patio to look at the brown Lab over the four-foot fence that bounded what was supposed to have replicated the neat and tidy yard Lexie associated with the happy families she'd envied in her childhood—the ones with a mother and father who didn't shout at each other or ignore their kids.

Instead, her once green lawn and thick, well-manicured shrubs looked as if a gigantic gopher had invaded them. Holes ten feet in diameter and three feet deep peppered the yard. The shrubs had been chewed down to mere twigs. It brought tears to Lexie's eyes to look at the destruction created by one dog.

"You should be ashamed of yourself, Rufus," Lexie chastised him, pointing to a recent hole just on the other side of the gate.

*"Rowr-rowr-rowr."* Rufus's growl told Lexie that he felt he had every right to try to catch those little gophers, even if it did mean she had no lawn left.

"Hasn't that procedure slowed you down at all?" Out of desperation, Lexie had had Rufus neutered two weeks ago in the hopes that he'd calm down. She'd even been optimistic enough to plant a few small flowers in one corner of the yard.

Rufus barked at her with the same cocky attitude. He'd been the one to laugh last. The surgery hadn't hindered him in the least. Her flowers had lasted one afternoon. And now she wouldn't even be able to breed him.

"All right, you reprobate, come inside and spend your energy on a rawhide chew for a while." Lexie opened the gate as far as she was able, given the mound of dirt behind it, and Rufus squeezed out, brown tail held high and wagging as if he were the best dog in the world and proud of it. Lexie wished the rascal would loan her a little of his devil-may-care attitude. She could use a boost of something about now.

"Everything's going to be okay," Lexie told Rufus, trying not to worry about money or her baby's health, trying not to wonder if Jackson could ever put Lexie and their children first.

The dog looked up at her and grinned in what Lexie chose to think of as agreement. At least he wasn't barking at her.

Heidi slumped against a kitchen bar stool as Lexie started pulling out the meager items that would eventually be dinner—two slices of Spam, an apple, noodles for soup, and a small hunk of cheese that became smaller after she cut away the moldy parts. Her next assistance check was due any day now. None too soon. She'd used her last coupon for milk this morning. The cupboards and refrigerator were nearly empty.

Lexie sighed heavily.

"What's wrong, Mom? Do you miss Dad?" Since Jackson's return, Heidi had been constantly asking Lexie about her feelings toward him. "I know I do."

"Actually, I was sighing because I thought I'd never have to eat like this again. Here, slice up this apple." Lexie handed Heidi the cutting board, a knife and the apple.

Heidi climbed onto the stool. "It's better than all those dishes you and Aunt Deb experiment with. At least I know what this tastes like."

"What are you talking about? You ate all your quiche last night. You'd never had that before." The meal at Deb's had been a success, with clean plates all around.

"Mom, I have a confession. Half my quiche ended up in my napkin."

Lexie plastered her palm to her forehead. Her little girl was nothing if not honest.

"I wouldn't have done it if Dad was living with us," Heidi added with a note of drama.

"Where did I go wrong?" Lexie moaned, only half joking.

"You divorced Dad. He knew how to make me behave." Heidi was only able to keep a straight face for a few brief seconds.

"Oh boy. You're piling it on so thick, I think I'm stuck here." Lexie pretended her feet were stuck on the kitchen floor before sinking carefully to the linoleum. "I'm trapped. Woe is me. Stop with the matchmaking lines already."

"Let's think of something happy." Sprawling across the counter, Heidi took a bite of the apple and grinned at Lexie.

"Tough crowd." Lexie rose with all the lumbering grace of a very pregnant woman.

"Try it on the new kid, Mom." Heidi bit into the apple again despite her huge grin. "If you take Dad back, things will go back to the way they were—when we had ice cream in the fridge all the time."

"I'd settle for a huge, juicy pot roast." Lexie could almost smell the spicy aroma.

"I'll bring some pot roast next time." Jackson opened the screen door. "I'm afraid all I brought today are Russian souvenirs."

Lexie's heart jumped at the sight of Jackson. He looked smart in his clean fire-resistant yellow shirt and green pants, so different from the grubby, smelly man who came home from fighting fires.

"Don't get up, Runt." He leaned over to hug Heidi on

her bar stool. "This is for you." He handed her a velvet bag the size of a football.

"Is the fire under control?" Lexie couldn't resist asking.

Jackson shook his head. "I've pulled so many eighteen-hour shifts, Sirus gave me a break."

"It's a baby toy," Heidi announced in a sour voice when she pulled a wooden doll out of the bag.

"It's collectible Russian folk art. Hand-painted. Hand-carved. Look, you open the top and inside is another doll." Jackson lifted the top half of the doll.

Heidi halfheartedly lifted the top off two more layers of dolls. "Thanks," she mumbled, clearly not impressed.

Jackson leaned closer to their daughter. "Since you don't like it much, how about you put it away? Someday, it'll be worth a lot of money."

"How much money?"

He ruffled Heidi's hair. "Wait and see."

Heidi looked at the doll with renewed interest.

"And this—" Jackson handed Lexie a flat bundle wrapped in paper "—is for you. I meant to give it to you the other night."

"You shouldn't have." Lexie didn't reach for the package, but she was intrigued.

"How will you know if I shouldn't have, if you don't open it?" He stepped around the counter so that he stood next to her, and lowered his voice. "Please take it."

Tentatively, Lexie took the light bundle and lifted the paper, revealing black folds of material scattered with bright pink roses. Setting the paper on the counter, she shook out the shawl. "Thank you, it's beautiful."

"Not as beautiful as you," Jackson proclaimed.

Lexie looked up into Jackson's warm green eyes and felt her cheeks heat—oh so aware of Heidi sitting across the counter from them. "You shouldn't be saying things like that to me," she said softly.

"It's about time he said stuff like that to you," Heidi countered. "Now, kiss her."

"Heidi Janine Garrett," Lexie warned, stepping back in case Jackson decided to take their daughter's advice.

Jackson laughed, the sound warming Lexie in ways a pregnant woman shouldn't be warmed.

"I need to make dinner. Heidi, please feed the dog when you're done eating that apple," Lexie directed, returning to the stove.

"Dad can feed the dog," Heidi said, the half-eaten apple forgotten on the counter before her.

"No, your father is a guest. He doesn't need to do your chores," Lexie countered, turning to look at Heidi and only Heidi. She wasn't going to risk meeting Jackson's eyes.

"But—"

Lexie wasn't up for an argument with Jackson watching. "We agreed that you would help me around the house. Need I remind you that the vacuuming still needs to be done?"

"Dad is not a *guest*." Anger tinged Heidi's young voice. "And you wouldn't be so helpless if you weren't having another baby."

"Heidi, that's no way to talk to your mother," Jackson admonished.

"That's the problem with her…and you!" Heidi jabbed her finger at Jackson. "Neither one of you talks to the other. You won't even try to get back together. And who suffers? Me!"

"Heidi—" Lexie began.

"You're ruining my life!" Heidi flew out of the room, ran down the hall and slammed the door behind her.

Lexie sank into a kitchen chair. Her heart was pounding and the baby was elbowing her ribs. Jackson sat down across from her.

"Welcome home," she said miserably.

"IT'S NOT LIKE I HAVEN'T SEEN HER upset before." Jackson got the distinct feeling that Lexie was uncomfortable with him witnessing his daughter's explosion.

Lexie challenged him with raised eyebrows.

"Okay, I haven't seen her quite like this," he allowed.

"And this is what happens when she has a training bra. Just wait until she's wearing makeup. I shudder just thinking about it."

Jackson eased into a smile. "There'll be a second one around to distract her then."

Lexie pulled her hair away from her face and captured the dark brown, silky mass with a hair clip that had been lying on the table. "Yes, but I'm sure the two of them will somehow manage to gang up on me."

The orange-and-white cat rubbed against the corner of the hallway, twitching her tail. Rufus's ears perked up and Jackson sensed impending disaster.

"Has she been like this a lot?"

"No... Yes... Off and on." Lexie stood and went around the counter into the main kitchen, as if that would end the conversation.

As soon as she moved, Rufus barreled toward the cat, which scampered away. Jackson could hear them scrambling around the back of the house, and then the cat's soft hiss of warning. Lexie sighed but didn't scold the dog.

Jackson suppressed the thought that Lexie's life was out of control. Lexie never let things get out of hand. "What's the problem other than a few wayward preteen hormones?"

"It's our fault." Her words sounded defeated, nowhere near her usual take-charge, optimistic self.

Jackson didn't know what to say. Rufus trotted back to the kitchen, his tongue hanging out. The dog turned golden eyes from one human to the other as if looking for praise.

Finally, Lexie turned to face Jackson. "When you left—"

"You asked me to go."

"—Heidi's grades started to slip."

"That was a year ago."

Crossing her arms, Lexie seemed to dare him to dispute her.

"Why wasn't I told about this sooner?" He stood up, kicking back the chair.

Startled, the dog backed out of his way.

"And don't tell me I was in Russia. She had to have gotten a report card before Christmas."

"She did. She promised to do better."

"Obviously that didn't happen."

"No, it didn't." Lexie stood, rigid and alone, as usual, but her blue eyes seemed huge and vulnerable. "She barely passed the fifth grade, and whenever I bring up school, ask her to help me when she doesn't feel like it or something doesn't go her way, she gets defensive and blames it on me or the divorce. It's so explosive, I just can't get used to it."

Weariness descended on Jackson. He rubbed his eyes. That way, he didn't have to register how completely Lexie had blocked him out of her life. "So who do you really blame? Me or you?"

Lexie turned back to the counter. "Just me," she said in a small voice.

That deflated Jackson's anger quicker than a dousing by a fire hose.

"It's not all your fault." Although at the moment, Jackson couldn't think of who else would be to blame, since he'd been the one kicked out of the house.

Lexie sucked in a shuddering breath, and, even from behind, Jackson realized she was trying not to cry. In three long strides, he was close enough to wrap his arms around her, pull her back to his chest and breathe in the flowery scent of her hair and the sweet smell that was Lexie's alone.

"Hey, now. Don't take all the blame," he whispered, remembering how his hands had taken on a mind of their own just a few days before and reacquainted themselves with her body. This time, he wrapped his arms around her from behind, planting his hands on her shoulders, nestling his cheek next to hers. "Heidi's just going through a phase."

Lexie's breathing was ragged. She sniffed. "Do you think so?"

"Damn straight. Of course, it might take a year or so." He'd witnessed his older sister's similar growing pains. He knew the phase would pass—in about four years or so. What he worried about more was Lexie. He'd never seen Lexie's emotions so volatile. She was in dire need of some tender loving care, and he was just the guy to give it to her. "Why don't you go take a shower or something? I'll fix dinner."

"I can't. What would Heidi think?"

"Maybe she'd realize that you are tired. It'd be a different story if you invited me in the shower with you."

Lexie stiffened in his embrace, then she was pushing his arms off her and stepping away. "That's not likely to happen." She turned around, regarding him suspiciously, ready for battle again.

"Didn't say it was." Today. "I just think you need some time to yourself. I'll make peace with the little gremlin and make sure she gets something to eat."

Lexie hesitated. Jackson smiled at her.

"Go on. When was the last time you didn't have to worry about a thing?" If she'd just let him, he'd ease some of her worries.

Her gaze fell to Rufus. "Even if I take a bath, I won't stop worrying."

"But at least you'll feel rejuvenated. How about it?"

Lexie gave a brief nod and accepted his offer of assistance. It wasn't much, but it was a start.

"Spam and soup again?" Heidi whined when she sat down at the table a while later. Her hair hung in wild, long tresses about her shoulders and her face was tear streaked. She gave one last complaint—a dramatic sigh—then she began to eat.

Lexie had yet to emerge from the bathroom.

Jackson wondered if Lexie and Heidi had been living on canned meat and noodle soup since she'd been forced on bed rest or if this was a recent development. Lexie was a great cook, but he'd eaten better food than this at base camps.

"Do you want to talk about it?" Jackson asked Heidi.

Heidi shook her head, keeping it bent over her plate. Jackson couldn't let the conversation, lame as it was, end there.

"How's dance class?"

"I had to quit. Mom said it was too expensive." Heidi's voice was filled with recrimination, as if it were Jackson's fault that she'd had to drop out.

Given Lexie's financial shortfall, Jackson had no problem laying the blame at his own door. "Let me see what I can do."

"Why? Do you care all of a sudden or something?" Heidi's sullen words were totally out of character with the sweet daughter he remembered.

Speechless, Jackson sat back in his chair.

Heidi's cheeks were red and her blue eyes watery, but her chin had a determined set to it. "You never came to a recital. Or a soccer game. Do you even know what instrument I play in band?" Heidi picked up her dishes and carried them to the counter. Then she turned and walked away, flinging over her shoulder, "Mom was right to divorce you. You're not my dad. You never were."

Her muffled footsteps on the hallway carpet were the only sound until she closed her door.

Something bitter grabbed hold of Jackson's heart. It

wasn't enough that he'd lost himself in the Siberian fire. He'd returned home to find he wasn't the man he thought he'd been. Not for Lexie, certainly. But to discover that his self-image as a father was wrong, too…well, that was another thing entirely. He hadn't thought his spirits could sink any lower.

When he finished eating, Jackson fed the dog and put him out in the back, taking his first good look at the damage to Lexie's yard. He'd never understood why she wanted a manicured lawn out here in the middle of nowhere, but it was disheartening to see what had once looked so neat and inviting so torn apart.

While he was leaning on the fence, the motor home he'd talked Lexie into buying caught his eye. It was parked at the far end of the property. Jackson had bought it with the idea that Lexie and Heidi could drive out to base camp so that they could be together at night in the summer when he was fighting fires. But the engine didn't run well and Jackson had never gotten around to fixing it. If Lexie's nagging of previous years was any indication, Jackson would have thought that would be the first thing to go, along with the race car frame he'd dragged home and numerous other good ideas he'd never followed through on.

His attention was drawn down the hill to the barn where the grass was knee high. Lexie was almost crazed when it came to the appearance of this place—or at least, she had been. The potholes in the drive, the overgrown grass, the demolished yard and the eyesore of a motor home—all were an indication that Lexie couldn't keep up the place alone—not when she was on bed rest and certainly not after the baby was born. Add the emotional state of Heidi, her academic woes, Lex's employment status…and Jackson could come to only one conclusion.

Lex needed him.

It didn't matter that she claimed she didn't, because she

did. No matter what she said or did, no matter how hard she tried to push him out of her life, Jackson wasn't going away. He'd find a way to fit into her life again, to prove his love to Lexie so she'd take him back.

# CHAPTER SIX

THE HOUSE WAS QUIET. Lexie had dozed off in bed after her bath, not even waking for dinner. She'd spotted more this past week than she had in a long time so she knew she needed the rest. Now the clock next to her bed read ten-thirty. The baby growing inside of her slept as Lexie lay in the dark. She would have been completely relaxed if not for one thing.

Jackson.

She had no idea if he'd left or not. Her head wanted him to leave the house, leave her heart, leave her with peace of mind.

*Liar!* Her heart ached for him every night after Heidi was asleep and no longer vying for her attention. She hoped that he was finally sleeping peacefully, undisturbed by nightmares.

The floorboards groaned on the other side of the house. That could mean only one thing.

Jackson was still here.

Well, too darn bad. She was in bed and she was going to stay there. Lexie pushed herself to a sitting position, dragged the pillows to the other side of the bed and lowered herself onto her left side, resting her tummy on one pillow and pulling the other pillow between her knees.

The baby poked her bladder once. Then again. Harder.

The urge to go to the bathroom became impossible to ignore. While she was pushing herself upright, her stomach rumbled. Not that the food in the kitchen held any enticement, but she had an obligation to stay healthy, which meant she had to eat…and face Jackson.

A few minutes later, Lexie was waddling down the hall in her sleep shirt, her chenille robe hanging open. The kitchen was at the other side of the small house and light glowed at the end of the hallway, beckoning her closer.

Jackson sat at the kitchen table. Charts, maps, folders, worksheets and pens cluttered the oak surface. He was asleep, his head pillowed on his arms, his arms resting on his work. Lexie almost placed a hand on his dark crown to wake him and send him to bed, before she remembered she'd given up that right.

She froze, her hand inches from Jackson's sable hair. Old habits apparently died hard. She pulled her hand back, but couldn't stop herself from studying his face in repose. The beard was so…so…adult.

Which was silly. He *was* an adult.

Lexie frowned.

Still, there was something different about him. Maybe it was that Lexie had never seen Jackson fill out paperwork before. He'd always been just another firefighter while they'd lived together, a man of action, a man gone from her life six to nine months of the year. The paperwork must be part of the job he was doing now. Another change that indicated Jackson was becoming responsible.

*Yeah, right.* Lexie backed away, rolling her eyes. She'd long ago given up on Jackson ever becoming responsible.

Sure enough, dirty dishes were strewn across the counter. Given the choice, Jackson probably would have left hours ago to hang out with his friends at the Pony. He wasn't much for sitting and relaxing at home.

She tiptoed across the kitchen and opened the refrigerator. Jackson had left her a small bowl of noodle soup. The baby stretched, crowding her lungs and making it hard to breathe.

"Are you okay?"

Lexie hadn't realized she'd made a noise until Jackson spoke.

"Just taking the baby out for her nightly stretch." Lexie removed her dinner and popped it into the microwave.

"You know it's a girl?"

"No. I just assume." As she'd assumed the baby she'd lost last year was a girl. Lexie shied away from the thought.

Jackson yawned behind her.

"Why don't you go on home? I can cover things from here on in."

Jackson snorted. "I don't have a place to go. If I go back to Mom's, I'll wake her because I don't have a key. And the thought of spending another night sleeping in the passenger seat of my truck sucks. In fact, I was hoping to stay here."

"You can't." Lexie did turn then, pulling her robe as far around her as she could, which wasn't far enough to cover her protruding stomach.

Jackson's smile was tentative, his eyes shadowed with sadness. "I was thinking about staying in the motor home."

"No way." Lexie sucked in much-needed air and started to say more, but Jackson stopped her.

"Hear me out. I need a place to stay. I can't get any sleep out at base camp."

Lexie couldn't meet Jackson's intense green gaze and think about sleeping arrangements, because she knew she'd just think about sex. With him. She clenched the worn fabric of her robe, as if that would guard against the traitorous feelings Jackson aroused in her. "You'd be closer to work in Garden Valley. It's an hour's drive back here. Why not stay in the Dew Drop Motel?"

"But I'd be farther away from you and Heidi."

She recognized the ache in his voice, saw the lines of worry around his eyes and felt a tug of compassion for him. Lexie struggled with the desire to have Jackson a safe distance away and the conflicting belief that her daughter needed her father as much as he seemed to need her. She wished she hadn't wandered out here in her bathrobe and nightie. It made her feel vulnerable.

Lexie sighed. Who was she kidding? She was big as a bear, unemployed and practically tethered to the couch. She felt vulnerable all the time now.

What was she going to do about Jackson?

"I'll pay rent. That ought to help you out."

Anger shocked her into looking at him. "I don't need your charity."

"If I was offering charity, I'd write you a check now without asking anything in return."

Lexie bit her lip and closed her eyes. She needed the money. But, oh, how she hated that Jackson knew she needed the money. Lexie could hear her mother's voice, full of recrimination, when a barely eighteen-year-old Lexie finally found the courage to confess that she was pregnant and marrying Jackson.

*"Don't be a fool. He won't stay with you."* Lexie's mother had scoffed all those years ago. *"Love… Love with a man doesn't last. You'll end up poor and alone with nothing to feed that baby. Didn't you learn anything from me?"*

Her second child kicked Lexie, bringing her back to the dilemma at hand. Taking money from Jackson wouldn't solve anything. "No."

Jackson washed his hands over his face. "I don't want Heidi and the baby to live on Spam and noodle soup."

She didn't want that, either. Lexie felt her cheeks heat. Still, her pride wouldn't let her give in. "It's only a little while longer. Thirty-four days until my due date. Then another six weeks and I'll be back at work."

"Two and a half more months." His smile was gentle,

his words were not. "That's great, Lex, but what about dinner tomorrow?"

"I'll manage somehow." There were too many reasons she couldn't let Jackson back in her life. First and foremost, she couldn't let him see that she still loved him. "Besides, that motor home never ran right. The electrical is shaky. I would have sold it before this if I could have. I don't even let Heidi play in there." Trouble was, she knew his proposal made sense. It was a business proposition. If she put it in those terms, it didn't seem so bad.

"I'll take care of it. I'll fix it up, and then you can sell it for more than five hundred dollars."

"You'll be living at the barracks, then? With the Hot Shots?"

"I'm not going back to the crew."

"You're giving up the Hot Shots? Permanently?"

He gave her a rueful smile and a nod. "I told you I was going to be a desk jockey."

"I guess I assumed it was just on this fire." Lexie should have been happy that Jackson wouldn't be risking his life every day anymore. It was what she'd secretly wished for. Except she knew how hard Jackson had worked to make the Hot Shot crew and how important it was for him to succeed where his father had met with the ultimate failure. It had been the dream he'd shared with her under the stars all those years ago. His quitting just didn't seem right.

Lexie didn't know whether to laugh with relief or cry in sorrow that Jackson's dream was coming to an end.

*LEXIE SNUGGLED TIGHTER against Jackson, as if she couldn't get close enough to him. He wrapped his arms around her and buried his face in her hair. For a time, Jackson was at peace. In the distance, he could hear crackling and knew this respite would soon end. Fire was creeping up on them. He looked over his shoulder in time to see it race down the mountain toward them. There was no escape.*

*"Run, Lex!"*

*Only, Lexie couldn't run. She was heavy with their child and unable to move fast enough. Jackson took out his Pulaski and hacked away at the soil, but it was hard as concrete.*

*His fire shelter blew away in the wind—*

Beep! Beep! Beep!

*He never should have taken her up in the mountains—*

Beep! Beep! Beep!

Jackson pulled his head out of the pillow and forced open his dry, gritty eyes. Gray sunlight filtered through the windows of the 1970s orange-and-green motor home. His watch alarm stopped beeping just as Jackson realized he was safe. He rolled onto his back. He wasn't out fighting a fire. Instead, he was one step closer to winning Lexie back, one step closer than he'd been yesterday.

Jackson wrinkled his nose against the musty odor that permeated the junker. It had never been in great shape. And now the motor home he'd held such great plans for was in horrible disrepair. It challenged his equilibrium as it listed to one corner on a flat tire. When he'd first opened the door to the motor home last night, Jackson had wanted nothing more than to slip back into the house and crawl into bed with Lex.

But that wasn't an option.

He swung his legs over the edge of the foam cushion that passed for a bed and his bare feet landed on damp orange shag carpet. That explained the odor. A glance upward revealed the culprit—the skylight sported cracked glass beneath a legion of pinecones. It must have rained during the summer and never dried out.

He turned one squeaky handle on the sink, but nothing came out.

With a sigh, Jackson gathered his clothes and shaving

kit. Nothing worked in the motor home—not the plumbing, not the electrical. He'd have to shower in the house. He wasn't about to show up for work smelling of stale fear.

Jackson turned the motor home door handle, expecting it to open. It spun loosely without catching. Well, hell. Jackson suppressed the urge to kick the door open. Wouldn't Lex appreciate the eyesore of a motor home with its door hanging off its hinges?

He glanced around, assessing his options and trying not to breathe in the mustiness too deeply. Now that he was fully awake and trapped, it was nearly unbearable. There was only one door, but there were several windows. Windows were always the second-best exit for a firefighter. Besides, the place needed airing out.

Jackson dumped his stuff back on the bed and went to work on his escape.

LEXIE OPENED HER EYES, wondering what had awakened her. It was just starting to get light outside—much too early for her to be up.

A noise. She'd heard a noise.

"Heidi? Are you all right?"

Heidi didn't answer. But someone called her name outside.

"Jackson?" Lexie mumbled. Maybe she'd been dreaming. Surely, she'd been dreaming. Why would Jackson be yelling for her? Lexie began the labored process of turning her swollen body over so that she could go back to sleep.

"Lex, wake up!"

Lexie pushed herself awkwardly out of bed. The voice was definitely Jackson's. Was there an emergency? Lexie opened the window above the bed and called, "Jackson?"

"Over here."

From Lexie's window, she could see the front walk, part

of the driveway and the motor home. Jackson was nowhere in sight.

"Where?"

"I'm stuck in the motor home," he said.

She'd warned him that he shouldn't stay in the darn thing. "The doorknob sticks."

"Now she tells me."

"I'll get the screwdriver," Lexie called back.

"Call Sirus first. Ask him to... Tell him I need him to stop by on his way to Garden Valley."

Unable to resist smiling, Lexie hurriedly put her clothes on. The mighty Golden was stuck in a motor home. If the other firefighters caught wind of this, he'd never live it down. And find out they would, if Sirus was coming by.

A few minutes later, screwdriver in hand, Lexie waddled around the front of the motor home and froze at the sight of Jackson's head, bare arms and shoulders hanging out of a window.

"What on earth happened?" Lexie walked around him, wanting to see Jackson from every angle. She struggled to contain a smile. "When you said you were stuck, I assumed you were still inside."

He wouldn't look at her. "The door handle is broken, so I tried to climb out the window. Now I'm wedged in tight. Can't go forward or back."

"Are you blushing?" Lexie hadn't seen him blush since high school.

"This is not my finest moment, Lex." He grimaced. "Did you call Sirus?"

"Yes. He's coming down with Logan."

"Just what I need," Jackson groaned. "An audience."

"I'm told it builds character." Taking pity on him, Lexie turned her attention to the motor home door. She jiggled the door handle a few times until it popped open. Then she loosened the screws on the knob and took the disaster-causing hardware off the door.

"Don't make it look so easy," Jackson grumbled.

Lexie stepped into the listing, smelly motor home and peeked at the half of Jackson, clad in jeans, that wasn't hanging out the window. His boots and shaving kit were dumped on the kitchen table and his clothes spilled out of his duffel.

"What are you doing, Lex?"

"Just checking to make sure you're fully clothed on this end." She also took a moment to examine the window frame up close, mindful not to touch him, although her hand itched to stroke his legs. "You know, I might be able to pop out this frame and get you out of there."

"Don't you dare."

"What's wrong? Don't you trust me?" With one hand supporting her belly, she climbed carefully down the steps so she could see his face, to see if he was taking his frustration out on her.

"I'd trust you with my life," he said softly, no trace of irritation evident in his expression. "I just don't want you or the baby to get hurt."

"Oh." He considered Lexie's safety more important than his freedom. The sentiment brought tears to her eyes. She was a mess of hormonal waterworks lately. To hide her reaction, Lexie sat on the bottom step of the motor home and fiddled with the doorknob. If he asked her to marry him now, she'd burst into tears for sure.

"Thank you," he said simply.

They didn't speak for a bit, during which time Lexie wondered about Jackson's patience.

After a moment, she allowed, "If I was the one stuck up there, I'd be spitting mad."

"Anger never did me any good. I was always a big kid that someone wanted to test himself against. Anger more likely put me into trouble."

"That's why you smile your way through everything."

"I suppose." Jackson sighed, adding after a moment,

"After my dad died, my mom wanted to make sure Theresa and I didn't get depressed. She'd worry and fuss if I wasn't smiling. I guess I just learned to smile, no matter what."

And he'd smiled all the way through the separation and divorce she'd forced on him last year, making Lexie believe he didn't care about their marriage. Had she been wrong?

The baby slugged her bladder.

Had she?

THE MOMENT HE'D BEEN dreading arrived.

A silver truck pulled up the driveway. Logan and Sirus climbed out, both dressed in wildland fire-fighting green pants and yellow shirts, and sporting huge grins. Like Jackson, the two men had taken a much-needed break from the noise and activity in base camp to sleep at home.

Logan hung back by his truck, rummaging around in the back seat.

"What the hell happened to you, son?" Sirus walked over for a closer look, examining Jackson as if he were a horse up for auction.

"Is this some new kinky sex move, Jackson?" Logan teased.

"Just get me out of here, would you? The window frame is permanently etched in my rib cage." Jackson had been propping himself up on his arms for what must have been nearly an hour.

"In a minute. We've got to document this *Golden* moment." Logan's grin broadened as he lifted a camera.

"Logan, I swear, I'm going to kill you when I get out of here." To hell with smiling.

"I think you can pry the frame out and give him an extra inch all around," Lexie said as she stood.

"Maybe we could try that old magician's trick and saw you in half," Logan offered.

Sirus slipped his fingers into the corner of the window and tugged on the frame. "You might be right, Lexie. Hurry up with the pictures, Logan. I've got a meeting to run in ninety minutes." The older man went into the motor home, presumably to get a good look at the situation from that end.

"Thanks for the sensitivity, Sirus," Jackson noted grimly while Logan snapped pictures. He was glad that he hadn't tried to climb out the window in his boxers.

"And one of the happy couple." Logan maneuvered Lexie closer to Jackson and took a few more shots.

Lexie laughed, the sound cheering him. He smiled down at Lex, rewarded for his pain when she grinned back at him. She'd been silent while they waited for his would-be rescuers, head bent over that damn lock. Jackson had been so embarrassed, he'd been at a loss for words.

When Lexie moved away, Jackson said to Logan, "I fail to see the humor in this."

"That's because it's your ass in a sling, buddy boy."

Sirus came out of the motor home, rocking it with each step he took. "All right, that's enough. Get me the tool-box, McCall."

"Everyone in camp is going to know about this by breakfast, aren't they?" Jackson said.

"Before. Long before," Logan promised as he rummaged in the back of his pickup again.

"Jackson, I may need you to go out in the field today." Sirus followed Logan to the truck.

Jackson gritted his teeth against the sudden, gut-wrenching anxiety. Feeling Lexie's eyes upon him, he gazed down at her.

"Was it that bad over there?" Her quiet question was meant for Jackson's ears only.

He didn't know what to say. He was determined not to tell anyone about Russia.

"You wouldn't tell me if it had been, would you." Lexie backed away with accusing eyes.

Of all the people in his life, Jackson wished he could tell Lexie, but he didn't want her to know what a coward he was. It was better that she suspect his secret than know the truth.

"Make Lex sit, will you? She shouldn't tire herself out," Jackson called to Sirus.

Lexie shook her head in disgust.

Sirus carried a plastic chair over from the porch for Lexie to sit on, positioning her so that she had an excellent view of Jackson's humiliation. As soon as she sank into the chair, Heidi and Rufus joined the party. The dog ran right up to Jackson, placing his front paws near Jackson's hands and sniffing at him with his extended nose.

"Get away, dog." Jackson pushed him off with one hand.

"Dad? Are you stuck?" His daughter's wide-eyed, awe-struck expression reminded Jackson of the time years ago when he'd taken her to see the elephants at the zoo.

Logan laughed heartily. "Yes, he's stuck, Runt. It's a sight to behold, isn't it?"

"I'll say." Heidi high-fived Logan.

Jackson gritted his teeth and pulled his lips into a tight smile. "You are so dead, Tin Man."

Logan ignored him.

"This is why we don't play in the motor home, Heidi," Lexie explained. "It's too dangerous."

None of the men spoke. Lexie had no idea the extent of danger they faced every day and Jackson, in particular, was happy to keep it that way.

"So, Runt, I was hoping we could do something to-night; just you and me." Jackson wanted to mend the bridges Heidi had burned last night.

Frowning, Heidi stared at Jackson for all of maybe five

seconds before dismissing him and turning to Logan. "Can Tess and Hannah come over this afternoon?"

Jackson's jaw dropped.

"Sure." Logan shrugged, his grin dimming. "As long as Lex can pick them up."

"I'll call Deb later," Lexie said.

"I don't think Lex should be driving," Jackson protested.

"I'm fine." Lexie frowned at him.

Great. The morning's truce was over. "When I told you earlier that I didn't want you to get hurt, you seemed touched."

Lex crossed her arms on top of her belly and arched her brows.

Jackson plowed on, despite his audience. "I'm just protective of you…of our baby."

"And if I just stopped driving, how would I get around? You're off fighting fires."

"Like, strand us, Dad," Heidi huffed.

"I'm *not* fighting fires," Jackson said through clenched teeth.

"He's a desk jockey, Lex," Logan butted in with a grin. "Oh, how the mighty have fallen."

"I'm well aware of what he does." Lexie's tone was firm. She wasn't giving in or accepting any backpedaling from Jackson.

"Logan, when will you learn that every person on a fire is important?" Sirus asked.

"I know that, Socrates. It's just that some of us are more important than others." Logan's response was sarcastic, but the sentiment would have been echoed by every Hot Shot from Anchorage to Miami.

"I just want you to be careful." Jackson tried once more to make peace with Lex.

"I'm always careful," Lexie replied, her expression stony.

Heidi leaned against the motor home. "For cryin' out loud, can't somebody free my dad so he can kiss my mom? They fight less when they kiss."

Jackson tried smiling again, hoping to lighten the moment with Lexie, but she left him to go inside the house.

"I'LL CALL DOWN to the motor home supply store in Boise today. I made a list of things it needs," Jackson promised, looking fresh after being freed from his window prison and taking a shower. "That thing has potential."

"Don't you think it's a lost cause?" By the look on Jackson's face, she wasn't sure if he thought she meant their relationship or the motor home, so she added, "Like all that other junk you've got out there. The broken treadmill that you said you'd fix. The empty brandy barrel you said you'd cut in half for planters. That old frame you bought when you and Logan were going to build a race car." She was still reeling from Jackson's revelation that he hid his emotions behind his smile. She'd never dreamed he'd hide himself from her, but what other explanation was there?

"I'm not giving up on the motor home. I'll look at the other stuff soon." Jackson picked an apple out of a bowl on the kitchen counter. "I'll stop by the store today on the way home and pick up some groceries."

Grabbing a sponge on the kitchen sink, Lexie began to scrub the already clean counters. "No need." She'd pick up a little food later if her government check showed up in the mailbox.

"Here." As if reading her mind, Jackson stepped beside her and thrust a check her way. "For rent."

Money. Lexie had to force herself to take the check slowly, as if she were an adult in full control of her destiny, not swaying on the brink of ruin.

"Five hundred dollars. That's too much." Lexie's cheeks flamed with embarrassment. It was enough to cover their debts this month and set them on the right track for next month. Reluctantly, she extended the check back to him.

"That's less than I'd pay to rent a room at the Dew Drop for a week." He leaned against the counter and shoved his hands in his pockets. His eyes held hers without a trace of recrimination. "Think of it as being for Heidi and the new baby."

Lexie blinked back the tears, trying hard to hold on to her pride. "I couldn't sell that motor home for five hundred dollars," she whispered, hand thrust toward him.

"You will when I get through with it. Take it, Lex," Jackson encouraged gently, his expression grave.

Lexie couldn't look away from Jackson. There was something different about him. The Jackson she'd been married to would have smiled and joked with her until she felt at ease taking the money. The Jackson she was no longer married to let her conscience determine what was right. And what was right had nothing to do with her foolish pride.

She blew out a defeated breath. "Thanks." Lexie tucked the check into her purse, avoiding looking at Jackson. But she couldn't let him go without asking, "Do you want to talk about it?" She was worried about him, more so after seeing his response to Sirus's casual comment about sending him out to the fire. She didn't think Jackson had noticed Sirus studying his reaction.

Jackson eyed Lexie warily.

She sighed. "Those dreams have been giving you trouble."

His jaw clenched.

"Forget I asked." She went to her room and closed the door.

Even as he continued to shut her out, the memory of the grave expression on Jackson's face when he was trying to give her the check wouldn't recede. Lexie was left wondering when she had stopped seeing Jackson for who he was and had started seeing him only as the man he wanted others to see—a carefree guy always willing to lend a hand. What she'd seen today was a man haunted by the past but determined to push on, sacrificing the job he loved.

That man's heart called to her own.

ALL DAY LONG, people greeted Jackson. People he knew from previous fires—firefighters, laundry crews, helitack crews, maintenance men—people he was just starting to deal with—meteorologists, biologists, reporters. He knew them, but he didn't feel as if he was part of any one group. The feeling of isolation was unexpected and unwelcome. He liked being part of a team.

Fire crews came to check in and left, full of an enthusiasm that Jackson no longer shared. It seemed odd to think there was a fire out there when he could barely smell the smoke, couldn't feel the heat and wasn't bone-tired at the end of the day from hacking away at fire lines and underbrush after hiking steep slopes with forty-plus pounds of gear strapped to his back.

And yet slowly, with certainty, they were winning the battle against the fire, even if Jackson wasn't seeing the results firsthand. Each day, the map they produced showed more completed fire lines. The thick red lines indicating untamed fire became shorter, while the thick black containment lines began to dominate the map.

Around four in the afternoon, Jackson ran into Logan and several Hot Shots standing in the chow line. They were all cleaned up and ready to go out on the night shift.

"Hey, Paper Jockey!" A grinning Spider slapped Jackson on the back as he passed.

"Hi, Golden, sir." Rookie waved with a weary smile.

Jackson acknowledged the kid with a nod, uncomfortable with his hero worship.

"Escape Artist! Got time for a cup of coffee while we eat?" Logan asked.

"Not a problem. I'll meet you at the end of the line." Jackson hustled over to collect Sirus's signature on a stack of paperwork, knowing that Silver Bend was due on shift shortly and therefore they wouldn't have much time to talk.

"You're doing a good job, Garrett," Sirus said. "Like a duck to water. Great second career move."

"No." Jackson instinctively drew back from the idea, even if it was something he'd originally pursued. He was still a firefighter at heart.

"Not that I mean any disrespect, but..." Jackson's voice trailed off. What did Jackson mean? He was a hazard out in the field, a liability to a Hot Shot crew without his head screwed on one-hundred-percent straight. He could only be useful behind a desk. But to admit that to someone like Sirus? Not in another lifetime.

"I've walked in your shoes, Garrett. Trust me, the move from the field to a desk job is a big attitude adjustment. Just keep in mind that life has a way of changing your priorities when you least expect it." Sirus laughed and slapped Jackson on the back. "Maybe I should have sent you out to the field today."

Jackson could only nod stupidly until he worked up enough saliva to speak, during which time Sirus looked at him strangely, almost as if he sensed something was wrong.

"I'm going to hook up with Silver Bend for a bit and then collect the last of the reports for tomorrow before I leave." Jackson managed to sound almost normal.

Sirus continued to study Jackson long enough to make him uncomfortable. Then he shook his head. "Sorry, I'm a bit tired today." He rubbed his forehead beneath his fire helmet. "Looks like we might wrap this one up soon.

Make sure we touch base on demobilization plans before you go."

"I will."

Sirus took a step away from Jackson, but then turned back. "You're not any worse for wear from that incident this morning, are you?"

"No." Why did Sirus have to bring that up?

"That's a nice family you have. Fire is hard as stone on marriages. Hope you can make it work." Sirus paused, seemed about to say something else, and then shook his head and gave a rueful smile. "I'm a sad example giving you marriage advice. Been down that aisle two times. It makes me wonder why I'd even consider a third Mrs. Socrath."

"A third? You are a brave man."

Sirus stared into Jackson's eyes for a bit, as if considering something, and then he smiled and looked out toward the smoke-wreathed mountains above them. "I have no problem with you heading back to Silver Bend every night as long as you get those reports out before you leave."

"Not to worry, sir." He was going to need one heck of an attitude adjustment if he took a permanent desk job. It wasn't so much the humiliation of the position—the work was important, he could see that now. It was his almost instinctual, knee-jerk mental reaction to the thought of being far from the fire, shuffling paper.

Was this job necessary to fight a fire? Of course.

Was it the heroic role he'd dreamed of since he was a little boy? Not by a long shot.

## CHAPTER SEVEN

"WHAT WAS THAT ALL ABOUT?" Logan asked, moving next to Jackson and tossing his head in Sirus's direction.

"I think Socrates was trying to give me sage advice."

"Ahh, one of those deeper-meaning-to-life discussions where you don't know what the hell he was talking about for years. Well, he's off giving notable quotes, so let's find a spot to take a load off. I've got a lot of miles to climb tonight." Logan headed for the row of tables to which the Silver Bend crew had already staked claim.

Grabbing a cup of hot coffee, Jackson followed, but then hesitated mid-stride beside the crowded table—unfortunately, right by the new kid.

Rookie scooted over to make room for Jackson. "I'd sure love to hear about the last time you were out here. Chainsaw tells me it was quite a ride."

Jackson stalled in both sitting and answering. Suddenly, he didn't want to be with the Silver Bend crew.

"Sit down, Golden," Logan encouraged. "You're acting like you've never sat at a picnic table before."

The group snickered.

After another moment of hesitation, Jackson sat down. After all, if he wanted to talk to Logan before he went on duty, he had to sit.

Jackson put on what he hoped was a decent smile. "You don't have much time before your bus leaves, Rookie. It's a long story. Maybe we should talk another time." Lucky for him, Rookie was the only one that wanted to hear his story. To everyone else, he was the guy who hadn't been around this fire season.

"With a lightning-quick ending, eh, Golden?" Spider chortled as he slathered his steak with salsa and horseradish sauce.

Somehow, Jackson managed to keep what he hoped passed for a smile for the grinning Hot Shots who'd been here with him a few years ago.

"Why is it they call you Golden?" Rookie asked, emboldened by the jovial mood at the table. "I mean, I get Chainsaw. That's obvious. And Spider, well, he can be creepy. And the heartless Romeo as the Tin Man makes sense. Well, it did take me a while to link him with the Wizard of Oz character. But you, sir, there's nothing golden about you."

Jackson stared across the table at Logan, uncomfortably aware of how close to the truth Rookie's statement was.

"Listen up, kid." Logan pointed his fork at the youngster. "Because I'm going to spin you a tale that is near legendary. That man sitting next to you. He's not a man. He's the earthly representation of our Hot Shot deity. When there's trouble, you want him right by your side because he embodies good luck."

Rookie looked at Jackson dubiously. Jackson could tell that the crew had been pulling the kid's chain a few times too many. Rookies were always fair game for pranks.

Logan continued. "The last time we had a fire out here, it was as if the devil himself was whipping up the winds, feeding the flames to jump across roads and rivers that are too wide for any lame-ass fire. This fire was one of those once-every-ten-year nightmares that made rookies like you shit their pants while trying to build a fire break."

A couple of the crew that had been there murmured, "Amen."

Rookie's eyes had grown wide and he'd lost interest in his dinner. The coffee in Jackson's stomach turned. He

didn't want to hear this. His jaw was clenched so tight it
had started to ache. He didn't want Logan and the rest to
make him out to be some kind of hero, but Logan kept on
talking.

"We're up on a slope, trying to discourage this dragon
from crossing a ridge and racing down to devour Garden
Valley by doing a little back-burning, when our Golden
here turns around and faces downhill. From our position,
if we look down, we can see the Payette River at the
bottom. I was figuring that we had maybe thirty more
minutes of work to do, making sure the base of the slope
had burned its way completely out. But Golden gets on
his radio and he starts yelling, 'Pickup! Pickup!' Then he
turns to us and orders us to hightail it up the ridge toward
the fire."

"Why?" Rookie had leaned forward, totally engrossed
in the story.

Logan propped his elbows on the table. "Golden felt
the wind shift. It was coming from below, off the river. If
the fire came around the ridge below us, raging like it was,
that wind off the river would funnel the fire up in an explosion."

"Storm King," Rookie whispered, gazing reverently at
Jackson, referencing a fire in Colorado that had claimed
fourteen firefighters in a deadly blowup in 1994.

"Mann Gulch," Chainsaw added, crossing himself out
of respect to the twelve firefighters who died in a similar
fire in Montana in 1949. "May they rest in peace."

Both fiery blowups claimed firefighters with little warning, their legacy a lesson about the dangerous combination
of upsweeping winds, funnel canyons and fire.

Jackson sipped his coffee and looked out over the green
tree line of the valley, willing himself not to think of the
smoke-filled skyline behind him.

"So two helicopters come to get us," Logan continued.
"The first picks up my crew of ten, packed in like sar-

dines. The second helicopter is being batted about by these winds like a mosquito. You know, in a situation like that, those helishot pilots do not want to set down. You have to leap up onto that bird with your pack and pray that you'll land at least partly inside and not mash your teeth on the door frame or the metal landing rail and fall back to the ground. So, Golden and his crew finally all get on board and the pilot takes off, swaying like Big Ben's pendulum. And this one guy, a rookie just like you, he doesn't have anything to hold on to and he tumbles out."

Rookie seemed to stop breathing.

"Nothing between him and a hundred-foot drop onto hot ashes—except our boy here." Logan gestured toward Jackson. "Golden had the smarts to grab on to the sissy strap when he got in, and he snagged that rookie before he plunged all the way over. And just as the rest of the crew is hauling this rookie's ass into the bird, a little rumble sounds below and it grows in volume until it's like a freight train. And the pilot is shitting bricks trying to get out of the way of this huge explosion racing up the funnel toward them."

"What happened?" Rookie breathed.

With effort, Jackson forced himself to sit, but his feet wanted out of there. Damn if this wasn't embarrassing as hell. What he'd done was stupid. He could have killed himself and that kid.

"The helicopter made it clear of the ridge. Looking back, I could see this fireball roll up behind the helicopter. I thought for sure they wouldn't make it. But I shouldn't have worried. They had Golden." Logan took a swig from his water bottle.

"You make me out to be some kind of hero, and I'm not," Jackson protested. "Any of you would have done the same thing."

Chainsaw shook his head. "I wouldn't have noticed the wind. With my chaps and saw pads on, it's so hot out there I can't tell where the wind's coming from sometimes.'' Men who operated the saws had to wear more protective gear than anyone else.

Ignoring them all, Rookie asked Logan, ''And the rookie?''

Logan shrugged. ''He quit after that.''

''Couldn't stomach the challenge,'' added Spider. ''Heard he's selling shoes in Boise.''

Chainsaw nodded. ''You took his spot.''

Rookie blanched.

''Don't let it bother you, kid. Your crew isn't fighting in any spot near as dangerous.'' Jackson knew that because he'd already received their daily assignment sheet from Rob.

Rookie didn't look encouraged.

''You know, I think Golden's right,'' Logan announced. ''He's not a hero. He's just an average guy that gets his ass stuck in motor home windows. Ain't that right?'' Logan held up a picture of Jackson and flashed it around the table.

The group dissolved into raucous comments and laughter.

''I paid an off-duty laundry tech to drive into town and have these developed. Pretty good, huh?'' Logan grinned.

''Give me that.'' Jackson snatched the photo out of Logan's hand. It was one with Lexie in it. They were smiling at each other as if sharing some private joke. Jackson slipped it into his shirt pocket.

Several Hot Shots protested. Some of them hadn't gotten a close enough look.

''Not to worry, folks. There's more where that came from.'' Logan produced a second picture, this one of just Jackson.

''Always have an escape route, eh, Golden?'' This from someone at the end of the table, referring to one of the ten standard fire orders for safety.

"Maybe your new nickname should be Cuckoo," Spider said after scrutinizing the picture. "You look like one of those birds that pops in and out of the clock every hour at my grandmother's house."

"Very funny," Jackson said. "I hope you're through because your bus just pulled in."

Immediately, men and women began stuffing the last of their meal into their mouths. They'd be on rations for their next meal, most commonly the military MREs—military meals-ready-to-eat—so hot, fresh food was a luxury.

When Logan made to follow the unit, Jackson pulled him aside.

"Is there anything I can do for Deb?"

Logan's expression immediately fell. He shook his head. "I don't even know what I can do for her. Her husband, Wes, took off when he heard the news. I swear, if I ever get my hands on that skunk, he'll pay for running out on her and those kids."

"How about if I stop by Deb's on my way home tonight," Jackson offered.

"That would ease my mind." Logan hefted his pack. "See you sometime tomorrow...Cuckoo."

Jackson knew better than to react to the nickname, or else he'd be stuck with it forever.

As Mary watched, Sirus dragged himself up onto a bar stool, looking worn out and in need of some sleep.

It was a quiet Friday night at the Pony. An out-of-town couple played pool. At the other end of the bar, a pair of female tourists, back from a day of rafting on the Payette River, and several firemen sat drinking beer while they watched the Seattle Mariners on television.

Swallowing her doubts, Mary brought Sirus a beer, carrying an iced tea for herself. "Taking a break from the fire?"

"Evening, Mary." Sirus looked up at her with a slow smile. "Why, yes, I am."

Tearing her eyes away from Sirus's, Mary took a sip of her cold drink, flailing for something else to say. "I hear you saved Jackson this morning. Something about him being stuck in a window?"

"Ah, yes. News travels fast around here."

"Heidi couldn't wait to tell me." Mary took another sip. "You've always been there for him."

Sirus shrugged.

"He used to idolize the Hot Shots that came in here. I suppose he was looking for a father figure after Jeremy died. I think Jackson would have worked for free just to hear the fire stories." Mary stared at a far-off wall, remembering how young and impressionable her son had once been. "Of course, Theresa was a different story. She wanted to date every Hot Shot that walked through that door. I wanted to pay her to stay locked up at home."

A waitress leaned against the counter and gave Mary a drink order. Mary mixed the two cocktails efficiently, without much thought.

"I've been meaning to ask you, Sirus—where did you get that scar?" Mary snuck a glance at Sirus and the light line that traced his temple.

He raised his hand as if to touch his scar, then lowered it slowly back onto the bar.

"Did you like being a firefighter's wife?" Sirus asked, instead of answering, spinning his beer in a slow circle.

"I...I don't think about that anymore. Our marriage seems like an old movie." Mary paused, wondering why Sirus would ask her about that. "I remember the laughter. We had fights, although I don't remember what we fought about. I do remember that I was the one who got angry more than him. And then I remember the morning they came to tell me..." The strength of the painful memory caught her off guard.

Sirus nodded slowly. "He was a good man."

"Thank you. I thought so, too." She went to serve another customer, and continued their conversation when she returned. "I haven't worried about Jackson these past few days, knowing he's working at base camp rather than out somewhere dangerous. Are you glad you aren't on the line anymore?"

There was an odd look in Sirus's eyes. He took a swig of beer before answering. "I don't want to lie to you, Mary. I do go out in the field."

A pit of dread formed in Mary's stomach, yet she wasn't sure why. Perhaps it was just his tone of voice that made her anxious. "But not to fight fires."

Sirus's dark eyes held hers. "I do what needs to be done."

Mary ignored the message. "But you're a commander. You shouldn't be risking your life." The void in her stomach was filling with something she recognized all too well. Fear. She coddled Jackson and the other Hot Shots because she believed that by cleaning up after them, washing their clothes and feeding them, she could keep them from harm. She'd never really coddled her husband, Jeremy—and she'd lost him.

"I can't ask men to do something I wouldn't." Damn Sirus's eyes. She thought she read pity there. "I can't lead without their respect."

Mary's heart was pounding, making her hands shake. She'd had no idea she'd react this way. "I thought you were safe. I thought... I can't do this. I lost Jeremy to the fire. And Jackson...he's different since he's been back. I know the fire took something from him in Russia. I just... I just can't do this."

She could tell by the pained look on Sirus's face that he knew what she meant. She couldn't risk losing her heart again if something happened to him.

"Well, that's that, isn't it," he said, before slipping off the bar stool and disappearing into the night.

BARELY AWAKE, but in urgent need, Lexie stumbled out of her bedroom and toward the one bathroom in the house. Drat if she hadn't almost wet herself. If she was lucky, she'd be able to relieve herself and catch another hour of sleep without fully opening her eyes.

Only, she wasn't lucky. The bathroom door was closed and the shower was running.

"Locked." Lexie jiggled the handle. "Heidi," she mumbled to herself as the baby bounced on her full bladder. Heidi and this baby were both early risers, like their father.

Crossing her legs tightly, Lexie reached up to the molding framing the bathroom door and retrieved the bent nail that would unlock the door. She returned the makeshift key to its hiding place and waddled quickly into the steamy bathroom, eyes still half closed from sleep.

"What's the first rule of the morning, Heidi?" Lexie asked as she hitched up her nightie so she could sit on the toilet.

For a moment, there was nothing but the hiss of the shower.

"Don't lock the door—" Jackson's deep voice carried over the shower spray. "Damn, I'm sorry, Lex. I forgot."

Lexie sat bolt upright just as she was starting to pee. She would have made a hasty retreat, but her pregnant bladder wouldn't let her. "Don't come out," she shrieked. Too late, her mind registered the large, masculine silhouette behind the opaque glass. She hadn't heard Jackson come back last night. He hadn't made it to dinner as he had promised, nor had he called. She'd tortured herself all day long thinking she'd made a mistake and given up on their marriage too soon, only to watch Heidi's heart break when Jackson didn't show up.

Lexie suppressed a groan. Even after he'd squelched hope in her heart, drat if part of her didn't want to see Jackson more clearly. She'd always been fascinated by his body.

Lexie scrunched her eyes shut. Where was her pride?

"What's wrong? Is there something you've got that I haven't seen before, Lex?"

He'd seen her like this before, all right. Bloated, splotchy, stretched and just plain fat. Why couldn't their first interaction after the divorce have been with her at her fighting weight?

"Lex, will you marry me?"

She opened her eyes and looked at Jackson's clothes hanging on the back of the bathroom door. "I'm almost through." Lexie finished her business and flushed.

Jackson howled as the toilet diverted cold water from the shower pipe. Just when Lexie was enjoying a little payback, something worse happened.

He shut the water off.

"I'm sorry," Lexie said, feeling anything but sorry. If only he'd stay in the shower or she could move her feet. Why had he asked her to marry him? How many more times was he going to torture her this way?

*What was she going to do when he stopped asking?*

For a moment, neither one of them said anything.

"Lex?"

"Yes," she said, looking at her blurred reflection in the foggy mirror.

"Did you do that on purpose?" Jackson asked.

"Yes."

"I thought so." He paused. "Do you want to tell me why?"

"No." Her feet finally acknowledged her brain's command to skedaddle. Lexie bumped into Heidi in the hallway in her haste to escape. She turned her daughter around and walked Heidi back to her bedroom.

"Mom, I have to go." Heidi dragged her feet.

"Your dad's in the bathroom."

"You were in there, too," Heidi noted, straightening.

"I thought you were in the shower," Lexie admitted. "Besides, he's about to get out. You don't want to see your dad in the buff, do you?"

"Did you?" Heidi turned and gaped at Lexie.

Lexie let just a touch of rebuke support her answer. "You know you can't see a thing through that glass."

"Did you want to?"

Lexie could feel her cheeks heating. "We're not married anymore," she replied firmly. His absence last night was a testament to why their marriage hadn't worked. She was a fool to believe for a moment that they could work things out.

Heidi considered Lexie carefully, making Lexie grateful that the closed blinds kept the room in relative darkness. "You could be married. You're having a baby together."

Lexie sensed Heidi's building resentment. "Heidi, you've got to stop thinking like that. I know it's difficult, but you have to accept the fact that we aren't together anymore."

Heidi snorted. She flopped onto her bed and hugged a worn teddy bear that Jackson had given her when she was a toddler. Lexie waited, knowing her daughter needed to vent.

"If you loved Dad enough to have this baby, why didn't you love him enough to stay married to him?"

"Sometimes love isn't enough." Sometimes, love didn't know when to give up. Jackson's return would be so much easier if she'd fallen out of love with him. Then she could stick to her plan of building a friendship with him.

"What would be enough?" Heidi asked, studying Lexie's face intently.

*A man who put his family above all others,* Lexie thought sadly, but only said, "It doesn't matter now."

"How can you say that? He's back."

"And he hasn't changed. He didn't come home last night, did he?"

Someone rustled in the doorway behind Lexie. She heard Jackson coming toward them. Out of the corner of her eye, Lexie caught sight of his shoulder. She moved farther away from him. She'd reinforce again this morning that they were through. Then she'd find someone to haul away that heap of a motor home so that he couldn't stay there.

"I'm sorry. I stopped by Deb's house last night and somehow ended up fixing them dinner." His voice sounded unbearably sad. "I meant to call."

"I knew you had a good reason, Dad." Heidi leaped off the bed and into Jackson's arms. "See, Mom?"

If Jackson had had any other excuse, Lexie would have held on to her anger. As it was, the emotion drained out of her so quickly that she had to sink down onto Heidi's bed. She told herself it didn't matter, that he could just as easily have stopped to fix Smiley's air conditioner or change the oil in Birdie's old clunker. But she couldn't begrudge a family in need.

She'd asked him to step out of her life because he was a hero to everyone but his own family. She loved him. She admired him. But it wasn't enough. She needed him to be her champion, at least once in a while.

Jackson's sorrowful eyes met Lexie's. Dark circles gave away the fact that Jackson hadn't slept well. Perhaps the nightmares had robbed him entirely of sleep.

Despite her resolve, it was hard for Lexie to look away.

JACKSON WALKED into the kitchen just as Heidi was putting her dirty cereal bowl in the sink. Lexie was nowhere to be seen. He had thought she'd understand why he'd been delayed. Deb needed all the help she could get, what with only two young girls and a slightly senile aunt to care for her.

"I thought you left," Heidi said. Despite supporting him with Lexie earlier, his daughter was back to giving him the cold shoulder.

"I found the dog sitting in my truck," he explained.

"He loves to go for car rides. We don't leave our windows down anymore because he can just leap right in. I think it's a pretty cool trick, but Mom's not impressed."

"I can understand why your mom would think that. Rufus was digging in the garden before he set sights on my truck. There's mud everywhere." Just what Jackson needed, another reason to be late for work. "Are there still rags in the utility room?"

Heidi shrugged.

The utility room was at the end of the hallway. In a hurry, Jackson opened the door quickly, surprising Lexie, who was spraying clothes with stain remover. The spray bottle clattered to the ground.

"Sorry," Jackson mumbled, bending to retrieve the bottle. "I'm looking for some..." His voice trailed off as his eyes registered the red stains she'd been treating. "Is that blood?"

Her cheeks flamed.

"My God, Lexie. Have you been bleeding? Is that why you're on bed rest?" Somehow, he'd gripped her shoulders without realizing it. He forced himself to relax his hold on her. "You didn't tell me anything—I didn't think it was that serious." Now he felt like a fool.

"I'm handling it."

"It's my baby too. I can't stop worrying just because you tell me to." He had every right to worry.

She pulled away.

Normally, this was where Jackson shut up, backed off, smiled and gave Lexie space, but normal hadn't worked all that well in the past year. He cupped her chin. "'Fess up. What's wrong?"

Lexie remained mutinously silent, her cheeks still flowered red as roses. Slowly, her blue eyes raised to his. "Okay. I'll tell you how *I* feel."

The implication being that he didn't share how he felt. She wouldn't want to know the extent of his failure and cowardice.

"The doctor put me on bed rest because I have an incompetent cervix. As the pregnancy progresses, the stress on it causes spotting and could eventually lead to a premature birth."

"I remember that happening to you with Heidi, but it seemed closer to your due date." He hadn't remembered it as being such a serious complication, but perhaps that was due to the naiveté of youth.

"Yes, it started sooner this time. I shouldn't worry, but…" Her voice trailed off.

Jackson waited for her to finish.

"It was much heavier than usual yesterday."

"Call the doctor." Jackson caught Lexie's arm and started dragging her out to the kitchen where the phone was. "You need to listen to your body."

"I've got an appointment with him next week." Lexie protested all the way down the hall, but when presented with the telephone, she dutifully dialed the doctor. Jackson stood next to her just in case she decided to bail on the call. She always had been one to downplay the seriousness of things.

"His service said he'd call back later." Lexie hung up the phone.

"Maybe we should go to the hospital," Jackson suggested.

"We'll wait until he calls back." Lexie smiled weakly. "Go to work. I'm sure it's nothing."

Jackson picked up the phone. "I'm not going in to work today. You need me more than they do."

THE DOCTOR FINALLY CALLED BACK, and Jackson set an appointment for Lexie for later that afternoon. He and Heidi watched television in the living room for a while without speaking, until Jackson got restless and wandered out to the motor home. It really was an eyesore, what with the window missing and the flat tire.

Jackson jacked up the motor home so that it no longer tilted to one side, and then he coaxed the engine into life and adjusted the timing. Frankly, he was amazed the thing started at all. Mid-morning, a truck pulled in from the supply store in Boise, delivering several large bundles and boxes full of replacement parts, including a new window.

Grateful for the distraction, Jackson set to work stripping out old parts.

Heidi wandered into the motor home and pretended to drive while Jackson tugged and tore out the old, mildewy carpet.

"Did you have any friends in Russia?" Heidi asked.

"Some." Ignoring memories he'd rather avoid, Jackson wrestled the old carpet and pad outside, where Rufus promptly sniffed it. Jackson began to sweep out all the dirt and carpet scraps left behind.

Before long, the dog was growling and tugging the ends, dragging the carpet across the ground.

"What about your friends in Russia, Dad?"

Jackson grunted, speech momentarily robbed from him when Lexie came into view. She paused outside the door to praise Rufus's progress against the carpet dregs. When she looked up, Jackson smiled at her, hoping to provide her some reassurance that things were going to be all right. He wouldn't let himself think otherwise.

Standing in the morning sunlight, Lex neither smiled nor frowned. One hand absently stroked her belly, covered today in a simple navy-blue T-shirt—one of his—and shorts. She met his gaze briefly before looking away, reminding him of her earlier accusation that he didn't tell her things.

"You had to have friends over there, Dad. You make friends everywhere." Heidi tried a third time. "Tell me about them."

Jackson couldn't ignore Heidi's questions anymore. She was making an effort, while he was trying not to wallow in the past.

Lexie peered curiously at Heidi through the gap where there had once been a window. Rufus popped his nose at Lexie's hand, seeking more praise. Slowly, Lexie knelt down to pet the dog.

It seemed odd to realize that Lexie hadn't asked him about his time away. He liked to think she'd respected his privacy, but part of him was hurt that she hadn't cared enough to ask him what he'd been doing for more than half a year. The closest she'd come was asking about his nightmares.

Aware that Lex was listening, Jackson began to weave a tale of Russia designed to please his daughter. "I was assigned to a team of firefighters." Jackson went back to sweeping, but kept an eye on Lexie.

Heidi twirled her fingers around the ponytail at the back of her neck. "Did they speak English?"

"A little. Mostly broken English." He moved to the front of the motor home, where Heidi sat in the driver seat, watching him in the rearview mirror.

"Broken English?"

"A word of English here and there. Someone might tell me to *give girl kiss*." Jackson tried his best Russian accent before leaning over to give Heidi a kiss on the top of her head. "There was a lot of gesturing, too. *You squeeze. You squeeze.*" Jackson made a series of gestures before hugging his little girl.

Heidi couldn't stop giggling. Lexie had come to stand in the doorway, hovering like a large butterfly.

"Were the fires big?" Heidi asked when he'd released her.

He sobered instantly. "The fires were wild and out of control."

"But not too much for you."

The fire had been a monster, flames roaring to the sky as if challenging God himself to stop them. The motor home suddenly felt too warm. Jackson gripped the broom tighter.

"Dad?" Heidi spun in her chair, a frown marring her small brow. "Are you okay?"

Still seeing the fire on the fringes of his vision, Jackson turned away and found himself facing Lexie—only, he couldn't bring his gaze above her knees. He knew that if he looked into her blue eyes, she'd see him for the coward he was. Her pity would kill what was left of the man inside him.

"I'd better finish this up before it gets too late." He walked to the back of the motor home and swept with more force than necessary. He couldn't look at either of them now.

After a moment's silence, Lexie said brightly, "Come on, Heidi. Time for lunch."

"Dad." Heidi made as if to follow, but then turned at the bottom step, the mere act drawing Jackson's gaze to hers. "You're stronger than the fire, aren't you? I mean, you always come back."

He almost hadn't come back this last time. He hadn't been strong. He'd been a fool. Russian fire had taught him how little and insignificant he was.

Heidi tugged on the hem of her pink tank top and bit her lip.

Knowing he had to give her some bit of reassurance, Jackson dug down deep inside for something to say.

"Your mom used to race. Did you know that? She was a cross-country runner, which means she used to race up and down these mountains."

Heidi's expression eased. "Was she any good?"

"She was good. She only won one race, but it was an important one for our school."

"Cool."

"I never had much time for sports, growing up. I'd always helped at the Painted Pony. When I finished training and passed the physical tests to become a Hot Shot, your mother gave me the one medal she'd won. She told me how proud she was that I hadn't given up, when it would have been easier to quit than to go on." Jackson grew more thoughtful as he remembered how honored he'd felt when she'd given him what represented her only racing success. "I carry that medal to every fire. That's how I know I'll come back."

"Wow." Heidi graced him with one of her sweet smiles. "You two were meant for each other."

Numbly, Jackson nodded, rubbing his hand over his aching heart, remembering Lexie's words when she gave the medal to him: *My love will always bring you home.*

Over near the house, Lexie shrieked. The orange-and-white cat scampered away into the bushes carrying something gray in her mouth.

"Marmy caught another mouse." Grinning, Heidi hit the ground running, calling for Rufus with a high-pitched "Here, boy!" In seconds, she was inside the house.

But Jackson saw what Heidi hadn't. Lexie was leaning against the corner of the house as if she needed all the support the wall could give. Jackson hurried over. As he came nearer, he saw pink-tinged liquid streaking down her legs.

"Are you all right? Lex? Lex?" He was halfway across the driveway when he realized the liquid was blood. He started to run. "Damn it, Lexie, answer me."

# CHAPTER EIGHT

LEXIE HAD PEED HER PANTS.

She'd been feeling fine one moment—well, the pregnant equivalent of fine, which was ungainly and achy—when Marmy had dropped that mouse on her foot and scared the pee out of her. Warm liquid seeped into her shorts.

At this rate, she was destined for almost five weeks of adult diapers.

She heard Jackson call her and turned, still somewhat dazed. Embarrassment started its hot creep up her neck.

"Sit down, baby. Everything's going to be okay."

Jackson didn't seem to realize she'd wet herself. He seemed to think it was something more serious. He guided her over to a plastic chair on the porch and lowered her into it.

"Breathe. That's right. How are you feeling? Talk to me."

Lexie laughed self-consciously as her gaze focused on Jackson towering above her. All this unexpected concern over a bladder-control issue. Sitting down had been a mistake. Wetness pressed through layers of her clothing. She wouldn't be standing up again without telling him what had happened to her.

"Can we talk about something else?" she asked.

"No. Listen, I need to know if you're okay. I need to know…" He floundered, and then gestured to her legs. "About that."

That's when Lexie looked down and noticed the blood-tinged liquid trailing down her legs. "Oh, no. What's happening?" she whispered.

Jackson knelt in front of Lexie, putting his hands on the arms of the chair. "Do you usually bleed like this?"

She didn't say anything for a moment. She refused to believe she was having the baby this early. Lexie's lower lip trembled. "I had an accident," she said stubbornly.

"Did you turn your ankle or something? I didn't see you fall." Jackson ran his hands down the outside of Lexie's lower leg from her knee to her ankle and then back up to her knee. She stiffened at his touch.

Lexie blew out a breath and admitted "I've wet myself." Her urine must have carried some blood with it. Lovely.

"I think it's more than that. Stay right there. I'll get a towel."

Lexie sat very still. She stared up at the clear blue sky and wondered why this was happening to her.

It wasn't long before Jackson was back. He began rubbing her legs dry.

"I don't smell anything. I remember how Heidi smelled when she was little and wet herself. Pungent. You don't smell."

"I would hope not." Affronted, she pushed his hands off her knees.

"Are you sure it's not your water?"

"Water gushes more. Much more. Remember how I made a puddle in the kitchen with Heidi?"

"Are you sure?"

She noticed him checking out her stained shorts and blushed.

"I thought we were having lunch." Heidi came out the front door.

"Heidi, get in my truck," Jackson instructed calmly. "We're going to the hospital."

"Is the baby coming now? So early?" Heidi looked a little panicked.

"I'm fine. Really," Lexie protested from her seat. "The baby is staying right where she belongs. Your father is overreacting."

"We're not taking any chances." Jackson stared hard at Lexie.

Lexie stood. Her sodden shorts felt baggy and heavy at her bottom. "I need to change."

"I don't think so. You shouldn't be walking around. We'll get you in the truck first, and I'll grab some dry clothes for you." Jackson escorted Lexie to his truck.

"Don't you have a blanket or something I can sit on?" Lexie asked, gesturing to the velour interior. "I don't want to ruin the seat if I have an accident."

"No." Jackson opened the door wider. "Get in."

"An old shirt?"

"Lex, you're not going to ruin a thing. The seats are stain resistant. The mud from the dog cleaned right up."

When she was buckled in his truck, Lexie turned to him and voiced her fear. "What if the baby's coming early?"

"We'll deal with it." Jackson took her hand and gave it a squeeze. "Together."


"YOUR WATER IS LEAKING, Mrs. Garrett." Dr. Stuart settled the paper sheet over Lexie's legs and snapped off his gloves. "You've dilated to three centimeters. There's no stopping you now. We'll need to induce to make sure things move along quickly."

Lexie reached for Jackson almost instinctively. His hand closed over hers, giving her fingers much-needed warmth in the cool hospital, bolstering Lexie's strength.

"The baby is fine, right?" Jackson asked, his brow wrinkled.

"I hear a sturdy heartbeat, but we need to run some tests. We'll get you admitted right away."

"You didn't answer my question."

"Mr. Garrett, that's because I don't know for sure."

*I don't know.* The words echoed in Lexie's brain until she wanted to cry out in frustration. She'd been so sure that the baby had caused her to wet herself. But that wasn't it at all. The doctor wasn't certain if her baby was going to be healthy, perhaps it wouldn't even live. Struggling to be rational, Lexie rejected those negative thoughts even as her emotional side clutched the possibility of loss and started to grieve.

How naive she'd been to have assumed this pregnancy would be as smooth as her first, that she'd be able to hold a healthy baby in her arms after nine months of waiting, given all the problems she'd had conceiving. The baby within her womb may never live beyond its first few minutes or hours of life.

Tears welled in her eyes and Lexie gripped Jackson's hand tighter, moaning softly as despair threatened to overwhelm her. She was glad that Mary had arrived and taken Heidi to the waiting room.

"Don't," Jackson said, gently holding Lexie's chin in his free hand and turning her face toward him. He smiled reassuringly, no trace of the emotional upheaval she was experiencing showing on his face. "Our baby is going to be fine."

Lexie stared into the depths of Jackson's bright green eyes, wondering how he could be so sure of himself, so resolute. He wasn't a doctor. Yet he looked at her unflinchingly and made her a promise—this baby would be fine. And, despite her panic, she believed him. She knew now why men followed him to fight against wildfires. He made them believe in themselves, gave them courage.

She attempted a smile that was much too wobbly, asking something of him that would most likely break her heart later. "Don't leave me."

"Never."

Despite everything she'd done to him—her kicking him out, demanding a divorce—he still loved her. Lexie glanced once at his wedding ring before making up her mind. She loved him enough to try again.

The next time he asked her to marry him, she was going to say yes.

NURSES AND SPECIALISTS CAME AND WENT through Lexie's room. A nurse administered an IV and strapped monitors to Lexie's belly to report the baby's heartbeat and contractions to the nurses' station. Jackson, used to being a man of action, sat by and did nothing aside from keep a smile on his face that seemed to give Lexie hope. She held on to his hand, occasionally squeezing his fingers when a comment from a specialist worried her, but otherwise, she didn't speak.

They were allowed visitors. His mother brought Heidi in, along with Sirus.

When Jackson gave Sirus a look that questioned his presence, Sirus shrugged and said, "I go where I'm needed. Besides, I thought it was time to give Rob a taste of what it's like to be incident commander, and NIFC didn't object."

"You insisted on driving me," Mary quipped, almost as if she were trying to distance Sirus for some reason.

Sirus didn't say anything, and the room was saved from an awkward silence by the appearance of the sonogram technician. He discreetly repositioned Lexie's blankets and gown, then ran his instrument across her belly before announcing, "It's a boy!"

Lexie and Jackson exchanged looks and laughed together for the first time in months. Her smile chased away the doubt in Jackson's heart. Everything was going to be okay with them. The mood in the room lightened considerably. Mary hugged Heidi, while Sirus leaned up against a wall and beamed.

"I guess we won't be naming him Henriette after all,"
Lexie said gamely.

"Whew." Jackson grinned. He swept Heidi up in a hug.
"How do you feel about having a little brother?"

"Sweet! I'll teach him how to raft and throw the ball
for Rufus."

His mother had tears in her eyes. Sirus moved closer
and put a hand on her shoulder. After a moment, his mom
reached up and gave his hand a squeeze.

"Life does have a way of moving you." His mother
struggled not to cry.

"When you least expect it," Sirus said softly, as if for
her ears only.

Jackson exchanged a glance with his mentor. Socrates's
interest in his mother seemed more than platonic. Was
Jackson reading more than was there or had Sirus's comments from the other day at base camp just put ideas in
his head?

Sirus gave Jackson the briefest of nods, as if confirming
that he was, indeed, becoming part of Jackson's family.

Okay, then. At least Jackson didn't have to worry about
his mother having an affair with someone that was after
her money. Sirus was a good man—with good intentions,
if this was the third marriage that Sirus had mentioned the
other day. Jackson rolled that around, trying to get used
to the idea of Sirus as his stepfather. Jackson supposed his
mother could do worse.

"Since Henriette is out, what would you like to call
him?" Lexie said, her voice wispy.

"Are you stuck on names beginning with *H?*" Jackson
pulled Heidi closer to Lexie's bed, wrapped an arm around
his daughter's narrow shoulders and reached for Lexie's
hand. For the moment at least, it seemed he had his family
back.

"I know it's sappy, but I like the idea of having kids
with the same initials." Tears glistened in Lex's eyes.

Lexie rubbed the small section of her stomach not covered by electrodes and belts, stroking the baby lovingly. He could tell she was worried. He was worried too.

His mother sniffed. In a minute, Jackson suspected the whole place was going to need a box of tissues.

"How about Haywood?" his mom offered, sitting forward.

Sirus's hand fell away from her shoulder.

Jackson shook his head. "Hayseed plowboy."

"Harley?" Heidi suggested.

"A tattooed, leather-vested man with a big belly?" Lexie laughed and Jackson relaxed, enjoying the moment.

Mary's brow furrowed. "Howard?"

"The accountant that embezzled all that money from Birdie? No." Jackson rolled his eyes. "Remember that guy Theresa dated? The bald guy?" Jackson racked his brain for the name of the boy his sister used to date. "Hunter, wasn't it?"

Lexie shook her head with a weary smile. "Yuppies killing Bambi."

"Good thing Theresa moved to Montana," Jackson said. "No one teases my sister about her dates, past or present, without a fight."

"I'll call her when I get home. She'll be worried." Mary wiped her nose with a tissue.

"Maybe we should go back to Henriette," Heidi said, giving everyone a good laugh.

Then Sirus spoke up, surprising everyone. "What about Henry?"

Jackson nodded. "Henry's not bad." It wasn't. And the fact that Sirus had proposed the name seemed to make Jackson's mentor even more a part of the Garrett family.

Jackson looked at Lexie to make sure the name was all right with her.

Lexie smiled. "I feel better now that we've given him a name."

Jackson knew what she meant. *Henry.* In that moment, their baby had become more of a person. And soon, Jackson would be able to hold him.

But the light moment didn't last. Things were happening too fast. The nurse applied an internal stimulant to Lexie to induce labor, then raised the hospital bed so that her feet remained higher than her head for an hour. By nightfall, Lexie had received two labor-inducing treatments with no action and was complaining of a headache.

"Maybe you should have eaten more," Jackson said, after Sirus had taken Heidi and his mother home. Lexie barely made a dent in her tray of hospital food.

"Maybe you should have brought me a pizza." Her words were flat and lacking energy.

"I could call for one now." Jackson would, too. He stroked her brow, pleased that she was letting him touch her, and taking every opportunity to do so.

"Don't. The doctor would freak out."

Jackson gazed at Lexie. "Would it help if I gave your tummy a massage?" It had been twelve years since their last prenatal course, but he still remembered how.

She blinked up at him for a moment, and he could see her debating. Then she pushed herself up and inched forward on the mattress.

Pausing only to take off his boots, Jackson climbed as gently as possible onto the bed behind her, making a V with his legs and easing her back against his chest. The flowery scent of her hair filled his nostrils, while her dark silky strands brushed his cheek and neck.

When he hesitated, she placed her hands over his and laid them over her tummy, careful of the straps and wires monitoring the baby's condition. "Here."

Jackson's heart beat faster at this connection with his son and the woman he loved. Lexie's hand made tiny circles with Jackson's hand, hovering around a lump.

"Near as I can tell, that's his bottom," she whispered.

"Which means his feet are over this way." Jackson let his hand slide across her tummy to the other side.

She turned, her blue eyes raised to his, dark with invitation, and he knew they were going to kiss. Slowly, savoring the moment of anticipation, he leaned over, sliding one hand around to the small of her back while the other supported her head. He pulled her closer until the curves of her body melded against him. Their lips made gentle contact.

*Home.*

No one knew Jackson the way Lexie did. She held on to him just the right way. Her breath wafted softly over his skin. And she accepted his kiss as if they'd never been apart. He settled her back against him with a contented sigh and continued to massage her belly.

"Do you remember the day you first spoke to me in Mrs. Faust's class?" Lexie asked.

"Attila the Hun's class?" Jackson searched his memory, coming up blank. "I must be getting old, I don't remember. Sorry."

"Logan was messing around with Bobby Braden before class and he bumped into me. Everything went flying— my books, my binder—"

"Even you. I remember now."

"You caught me." She took his arms and wrapped them tighter around her. "You were my hero then."

Jackson paused. He'd been about to ask her to marry him again. But he wasn't anybody's hero.

"YOU DIDN'T HAVE TO DRIVE ME, Sirus," Mary said, filling the silence left when Heidi had drifted off to sleep in the back seat of Sirus's truck.

"You seemed upset when they called. I didn't want to hear you'd driven off into some gully because you couldn't keep your mind on the road."

Mary was impatient, on edge. After the way she'd admitted her fears to him earlier in the week, Mary was sure she was the last person Sirus would want to be with. He'd been having an early dinner meeting in the Pony when Heidi called with the news that Lexie was being admitted to the hospital. He'd noticed that the call had shaken her and had offered to come with her to the hospital.

He'd been a rock for her to lean on all night, and she appreciated it. At the same time, her feelings for Sirus made her uncomfortable. He was a wonderful man, so thoughtful and kind. If only he didn't have such a dangerous job.

Sirus slowed for a bend in the road, and Mary bit her bottom lip to keep herself from saying anything else that would only come out looking foolish or ungrateful.

"Any news about the fire?" Mary asked after a few more miles spent wondering how long it would take for her to shake her infatuation with Sirus.

Sirus chuckled. "It seems to be fighting back. Just when we think it's coming under control, the winds help it jump a line or airborne sparks land in a tree down some impossibly steep slope and it regains momentum."

She could tell by his tone that Sirus was comfortable with the fire, as if he were confident they'd win and was amused by its behavior. It was so like a Hot Shot, former or not, to have a cavalier attitude about facing death.

She would not start another discussion about the danger of fire fighting. "Do you know how much longer base camp will be running?"

"Can't really say. It all depends on the fire."

"I hope for your sake it closes soon, although business has been so good, what with the crews passing through town, that I'll be sorry to see them go."

"But things will settle down to normal."

"I used to think Lexie and Jackson together was normal. And then it wasn't. Little Heidi was a ray of sunshine until she started *maturing* this past year." Mary flexed her fingers. "And after years of working at the Pony, the joints in my fingers are starting to ache. I don't think I know what normal is anymore." She turned her head to look at Sirus, surprised to find him half smiling.

"I do appreciate your perspective on life, Mary."

Mary accepted the compliment, comforted by this moment of peace. She felt closer to Sirus than ever before, but knew somehow that the feeling wouldn't last.

"Have you…Have you noticed a change in Jackson since he's come back?" he asked, changing the subject.

Mary shifted in her seat. "What kind of change?"

Sirus didn't answer, just continued to drive.

Mary had noticed a difference in her son. Jackson was a born storyteller. He could mesmerize you with a story about reading a book if he wanted. Yet, he'd said nothing about his Russia trip. Absolutely nothing.

"Do you remember what happened to Jeremy the summer before he died?" Sirus prompted.

Mary closed her eyes against the memory, but it came anyway. The night sweats, the brooding, the way the bravest man she knew—her husband—admitted he was afraid of fire. Sirus and Jeremy had served on the same crew. Sirus had to have seen something different in his friend as well.

"You think Jackson's lost his nerve? Is that why he's working for you?"

"He's working for me until a crew supervisor position opens up, although he's applied at NIFC for a full-time position in Incident Command. But when I asked him about taking on a permanent role, you would have thought I'd asked him to dance naked in base camp." Sirus sighed. "I'm not sure what's going on with Jackson. I'd like him to talk with someone. NIFC has some great counseling programs."

"But why? I'm happy that he's in less danger working in IC. Leave him be." Mary didn't want to admit that

Jackson might be fighting the same demons his father had. She'd always blamed Jeremy's pride for his death. Jeremy hadn't wanted to quit because he felt he'd be less of a man if he gave in to the power of his fear. So he'd continued to fight. The fire had won.

"Mary, we both know he's more valuable to the Forest Service out on the line than at base camp."

"His life is more important than his value to the Forest Service."

"You wouldn't say that if your house or your life was in danger. You'd want Jackson in charge."

Mary's heart sank. Is this why he'd come to the hospital—to talk about her son and his job? "That's why you came tonight, isn't it, because of Jackson."

"Mary, we've known each other a long time. I enjoy your company. And I'm awful fond of your little family." Sirus spoke deliberately, slowing his truck as they entered town.

"Fond enough to use me to convince Jackson to go into counseling for the good of the Forest Service?"

"You're taking this out of context. I could drive you home, give Heidi a little more time to sleep, and we could talk about it." He pulled into the Pony's parking lot, next to Mary's Subaru wagon.

"There's nothing more to say. You can drop me off here. People would talk if my car was parked out here all night."

"People always talk, especially in this town. You think they haven't noticed me spending all my free time at the Pony?"

"Yes, but—"

"*But* is just a little word, and hearing you say it so often is frustrating. Eighteen years ago, things were different. There were fewer safety precautions in place and fewer options available when a firefighter lost his nerve. I don't allow the past to rule my life and, damn it, neither should you.''

Mary gasped.

"Why are you cussing?" Heidi stretched in the back seat. "We're here already?"

"We seem to have gone about as far as we can go," Mary said, gathering her purse and climbing out.

WHEN DR. STUART CAME to check on her at two in the morning, Lexie announced, ''We've decided to call the baby Henry.''

Dr. Stuart looked less than pleased that they'd named the baby. Lexie was reminded of a stray cat she'd fed for a time when she was a kid. Her mother had cautioned her not to name it, but Lexie had done so anyway. "It'll just hurt that much more when he runs away or gets hit by a car if you give it a name," Lexie's mother, ever practical, had warned her.

Lexie hadn't wanted to listen. Back then, Lexie had been an optimist and searching for any love she could get. She'd named the cat Ruffles and she'd played with him every day. Until a few weeks later when she'd found the cat's lifeless body in the gutter of the busy street they lived on.

Now Dr. Stuart seemed to be doing much the same as her mother, sending shafts of doubt to the foundation of Lexie's hard-won optimism. "You have a delicate constitution when it comes to babies, Mrs. Garrett, as we learned from that miscarriage last year. We always take every precaution in a situation like this, but…''

To Lexie's dismay, the doctor droned on.

Jackson's expression had turned to stone. He nodded curtly to the doctor when he'd finished his "don't worry, but don't get your hopes up" speech, but didn't say a word.

"I'll check on you in a few hours." Dr. Stuart disappeared out into the hallway, leaving Lexie alone with Jackson.

"What's he talking about, Lex?" There wasn't even a trace of a smile on Jackson's face.

Lexie chose to ignore Jackson's question, looking instead at the muted television. What could she say? She'd been pregnant twice in the past year and hadn't told him either time.

"It doesn't matter now," Lexie said wearily, when she couldn't stand the silence any longer. "It's in the past."

"Was it mine?"

Lexie nearly cried out because his doubt cut her heart. "How can you ask that?"

Jackson didn't say a word, didn't make light of the situation or tell her it didn't matter. The silence between them became unbearable, as it never had been before, because Jackson had never stared at her with so much raw pain in his face. She could feel his betrayal as surely as the ache in her heart.

She should have told him.

"When?" he asked in a cold voice.

Lexie shivered. In all their time together, he'd never been this disappointed in her. But she'd been the one whose expectations weren't fulfilled. He'd been nowhere to be found when she needed him most, when she was scared, bleeding and alone last summer in this same hospital. The memory gave her strength.

"Do you remember the day I asked you to move out?" Lexie held her head up and met his steely gaze squarely. "I asked you to meet me for lunch. We'd grown so distant. I'd just found out about the pregnancy and I was ecstatic about the baby. I thought it was a sign that we were meant to be together. I thought you'd be happy." Her fingers gripped the blanket. "I wore your favorite dress. And I sat at Giseppe's for an hour while I waited for you. I drank so much water that I had to use the bathroom. Only, when

I went to the bathroom, there was blood." Lexie closed her eyes. "So much blood." Lexie remembered how scared she'd been. How alone she'd felt. "I called Dr. Stuart and he met me at the hospital. No one knew where you were. Dr. Stuart told me there was no hope for the baby, so I had the procedure and went home later that afternoon. Our baby—my sign that we were supposed to be together—was gone."

"You never said a word." His words were clipped.

"I'm sorry I didn't tell you. I really am. I've had to live with the guilt all this time."

"The same way you lived with the guilt from this baby?"

"Maybe it wasn't the 'keep me up at night' type of guilt, because I thought I was doing the right thing for both of us. You didn't want to be in this marriage."

"That's not true!"

"Isn't it? Where were you?" she cried, her pain echoing in the spartan hospital room. She'd never asked him that before. She hadn't wanted to know. If he'd let Lexie and their baby down because of something as trivial as helping a friend stack a load of firewood or shooting the breeze with a buddy over a beer, Lexie didn't think she'd ever be able to forgive him. So she hadn't asked, because not knowing gave him the benefit of the doubt. Until now.

"You were never home. *Never.* The only thing that mattered to me then was that you hadn't been where I needed you. You weren't there for me or Heidi, so why should we let you come home to sleep? Where were you, Jackson?"

Instead of answering or arguing, he spun away, his footsteps hollow as he left her.

"You were supposed to be my hero," she said softly, realizing that he'd never ask her to marry him again.

NOW HE KNEW what Lexie really thought of him.

Not much.

Jackson wandered around the halls of the hospital in a daze. He'd written off her secret pregnancy to their divorce and his being half a world away. But she hadn't told him about the other pregnancy last summer. She'd talked about "signs" and him not being around. Well, he was around now, wasn't he?

Would he stay?

Would she let him?

Somehow, Jackson ended up in the cafeteria, staring at the limited choices offered by the coffee machine. What he really wanted was a stiff drink and someplace dark to crawl into so he could lick his wounds in private.

How could he even pretend she still loved him, when Lexie had deceived him twice in one year? He was deluding himself.

Thick black coffee poured out of the machine before Jackson even realized he'd inserted money. He took the steaming hot cup over to a table by a window, turned a chair so that his back was facing the rest of the deserted, sterile room and then stared at his empty reflection.

Why would Lexie keep a pregnancy and miscarriage from him? She'd gone through something devastating, physically and mentally. And she'd done it alone. He'd had no idea that she was grieving or upset over more than his standing her up.

And she'd been prepared to do it again while he was in Russia.

Jackson propped his feet on a chair and tilted his head to the ceiling, searching for clarity in a world that had suddenly become too murky to navigate. With the fingers of his right hand, he spun his wedding ring slowly around his left finger.

Bit by bit, fragments of conversation came back to him. Lexie considered him an absentee father and husband. Maybe there was something to that accusation; Jackson certainly couldn't refute it. Lexie was so competent, so good at doing things on her own, that Jackson often jumped at the chance to help a neighbor in need. She'd been searching for some sign that they should remain together instead of asking him flat out to behave differently. She'd shut herself off from him.

Jackson took a sip of the bitter-smelling coffee and burned his tongue.

And yet, Lexie hadn't shut herself off totally. It was clear she wanted someone that was around more than six to nine months out of the year. Perhaps she even held out hope that he'd be that someone.

And she *did* need him. But he had no guarantee that she'd let him back if he traded a field position for a desk job.

Except...she'd let him kiss her, let him touch her, let him wrap her in his arms.

Jackson shook his head. He was probably just trying to convince himself that she still cared. If she didn't hold any love for him, then he should have perished in the Siberian fire.

Damn it. If there were signs to be read, he couldn't ignore that one.

Jackson just wasn't convinced he could withstand the battle back into her heart.

Tightness on her stomach awoke Lexie. She pushed herself upright to escape the sensation, until she recognized what it was. A contraction. She tried to breathe evenly until her muscles relaxed.

"Jackson," she whispered, looking quickly around the room. The hospital was quiet at this time of night and no one answered her. Then she remembered how hurt he'd been when she'd told him about the miscarriage.

For a few hours tonight, the unsettling feelings, the

doubt, guilt and loneliness had vanished. With Jackson's arms wrapped around her, her worries had slipped away. He'd talked to her about things other than his schedule. For the first time in over a year, she'd felt at peace, despite her concern for Henry.

The lights snapped on in the room and a nurse walked in, pulling the door closed behind her. "I was wondering how strong those contractions had to be before they woke you up. I guess we're having a baby." She washed her hands in the bathroom sink, and then approached Lexie with a *snap* of plastic gloves. "Let's see how far you've dilated."

Lexie looked at the ceiling while the nurse performed her exam.

"Where's that husband of yours gone to?"

"I don't know." Lexie didn't dispute the nurse's assumption that she and Jackson were married. She tried to imagine Jackson walking down the hallway, out the door and out of her life forever, but she couldn't. He wasn't the kind of man who turned his back on someone in need.

"Five centimeters. I'll wake the doctor and page your husband. Plenty of time yet."

Forty minutes later, Lexie fought unsuccessfully to relax. Her labor pain was nearly unbearable. She was a wimp, through and through. And it was only going to get worse.

Only the presence of Jackson, sitting silent and rigid in a chair near the door, kept her from moaning like a weakling. He hadn't said a word to her. In fact, she wouldn't have known he'd returned if the nurse hadn't acknowledged him. She supposed his silence was no more than she deserved for keeping their loss from him.

Jackson had come back to Lexie, yet she was still very much on her own.

The doctor and nurse walked in. The nurse carried a tray with a syringe of medication to numb the pain and put her back in control. Lexie was a sweaty mess, not a glow about her, and she felt as if she could scream for days and days. At the sight of almost certain relief, Lexie bit her lip so hard she tasted blood.

"Hurry," she murmured half to herself.

"How are we doing, Mrs. Garrett?" The doctor had a mask around his neck and gloves ready to snap on.

"These contractions aren't pretty. Oh, no. Here comes one." Lexie panted and puffed her way through the searing pain. "There's so much pressure all the time."

"Sounds like back labor," the nurse said, tapping the syringe to remove any air bubbles. She made the announcement nonchalantly, as if she were commenting on a mild change in the weather. The nurse was slender and pretty, and probably never had experienced childbirth from this side of the birthing stirrups.

Lexie's body shuddered with the intensity of a particularly sharp contraction that turned into something even stronger.

"Oh no, I have to push!" Lexie shrieked.

The nurse tossed the syringe back onto the tray—unused—which only increased Lexie's panic. The pain was excruciating with no medicine to numb her to it, no hope of regaining control. The room receded into a backdrop—

"Baby, breathe. Focus." Jackson's voice cut through the cloud of pain.

The urge to push diminished ever so slightly. Things came back into focus. Peach walls. Tacky wallpaper.

"You're doing fine." The doctor's voice was cool and detached. He probably never had felt anything like what she was going through, either. "Don't push yet, Mrs. Garrett."

"You're kidding me, right?" Lexie panted as the worst of the contraction passed. If she ever had another baby, she'd insist on a doctor and nurse that had been through the process themselves.

"We need to get the Neonatal team in here for the baby." The doctor nodded to the nurse, who had run over to the telephone mounted on the wall. "We need to keep the baby inside you until they get set up."

The nurse was already telling someone on the line to "Get here, *stat*."

"Where are they? Are they close?" Lexie asked.

"They're just down the hall," Dr. Stuart said.

"Ow!" Lexie nearly jumped as something poked her nether region.

"Local anesthetic for the episiotomy," Dr. Stuart explained without looking up.

Before Lexie could think much more on that, another contraction built, nearly stealing what little air she was managing to get in her lungs. Lexie didn't think she could handle not pushing again. She was on the verge of losing control completely and she had no way to stop herself.

As if sensing her panic, Jackson gripped her hand. "Breathe for Henry, Lex."

*Henry.* Much as Lexie wanted to push this baby out, she had to stay in control, even if it was only for a few more minutes. Lexie thought she managed to nod. Her body trembled so violently, she didn't think she could speak.

The nurse and doctor moved Lexie into position on the birthing bed. Three people in scrubs entered the room and stood by the empty bassinet with a full view of Lexie's privates. She didn't care how much they saw of her, as long as she could push this baby out.

"Mrs. Garrett, on the next contraction, I want you to push for the count of five and then relax through the rest of it."

"No way." Lexie's muscles were spent, sweat covered her skin. Women had actually given birth without medicine? Lexie couldn't recall hearing a single woman telling her she'd done so.

"Mrs. Garrett—"

"Lex, you can do this. Look at me."

Jackson's face was down close to hers. She wanted to shove him away.

"No." She wouldn't look at him. "You're supposed to be on my side. I want to push and never stop. Tell them I need to push," she pleaded.

"You can push. You can push all you want for five seconds. I'll count and then you squeeze my hand instead of pushing. Henry needs you to do this," Jackson said.

She had only just registered his words before the next contraction hit. She pushed against it with all her might.

"Four...five. Squeeze my hand, Lex. Stop pushing."

Lexie screamed and began to pant. She clenched Jackson's hand so fiercely that she worried his fingers might be crushed, but she wasn't letting go. Finally, the pain receded.

"Great going, Mrs. Garrett. You get to push him out for me next time, okay?"

The pain had barely receded before it built again. "Here it comes." Lexie's voice sounded panicked even to her ears. They must all think she was nuts.

"That's right. Push, push, push," the doctor encouraged.

Straining, Lexie gave it her all, anxious for the pain to end, ready to see her son and make sure he was fine, as Jackson had promised.

After what seemed like forever, the pressure ebbed, and then Lexie collapsed back in the bed. She couldn't see the baby, had only glimpsed him as the doctor placed him on the edge of the bed between her legs.

"There he is." Jackson leaned forward, then looked back at Lexie. "There's our boy." He stepped closer to the doctor, perhaps expecting to cut the cord. He'd cut the cord for Heidi.

"I'll be cutting the cord, Mr. Garrett. Nurse—" Dr.

Stuart efficiently clamped both ends of the cord, severing the connection between Lexie and Henry.

"We need some time, Mr. Garrett." The nurse guided Jackson back toward the head of the bed.

Jackson's brows pulled together with worry. The people around the bassinet were crowding forward. One man reached for her baby. Lexie didn't even know his name. This was so terribly different from her first pregnancy, where things had generally been relaxed and she knew everyone in the room by name.

Lexie lifted her head so that she could get a look at Henry. She had to tilt her head to see him past the sea of bodies around the table they had laid him on. "He's so small...and blue." Tears sprang from her eyes. "Jackson, he's not breathing."

# CHAPTER NINE

"WHAT'S WRONG WITH HIM?" Jackson stared helplessly as he watched every parent's worst nightmare play out in front of him.

His child wasn't breathing.

He watched the thin, grayish blue baby that hadn't howled a challenge to the heavens when he slid out of Lexie's womb. He watched the technicians or specialists or whoever they were slip tubes down his child's throat and poke needles in his tender skin. He wasn't used to watching. He was used to responding, reacting, taking charge.

"What are you doing to him?" Jackson demanded.

The birth of his child—an event that was so beautiful the first time he'd experienced it—had been marred. First by Lexie's betrayal, then by the unthinkable.

What if Henry died? Jackson tried to choke back his doubts. He'd only just found out about the child he'd lost last year. He hadn't even had time to grieve. Maybe a man like him, a man who'd taken unthinkable risks and paid for them with the life of another, didn't deserve any more miracles.

Suddenly, Jackson's throat was too dry to swallow.

"Mr. Garrett, we need you to back away and give the team room."

It took a moment for Jackson to realize what the maternity nurse was saying. He hadn't been aware that he was standing at the shoulder of one technician.

"Sorry," he mumbled.

He looked at Lexie. The doctor stood between her legs delivering the afterbirth, while Lexie cried quietly. "Why didn't you tell us he was sick?" Jackson looked around the room, willing someone to answer. Jackson didn't look at Lexie again. He wanted to be strong, and positive, and a man. He didn't want to cry.

"What are they doing to him?" Jackson asked again. The question was directed at anyone and no one. He paced the floor, filled with helpless energy.

"Your son is having trouble breathing on his own. Please let them do their work, Mr. Garrett." Dr. Stuart said this without looking up from Lexie.

*Lexie.* Jackson snuck a glance at her face.

She made a groaning sound when their eyes met.

"You don't think he'll make it," she said.

"I didn't say a word." How did she read him like that? Jackson spun away and paced to the door. He could leave. He could just walk out into the hallway and wait until it was over.

Leaving two people in the room that needed him.

Jackson turned back around. Reluctantly, his gaze returned to Lexie. His chin lifted. "He'll make it."

"You don't believe that," she accused.

"Why would you say that?" He looked at the odd pattern of her hospital gown sleeve so that he wouldn't have to look her in the eye.

"Because I can see it in your eyes. You never smile with your eyes when you're just being polite." Her hair was plastered to her forehead, her face as pale as the sheet.

"There is no difference in my smile. A smile is a smile is a smile."

She wiped away a tear almost angrily. "Don't give me that. You have a smile for every occasion."

"Cut the crap, Lex. You're reading more into things than are there." Only, that wasn't true. He didn't want her to be able to read him, not now, when he was so near emotional collapse. He'd finally realized she couldn't possibly love him, and now his son might not last through his first hour of life.

"Mr. and Mrs. Garrett! Now is not the time," Dr. Stuart snapped.

"I want to help my son," Jackson said hoarsely, his fists clenched at his sides. "I need to help my son."

"Unless you're a specialist with premature babies, there's nothing you can do right now." Dr. Stuart's eyes held Jackson in place. "Sit down, Mr. Garrett, or I'll have you removed from the room."

Jackson sank into a chair and cradled his head in his hands, unable to shake the feeling that all was lost.

"YOUR BABY IS STABILIZED and in our Neonatal Intensive Care Unit," the nurse said as she came back into the room. "Would you like to see him?"

"Yes." Lexie and Jackson spoke at the same time.

They'd been sitting in silence for nearly an hour. Occasionally, Jackson would pace the hallway, but he always returned to her.

For now.

Lexie pushed herself into a sitting position, ignoring the white-hot numbness between her legs. The doctor thought she might have mild nerve damage from the quick onset of labor. If this was mild, Lexie felt sorry for women with more severe nerve damage.

Jackson took her arm as her bare feet hit the floor, which was good because her legs shuddered and buckled.

"Do you need a wheelchair?" the nurse asked.

"No." Lexie preferred to rely on Jackson as long as he let her. "I'm sorry," she said to Jackson, looking at the toes she hadn't seen in months. This should have been a joyful time. Right now she should be reveling in details like how much her baby weighed or how long he was.

Instead, she was experiencing dread because her baby's life was in danger.

"You're exhausted. Lean on me." Jackson's words were comforting even if his tone was cool.

They walked down an endless, empty hallway. Lexie wheeled her IV stand awkwardly along beside her. At this time of night in the hospital, there weren't many people up and about. Lexie gripped Jackson's arm so tightly that she thought he might complain, but he kept silent, and once more, Lexie felt the chasm widening between them.

When they got to the NICU, a different nurse took them to a side room.

"Please scrub up every time you come in to visit. All the way up to your elbows."

Lexie washed up, being careful of the IV tube in her hand, and tried not to cry.

The nurses spoke softly behind her. Lexie only caught one word—*emotional*. She certainly deserved the label. She'd been out of control during the delivery, and later unable to resist taking Jackson to task for thinking Henry would die. She had depended upon Jackson to keep believing in Henry and when he hadn't, she'd been overcome with fear for their child.

They were escorted into a large room with eight small, tall beds and high-tech equipment lining the walls. It seemed chillier in here—all these tiny babies with tubes and wires and noisy machines attached to them.

*Is this where babies come to die?*

Unaware of Lexie's agitation, the two nurses led them to an open bed with a diminutive baby in it.

One nurse took out a Polaroid camera. "Smile," she said, and snapped their picture without waiting for them to respond. "Now the nurses will know who—" she leaned over to read a card taped to the plastic bed "—Henry's parents are." Then she left the room.

The other nurse checked Lexie's ID bracelet to Henry's, making sure they matched.

Her baby's breath came in shallow gasps, as if he had to fight for each little amount of air. If it weren't for the identification bracelet and the card with his name on it, Lexie wouldn't have recognized this child as her own. The tubes and tape attached to him covered any features she might have recognized.

The remaining nurse went on to explain the monitors located above Henry's bed and the different wires, tubes and leads attached to his frail body. As soon as the words were out of the nurse's mouth, Lexie promptly forgot what they meant. All she could think of was how delicate her little baby was and how strong he would need to be to survive.

"How long is he going to be like that?" she asked, hugging herself and willing her legs to hold out now that Jackson wasn't supporting her.

"You'll have to talk with the doctor about that."

"I want to hold him." Lexie choked on the words. How could she bond with her baby if they wouldn't let her hold him? How could she give him strength to survive without cradling him close to her heart?

The nurse shook her head. "Not until the doctor approves it."

"When can we ask the doctor for permission?" Jackson asked, his expression grim.

He took Lexie's hand in his, and Lexie sagged against him in relief. He'd find a way to place Henry in her arms.

"The doctor comes in every morning."

"What time?" Jackson probed.

"Sometime between seven and ten." The nurse's responses were as coldly detached as the stony expression on her face.

Lexie was supposed to leave Henry with her?

"Three hours." Lexie frowned, glancing up at Jackson. "Should we make an appointment?"

"He doesn't take appointments at the hospital, he makes rounds. If you want to see the doctor and you miss him, tell your nurse. He'll try to come by when he knows you're here."

Lexie blinked back tears as a nearly overwhelming feeling of hopelessness engulfed her.

The nurse continued with her list of instructions. "You can be in NICU anytime round the clock, except from six to seven when the nurses are preparing reports for shift change."

Lexie looked down upon Henry, so small and helpless, almost lifeless. She put two fingers on Henry's little foot. Unlike Heidi's plump newborn feet, Henry's feet were thin and bony. She stroked the top of his foot with her fingers, as close as she could come to comforting her baby, to reassure Henry that she loved him and to give him the will to survive.

The nurse looked up from scribbling something on Henry's chart. "Don't do that."

Lexie froze. "Did I do something wrong?"

"Preemies have very sensitive skin, Mrs. Garrett. You can touch him, but don't stroke him."

"It's not as if I've never had a baby before. Babies love to be touched. In fact, I've stroked this one almost constantly throughout my pregnancy."

The nurse raised her eyebrows and shook her head again.

"Why do you even let parents on this side of the glass?" Lexie protested. Anger rose beyond her pain, heartache and exhaustion.

Jackson released Lexie's hand and wrapped his arm around her shoulders, giving a warning squeeze, cutting off her further protests. "What else do we need to know?"

The nurse eyed Lexie as if gauging a misbehaving child,

before returning her attention to Jackson and his smile, which seemed to be working, since the nurse's expression relaxed a little. "Well, you'll need a breast pump. The one from the hospital is about ten times more efficient than any over-the-counter model. If you decide to rent it, you'll need to buy the tubes and cups to go along with it. I'd recommend pumping both sides at once. Although Henry is feeding through an IV right now, the next step is your breast milk, Mrs. Garrett, and we'll need a lot of it."

"We'll take care of that right away." said Jackson.

His reassurance irritated Lexie. Whose breasts were they, anyway?

"Freeze the milk in plastic bags that fit in baby bottles. You'll need a twist tie to close them at the top. Bring a supply of milk with you every few days in a cooler and we'll store it here."

Lexie frowned. "You make it sound as if he's going to be here a long time."

The nurse gave Lexie one of those looks that made you feel as if you were a moron and not getting the message. "We give everyone the same instructions here, Mrs. Garrett."

Lexie doubted it. She cast her gaze around the room at the other babies. She pointed at a chubby baby in a bed near Henry's. "How long has that baby been here?"

"Mrs. Garrett, I'm sure you understand about confidentiality. I can't discuss any of the cases here other than your own."

"You've been very helpful," Jackson said, again putting his arm around Lexie.

She wanted nothing more than to lean into him and take some comfort in his strength, but that wasn't what he was offering. He'd put his arm around her to manage her temper.

The nurse continued. "When you come in, talk a lot to your baby. He's been hearing your voice for a long time now, and even if he doesn't react visibly, it's very comforting."

"Please. I want to hold him." Lexie fought tears once more. She was so frightened and just wanted the reassurance of her baby in her arms. If he died without her ever holding him, she wouldn't forgive herself.

"I'm sorry but you won't be able to do that until he's more stabilized."

"How soon?" she blurted. "He needs me."

"I can't answer that. Each baby's progress is different. That's something you can ask the doctor about."

Jackson began urging Lexie toward the door. "You need some rest, Lex. We'll come back later."

"Oh, Mr. and Mrs. Garrett, one more thing. There's a service down the hall. Some parents find it helpful to talk to someone about their feelings while their babies are in NICU."

"You mean a therapist?" Lexie asked, shocked.

"A counselor."

Someone assigned to people who couldn't handle the crisis in their lives. Lexie remembered all the detached social workers assigned to her after her father left. Their probing questions. Their penetrating stares.

"Get me out of here." Lexie's wobbly legs shook even more as the adrenaline of anger coursed through her veins. When they were back in the hallway, she turned to Jackson, unable to contain herself any longer. "She thinks I'm a nutcase. She probably thinks you're a nutcase, too."

Jackson seemed to freeze, although why was a mystery. It wasn't as if he had anything to hide. He was handling this better than she was. "Maybe it's like she said, just the standard instructions they give."

Lexie shook her head vehemently. "No, no. The delivery room nurse was talking about us when we came in. She thought we were emotional."

He put his hands on her shoulders. "We almost lost our baby back there, Lex. We still could."

If only Lexie could turn back the clock. She wanted to lean on Jackson more than anything, but the tragedy of last summer and Henry's horrible situation had divided them. Jackson didn't seem ready to bridge that divide. Lexie selfishly drew strength from the warmth of his hands.

"I swear to you, Henry's going to make it."

"Lex, you can't keep him alive by sheer will—"

She yanked her shoulders free and stepped back. "Don't let me even hear you talk like that. Not ever again." She pointed back toward NICU. "*Henry* is going to live. We're going to take him home. I'll get his crib and bassinet out of the garage. You'll see. He's going to grow up to hike and raft and play baseball. You just wait and see."

Lexie turned on her heel and walked down the hall, dragging the pole with her IV tube with her. Tears were streaming so thickly out of her eyes that it took her a few minutes to realize that she was walking alone.

JACKSON WATCHED LEXIE walk away. How could she have such unshakable faith that their small, weak baby was going to make it? Hadn't she seen how blue and unresponsive he was at birth? Hadn't she seen all the tubes and expensive equipment hooked up to him as if he were on his deathbed?

Jackson's thoughts bounced from one mind-numbing possibility to the next. Brain damage, deformities, handicaps, hostile words from kids who couldn't help but point out Henry's deficits.

*Maybe he'd be better off not surviving.*

Turning back to the NICU, Jackson stood at the door looking in. He wouldn't wish such a hard life on anyone, but he didn't want to lose his son.

*Henry is going to live.*

Her words taunted him, begging him to believe, though she'd taken away his ability to hope for the future. She believed in this baby in a way Jackson couldn't.

Jackson spun the band of gold on his finger in a slow circle.

He just wished she'd believe in him.

AFTER THE SUN ROSE that morning, Lexie staggered back to NICU in her hospital gown, unable to ignore the numb throbbing between her legs. The medicine she'd been given with breakfast had only managed to take the edge off the pain. At least the IV was out of her hand.

A new team of nurses was working. Lexie couldn't believe how relieved she felt that no one who had witnessed her meltdown last night was here this morning. She scrubbed up and then entered the closed room.

"It's Henry's mom." A nurse looked up at her and smiled.

The woman had a kindly face, but she was sliding a tube down a baby's throat, making Lexie want to gag. The tube was attached to a funnel, into which the nurse poured something thick and yellow, something that looked a lot like breast milk.

"Go over and say hello to your little guy. We'll be with you in a minute." This from a nurse who was placing a stethoscope on a baby in the corner.

Lexie walked over and looked down at Henry in dismay. She barely recognized him from last night. He was swollen everywhere, even his face. He didn't even have the dignity of a diaper.

The nurse with the stethoscope brought Lexie a stool. "Hop on up. You can put a hand on him, but don't stroke him. His skin is very ticklish." She studied Lexie critically. "I'm only going to let you stay about thirty minutes this time. You look a little pale. Did you bring water with you?"

In the midst of hitching herself up onto the wooden stool, tears pressed at the back of Lexie's eyes. She had never experienced anything so frightening, had never felt so helpless as she did now—having a sick, unresponsive baby. She was as vulnerable as Henry.

"I ate breakfast before I came. I drank plenty." As much as she could choke down, what with worrying about Henry and trying to keep her heart from breaking over Jackson's rejection—of both Lexie and their son.

The nurse nodded. "All right, then. An hour, if you can take the stool." The way she said it made it sound like some sort of challenge. Then her voice softened. "Would you like me to explain everything to you again?"

Her kindness was almost worse than the previous night's nurse barking orders. Lexie sniffed to keep the tears at bay. "Please."

The nurse discreetly handed her a tissue. "This tube in his trachea helps him breathe. We refer to it as intubation. The tube is connected to a respirator." She pointed to a machine on the counter. "Many preemies can't breathe on their own. Usually if they're born more than five weeks premature, they have RDS—respiratory distress syndrome. That's when babies aren't mature enough to produce surfactant, which is the fatty substance that coats the tiny air sacs in the lungs and prevents them from collapsing. In addition to that, Henry's got an infection in his lungs, similar to pneumonia, so he may have this respirator to help him breathe for quite a while until that clears up."

The tube and mouthpiece seemed far too large to be forced into her baby's throat. Lexie worked hard to swallow, and forced herself to watch and listen.

The nurse—Helen, her tag said with a flourish of heart stickers—continued. "Several times a day, Henry's lungs will be suctioned. The first step is to get the medicine into his lungs to loosen the mucus from the wall of the lung. The second step is rather alarming the first time you see it. The technician pounds on Henry's chest and back. He does that to detach the mucus in Henry's lungs before suctioning it out.''

Lexie must have looked frightened, because the nurse patted her arm. "Trust me, he's not as fragile as he looks. And the benefits are worth the discomfort." She pointed to Henry's little hand. "Doctor put a catheter in his hand so we can check his blood gases several times a day. We monitor the amount of oxygen and carbon dioxide circulating through his system so that we know how Henry's illness is affecting the acid content in his blood."

Lexie reached out to lay her fingers on Henry's little forearm but didn't rest any weight on him. His arm was taped to a sandbag the size of a man's wallet. She gave the nurse a questioning glance.

"I know it looks cruel, but it keeps his hand in place. Hopefully he won't have to be strapped for long." Helen's smile was perfunctory, as if she didn't want to encourage Lexie with more than words but someone had told her to deliver this last piece of information with a smile.

"He's also got two leads on his chest and one on his foot, so we can monitor his heart rate even if one comes loose. There is at least one nurse here at all times, if not two, and if he stops breathing or his heart stops, an alarm will sound. Usually the alarm wakes up every baby in the place, including the one that set it off."

"That must keep you on your toes," Lexie observed. Uncomfortable with her fingers on Henry, she clasped her hands in her lap.

"We don't over-caffeinate ourselves in this ward, that's for sure." Helen smiled more genuinely this time. "His main IV is in his belly button. That's how we're feeding him and giving him medicine. Since his veins are so small, we've got a backup line in his other arm, just in case."

"After what the nurse told us last night, I suppose breast-feeding is out." Lexie said it half jokingly, but it caused her a pang of remorse. She longed to cuddle Henry to her breast and comfort him. His treatment seemed so barbaric. If that were her with all those tubes in her, Lexie doubted she'd want to live.

The thought scared the bejesus out of her.

"For a while. But you'd be surprised at how quickly these little guys respond to treatment." Helen checked Henry's chart. "Just talk to him. He's heard your voice all through the pregnancy, so it will comfort him." Then she left Lexie alone with her son.

Lexie looked around at the other babies in the room, hoping that she'd see them with different eyes than the night before, hoping that someone else's baby was smaller and sicker than hers. Ashamed of the thought, Lexie bit her lip and forced her gaze back to Henry. She lay her fingers over his thin ankle and foot, the only place where tubes and leads weren't attached.

"What a brave little guy you are," Lexie said self-consciously, acutely aware of the two women in the room going about their duties in silence.

When her words didn't garner any reaction from Henry, Lexie almost couldn't keep herself from crying. Somehow, this must have been her fault, or fate must want to test her. If it was the latter, Lexie prayed she wouldn't fail. Sitting next to her swollen, tiny, ailing baby was the hardest thing she'd ever done.

"You'll get better soon." Lexie spoke halfheartedly, resisting the urge to check and see if the nurse was watching her.

The door to the ward swung open. A tall, thin woman in street clothes with a hospital badge hanging from her neck entered. She wore glasses with large frames, and a skirt and blouse that were a bit outdated. A zippered portfolio was tucked in the crook of her elbow. She wasn't a nurse. In fact, she looked like the kindhearted ineffectual social workers from Lexie's youth.

"Mrs. Garrett?"

With plunging spirits, Lexie realized this had to be the hospital's counselor. If she hadn't been subjected to so many counselors and social workers in her youth, the idea might not have sent her into a near panic.

Lexie studied the woman a moment before acknowledging her, needing time to collect herself. She didn't feel up to the task of appearing optimistic and well-balanced. Her life was a mess: her baby was ill, her finances were on the brink of disaster, and she was in love with her ex-husband. Lexie longed to tell the woman to go away, but knew she couldn't. Counselors were trained to collect the information they needed for their reports. Evaluate and recommend. That was their motto.

"Yes," Lexie finally answered, modulating her monosyllabic reply to sound like a fully functional adult.

The woman crossed the room, her thick heels clicking ominously on the linoleum. She stopped on the other side of Henry's bed. "I'm Edna Higgins, with Patient Services."

Lexie nodded, pretending she had no clue who Edna was. "If you're here about insurance, you'll have to talk with Jackson."

Edna's patient smile indicated she wasn't as callous as some of the other social workers Lexie had dealt with. "I'm not here about billing, Mrs. Garrett. I'm here to see how you're handling all this." Edna gestured around the ward. "It can be overwhelming."

"That's an understatement." Lexie clenched her fist and slid it under her leg, grateful that her hospital gown hid it from Edna's view. She blinked back the tears, refusing to cry in front of this woman.

"How are you holding up?"

Something raw and angry clawed at Lexie's insides. She wanted to tell Edna that she'd just given birth less than twelve hours ago, that she was tired and sore in places she didn't want to be sore in, and that her heart still hadn't recovered from the sight of her baby not breathing. Instead, she said, "I'm fine."

Edna's eyes swept over Lexie with the practiced ease of one trained to observe. Lexie knew that the counselor was registering the fact that Lexie perched stiffly on a dunce stool and sat on her fist. Lexie eased her hand into her lap. Edna's eyebrows raised, but she didn't say a thing.

"It's tough seeing little babies with all these things attached, isn't it?" Edna looked down at Henry.

The fishing tactic. Case workers probed and pushed until they found your weak spot and made you blubber like a baby. Lexie hadn't sought marriage counseling for just that reason. There was nothing as humiliating as breaking down in front of a total stranger. Well, that wasn't happening today. She wasn't the psycho woman from last night. She laid a careful hand on Henry's little foot and struggled to calm her breathing. His skin was soft, and touching him was somehow soothing.

"He'll make it," Lexie said confidently. She'd make sure of it. "He comes from stubborn stock. Don't you, Henry?"

Lexie gave Edna a matter-of-fact look. When their eyes met, an understanding seemed to pass between them. Lexie knew without asking that Edna recognized she'd been in counseling before.

"I'll let you know if I need anything. Thank you for coming by, Edna."

Edna smiled. "You take care of yourself, Mrs. Garrett."

Lexie spent another half hour sitting with Henry, until she couldn't stand to sit anymore. In that time, Henry didn't do anything more than exist.

Lexie told herself that was enough.

NOT MUCH LATER on Sunday morning, Jackson stood outside NICU, Sirus having granted him as much time off work as he needed. He'd gone by Lexie's room at the hospital first, but she'd been sleeping and he hadn't wanted to disturb her. From the window, he could see tiny babies covered with patches, wires and tubes. Unlike the babies in the hospital's other nursery, these infants didn't move even to stretch their arms.

Slowly, meticulously, Jackson scrubbed his hands and forearms. With measured steps, he entered the NICU. Two nurses glanced up from scribbling on charts when he came in.

Jackson nodded in Henry's direction. "That's my son." He edged closer to the bed, carefully avoiding looking directly at the helpless body and the myriad of tubes attached to him. The sight of his son scared him to the core because he had no idea how to help him.

There were no chairs next to Henry's bed. Had his son been frightened, laying here all alone?

Shoving his hands into his pockets, Jackson leaned against the counter. "Has the doctor been in yet today?" He watched Henry's heart rate and breathing patterns on the monitors.

"The doctor came by earlier on rounds. He might still be here." One of the nurses spoke without looking up from sliding a tube down a baby's throat. "Your boy's had a rough time."

A man in cowboy boots and faded blue jeans darted in the door. "Have you seen my pager, Helen?" Jackson recognized him as one of the team that had been at Henry's birth.

"No, Dr. Kelly." Helen looked up from her task. "Do you have a minute? I think Mr. Garrett would like a word with you."

"Ah, Mr. Garrett. I meant to drop by this morning to speak with you about your son. Good to see you here. The more time you spend with your child, the better." The doctor looked entirely too young to be in charge of the NICU. He couldn't be much older than Jackson.

Jackson shook the doctor's proffered hand and got right to the point. "I have a few questions."

"Shoot."

"How sick is my son?"

Dr. Kelly reviewed Henry's chart before answering. "I'm not going to kid you. Your son is very sick. He's got a long road ahead of him. RDS, pneumonia, brady-cardia."

Jackson held up his hand before the doctor baffled him with too much medical jargon. "Just tell me two things in plain English." Jackson gathered what little courage he had and forced himself to ask. "Will he recover, and what permanent side effects will he have?"

Dr. Kelly met Jackson's gaze squarely. "Preemies are amazingly resilient human beings. Their lungs and circu-latory systems aren't ready to support their little bodies outside the womb. But given time, they strengthen." He shrugged, then placed a hand on Henry's leg. "A little guy like yours…you'll be amazed at his progress. You'll come in one day this week and some of these tubes will be gone. He'll still be incredibly small, though—fragile by the standards of a full-term baby."

None of which answered Jackson's questions. "Will he live?" He forced himself not to look away, clamped down on the feelings of betrayal. He should believe unequivo-cally that his son would live, but he couldn't. Yet, Lexie needed his conviction to support her own, to lend Henry their strength.

"Nothing in life is guaranteed, Mr. Garrett. All I can say is that I feel very good about Henry's chances."

"And permanent damage?" Jackson asked through grit-ted teeth.

"Hard to tell. I don't suspect any, although some stan-dard problems include vision, and cognitive prowess, but that usually occurs in extremely early deliveries, which yours was not. However, preemies often lag behind other children in their development, particularly in the first year." The doctor talked a mile a minute.

Jackson resisted looking at Henry by staring at the doctor.

"Don't be fooled by the way he looks today, Mr. Garrett. You've got one strong baby here."

His words were at odds with Henry's appearance. Jackson finally stared down at his baby. If it wasn't for the shallow rise and fall of his chest, Jackson couldn't have said if he was alive or not. "How...how does something like this happen?"

"There are lots of possibilities, mostly stemming from viruses transmitted through the mother. Toxoplasmosis is the most common cause in babies born with lung infections. For example, if your wife gardened in an area where cats defecated or cleaned out a litter box during her pregnancy, she could have been infected with a parasite that would eventually transfer to Henry's lungs."

Cat shit. Jackson leaned back against the counter with a thump. He'd given Heidi a kitten, and she'd told him Marmy had been using the house as her own personal litter box. Jackson had been the cause of Henry's illness.

He'd put his son's life in danger.

A new addition to his stack of recent failures...Jackson had never felt so worthless.

Someone knocked on the window. Jackson glanced up to find Logan standing on the other side of the glass. The doctor had left while Jackson was lost in thought. Slowly, Jackson made his way to the door.

"Hey, I brought Deb in to get some tests run and decided to come see your little urchin." Logan beamed as if he were as proud of this baby as Jackson should be. "I brought him a gift. Can I deliver it personally?"

Logan took a small stuffed brown bear out of his back

pocket. It was about the size that Marmy had been as a kitten. Another wave of guilt and sorrow threatened to overwhelm Jackson.

"Make sure he scrubs," a nurse called from behind Jackson, even as he'd been about to refuse his friend entry.

Mechanically, Jackson led Logan through the ritual cleansing and then over to Henry's bedside. The bear and the boy were each so tiny that they both fit in the small plastic bassinet with plenty of room to spare.

"You okay with this?" Logan asked, gesturing to the wires, leads and machines keeping Henry alive.

Jackson found it hard to speak. He was far from okay with any of this. He made a noncommittal motion with his head.

Luckily, Logan didn't wait for him to speak. "This is scarier than a wall of fire. I mean, look at all this. And he's so minuscule, his head isn't even as big as my fist. He's going to make it, isn't he?"

All Jackson could think of was failing Alek and watching him run to his death. He was going to have to watch Henry die, as well, despite the doctor's reassurances, despite the expensive equipment—

"He's going to be fine, Logan." Lexie's voice was coolly confident.

Jackson turned at the sound and met her indecipherable gaze. He deserved her scorn and so much more. He was the reason that Henry was going to die. He'd failed as a father. He forgave her right then and there, for the secrets she had kept from him in the face of his mistake.

Logan gave Lexie a gentle hug. "Couldn't keep the little bugger incubating any longer?"

Lexie didn't break eye contact with Jackson. "He's definitely a boy with a will of his own, just like his dad."

Jackson's mouth was dry as toast and his knees felt like rubber. His heart seemed to be racing against an unknown opponent as Jackson realized that he'd put two lives in inescapable danger. What more proof did he need that he was no good? He didn't deserve Lexie. And yet, if he didn't have her by his side, what was the point? She was his lifeline.

He took one deep breath. Then another.

Lexie.

She stared up at him with such clear blue eyes that his heart leaped toward hope. That's all he had to keep him going. She'd stopped believing in him when she miscarried last year, but she had loved him once.

He took another breath.

There was hope if she loved him…even a little. If only he could figure out what had made their love work all those years ago.

# CHAPTER TEN

"YOU TELL ME YOUR SAD STORY and I'll tell you mine," Logan said to Jackson as they sat in a fast-food restaurant down the street from the hospital.

"Which sad story?" Jackson seemed to have many. "Wife? Career? Baby?"

"Well, Lex seems convinced the baby's going to make it."

Jackson shrugged.

"What does the doctor say?" Logan popped a french fry into his mouth.

"He says I'm the one that made him sick." Jackson wasn't feeling so hot right now himself.

Logan stopped chewing.

"Pregnant women aren't supposed to come into contact with cat shit. It's very bad news for the baby's lungs." Jackson pushed his fries around on his tray.

"And you gave her that kitten before you left." Logan considered that for a moment. "What does Lexie say?"

"She doesn't know."

Logan raised his eyebrows. "What do you think she'll say when she finds out?"

"As long as Henry makes it, I think she'll forgive me." *Please, God.*

"You're wrong there, buddy. I think she'd forgive you no matter what. It's not as if you had this wealth of knowledge about the impact of cats on pregnant women before the gifting process." He slurped his soda. "Or even knew that she was pregnant."

"I hear you. It's just that I can't look at Henry and see him forgiving me."

Logan shook his head. "Oh, man. You've got to shake this one off."

"As if you can shake off Deb and her problems?" Jackson knew it wasn't fair to remind Logan of his dying sister, but he couldn't take much more talk about Henry without losing it.

"That's entirely different." Logan's words became oddly flat. "She found out she was sick right after you left the States. She called me and asked if I'd take her kids when she dies." Logan stared at Jackson with hard, empty eyes. "Just like that. No pulled punches, no soft pedaling."

"That's Deb for you." She didn't hold things in. Logan was the one who stewed. This had to be eating at him. "What happened to her husband?"

"Wes ran off with a cocktail waitress when he found out Deb was sick. Not that it matters. He was a deadbeat dad and was never home, being a truck driver and all."

Logan's disdainful attitude about Deb's husband not being home because of his job struck an unexpected nerve with Jackson. He was still vulnerable when it came to how he saw himself as a husband and father. "Deb doesn't care that he's gone?"

"Right now, all she seems to care about are her kids."

Jackson couldn't imagine being nine and knowing his mom was going to die. It almost made his fear for Henry's survival pale by comparison.

"How long does she have?" Jackson didn't really want to know.

Logan chewed on his cheek. Finally, he admitted, "The doctor says it could be anytime now. The tumor is lodged around her cortex. She used to have the most god-awful headaches when we were kids. I wonder…I wonder if she had something even back then." Logan swallowed.

"Custody's a big responsibility."

"I haven't said yes." Logan wouldn't look at Jackson. "You know how this works. We're here today, gone five states away tomorrow, back home with a duffel full of dirty laundry next week. That's not the life for a father figure."

Why hadn't Jackson seen earlier that Hot Shots weren't cut out to be dads? Logan, who'd sworn never to have kids of his own, knew it. "Shouldn't you at least be with them now? You could take some time off."

"Right now I'm the only means of support for Deb."

"So, who's taking care of the family? When I stopped by the other day, no one was there but Aunt Glen and the girls. You do realize that Glen—"

"Is living half her life in an alternative reality? Yes." Logan pushed away his food. "Let's talk about something else. When are you giving up that bullshit IC job and coming back to the team?"

"I'm not coming back." If anything, his discussion with Logan had shown him how ill-suited the job was to fatherhood. Jackson's throat tightened with regret.

Logan scoffed. "Guys like you and me don't quit fire. It runs in our veins. Come on, Lex will understand. She'll be too busy taking care of this baby to even miss you during fire season."

Jackson was starting to feel nauseated just thinking about fire. "Thanks for the pep talk, but I can't go back on the line."

"I'm going to talk with Lexie about this. She'll understand."

"Don't." Jackson said the word more vehemently than he'd meant to. He couldn't say how tough this was because that meant admitting he'd lost his nerve even though he hadn't lost his love of fire fighting.

Logan leaned back in his chair. "Hey, no big deal. I'll still be your friend if you quit."

The word *quit* echoed in Jackson's head hours later.

"HOW ARE YOU DOING?" Deb stood leaning against the door frame, looking as if she was using the wall to hold her up.

"Good," Lexie responded, propped up in bed. She turned off the hospital television. "How about you?"

"Well, I seem to be the human pincushion today. I'm a little short on blood and other bodily fluids. Mind if I sit down for a bit?"

"Get your butt over in the chair before you collapse. I'd help you, but my legs resemble Jell-O today. I wouldn't be much help."

"Pick me up if I fall, then, would you?" Deb made her way gingerly over to the chair next to Lexie's bed.

Lexie didn't really believe Deb would fall. Her friend was too stubborn. Lexie poured Deb a glass of water. "Drink this. What did the doctor say?"

Deb slouched in the chair and looked at the ceiling. "Not much. Yours?"

"They tell me enough to confuse me. They say it's up to Henry. How can a little baby decide if he's going to live or not?"

"He's a survivor, Lex."

"How do you know that?"

"Because you and Jackson are two of the most hard-headed people I know."

Raising her brows, Lexie challenged Deb's statement.

"Along with Logan and me," Deb allowed with a smile. "Did Jackson ask you to marry him again?"

Lexie nodded, unable to speak.

"And you said no again?"

Lexie started to cry.

Deb patted Lexie on the arm. "Are you crying because you're happy or sad?"

"He'll never forgive me," Lexie said between sniffles. "I should have told him things."

"He was on the other side of the planet. What good would it have done to tell him you were pregnant?"

"You're the one who told me I should tell him."

"Do you want me to talk to him?"

"No. We're not in the ninth grade anymore."

"I'm glad you said that first. So just walk up to him next time you see him and tell him you love him. You be the one to propose to him."

"I can't do that. What if he says no?"

"How many times has he asked you to marry him since he's been back?"

Lexie paused to count. "Four times."

"When you said no, did he rant and rave? Fall to the floor in tears? Laugh and say, just kidding?"

"No."

"Of course not. Because he's just going to ask you again. You two have this special love that is beyond the crap that life throws your way. I wish I could have found something like that."

"I'm sorry. Here I am, blubbering about my troubles. And…" Lexie started crying again.

"I promised myself a long time ago that I wasn't going to cry the rest of my life away, so you just stop the waterworks right now." Deb looked as close to tears as Lexie had seen her in months. "I have something important to ask you."

"Anything."

"You should try remembering that word and use it when Jackson is around."

Lexie took a deep breath and hiccuped.

"Better." Deb sat back in the hospital chair. "I haven't seen Wes in months. I left him a message on his cell phone saying that I didn't want him to have custody of the girls. I've asked Logan to be their legal guardian."

"He'll do a wonderful job."

"I think I shocked him by asking. I talked to him about it a few months ago, and he kind of got this glazed look on his face. I could tell he was thinking of our dad. He seems to think he's carrying around the defective McCall gene, the one that makes men abusive to women and children.''

Deb's dad had taken out his frustrations on his wife and two kids, culminating in one particularly ugly day when he'd argued with his wife, shot her, and then shot himself.

"Logan would never hurt those girls." Lexie rose to Logan's defense.

"I know that. You know that. I don't think Logan knows that. Why do you think he doesn't keep a steady girlfriend? He's got a hang-up a mile wide over this heredity thing." Deb stared at her feet. "If he doesn't come through for me before...I want you and Jackson to help Logan with the girls. They don't know their dad. And he doesn't want them.''

"Of course I'll help Logan. I'm sure Logan won't bail on his duty. But what about Wes?''

"He doesn't want me or them." Deb's voice was small. Then her attention focused on Lexie. "I don't want to ask you to take this on alone. I mean, I know Logan can depend on you to help with Tess and Hannah. But I'd feel better about it if you had someone to lean on, someone like Jackson.''

"WHAT ARE YOU DOING with all this junk?" Heidi asked. The garage was filled front to back with boxes, bags, piles of things, blankets of dust and lacy cobwebs.

"Looking for the bassinet for Henry." If Henry came home, he would need a place to sleep. Whether his son came home or not, when Lexie returned to find the bed set up, it would ease her mind.

He was also looking for the key to her heart. He wondered about Lexie's charge that he was an absentee husband and dad. He wanted proof that his marriage hadn't been a farce from day one. They'd been in love once. Jackson wanted to remember why.

He'd uncovered many memories as he searched the garage looking for Heidi's bassinet. The Christmas boxes were piled in front. There was a stack of board games three feet high with a bag of stuffed animals on top. He lifted a purple sleeping bag out of one storage bin.

"Whose is this?"

"Mine," Heidi said.

"Have you ever used it?" It looked brand new to Jackson.

She shrugged. "When I go to friends' houses."

"When I was a kid, my mom and dad took us on lots of camping trips. I don't think my sleeping bag ever looked that new."

"You haven't taken us anywhere." Heidi's comment was a borderline whine.

One more strike against Jackson as a good dad. Jackson smiled, trying to coax his daughter and himself into a better mood. "Doesn't roasting marshmallows over at Tess and Hannah's count?"

"Nope." Heidi poked her nose into a box.

"So you think I'm a disappointment as a dad?" He asked the question only half jokingly, needing reassurance from his daughter.

"Can we go camping tomorrow?" she asked.

"No."

"Then, you're a disappointment."

Jackson's heart almost stopped beating, until he caught Heidi's grin.

"You set yourself up for that one, Dad."

"Ha, ha. Very funny."

Jackson returned to his search, continuing to move boxes and things from the garage out into the driveway, pausing every once in a while to look at the motor home. Spider and Chainsaw had spent part of their morning off helping him lay down the carpet and put in the new window.

It seemed odd to be here when Lexie and Henry were still at the hospital. He made a few subdued calls this morning to his mom, his sister and Sirus, but beyond that,

Jackson felt as if he could be doing more—for Lexie and for his son.

Heidi seemed content setting up a board game and playing by herself.

"Why can't we go camping tomorrow?" Heidi pushed after a bit.

Bent over a box, Jackson stopped digging to toss a dark look her way. "Because your brother is in the hospital."

She shook dice in a cup. "Dad, I don't think he's going to miss us. You told Grandma he doesn't even open his eyes."

"Don't be smart."

"If I was smart I would have figured out how to go camping by myself. No one around here's going to take me."

Jackson straightened. "Heidi, I'm sorry your mother and I had to ruin your life with this divorce. I'm not all that happy about it, either, but you don't hear me whining. And listening to you piss and moan doesn't help. Now, zip it or you'll be looking at the back side of your bedroom door for a month."

Heidi grumbled something about just joking, but Jackson knew she hadn't been. The crash of the dice on the game board followed by the sharp snap of game pieces confirmed her true state of mind.

"Have you found the bassinet, Dad?" Heidi asked after a long silence. She had abandoned her game.

"No."

"Why are you opening up all these boxes? Does it fit in a box?"

Heidi slipped her hand into his—forgiving after their recent tussle, or just trying to suck up, Jackson couldn't be sure. He chose to believe the former.

She leaned into him. "What does the bassinet look like?"

"White."

"Like my old doll bed?" Heidi asked.

"Maybe." Jackson had no idea what Heidi referred to.

Heidi bent to pick up a small box. "You can't see anything the way Mom stacks stuff." She carried the box out to the driveway.

Jackson continued to dig through the layers of possessions his family had accumulated over the years. As he did so, his progress became slower. He was a man obsessed with unlocking the key to the love he once had, opening every box and bag, looking inside to see if he had any part in it, if it struck a chord in his memory.

There was an entire box filled with tiny sequined costumes. He pulled out a bright blue-and-white sailor suit. Jackson swallowed his pride, turned and asked Heidi, "Yours?"

Now she was sitting in the corner of the garage playing a game of solitaire with a deck of cards she'd found. Beside her, Marmy licked her paws. One quick glance at what Jackson held and Heidi was back to her game. "From my first year in dance." Her tone indicated he should have known that.

"It would be nice if they'd have a winter dance recital," he grumbled.

"It's a two-hour show once a year, Dad. Mom makes it every time."

He turned back to his task and dug through a box of toys, some of them sticky and worn, others looking brand new. Beneath the toys was a yellow dress. Jackson fingered the smooth, shiny material.

"Now, this is something I remember."

"What's that?" Heidi moved closer, her flip-flops snapping with each step.

"Your mom's prom dress." Jackson stood and shook out the dress.

Heidi's eyebrows rose an inch. "She was fat."

"No, she was beautiful," Jackson corrected, falling into the memory. "We got married on Easter weekend."

The prom was in May, and Lexie had been plump and

showing at five months pregnant. They'd already won the fight to allow Lexie to finish school at Silver Bend High. Jackson's mother and friends had argued Lexie's case. Lexie's mother had washed her hands of Lexie as soon as she'd heard she was pregnant. Only the fact that they'd gotten married had swayed the board to allow Lexie to stay in school. But they hadn't budged on the prom. Jackson supposed they hadn't wanted Lexie to become a poster girl for teenage pregnancies.

Lexie had been crushed.

"I took her out for a special night. I rented a tuxedo and made her wear this dress. I drove her all the way down into Boise for dinner and then I took her dancing." At their garage apartment on his mother's property, he'd turned on music, lit candles, and they'd danced. Jackson had made sure Lexie understood that evening how precious she was to him, trying his best to ease the pain of her exclusion.

Yes, Jackson remembered that. He supposed he had been something of a hero to her back then. He was far from being a hero now.

LATER THAT AFTERNOON, Jackson entered the tent housing Incident Command at the base camp of the Garden Valley fire. It had been a toss-up as to where to go—down the hill to see Lexie and stand strong next to her as she kept vigil for Henry, or return to the fire. Knowing he'd disappoint Lex if he couldn't wholeheartedly believe in Henry's recovery, Jackson chose the fire.

"Didn't expect to see you here, Garrett," Rob said from behind his desk. He crunched on a potato chip. "Congratulations. It's a boy, right?"

Jackson mumbled something in the affirmative and proceeded to weed through the paperwork on the Command desk. "Where's the most recent map?" Having been away from the fire for two days, Jackson had no idea what to make of any reports without looking at the map with its fire and containment lines.

"Got one right here." Rob waved the colorful paper, waiting for Jackson to walk over and get it.

Jackson looked at the expanded containment lines and frowned. "The fire broke through again?"

Rob scowled. "Damn winds rode the fire up steep slopes and crossed our lines before they were complete. I know you don't agree with putting crews on those steep ridges, but it's got to be done or the fire wins."

"It's a risk," Jackson countered. He knew better than most the dangers of fighting fires on such rough terrain, where a firefighter almost needed rock-climbing skills to ascend, making a speedy escape that much more impossible.

"We didn't control this beast. She's hot and moving. I guess we're not winding down yet," Rob said. "And soon we'll have no choice but to fight on the ridges."

Jackson flipped through the weather reports and fire-behavior prediction sheets. "It doesn't look good the next few days. High winds. More lightning to the north. We could get a whole new set of fires." Sometimes the fire moved so quickly through a patch that it didn't burn the trees and scrub completely. A new fire could come back through and burn the same land again. Just the thought of having to fight fires on beds of ash where a firefighter might sink up to his knees in charred debris deflated what was left of Jackson's spirits. "Does Socrates know?"

"Yeah, he got the happy news this morning."

"We'll have to pull some crews back in. Maybe call in some water buffalo," Jackson said, using the term for private Hot Shot crews. Although they had to pass similar tests to qualify for the job as Forest Service and Bureau of Land Management Hot Shots, the government-employed fire crews considered the private crews of lesser quality.

Whether deserved or not, the reputation associated with

private crews was of them sitting and drinking water back at base camp rather than champing at the bit to see some action—hence the nickname, water buffalo. Add to that the current political practice of disbanding government teams—replacing them with water buffalo—and the belief that private crews were higher paid, and it was no wonder government firefighters resented them.

Jackson sorted through mounds of paperwork. Everything seemed to support that they needed to approach the fire with more aggression if it was to be contained. It meant sending more men and women into danger. Jackson's heart thumped so loudly in his ears, he wondered if Rob could hear it. But the operations chief had already turned his attention to his own stack of paperwork.

Around dinnertime, Jackson made his way out to the chow line, filled his plate with steak and salad, then found an empty table at the edge of the dining area and picked at his food.

"Can I join you?"

Jackson squinted up. With the fading afternoon sun behind the broad-shouldered man and his earnest tone of voice, for a moment, Jackson was reminded of Alek. A sudden realization that the feeling of helpless responsibility he carried for Alek was incredibly similar to the burden he carried for Henry caused Jackson to close his eyes to keep from doubling over in pain.

"Golden? Sir? It's me, Rookie." The newest member of the Silver Bend Hot Shots stepped closer, blocking out the sun so that Jackson could now make out the young man's features.

"I'm afraid I'm not much company today," Jackson managed to say.

"I don't talk much, sir."

Jackson doubted that. Rookie had the eager look about him that said he was waiting to be filled to overflowing with fire stories. But true to Rookie's word, they ate in silence.

Gazing up at the tall pines, Jackson wondered how Lexie was dealing with Henry alone at the hospital. Guilt prickled at his conscience, until he reminded himself that he wouldn't be much use to her. The only thing he could offer her was a shoulder to lean on when things worsened. He hoped that would be enough.

"Have you ever been burned, sir?" Rookie had to repeat the question twice before Jackson heard him.

He shrugged. "Everyone gets burned. It's one of the hazards of the job. Did you get toasty?"

"Yesterday." Rookie held out his hand proudly and peeled back the bandage, as if the series of red blisters on the back of his hand was a badge of courage.

"You weren't wearing your gloves," Jackson surmised.

Rookie smirked, as if only wusses wore the protective covering. "Well, no. It was hot and the fire wasn't that close."

This kid was never going to make it past his first season. "Have you seen Old Man Caruthers working over at the laundry?"

"Sure. I just picked up my stuff from him."

"Seen how blotchy his hands are? Big streaks of pigment missing?"

Rookie nodded, still not getting it. "His hands are something else."

"His hands are the results of burns. Watch how he grabs the bags next time. He can barely close his grip, his hands were baked so bad. Hot Shots are given equipment for a reason, not just for something extra to lug around."

The young recruit's face reddened and he stared down at his food. Jackson thought he might finally have taken some of the bluster out of the kid's sails, until Rookie spoke.

"I realize I can be a pain. I ask a lot of questions because, quite frankly, I never dreamed I'd make the cut to be here. Some people find me irritating. But at least they have the balls to tell me to shut up. I don't need to be put

down in a roundabout way by you or anyone else.''
Rookie stood rigidly and took his tray to another table.

Jackson sat for a couple of minutes watching Rookie's
back, thinking about his words. It didn't take long for
Rookie to start asking people at the other table questions,
getting them to open up. It was clear the young recruit
loved fire fighting. Perhaps the kid wasn't as vulnerable
as he looked. He sure as hell wasn't nearly as green as
Alek had been.

"Maybe I was wrong about that kid," he said, chuck-
ling at the revelation.

"DO YOU KNOW WHAT, Grandma? I don't want Dad to go
back to fighting fires. He's never home." Heidi's words
were full of accusation. "It's not safe."

"Heidi, it's not that he doesn't love you just because
he isn't around. He's a hero. He's always wanted to save
lives by fighting fires."

Mary and Heidi sat around the coffee table in Lexie's
living room playing cards. Mary had lit a fire in the fire-
place and popped popcorn. Rufus sprawled in front of the
hearth on his back, mouth open to bare his teeth in what
Mary had come to think of as his version of a smile.
Marmy, the cat, was curled up in a chair near the dog, as
if daring him to wake up and chase her.

"I guess," Heidi said with another shrug.

"It's true," Mary said firmly. "Ever since he was a
little boy, he's been taking care of people. What would he
do if he couldn't take care of people anymore?"

"He could take care of us," Heidi said softly.

"He does that in many ways you don't realize, dear."
Mary gathered up the cards because it was clear that this
wasn't a battle she was going to win tonight. "Time for
bed."

Once Heidi was tucked away in her bed, Mary brewed
some coffee. After pouring herself a cup, she settled back
down on the couch with the newspaper. Her entire week-

end schedule had been thrown off-kilter. She'd had to call in extra help at the Painted Pony so that she could be at the hospital Saturday, and then had stayed with Heidi much of the day so that Jackson could go back and be with Lexie, then spend time out at the fire. Mary hadn't been able to sit and enjoy a cup of coffee with her newspaper all weekend.

Tonight, she'd missed her weekly bridge game, although that was a bit of a relief, since she didn't have to face Sirus. It had been bad enough to have Sirus take her to the hospital acting as if he were her husband, only to find out he was worried about Jackson.

Rufus lifted his head and cocked his ears.

"What is it, boy?" Mary listened. Then she heard it too. The sound of tires crunching over gravel. "Jackson must be home." Following Rufus, she pulled open the heavy door.

Rufus growled low in his throat.

"Evening, Mary."

"Sirus." Mary's knees suddenly felt very unsteady.

He stood in the moonlight, looking tall and handsome. Rufus growled again. Mary shushed him and flicked on the porch light, hoping it would chase away some of the attraction she felt.

No such luck.

With the benefit of more light, Rufus stepped out and sniffed Sirus's work boots. Satisfied that Sirus was no threat, Rufus trotted over to the bushes.

Traitor, Mary thought, watching the brown dog retreat.

"What brings you out here at this time of night?" She locked her knees together and tried to hide how her insides warmed at the sight of him.

"You."

Mary allowed the one word to stand between them, allowed herself to believe that she hadn't made a fool of herself over him more than once.

"I heard you were looking after Heidi and I thought you might need something."

Of course, he was just being neighborly. Everyone in Silver Bend pulled together and watched out for one another. Mary could think of over a dozen instances when Sirus had helped someone less fortunate or lent a hand to a family in need.

He drew in a deep breath. "And I wanted to apologize for the other night. It's a rough time for you and your family. Not the best time to be arguing with folks you care about."

Taken by surprise at his apology, Mary stared at Sirus stupidly for a moment or two. "Oh... I'm...I accept, thanks."

Sirus thrust his hands in his pockets and rocked back on his heels. Silence fell between them. Mary wondered if Sirus was trying as hard to stay away from the topic of firemen, safety and Jackson's state of mind as she was.

"Missed you at bridge tonight. Wasn't quite the same sitting across from Smiley."

Mary laughed a little. "I don't suppose it was."

He stared at her for a moment as if waiting for something, until Mary was reminded of the manners her mother had tried to instill in her all those years ago.

"Would you like a cup of coffee? I know it's late, but I haven't had any all day. It's a weakness of mine. And I just poured myself a cup." Mary snapped her mouth closed and resisted the urge to roll her eyes at her own behavior. Babbling on as if she were an infatuated schoolgirl. What must Sirus think of her? And why on earth did he continue to bother with her?

"I'd love some. Thanks."

Mary stepped back to let him inside. Sirus walked up to the welcome mat, then paused and looked behind him as if checking to see who might be watching.

Mary peered past him into the darkness. Although she knew Birdie, Marguerite and Smiley would be dying of interest, she doubted they'd be hiding out in the dark, spying on them.

Sirus whistled. "Come on, pup!"

Mary had forgotten all about the dog. With a last snuffle and a crackle of branches, Rufus came running.

Mary found herself in the kitchen pouring coffee. She lifted the mug and was about to carry it into the living room when she remembered her Sirus-and-coffee fantasy. Did she dare heat up her blood any further? From the kitchen, she could just see the back of Sirus's gray head.

What did she have to lose?

Mary opened the highest cupboard above the stove hood and reached for the bottle of whiskey she knew Jackson kept there. There was only about an inch in the bottom.

What was she doing? Her imagination was already overactive when it came to Sirus. She didn't need alcohol clouding it further. Before she could put it back, she heard something behind her and turned.

"Sirus." She nearly dropped the whiskey bottle.

"Need any help?"

"No...I was..." Looking at Sirus standing so tall and strong before her, Mary couldn't stop herself from letting her eyes coast down and up the length of him. Her cheeks heated. "I was just debating whether or not to warm up the coffee."

"I think it's just what we need, don't you?"

In two steps, Sirus was by her side and had taken the bottle from her. He gazed down into her eyes, and Mary held her breath, thinking he was going to kiss her.

"Just what the doctor ordered."

His smile built slower than molasses, slower than the temperature that spiked in Mary.

"Oh my," was all she managed to say.

The kitchen door swung open and Jackson stepped in, looking haggard. Quick as lightning, Mary backed into the corner of the kitchen and tried to appear as if she were the staid grandmother she'd been these past few years and not the baby-sitter who was about to make out on the couch with her sixty-year-old boyfriend.

No one spoke.

Sirus raised his eyebrows at Mary, then took charge of the situation. "When can I see that baby of yours, Jackson?"

Jackson shrugged.

Turning to Mary, Sirus said, "Have you been down to see your grandson yet, Mary?"

"Not yet."

"How about I take you tomorrow? Would that be all right, Jackson?"

After a moment, Jackson nodded.

"That's settled, then," Mary said, suddenly afraid that Sirus might use this time to question Jackson about his state of mind. "Well, it's late. Thanks for coming by, Sirus. I enjoyed your company." She poured his fresh cup of coffee down the drain.

As she opened the front door for Sirus, he cupped her chin. "You owe me a cup of coffee, Mary. And when we have it, we will talk all this through."

# CHAPTER ELEVEN

ON MONDAY, Jackson brought Heidi with him to the hospital to pick up Lexie. Heidi was excited about seeing her mom and little Henry, chattering all the way down the hill into Boise.

As they walked into the hospital, Heidi lagged behind. She stared into the long row of windows fronting the gift shop.

"Dad?" she said, then looked back into the store, pressing her face against the glass. "We should get Mom some flowers. She loves flowers."

Jackson silently berated himself for not thinking of buying Lexie flowers sooner. He hadn't seen Lex since yesterday and they hadn't parted on the best of terms. He'd left her in NICU and gone off with Logan for lunch.

"Oh, and a bear for Henry. A blue one." Heidi pressed her nose back to the glass. "That one, Dad. That big one. He's almost as big as me."

The bear was huge and grinning, with a wide bow tie proclaiming, "It's a Boy!" Jackson didn't want to buy a bear, especially not the one that was as big as Rufus. It wasn't the money. It was the fact that his kid might not make it through the week. That grinning bear might be buried with Henry.

Jackson forced himself to breathe at the heart-wrenching thought, fighting back the guilt.

"Please, Dad." Bright blue eyes gazed up at him pleadingly.

"Can I talk you out of the big one, Runt?" That bear was for proud dads and healthy kids—boys who had a bright future ahead of them.

"He's the only boy in the family." Heidi's eyes were wide. "Except for you…and Rufus. I've got a ton of toys, but he has nothing."

Jackson kneeled. "Are you sure that bear's not for you, Heidi? I mean, it's not as if Henry's going to be able to enjoy it." If he bought Henry that big bear and things didn't go well this week, Jackson would lose everything— who he was and who he loved.

Heidi's expression became more innocent, if that were possible, and she shook her head, sending her riotous ponytail flying. For the first time in nearly two days, Jackson almost felt like laughing.

"I don't know. His bed is pretty small." Jackson put a hand on Heidi's shoulder. "You know that bear's too big for Henry, don't you, Heidi?"

Heidi shrugged, glanced at her toes and then looked Jackson squarely in the eye. "You should buy what you think Henry will like because he's going to have it for a long time."

Cold goose bumps that had nothing to do with the air-conditioning rippled over Jackson's skin.

"YOU SHAVED YOUR BEARD," Lexie exclaimed, when Jackson and Heidi arrived at the hospital to take her home. "And cut your hair." She couldn't take her eyes off him. He'd been handsome with the beard, but the familiar lines of his chiseled features looked great…if she ignored the dark circles under his eyes.

"He wouldn't let Smiley do it. I think someone should give Smiley a chance," Heidi said.

"Not anyone in this family," Jackson vowed.

Still staring at Jackson, Lexie hugged Heidi tight. "I missed you, sweetie."

When she released Heidi, Jackson thrust a small spring bouquet toward her.

"These are beautiful. Thank you." The sweet smell and bright colors were like a breath of fresh air, lifting her spirits, even though Jackson's eyes seemed shadowed with worry. "I like the look. I can see your face." And all his cares. After a moment, Lexie tentatively reached out a hand, then ran her fingertips over his pale, smooth jaw, reacquainting herself with his features.

His eyes seemed to brighten. "I'd shave my head if it would make you happy."

"Seriously, Dad?" Heidi sounded doubtful. "We brought you clean clothes, Mom. Hurry up and change so I can go see Henry again."

"Give me a minute." Somehow, Lexie didn't think the worry lines etched on Jackson's face would ease if they got back together, but she still wanted to try. If only Jackson could believe in their son's chances for survival, maybe then he'd believe in their chance for love. If he didn't ask her to marry him today, she'd ask him tomorrow.

A short time later, they were on their way back to Silver Bend. Lexie spent the drive home from the hospital clutching the spring bouquet and keeping a smile pasted on her face. Heidi looked at Henry's picture, a Polaroid the hospital had given them, and kept asking questions.

"Why did they sandbag his arm? Why wasn't he wearing a diaper? Do all those wires hurt?"

Her young daughter's questions were insightful and painful to hear. Heidi had a right to know just how serious her brother's condition was, but it was difficult to explain while trying to remain upbeat. With the optimism of a child, Heidi didn't seem very worried that her brother wouldn't make it.

Behind the wheel, Jackson was oddly silent, leaving the difficult task to Lexie. She could almost feel him listening to her careful answers, and wondered if he still doubted Henry was going to live. He'd bought Henry a blue bear the size of a toaster and a small baseball glove that they'd left sitting on the counter in NICU. The bear wore a ribbon bow that proclaimed, "It's a Boy!" Could it be that Jackson had discovered his own faith in their son?

Finally, they arrived home. Lexie was suddenly struck by a wave of sadness. She climbed gingerly out of Jackson's truck and headed into the house with leaden feet. She shouldn't be coming home without her baby. She trundled down the hallway and stopped in the doorway to her bedroom, staring at the bassinet next to her bed.

"We pulled it out of the garage yesterday," Jackson said, setting the rented hospital breast pump inside the door behind her. "I cleaned it up and put the little sheets in the wash."

Lexie found herself standing beside the empty baby bed.

"Why don't you get some rest?" Jackson suggested behind her. "I'm going to take Heidi into town to pick up groceries and a movie."

Lexie half turned and looked at Jackson. He still stood in the doorway, looking at the bassinet much as she had, in utter disappointment.

"I'm sorry I didn't tell you about being pregnant," she said simply.

"I'm sorry, too."

Jackson's voice sounded raw and so unlike his own that Lexie paused to think about whether he'd actually said something.

"I let you down." Jackson's eyes were filled with tears. "I realize I've done it more than once. And now, he's so sick."

This, she thought, explained his distance. The silence. The way he wouldn't look at her until now. He was breaking inside just as she was over Henry's illness. Lexie almost cried out with relief. She'd assumed he'd given up on her and Henry at the time that they needed each other the most. She'd almost forgotten how hard he could be on himself.

"It'll be all right." Lexie forced the words past the lump in her throat. She wouldn't hold anything back if he came across the room and held out his arms to her.

"I'll try to remember that" was all he said before he closed the door.

"I'LL DO THE DISHES, Mom. You've done enough for one day. Sit." Jackson took his mother's shoulders and guided her around Rufus to the kitchen table.

Mary sat willingly. Her face seemed more lined than usual and she'd seemed a bit preoccupied during dinner.

"I feel as if we're wearing you out, what with watching Heidi while running the Pony."

"Well, it's a bit more draining than usual, but I'm hanging in there. You?"

He made a noncommittal noise and let the water fill the casserole dish his mother had brought over. Whatever her Tater Tot casserole lacked in nutrition it made up for in tasty fat content. Still, it beat his cooking, and Lexie hadn't been up to preparing anything for dinner. She'd slept all afternoon. Jackson would have liked to have done so too.

The *SpongeBob SquarePants* nautical theme song drifted out from the living room. If he turned his head, he could see Heidi sprawled on the couch, her bare feet propped up.

"You look tired, dear. Have you recovered from your trip? You know, I have no idea what you did over there."

"We fought fires," he began tentatively, casting about for a tale of his experiences that didn't involve Alek. And then he couldn't think of anything else to say.

In response to his silence, his mother seemed to choose her words carefully. "Have I ever talked much about your father being a Hot Shot all those years ago?"

His mom's question came out of the blue. "A little."

"I don't think I ever told you that he was thinking about quitting because of the awful scars."

Jackson frowned. "I don't remember any scars."

"These weren't visible scars, Jackson. These were marks on his soul."

Jackson shut the water off and busied himself with wiping down the sink so he wouldn't have to face his mother. He was sure he didn't want to hear whatever she had to say next.

"He saw a family die while he was trying to protect their house." Her voice was matter-of-fact, devoid of recriminations or pity. "He was on one side of the fire. They were on the other."

Jackson did turn then, his stomach protesting against the greasy dinner he'd eaten.

"In a way, I think he blamed himself for their deaths. Before that happened, he couldn't wait to be called to a fire. Afterwards, he had to drag himself out there. In the end, I believe he probably felt the fire deserved to claim him."

Jackson rubbed the back of his neck. Great. He came from a line of cowards. That didn't make him feel any better. "Are you trying to tell me something, Mom?"

"I'm trying to tell you that you have to find a way to let go of some of whatever you've been carrying around. I don't know what it is, but I see it in your eyes, the same burden your father had. I don't want you so overwhelmed with it that you compromise the way you want to live."

"Mom," he warned.

She held up a hand. "I'm just offering some advice, not telling you what to do."

"If you're talking about Lexie and fire fighting, I've already decided. I'm giving up fire fighting." It sounded like a lame cop-out.

"If that's what's bothering you—" His mother's smile

lacked warmth, as if she didn't quite believe him. "Well, then. You should be happy, shouldn't you."

*THE HEAT WAS INESCAPABLE.*

*"We've got to get out of here!" Jackson reached for Lexie's hand, but it dissolved as he closed his fingers. She stepped back, closer to the flames. Strands of her hair lifted in the air, fanned by the waves of heat rolling from the fire.*

*"Not without Henry." Her voice was calm, as if she had no idea the monster was nearly upon them.*

*Jackson looked down at the red soil at his feet, at the baby with wires and tubes nearly covering his frail body, shielded from the fire by Jackson's backpack. If he picked him up, Jackson knew the machines keeping Henry alive would be disconnected—all hope lost. But there was no hope here, in the midst of a sea of flame.*

*"He won't make it. We can't save him and ourselves. He needs more than we can give him."*

*"If that's true, then you go. Save yourself." Lexie stood alone against the flames. Only, she wasn't alone. Heidi was there, sheltered in the sweep of Lexie's arm.*

*Jackson looked down at Henry one last time. Small, delicate eyelids lifted. Solemn green eyes focused on Jackson. Flames raced to his left. There was no escaping if he didn't leave now. He looked at his family one last time…*

Jackson sat up in the motor home, drenched in sweat. Images of fire, smoke and helplessness consumed him. His heart pounded against his ribs as if he'd just run up a steep slope with full gear.

"I wouldn't leave them," he said to the night, refuting what his mind insisted—he wasn't a good father, had failed as a husband. Struggling for breath, he repeated, "I wouldn't."

The words couldn't erase the sorrowful burden of guilt and defeat.

LEXIE AWOKE MORE HOPEFUL than she'd felt in days. Sleeping in her own bed had helped, but it was the knowledge that she and Jackson still had a chance at happiness that made her spirits lift. They'd go together to the hospital this morning, sit with Henry and give their son the strength he needed to get better. Then she'd ask Jackson to marry her.

Even waking up to a nightgown wet from her milk couldn't upset her. This was a new day—for Henry and her marriage. She heard Jackson making coffee in the kitchen and went to make the day's plans with him.

"Good morning," she said when she entered the kitchen, infusing her voice with cheer even though the sun hadn't fully risen over the mountains yet.

Jackson started, spilling the coffee he was pouring on the counter.

"I didn't mean to scare you," she apologized, grabbing a sponge to mop up.

"It's all right." Jackson seemed to look at her differently, as if staring at something he knew he couldn't have, something he'd lost. He fingered his wedding ring.

Lexie's spirits plummeted. She forced her lips into what she hoped was a reassuring smile. "You know, if you give me a few minutes, I can be ready to go."

"Ready?"

Her mind finally registered that he was wearing fire clothes. The first chill fingers of disappointment settled on Lexie's spine. "Ready to go to the hospital."

Jackson's gaze dropped to the linoleum. "I'm not going, Lex."

"What? Why not?"

He looked everywhere but at her. "I've missed enough work already. If I want this job permanently, I need to make a better showing."

"But—"

Green eyes finally lifted to hers. "Henry will get better with or without me."

"That's not true." If nothing else, she needed Jackson. Somehow, she'd make him see that was enough. In time, as Henry got better, he'd believe.

His expression turned more grim, irritation crept into his words. "Lex, you made the rules, not me. I'm going to make this work. And to do that, I need this job."

*I need you with me.* She almost screamed it at him. Certainly, in her head the words came out as a shriek. She couldn't get anything past her dry throat. And yet she had to. She drew a deep breath. "Do you like it?"

"Like what?"

"Your job with Sirus. Do you like it?"

"It's a job. It'll pay the bills."

"That's not an answer."

Jackson turned toward the door, making Lexie fear he was going to walk away from her, but then he turned back. "Does it matter if I like it or not?"

She stared at him in silence.

"What's the right answer, Lex?"

"The truth," she said softly. Lexie rubbed her hands up and down her bare arms as if trying to ward off the chill of the morning. She met his gaze with her chin lifted. "Do you like it or not?"

"I'm a firefighter, not a paper pusher." His admission held more than a trace of bitterness.

Finally, the truth comes out. "I thought so." He'd kept his feelings from her for so long, she was grateful that he'd told her, even if it wasn't what she wanted to hear.

Jackson fingered his truck keys. "I'll try and get down to the hospital later, maybe tonight." He smiled at her and took a step toward the door.

Lexie had to look away; otherwise, she would have embarrassed herself by throwing herself at him and begging him to come with her. She crossed her arms over her chest and stood up straight. She was used to handling things on her own, wasn't she? Pride told her to let him go, that allowing him back into her life meant returning to the status quo, and that wasn't good enough. She wouldn't be asking Jackson anything.

"Do you promise?" Lexie blurted before she could catch herself.

"What?" He stopped mid-stride.

Why was she putting herself through this? She knew he wouldn't show, even if she made him promise. Something would come up, as it always had.

"Never mind."

Jackson hesitated. In the past, he would have smiled and promised her the world without hesitation. All those times she had waited for him, all those times Heidi had waited for him. And now Henry would have to stand in line as well.

"I want your promise that you'll go see him tonight. I don't care what happens at work today, at the fire, or with someone else's broken-down car. I want you to promise me that *our son* will hear your voice tonight." Her chest heaved, but she kept her chin up.

His eyes were haunted. He reached out to cup her face with his hand. "I'm no use to him, Lex. We both know that."

She closed her eyes so that she wouldn't cry. "That's not true."

But he hadn't heard her.

He was gone.

SOMEONE FROM INCIDENT COMMAND had taken over Jackson's role while he was gone over the weekend. Jackson sat in the Tuesday morning briefing with nothing to do but listen. And he didn't listen well. His mind kept replaying the disappointment on Lexie's face when he was leaving her.

He was such an idiot. He should have agreed to anything she wanted, just to get her back. Only, that last nightmare had shaken the last bit of self-worth from him. She deserved better than the big zero he'd become. He couldn't even stand next to Henry's crib and pretend he wasn't responsible. He was afraid she'd see the truth.

Sirus pulled Jackson aside after the meeting. "You don't need to be here. Why don't you take some time off?"

"I'll go crazy if I do. I need something to occupy my mind."

Sirus frowned. "What about Lexie?"

"She's at the hospital today." She was the strong one. Throw an obstacle in her path and she'd survive.

"And you? When are you going?" Sirus asked.

Jackson shifted his weight. "I...might go later."

"All right, you can go tonight with Mary and me."

"With you?"

An aide brought Sirus a clipboard full of papers. The older man began to scan through the pile, signing as needed. "Yep. The nurse said we can't visit little Henry without you or Lexie there, too."

Jackson rubbed the back of his neck. "One big happy family."

Sirus sent him a disapproving stare. "Don't get smart with me, Garrett." Sirus looked back down at his clipboard. "Since you're free on the duty roster today, I'm going to send you with the volunteers to the lower meadow to build a fire break roadside. They could use your expertise."

For the life of him, Jackson couldn't remember where the fire line was. He resisted looking at the day's map clutched in his hand along with the other reports. The muscles in his shoulders tensed. The fire couldn't be too near the meadow; otherwise, Sirus wouldn't be sending volunteers out there. Still, his heart pounded at being within sight of the fire.

"Take the van and that group over there, and quit complaining. It's not as if I was sending you out on the line. See you around dinnertime."

Jackson's mouth was suddenly parched. He spun away before Sirus noted his panic, drinking in air in big gulps. Irritably, Jackson mumbled under his breath, "Maybe we can play some catch while we're at it, *Dad*." Too late, he realized Sirus was right behind him.

"I'm going to consider that a serious invitation, Jackson. Dig up some gloves and a ball by chow time."

Silently fuming, Jackson walked faster to the van. The volunteers turned out to be a group of teenage Eagle Scouts. Most of them had brought gloves and shovels. The others leaned on garden-variety rakes that wouldn't make it through the morning. Jackson hoped their parents didn't expect the tools back.

He drove the group to the lower meadow on an unpaved fire road, having to pull over twice to let a school bus with real firefighters pass on the way to the lower fire lines. The boys snapped gum, tried to catch glimpses of female firefighters and generally irritated the hell out of Jackson when he normally would have been happy to answer their questions and cajole them into good behavior.

If this was his penance for past sins, so be it.

WITH ONE HAND GENTLY RESTING on Henry's leg, Lexie kept vigil next to his bed. Helen and another nurse went about their duties with the other sick babies. For the most part, both nurses ignored Lexie. Sometimes Lexie hummed, sometimes she talked to Henry, but she always kept one hand on him.

She read the vital statistics that she hadn't been told at his birth—four pounds, twelve ounces and seventeen inches long. It was posted on his chart, along with his current weight—four pounds, six ounces.

Time passed slowly.

Her son seemed almost lifeless. When she thought the nurses weren't looking, Lexie would run her fingers down the tiny bit of Henry's cheek that wasn't covered with medical tape holding his respirator tube in place. Then Lexie looked for any response to indicate he might be alive and feeling her tickling caress.

But Henry didn't move, gave Lexie no sign of hope to cling to. Why had she been given this baby after years of trying to get pregnant, only to have him taken away? He had to survive. Life couldn't be that cruel.

Only, life *had* been cruel. She'd been blessed with Jackson's love, just to have her faith in him falter. Now, when it seemed as if they were being given a second chance, there were too many obstacles between them. She loved him with all her heart. She liked having him around more often, appreciated the help he gave around the house, but there was a sadness in his eyes that even Heidi didn't seem to lighten.

And he'd stopped asking her to marry him.

At her feet, Heidi shifted to sit cross-legged on the floor while she read a book. Heidi wouldn't last much longer. They'd spent a few hours with Henry in the morning and gone outside the hospital for lunch at a fast-food restaurant. Lexie was lucky her daughter had been patient this long.

Someone stopped in front of the big window facing the hallway. Lexie glanced up, then wished she hadn't.

Edna Higgins. The thin woman smiled at Lexie, checked her watch, then scrubbed up and entered the NICU.

"How are you today, Mrs. Garrett?"

As Lexie exchanged greetings with the social worker, Heidi stood up.

"Any progress with little Henry?" Edna's expression was as kindly as her words. She was unlike any social worker that Lexie had come across in the past.

Lexie pursed her lips and shook her head, not trusting herself to speak without releasing tears of frustration. She'd cry in the privacy of her bedroom later. Not here, at the hospital, and especially not in front of her kids.

"It might be comforting to know that I've heard the first few days are the most difficult, when the baby is so heavily sedated they don't do much."

The counselor's words explained a lot and made Lexie feel better.

Edna smiled at Heidi. "You must be Henry's sister."

Heidi bobbed her head. "Do you know when my brother can come home?"

"No. There are only two people that can answer that—Henry, and Henry's doctor."

Lexie gazed down at her son, willing him to want to do better. She cupped the crown of his head with her hand, careful of the wires placed there. The soft fuzz of his dark hair against her skin reassured her that he was a real baby. She'd noticed his hair swirled at his right temple. He'd have one heck of a cowlick when he got older.

"I'd like him to come home soon," Heidi said, melting Lexie's heart, until she added, "Because it's really boring here." Heidi paused, then sighed dramatically. "But I suppose he'll need these wires and stuff for a while."

Edna's smile never wavered. "I think you're right. And when he comes home, chances are he'll have at least one belt or wire."

This was news to Lexie. She'd assumed that when Henry came home, she'd be free to cradle him in her arms without the deterrence of wires.

"Is your husband here? I haven't had a chance to talk with him." Edna pushed her glasses back into place.

"He's working today." She didn't refute the assumption that Jackson was her husband. Lexie put an arm around Heidi. "He's hoping to come by this evening." At least, Lexie was hoping he'd come.

"I'd love a chance to talk with him," Edna said.

Lexie hoped she would too, and said as much. Perhaps Edna could make Jackson see how badly Henry needed him.

"My dad's a busy man," Heidi supplied. "He just got back from Russia."

"How interesting." Edna smiled in a way that encouraged Heidi further, giving her center stage.

"He's a firefighter. A really good one, even though fires can be pretty dangerous. He always comes home in one piece."

Smiling at the pride evident in Heidi's words, Lexie rubbed her daughter's shoulder, wishing her words were true. Jackson seemed to have returned from the fires in Russia with a piece of himself missing. Lexie didn't have any idea how to help put him back together.

Or if he wanted her to try.


JACKSON AND HIS SCOUTING TROOP hacked down and cleared away weeds and brush ten feet on either side of the road. Very few people went by. At one point, Rob drove past in a green Forest Service truck heading back to camp, waving but not stopping.

By lunchtime, Jackson estimated they had cleared barely an eighth of a mile. It was slow work, and the boys were starting to complain. A volunteer brought out a box of sandwiches, chips and sodas, which helped the troop's morale and got Jackson off the hook as far as playing catch with Sirus.

"This is so boring. Did they just, like, give us the most lame job or does somebody do this all the time?" a big-boned boy asked Jackson. His name tag dubbed him Brian.

"This is one of the jobs we do when we aren't fighting

fires. It's important. If a fire starts out here, clearing the brush like this keeps the fire from jumping the road," Jackson explained.

"Yeah, but it's boring," Brian said, leaning on his shovel.

"Well," Jackson smiled, recognizing the stall tactic. "We usually sing."

"Please don't start 'Kumbaya,'" another scout—Jackson thought his name was Dustin—pleaded.

Jackson chuckled. "How about 'SpongeBob Square-Pants'? Anybody know that one?" Jackson jumped right into his best imitation of Mr. Crab singing the opening line. *"Are you ready, kids?"*

There was a pause when Jackson doubted the teens were going to play along.

Then Brian said rather halfheartedly, "Aye-aye, Captain."

*"I can't hear you,"* Jackson prompted with a grin.

Most of the boys started in on the song, making up words when they weren't sure of the lyrics. The work went more quickly after that.

While they were deciding what else to sing, Jackson straightened and breathed in deeply. "Do you smell smoke?" he asked the scoutmaster, the only scout in uniform with no name tag.

The older man sniffed. "Not any more than I have all day."

"Keep working." Jackson hurried up the road and around the bend. The smell of smoke was not only stronger, but there was a smoke trail. The sun warmed his shoulders, yet something cold shivered across his heart.

There was a fire nearby.

The smoke drifted over the bushes to the right of the road. Wood crackled and popped. Jackson was sweating now. Not the honest sweat from clearing brush, but the cowardly sweat that clung to the body as tightly as the fingers of death.

With footsteps weighted down with dread, Jackson stepped off the dirt and gravel road. Sparse, dry tufts of grass crunched beneath his feet. There was a slight rise behind some bushes, and then he knew the ground swept away, down into the meadow, with nothing between the lower meadow and the slope but a narrow stream bed.

The smoke was thicker now than it had been when he'd first seen it—an indication the fire was gaining strength. He could hear the crackle of fire eating fuel, could almost feel the heat increase.

His gut clenched, seeming to put a viselike grip on his legs; he couldn't get them to move.

The singing behind him stopped as the first of the boys rounded the bend.

"He's just going to take a leak right there in front of us?" one of them said.

Kids were so quick to judge. It was almost funny. A smile tugged at the corners of Jackson's lips.

Air flowed back through his lungs. His feet moved. One step. Two. The scrub was thicker here, and nearly up to his waist.

Dark smoke burned his nostrils. There was no mistaking it. Fire.

"Hey, is that smoke?"

"There's a fire over there!"

The sound of excited voices and pounding boots descended upon Jackson just as he pushed aside the brush and peered down the slope toward the meadow.

A kindergarten fire. That's what his Hot Shots called a fire that small. Merely twenty by twenty, the fire had eaten up most of the sparse tufts of grass and had started on the bushes at the end of the meadow, the bushes at Jackson's feet. The fire would have spread farther as dry grass was one of the most combustible fuels, but the small creek was a momentary barrier. When the fire got larger, it would jump that creek.

"What do we do?" The scoutmaster stood next to Jackson.

"We can put that out," one of the boys said.

"Yeah," someone seconded.

"How safe is it?" the scoutmaster asked.

Jackson put out a hand to stop a boy from stepping into the meadow. They were just kids out to earn a badge for the day. No one expected them to actually fight a fire.

This fire was small enough that Jackson could have put it out by himself a few months ago. It was a slow burner. The grass was spread out in clumps and the wind was barely blowing. The fire had just reached the bushes. The bushes were what would get it going and keep it alive. He needed to establish a perimeter.

His head pounded. He couldn't seem to pull his eyes off the flame. He hadn't seen a fire this close since Russia. The pop and sizzle of dry, burning wood was mesmerizing.

"Jackson?" The scoutmaster's voice again.

Jackson felt a hand on his shirtsleeve. "Jackson?"

He clamped down on the fear and let his training kick in.

"Brian, go back to the van and use the radio to call Dispatch. Take two others with you. Tell them we're above the lower meadow and found a small fire. Tell them we'll call back in fifteen minutes with an update but that it looks containable. Send someone back with their answer." Jackson knew there were other priorities, bigger fires to deal with, but they might have someone around base camp to send out, just in case. Three boys ran back to the road.

"Dustin, you and the others stand there by the road. Flag down anyone that comes by."

The anxiety was bearable while he was giving orders.

Jackson turned to the scoutmaster. "Use your shovel to toss dirt on the flames over by the creek. Don't step on any hot ash."

Jackson pushed his way through the brush, ignoring the way branches tugged and tore at his clothing. Gripping his Pulaski, Jackson began to hack away at the bushes that had already caught fire, tossing them into the burned-out area behind him. It was quick work, and before any of the boys came back from the van, the two men had made a two-foot-wide barrier around the fire.

"They want to know if you'll need backup." Brian was out of breath when he returned.

"No." Now that the bulk of the work was over and the fire was burning itself out, Jackson didn't want anyone to come out and see what a wreck he was—sweating more than he should be, his hands shaking.

He and the scoutmaster cleared a wider line around the little fire, then tossed more dirt on the meager flames at the edge until it burned out.

"How did it start?" one of the boys asked. "We're nowhere near the real fire, are we?"

Jackson looked up at the mountain looming large before them, smoke hovering over the lower slope like a low fog. He wiped the sweat from his brow. "This *was* a real fire. The big fire is over there. It's possible that the wind carried a spark down here. In which case, there might be more fires like this one." Jackson spun in a slow three-sixty. Nothing indicated there were other fires in the area. No smoke plumes. No snapping, hungry flame.

"Brian, go back and tell Dispatch that we'll walk through the area looking for other fires, but that they need to send a crew. Then bring everyone back up here."

Brian nodded and ran off.

"These kids aren't in any danger, are they?" the scoutmaster asked.

Jackson wiped more sweat off his brow. "We're just going to walk the road a bit. Nothing to worry about."

Jackson wished he could take comfort from his own words.

# CHAPTER TWELVE

"WHAT HAPPENED TO YOU, DAD?"

Lexie turned from the stove, checking Jackson out from head to toe, her heart sinking. He stood in his thick socks, his yellow Nomex shirt grubby and stained, his dark-green pants streaked with soot. "You fought a fire."

Jackson didn't say anything, didn't look at either of them. His gaze was distant and unfocused. Standing in the doorway, he looked as if he might collapse at any moment. His face was paler than usual, but perhaps that was because he'd just shaved his beard.

Lexie took a step toward him. "Jackson, are you okay?"

His gaze flickered to her and then away.

"Grandma's coming over and she's bringing Sirus, too. Then we're all going down the hill to Boise." Heidi scooted past Jackson as she finished setting the table. "Ew, you smell like smoke and stinky sweat."

Without a word, Jackson headed down the hall to the bathroom.

"Did I hurt his feelings?" Heidi asked.

"I don't think so, honey." This wasn't like Jackson. He smiled, joked and told stories about the fire that made it seem just like another day at the office. It was at that moment that she remembered his nightmares and the way he'd looked stricken when Sirus suggested he was sending him out on the line.

Lexie paused while mashing potatoes. Something was dreadfully wrong.

"When is Dad moving back in?"

Lexie avoided answering. "Why don't you feed the dog?"

"I fed him yesterday. Why won't you let Dad come back home? We could be a family again. I wouldn't have to do all these chores. It's like I'm your slave or something."

"Heidi, please. Let's not fight over this. Just feed the dog."

"Fine. But when Henry gets older, he's going to have to feed Rufus."

Lexie left Heidi and went down the hall. She didn't realize where she was going until she rested her hand on the bathroom doorknob. The shower spray pounded the bathroom wall.

She was a fool, loving a man who couldn't love her back the way she needed him to. Yet, she couldn't deny that he needed her now.

With an unsteady breath, Lexie turned the handle and pushed the door open.

Jackson sat hunched on the lid of the toilet, his head in his hands. His shirt was unbuttoned and hung open.

Lexie shut the door behind her. As the lock clicked into place Jackson jerked his head up. The sight of his pale face, eyes filled with unshed tears, brought Lexie to her knees in front of him.

"What happened?" She took his hands, alarmed to find them cold and trembling.

Jackson shook his head.

"Did someone…die?" Had they lost someone she knew? Logan? *God, don't let it have been Logan.* Deb and the twins needed him.

Jackson shook his head, but Lexie felt no relief.

"Please." She rubbed his hands with her own. "Tell

me. Are you all right? Are you hurt?'' She didn't see any blood or bandages. Her attention kept coming back to his eyes. Their green depths were haunted, as if they were privy to some horror only he could see.

Instinctively, her arms wrapped around him as she rose awkwardly from the floor. He gave a shuddering sigh and curled her into his embrace. Lexie made soothing noises, murmuring words of comfort much as she had with Henry earlier. He didn't cry, simply nestled his head in the crook of her shoulder and held her tight.

''You're fine, Jackson. You're home. It's going to be all right.''

Jackson shook his head. She thought she heard him mumble something, but he held her tighter, almost squeezing the breath right out of her. She ran her hands up and down the length of the strong, tense muscles of his back, willing him to relax.

''I had to do it,'' Jackson said finally, when his shaking had subsided a bit.

Lexie didn't want to imagine what Jackson had to do, to hear about the horrible thing had taken him to the brink of collapse. She ran her fingers over his hair, feeling the grit and smelling the smoke that was proof he'd been close to a fire, if not actually fighting one.

''I almost lost it out there.''

Lexie kissed the top of his forehead.

''A grass fire...so small.'' He clutched her tight. ''And I almost lost it.''

''What were you doing near a fire?''

''Eagle Scouts, just kids. We were clearing brush away from a fire road.''

''You're all right,'' Lexie reassured him. ''You're safe. Let's get you cleaned up.'' The room was filled with steam. The shower's hot water wouldn't last much longer.

With deliberate care, she encouraged him to get up,

helped him off with his clothes and steadied him when he stepped into the shower.

"I'll get you some clean clothes."

Jackson stood in the shower, his palms braced against the wall, but he didn't answer.

AS THE WATER STARTED TURNING COLD, someone knocked on the door. Jackson turned off the faucet and opened the shower stall door far enough that he could reach a towel.

"I'll be out here if you need me," Lexie called through the door.

Standing on legs that felt like rubber, Jackson dried off and dressed himself in boxers and a pair of knee-length cargo shorts. When he opened the door, Lexie stood there, as promised.

"Let's get you in bed."

To his surprise, she began to escort him across the hall to her bed. He dug in his heels. "I can make it out to the motor home. The worst is over."

"You need a good night's sleep in a real bed between sheets, not in a sleeping bag."

It did sound enticing. Cool sheets, and a mattress with springs, not foam. Jackson's feet moved again. She pulled back the covers and helped him into bed as if he were an eighty-year-old invalid, instead of the man that used to be her strong husband.

"Do you want to talk about it?"

Jackson's stomach turned. "I think I said enough in the bathroom."

She gave a resigned sigh and turned to go.

"Wait...I... This job is killing me."

Lexie turned back around slowly.

His brain had stopped filtering his emotions. "I need to *work* at a job. I have calluses on my hands and a sun-burned face. Who am I if not a firefighter?"

"I don't understand. This morning you said you hated

your job. Now it sounds as if you've made up your mind to go back to the Hot Shots. All that's stopping you is an open position.''

"I haven't...I can't." He cursed under his breath, wondering how much he could tell Lex without looking like a coward.

"Tell me. Did something happen to you over there?"

"This isn't easy for me, Lex." He sat up in bed and tried to find the words to make her understand. He blew out a frustrated breath.

She didn't say anything for a minute, and then she spoke so softly that he had to strain to pick up her words. "You might just need to follow your heart."

"It's not that simple. My heart and I come with baggage. Everywhere I turn there's baggage." He ran a hand through his short hair. What would she think if he told her the truth? That he'd lost faith in himself, lost his nerve to lead. There was no way to know without baring his soul to her. Gazing into her clear blue eyes, he knew that if he wanted her to marry him again, he couldn't hold anything back.

"I fought some fires when I was overseas. Sometimes with equipment that was so old and outdated...it was laughable. Sometimes...the men I was supposed to train had nothing but their bare hands and sheer will to save their town from an approaching fire. These places were so backwoods, they didn't have but one telephone per village. And they thought they could stop a raging forest fire?" Jackson shook his head.

"How could I not help people with that much heart?" He took a deep breath before continuing. "There were six of us out fighting a fire. The slopes weren't as steep as some places I've seen, but the forest was dry, so it burned quickly once it caught. When we started out in the morning there was no wind, but by mid-afternoon it was whipping up pretty bad. The ash in the air was so thick, it almost seemed to be snowing." It wasn't hard to remember what happened earlier on that fateful day. "We were just completing a fire break when I thought I heard something up on the ridge. At first, I thought it was a bulldozer or fire truck coming up the other side to help us, but it wasn't. It was fire. This fire looped around the ridge and was coming back down at us. It took me a minute to realize we were trapped."

Lexie seemed frozen in place.

"My Russian crew had nothing. They were wearing Nikes, for cryin' out loud. Step on smoldering ash with tennis shoes and the soles will melt to your feet fast enough to make your head spin. What was I thinking, taking these guys out to fight a wildland fire? It was clear to me that they were all going to die." Jackson took a deep breath. "That I was going to die."

"You made it out." Her unspoken question was, what happened to the other five?

"I came up with some cockamamy scheme and was just damn lucky, that's all. We had no backup, no other support, no way out. Hell, I couldn't even understand the Russian coming over the radio. They could have been telling us to get out and I wouldn't have known the difference. The crew assumed I knew what I was doing." Jackson sucked in a breath. "All of the crew but one...Alek. He was so young, so proud to be chosen to fight fires. He used to follow me around sometimes, asking me questions in broken English about America, about fire fighting. None of the others had his enthusiasm."

"What happened to Alek?"

He had to work up enough saliva to keep talking. "We'd just finished setting up the fire shelter and were all climbing in, when he lost it." Jackson could still see Alek's dark-eyed, horror-stricken expression. "He didn't believe we'd survive. He thought we were in for a slow death, so he ran downhill. Into the smaller fire."

Lexie reached for Jackson's hand and sank down onto the bed next to him.

"Oh my God, Jackson. Into the fire?"

He gripped her fingers tight. In his mind, he could see Alek running, casting glances back over his shoulder at the crew, ignoring the pleas of Jackson and the rest of the team. "Maybe he thought it would be quicker that way. Maybe he was so scared he didn't know what he was doing. I'll never know, because Breniv and Levka dragged me down and pulled the fire shelter over us." The roar of the fire had been so loud, they hadn't heard Alek's screams—but Jackson could imagine. He'd heard men scream from burns before.

Lexie shook his hand sharply. "You blame yourself. If those men—Breniv and the other one—if they hadn't held you down, you would have ran after Alek, wouldn't you?" Her eyes were filled with tears.

Jackson clenched his jaw. He would not accept excuses. "I should have noticed how scared he was earlier. I'm responsible for the safety of every crew member."

"Like the captain of a ship? Jumping overboard after him and being lost at sea as well when someone loses it?" She reached out to stroke his cheek, her voice gentling. "You wouldn't have come back."

Jackson lay his hand over hers, breathing in the flowery scent of perfume at her wrist. "I know what you're trying to do—make me feel better—but I was supposed to be in charge of these men, make decisions to keep them safe. Instead, I was an egotistical bastard who believed there were no risks too great for me, and I almost got them all killed."

"Yet, this crazy scheme of yours saved the lives of most of your crew and brought you back home?"

He held her gaze, willing her to understand. "How can I trust my judgment anymore, Lex? What if I take a team up a ridge and we get trapped? What if I decide to order back-burning when I really need an airdrop?''

"Didn't you tell me these Russians had nothing to fight fires with?"

He closed his eyes. "It was pitiful."

"And here in the States, don't you have the latest weather reports and different types of teams to attack fires?''

"It doesn't matter. The decisions I make on the fire line are life and death. Think about that. Life and death. I can't go out there again.''

"As far as I know, you've been in charge of men before. You've saved lives. What you've got to decide is whether or not you want to continue taking that responsibility.''

"You don't understand." He hadn't even told her about his role in Henry's illness.

"Don't I? You're not going to try. You're going to settle for a job that you don't like and be miserable the rest of your life.''

A KNOCK ON A DOOR awakened Jackson from a restless sleep. Blinking heavy eyes, he took a moment to get his bearings. He slept in his own bed. The bed he'd shared so many years with Lexie. The sheets carried her sweet scent, but she was nowhere in the room.

The door pushed open and Sirus entered. "I need to talk to you, Garrett. I'll be in the back."

"Where's Lex?" Still half asleep, Jackson ignored Sirus's command.

"She's in the living room. Meet me in back in two minutes." Sirus closed the door without waiting for Jackson to acknowledge or agree to his request.

Jackson rolled into a sitting position, cradling his aching head in his hands. Wasn't this pleasant? His boss seeing him broken. If Jackson didn't know better, he might think

Sirus set up that small fire just to test him. It seemed unlikely that a spark had traveled so far down the mountain and started a brushfire on the same road that Jackson was working on.

He swore.

On legs that still felt spent, Jackson made it to the door, pausing only to pull on a T-shirt Lexie had left for him. Anger building, he spared Lexie and his mother a brief glance as he passed through the living room.

The screen door banged behind Jackson before he accused Sirus. "How did you know?"

From his perch on the picnic table, Sirus raised his peppery eyebrows. "Know what?"

"Know I'd lost my nerve." The words spilled out bitterly. "Does everyone know?"

Sirus opened his mouth to deny it.

"You started that fire today, didn't you. You sent Rob out to start it," Jackson accused. "I bet you thought your brand of tough love would cure me or something." Jackson fell back against the wall of the house. "You were wrong about that one. No matter what you say, I'm washed up. And that prefab fire was a joke."

Sirus frowned. "Did one of those Eagle Scouts conk you on the head with a shovel? Not only would I never put you in a situation I knew you couldn't handle, but I'd lose my job if I deliberately set a fire. I've suspected something was wrong. I'm just sorry you didn't tell me about this *problem* sooner."

All Jackson could comprehend was that Sirus knew he couldn't handle a fire. Since he'd been back, no one had doubted his ability, that's how well he thought he'd been covering his fear. Jackson suddenly had the urge to punch something. How dare Sirus lose faith in him?

Feeling betrayed, Jackson walked to the corner of the house before turning back to face his mentor. "Somebody set that fire. The winds would have had to blow a hell of a lot harder for a lone spark to ignite miles down the hill.''

"You know as well as I do that stranger things have happened." Sirus frowned. "You put it out, didn't you?"

"I put it out and then I puked in the bushes for five minutes. I don't even remember driving home."

"So, you did put out the fire?"

Jackson rubbed his face. "I know you're not deaf. I told you I barely made it."

"But you did it."

"You know, this is getting old. That fire could have spread and someone could have gotten hurt. I busted my butt trying to make sure we contained it."

"You did your job today. What else do I need to know?"

"Don't try any psychoanalysis with me. I didn't feel that same adrenaline rush I used to get from fighting fires. It was fear for the safety of those kids that forced me to fight. I wanted to be anywhere but there." Jackson paced to the back door.

Who had he become?

Sirus stood up, lowering his voice. "There are all kinds of reasons to fight fires and people approach the job with all different emotions—fear, anger, determination. Don't tell me you don't think back on that fire now with a little bit of a rush. You always loved a challenge, and this was the ultimate test. You didn't think you could do it, but you did. I'm proud of you."

His words gave Jackson pause, but he'd lived with the fear and doubt clutched so tight inside the past few weeks that he couldn't let go that easily.

"It was a piddly little fire barely bigger than my living room. I'm amazed I found it at all. As for a rush, if you call cold sweat on a hot day a rush, I guess that's what happened."

"You're not as bad off as you think." Sirus placed a

hand on Jackson's shoulder. "Trust me. You have a knack for fire fighting that's uncanny. To be honest, I've always been jealous of your talent."

At the moment, the thought of anyone envying Jackson's fire-fighting ability was hard to swallow. "I'm not Luke Skywalker to your Yoda. The Force is not with me."

"You've always been the one people rely on. You did what you had to do today. You didn't collapse into a puddle of quivering jelly. You beat the doubt."

"Look, whatever. It's done. All I know is, I'm no good to anyone right now. That fire today proved my Hot Shot career is over." The words left a bitter taste in Jackson's mouth.

Sirus just shook his head as he walked past him into the house. "I hope for your sake that you're wrong."

"YOUR SON NEEDS YOU more right now than Jackson does," Sirus said, herding Lexie out the door with Mary and Heidi. He'd already told the Garrett women that Jackson was still under the weather. "Let's give Jackson a little more time to recover."

On the drive down to the hospital, the adults were quiet. Heidi took the spotlight, chattering and telling stories in a way that lightened things, or would have if all of them hadn't been worrying about Jackson and Henry.

"Your little guy has decided to show you some color," a nurse announced when Lexie introduced herself upon entering the NICU. "Just watch. Every fifteen minutes or so, half his body will turn bright pink and the other will pale."

"What does that mean?" Lexie asked, a trifle concerned.

"It's called the Harlequin effect, at least around here. I've heard every explanation under the sun, from poor circulation to awareness of his surroundings to apnea. Take your pick, but it's really nothing to worry about. Provides more entertainment than anything.''

Lexie gazed down at her little baby and placed her hand ever so gently over his lower leg. ''Hello, sweetie. I hear you can do tricks.''

Amazingly, as she watched, Henry's tiny body began to change color. It looked as if someone had drawn a line from his nose to his penis, with the right side flushing and the left side looking almost translucent.

Tears filled Lexie's eyes. It was the first time she'd seen Henry do anything other than lie still. ''Oh my gosh, Henry. That's beautiful. Wait until we tell your dad about this.''

''I almost wish I had a camera. Almost. This entire setup just about breaks my heart.'' Mary looked around the room, then to the window where Sirus and Heidi stood watching them.

''He's a good man,'' Lexie said.

Mary blushed almost as pink as Henry. ''It's not like that. We're just friends.''

''He wants something more, Mary. It's as plain as the nose on your face.'' Lexie leaned down to Henry with forced perkiness and stroked Henry's ear slowly. ''Isn't it, Henry?''

''He's everything my heart can't take again. Besides, I've shut him out so many times, he's not going to try again.''

''I seem to remember you telling me that being in love with a man was like dancing. It doesn't always appear to be what it is. And if you rely on the man to lead all the time, you're liable to get your foot stepped on.''

''Good heavens, when did I tell you something like that?''

Lexie forced a smile past the sadness, leaning closer to Henry. ''I think that was last year when you tried to get me to take Jackson back. Henry, I was dead set on not leading or following your father's dance steps." Now Jackson was no longer trying to get her to dance.

"Well, if we're making confessions to your young man, I'd just like to go on record as having tried to follow and tried to lead. I got my toes stepped on every time."

"Ah." Lexie picked up Henry's little foot, no bigger than her thumb, and held it in her palm. "So there was at least one time that you two were in step."

Mary sent a quick glance in Sirus's direction. "It was just my imagination."

"Maybe, maybe not. Oh, look, Mary. He's doing it again."

The color blossomed on little Henry's skin, as bright as the hope his changing hue sent to Lexie's heart.

Sirus and Mary traded places after a while. Lexie couldn't help but look at him in a different light since Mary's confession. Her heart held hope closer now that Henry was actually doing something—even if it was only some unexplained trick of his system, it was better than having him lie there. That must have been why she started teasing Sirus.

"Henry, did you know that Sirus has intentions toward your grandmother?" Lexie flashed a smile at Sirus.

"Now, what makes you think that?" Sirus asked, but he was half smiling, too.

"Oh, I don't know. The way you look at her? The way she blushes when she looks at you? The way you hold her hand or touch her when you think she's having a weak moment? Am I close?"

Sirus chuckled. Seeing him this way, Lexie could imagine him thirty years earlier—a heartbreaking Hot Shot.

"I suggest you make your intentions clear before Mary drives herself batty with second-guessing." Lexie lay her knuckles gently against Henry's cheek. His face was still swollen. His eyes were shut tight against the outside world. It would be wonderful to see his eyes open.

"It's not that simple. Mary's afraid that she'll lose another husband to fire."

That statement got Lexie's total attention. "Oh."

"Exactly."

Frowning, Lexie expressed her confusion. "I thought that as incident commander you don't fight fires anymore."

"So did Mary. But every day I go out and take a look at the fire. If there's a crew out there, I try to spend some time working next to them. I get a good feel for the fight that way. I listen to their successes and their complaints." By the intense way Sirus was staring past her to the window, Lexie could tell he was looking at Mary.

"That doesn't sound so bad."

"Mary never gave me a chance to explain. She just shut me out."

"Then, I guess you need to make sure she listens this time."

"CAN I HELP YOU?" the nurse asked Jackson as he entered the NICU.

"I'm Henry's father." He didn't feel as if he deserved to be Henry's father. He wouldn't even be here tonight if Lex hadn't wanted him to promise that he'd come.

"It's kind of late to be visiting, isn't it? The rest of the family left about an hour ago." It was the same sour nurse that had been working the night Henry was born.

"I work odd hours." Jackson moved slowly across the room to his son's bed, curbing the fear that he might discover Henry wasn't breathing. "How's he doing?"

"He's having a good day, very few alarms or episodes."

Jackson looked down at Henry. "Can you ever forgive me?" he whispered. Maybe if Henry forgave him, he could move on, get healthy, have a fair chance at life.

Henry continued to lay still. If the baby heard, Jackson had no way of knowing.

"Isn't it hard to work in here when these babies don't react to anything?" he asked.

"Oh, they react. Even little Henry." She wrapped her stethoscope around her neck and joined him at Henry's bedside. "Look at his heart monitor. See the rhythm?"

Jackson watched the red line on the monitor stroke steadily up and down.

"Put your hand gently on his head, right across his crown. That's it. Now lean over and talk to him in a low voice, but keep one eye on the monitor."

With his hand cradling Henry's head, Jackson leaned over and started talking. "You know, I think you're really going to like baseball. It's the all-American sport where you can crush a little ball with a big stick."

"Look. Do you see?"

Jackson focused on the monitor. "Is his heart beating faster?"

"It sure is. Keep talking. He's perking to life for you."

"He is, isn't he. That's amazing. Henry, how do you do that?" He straightened, keeping one hand on Henry's crown. "He won't get too excited, will he?"

"No. And he'll get tired of it after a while too, just like any other game."

"Thank you." She'd given him a precious glimpse of hope.

Thirty minutes later, Jackson was leaning on the outside of the glass window at the NICU, taking one last look at Henry before he drove home, when someone burst through the outer doors.

The thin woman looked Jackson up and down through large rimmed glasses. "Are you Mr. Garrett?"

Her question caught him off guard. "Yes."

"I'm Edna Higgins," she said somewhat breathlessly as she offered him her hand.

Trying not to frown in confusion, Jackson shook her hand.

"I'm the hospital counselor. I talked with your wife today and she said you'd be coming by later." Edna paused to swallow. "Whew! My son just finished a football game down the street, and I ran in to see if you were here. I hadn't realized how out of shape I am."

Pasting on a smile, Jackson asked, "Is there a reason you needed to see me this late at night?"

She smiled back. "No, not really. I've been visiting with your wife, and I hoped you and I could chat. How is everything?" Edna peered at him closely. "You look tired."

"It's been a long week." Jackson's smile stayed in place. He could tell this woman was fishing for something. She seemed innocuous, but she was too focused in her questioning.

"Your wife said you're a firefighter."

"Not anymore. It was too hard on our marriage." Jackson crossed his arms over his chest. "I'm in fire management now."

"How do you feel about that? I mean, it must be difficult meeting all the qualifications of fire fighting and then giving it up."

"It has been tough," he allowed, because he suspected she wouldn't let him sugarcoat his answers.

"Every change is, don't you think? My son is a junior in high school. He switched schools this year because he was offered a scholarship at a private school. He's had to make new friends, learn a new school system—not to mention the new football playbook."

"How's he doing?" Jackson was curious despite himself.

Edna's smile had more life to it this time. "He's doing well. I enrolled him in summer school to give him a head start. There are times when he's very frustrated, maybe even scared, but he's learning how to deal with everything. Some of his old methods don't work and he's surprised when he tries something new and it meets with success.''

"Are you giving me a bit of advice, Edna?"

"In a roundabout way, Mr. Garrett. We have over three hundred babies come through this ward every year. That's more than three hundred families whose lives are turned upside down by a change in expectations. Most of these parents had no idea they'd be facing a medical challenge with their baby. Some of the treatments and doctor visits last long into the first year. It requires understanding on the part of families to stay strong, and balanced, and loving. It helps to talk about it, even if it's to break down and cry on someone's shoulder while admitting your fears. It doesn't necessarily mean you're weak, it just means you need to give your emotions an outlet.''

Jackson's arms tensed across his chest. Her speech was hitting a little too close to home.

"Well—" she pushed her glasses back up on her nose "—I need to get back to my family. I just wanted to let you know that I'm here if you need someone to talk to other than your wife.''

"Thanks," Jackson mumbled, staring back into the NICU and wondering if giving his emotions an outlet would let him move on. And if so, where? Back into Lexie's arms? Or someplace where she was forever out of his reach?

## CHAPTER THIRTEEN

MARY WAS JUST GETTING OUT of the bathtub late that night when the doorbell rang. She tightened the belt on her worn flannel robe and finger-combed her short hair into place as she opened the door.

"Marguerite, if that's you, no, I don't want to have drinks with some hottie you found down the hill... Oh, heavens." Eyes wide, Mary clutched her robe tighter about her neck.

It was Sirus.

He scratched his head and his cheeks seemed to pinken beneath his tan. "Can we do that again? Because what I had planned to say doesn't go with what you just said. And now I see I may have interrupted something."

Mary blinked. "What did you plan to say?"

"Would you like to share a cup of coffee?"

Mind racing in debilitating circles, Mary glanced back at her kitchen. Wouldn't you know it? "I'm out of coffee."

"Well, I didn't exactly expect you to make any. I brought some." He leaned over the small table next to her front door and picked up a cardboard tray with two gourmet coffees on it. "I've had a lot on my mind lately, and it seems that whenever we talk we misunderstand each other or get interrupted."

"Oh, how sweet." Mary recognized the coffee shop label on the cups. He'd driven fifteen minutes down the hill just to get these. She stepped back to let him in. "You didn't have to drive all that way."

His tentative smile gave away his self-consciousness. "I did. You're important to me."

Sirus walked past her, and she had to hold on to the doorknob with her hand to keep her knees from buckling. He was one prime piece of man. He set the coffees down on the coffee table, and then pulled something out of his jacket pocket.

"I thought after the first few sips we could warm the coffee up with something." He held up a flask of whiskey.

Mary's insides heated at the idea. It took her an embarrassing amount of time to realize that she still held on to the door, which was propped as wide open as her mouth. She shut the door, suddenly conscious of the fact that she wore an old bathrobe over her bare-naked self.

She took a deep breath and turned around. "Perhaps I should go change."

"If you like," Sirus said, his brown eyes seeming to burn over her. "I don't mind if you don't wear a thing…I mean…whatever you want to wear is fine." He reached for a coffee and handed it to her. "Just come sit with me a minute. You keep distracting me when you move."

Mary sank into the opposite end of the couch, absorbing his remark. "I should probably tell you that I agree with your suggestion for Jackson. If talking to someone can erase the hollow look in his eyes, then he should do it."

"Well, that's good to hear, although that's not the real reason I came. I was talking with Lexie tonight and she had an interesting take on the two of us."

"She thinks we should be dating," Mary blurted.

"I don't plan on dating you, Mary."

"You don't." Her voice came out all tiny and insecure.

"I have more permanent plans than that. First, though, you need to understand what I do when I'm out in the field for IC." He took a deep breath. "I check on the men and women that are working the front line, just as I check that everything's going well with the crews that run base camp or our supply chain. It's not that I'm out fighting a fire every day—weeks may go by without my ever picking up a Pulaski. But it could happen. This is a personal business, and I've found people work that much harder for me if they believe I care about them and that I wouldn't order them to do anything I wouldn't do myself."

"Everyone knows you care, Sirus."

"Do they?" He stared at her, then his voice deepened. "Do you?"

Mary looked down at her hands, tangled in the ties of her robe. "We've always been friends," she said cautiously, still stinging from his comment about not wanting to date.

"I'm glad, because I want to spend the rest of my life with you."

"But...but...we haven't...what if I disappoint you?"

"You could never disappoint me, honey. Just to make sure, though, why don't you slide over here closer to me and you'll see what I have in mind."

Mary nearly fainted. "Are you...are you making a pass at me?"

"Only if you're receiving." He held out his hand. "Come on over, Mary. We've waited a long time to be in the right place at the right time."

Mary put her hand in his, watching as his long, tan fingers wrapped themselves around her paler, smaller ones. He'd been her rock many times during the past few days. She hadn't realized how much she'd come to rely on him, how much she wanted to rely on him.

He tugged gently and she scooted over until her hip touched his. His body was hard and warm next to hers. Her fingers crept up to the neck of her robe as she mentally searched her wardrobe for anything the least bit sexier than this.

"What are you thinking about?" His arm had somehow managed to come up over her shoulders.

She took a sip of her coffee and snuggled into his chest. "I was thinking that I'm too old to own a thong or anything lacey, so it's a good thing you'll take me as I am." Mary snuck a peek up at Sirus, pleased to find him grinning.

"Honey, I'll take you any way you'll let me."

Mary sighed as his lips descended to meet hers. She was more than ready to dance.

"TAKE ME TO THE HOSPITAL."

Lexie's words sent a shaft of fear down Jackson's spine. She stood in the hallway, fully dressed at five o'clock in the morning, greeting him with a request that could mean only one thing.

Still, he ignored the overwhelming premonition that it was Henry's time and asked, "Are you all right?"

"I'm fine, but the nurse just told me Henry didn't do well last night. I'd drive myself, but—"

"Let me call Sirus and tell him I won't be coming in." So, this was it. He'd try to be strong for Lexie, but Jackson wasn't prepared for his son's death. Not after last night, when he'd seen what a fighter Henry was.

Jackson had spent a sleepless night in the motor home, but this time it wasn't because of nightmares. He'd been thinking about what everyone had been telling him. Could he face his fears and will his courage to return, as Lexie, Sirus and Edna seemed to believe? He still wasn't sure. But he knew he couldn't shirk his duty and let Lexie go to the hospital alone today.

When they arrived at the hospital, Lexie reached for Jackson's hand, hanging on tight until they got to Henry's ward. Once inside the NICU, the nurse Helen stopped what she was doing and came to stand next to them. The second nurse left the room. They all gazed down on the sick baby. It seemed as if there were more tubes than ever attached to his frail little body.

Henry wasn't as swollen today as he had been last night, but he had marks on his cheek from the tape that had held the tube down his throat. New strips of tape had been applied.

"He had one heck of a night. The doctor thought he might be strong enough to breathe on his own."

Jackson must have made a sound of disbelief, because Helen looked at him. "I left him after eleven and he was fine. He had his tubes in and he was fine," he repeated.

Jackson felt Lexie's questioning gaze. He was sure she hadn't known he'd come to the hospital.

"These babies surprise you, Mr. Garrett. Some thrive on a challenge." Helen shrugged. "Some go at their own pace. Anyway, he's stabilized now and ready for some attention and TLC."

As the nurse's words sank in, Jackson stood ramrod straight and tried not to look at the tiny thing that was his son. Henry had once more dodged death. Anger roiled in Jackson's stomach at the injustice of it all. "Why on earth did the doctor think he was strong enough? Just look at him. I can't even see his eyes, much less the bones of his face."

Helen backed up a step, obviously unprepared for his anger.

"It's a fine line we walk, Mr. Garrett." Dr. Kelly had entered the room in his jeans, cowboy boots and green scrub shirt, followed by the other NICU nurse. "If we leave your son on a static treatment too long, he won't progress. His lungs might scar."

"He's three days old. I won't have you killing him." Jackson may not have been able to stop Alek from killing himself, but he could protect his son.

"Henry had a difficult time, but he was not at risk." The doctor was annoyingly calm.

Jackson opened his mouth to argue that they were very much putting his son's tenuous hold on life at risk, but Lexie placed her hand on his arm.

"Please" was all she said.

Dr. Kelly looked first at Lexie and then at Jackson, then back to Lexie. "Maybe the night shift nurse gave you the wrong impression."

"I'm not sure who to believe right now," Jackson said, looking around the room searching for something, anything that might help him defend his son. "Maybe we should transfer him to another hospital. One with more experienced staff." Jackson gave the doctor a once-over.

"Stop right there. Let's discuss this in private." Dr. Kelly led them out of the NICU and into a waiting room down the hall. He sat in a chair, leaving Lexie and Jackson the couch.

Lexie clasped Jackson's hand.

"If there's one thing I know, it's premature babies. I've been in charge of this ward for three years now, with four years of experience prior to that. And no—" Dr. Kelly gave Jackson a sharp stare "—I was not the only one to apply for the job."

"What we strive for here is a delicate balance between high-tech care and the nurturing babies need to thrive." The doctor leaned forward, resting his elbows on his knees. "You've got to trust me. We are highly qualified to make your son well. Sometimes we make tough calls about when to switch from one type of care to another. How your baby reacts tells us a lot about him. Will he be an out-performer and able to accept challenges early—meaning he could go home sooner? Or will he be a wait-and-see tyke—meaning he doesn't take change well and his treatment needs to move at a slower pace? We'll do everything in our power to bring your baby to a point he can go home."

"On the other hand, these babies respond to love, love,

love," Dr. Kelly continued. "I know it's hard, but the more time you can spend here with him, touching him, talking to him, singing to him, the better. It's not easy to be here so often. As I understand it, you have another child?"

Lexie nodded. "Heidi. She's eleven."

"Talk a lot to Heidi about the importance of the time little Henry needs. She's old enough that she can come visit and help keep you company while you're here, as long as she's quiet. I just can't stress enough the importance of you being part of Henry's recovery. Preemies take treatments better, are calmer and have a better chance for success when they know their parents are around. I don't want you to be seeing us giving him as many treatments next week. In order for that to happen, we need to see a lot of you at Henry's side."

"I wish like hell that I could believe you. But how am I supposed to do that when my son is about as responsive as a fallen tree?"

"JACKSON, WHY ARE YOU IN SUCH A HURRY?" Lexie asked. They were speeding up the hill toward Silver Bend, had been speeding since they'd left the hospital.

Jackson's jaw was clenched.

"Could we slow down?"

It almost seemed as if Jackson pressed the gas pedal harder. The wheels squealed around a sharp bend in the road. Lexie gasped and gripped the door handle, keeping her silence until they turned down their driveway, where he barely seemed to slow down.

"Jackson." Lexie almost cringed at the raw fear in her voice. She sounded weak and pitiful. She hadn't been any happier with the outcome at the hospital than he had been, but they had to work within the system, not fight it.

He brought the truck careening to a halt in front of the

garage. Dust billowed around the vehicle and then settled on the shiny black exterior, dulling its finish.

"It's over, Lex." His words sounded flat.

"How can you say that?" she whispered, feeling a wave of despair. How could he even think it?

"Back at the hospital when I referred to Henry as a fallen tree... Well, I'm the one who chopped him down. I'm the one who took away his chance at life before it ever began. I thought maybe I could get you to forgive me, but I can't even forgive myself."

"What are you talking about?"

"I'm no good for you. My being with you creates nothing but problems."

"That's not true."

"Isn't it? Shall I run through the litany of burdens I've given you to bear?" His green eyes were bloodshot. "I got you pregnant. You lost your job because of that."

"Jackson—"

"I gave you Marmy and Rufus because they were adorable little substitutes for the babies I couldn't give you. Maybe on some level I wanted that to be enough for you. Well, look how that turned out. Rufus ruined the yard you loved so much. And Marmy—" He swallowed. "Cleaning up after that little cat made Henry sick. It might even kill him. How's that for responsibility?"

Lexie took only a moment to process this news. "You couldn't know. I didn't realize I was pregnant until I was almost three months along."

He gripped the steering wheel tighter. "You want someone who's home every night for dinner. You want a normal life. I can't give that to you because *I'm* not normal."

"I want you to be happy. I don't care what job you have. I'll help you deal with this." Tears streamed down her face.

"I don't know how I'm going to deal with anything,

Lex. I just know I can't face it when I'm standing in the way of your happiness and Henry's progress.''

She shook her head. "You're not."

"I don't trust myself to fight a fire—how can you trust me not to go postal on you?"

"You're not crazy."

He pounded the steering wheel. "I can't do this anymore, Lex. I look at that sick baby and I don't know what I'd do if he died. I don't want him to wake up from that anesthesia. If he develops a personality and I become attached, I couldn't lose him. I'd go over the edge."

"Jackson, that means you care. You love him."

"No! It means I'm only holding on to sanity by a thread. Don't you see?" Jackson grabbed her shoulders. His fingers dug into her flesh. "I can't sleep at night because I lost Alek. I dream horrible things. Seeing Henry in that hospital is harder on me than what happened to Alek. If he dies..." Jackson's eyes glazed over and his breath came in ragged gasps. "If he dies, I'll be of no use to anyone. I can feel it."

"I won't let him die." She'd never let either of them go.

"No one can promise me that. Not the doctor. Not you." He released her. "I just need to go away. Permanently."

He was starting to scare her. "Don't do this."

"Do what? What am I supposed to do when I feel like crumpling at the mere mention of fire? I feel the same when I look at Henry. I'm helpless. It would have been better if I'd died in that fire in Russia."

His words sent a cold shiver down her spine. "Don't say things like that. Come inside, Jackson. I'll make a pot of coffee and we'll figure this out."

After a painful minute of silence, he shut off the engine. Lexie breathed a sigh of relief, and climbed out of the truck when he did. But he headed for the motor home, not the house.

Dread gripped her heart. "What are you doing?"

He ignored her and practically ran into the motor home. She followed, but by the time she got to the door, he'd packed up what few possessions he carried with him and was starting back down the steps. Taking off, just as she had feared.

"You're leaving me? Now?" She'd never felt so empty inside. "You can't. I need you."

Halfway to the truck, he stopped and turned around. In two deliberate steps, he stood in front of her. With a touch so gentle she almost cried out in anguish, Jackson cupped her chin in his palm. He pressed his lips to hers with featherlight care.

"You've never needed me as much as I've needed you, Lex." He pressed something into her hand. "You were right not to tell me about the other baby. You'll all be better off without me."

"Don't" was all she could manage to say, before he climbed into the truck and left her.

"GARRETT, GET OFF THE PHONE."

Ignoring Sirus's command, Jackson continued reading information to the personnel department in Boise. He had no idea how he ended up here after leaving Lexie. He supposed work was the only thing he had to hang on to at the moment, the only distraction that was keeping him sane.

"Now would be a good time," Sirus prompted.

Jackson looked up to find a crowd of people milling around his desk, including Sirus and Rob. They were all smiling at him as if he'd done something wonderful.

"What's up?" Jackson asked when he finished his call. He tried to look casual, but he had a sinking suspicion that they were going to congratulate him on becoming a father again—and Jackson wasn't celebrating that fact.

"You didn't tell us you were a hero, man. You're a wasted resource behind this desk," Rob said, slapping him on the back.

Jackson's gut clenched. "I'm far from a hero."

"Well, the Russian government seems to think you are. Turns out you saved four men in some wildland fire." Rob handed Jackson a small, hinged box just large enough to hold a man's watch.

Or a medal.

Jackson hadn't shown up for the medal ceremony in Siberia. He didn't deserve a reward. He hadn't gotten all his men out. He wasn't about to take any accolades now. Some detached part of his mind registered that the smiles of the Incident Command staff were starting to fade. His sixth sense, the one that used to serve him well in a fire, made him apprehensive. These people had been good to him. He should just take the damn medal and be done with it. They'd never know he was a coward if he just played nice, smiled and let them think what they would about it. Yet, his hands remained on the desk in front of him.

"Where'd that come from?" Jackson said finally.

"Today's mail from Boise. They called me immediately when they realized what it was." Sirus's voice was subdued. He reached for the box, which was still in Rob's huge hand. "May I?"

Jackson nodded stiffly.

"What happened?" someone in the back asked.

In a heartbeat, Jackson returned to that fateful day. The air was so dry and filled with ash, it almost hurt to breathe. Breniv's grim face was streaked with soot. The fires were converging, winds whipping from one direction to another, driving the fire and holding it back, teasing them with certain death.

Jackson wasn't even sure his idea was going to work.

He'd never heard of anything like it. It was just a last-ditch kind of plan. What if it didn't succeed?

He'd never see Lexie and Heidi again.

"Time to get back to it." Rob's resounding voice returned Jackson to the present.

Oh, hell. He'd been sitting here like an idiot with a roomful of people staring at him. He'd as good as hung a sign on himself saying, "I'm tainted goods."

Despite the awkwardness, or perhaps because of it, the group quickly dissipated, leaving Jackson and Sirus alone. Jackson's eyes drifted to the picture taped to his in-box, the one of him stuck in the motor home with Lexie smiling up at him.

"You're doing a great job here, Jackson. Might even replace me someday," Sirus said.

*Never.* Jackson barely kept from shouting the word. He was not a paper-pushing desk jockey. Even if he never fought another fire. This wasn't the job for him. He'd find something else.

Sirus gave Jackson a thoroughly speculative look. Finally, he asked, "That bad, eh?"

Jackson didn't pretend to misunderstand him. "I shouldn't have let them fight that fire in the first place. They were under-trained and under-equipped."

"Fuel?" Sirus asked, meaning what the fire had been burning.

"Mountain pine. Three years of drought. Dry as beached driftwood."

"You must have had something other than the men."

Jackson gave a rueful laugh. "Shovels with cracked wood handles. And one chainsaw. We shored up a crevice and used my fire shelter." The shelters were made to endure hours of heat, but no direct flames. They'd been lucky that the crevice had crossed the fire line they'd been making. Luckier still that no trees burned on the slope above had fallen on top of them.

"No fire trucks?"

Jackson was going to be sick. He couldn't take Sirus's criticism and he couldn't answer him, either.

"No bulldozers? No air support?"

Jackson looked the complete fool and he knew it.

"No escape route?"

"I know what you're going to say. We might just as well have gone out to fight that fire with our bare hands. But that's all they had. And I thought I could teach them something about fighting fires, something that would make a difference."

"Garrett—"

"It was idiotic. Egotistical. I know."

"Jackson," Sirus said again.

Here it comes. Sirus rarely called Jackson by his first name.

"You went out and fought a fire like they did in the old days and you came out alive?"

Jackson nodded. "Yes, sir."

"Hell, boy, I'd say that makes you a hero." Sirus thrust the medal under Jackson's nose.

"But—"

Sirus set the box on the desk in front of Jackson. "A firefighter assesses risk before, during and after a fire."

"But—"

"I want you to send out a report detailing what happened."

Jackson's spirits sank. Tell everyone what a fool he'd been?

Sirus put his hand on Jackson's shoulder. "Whatever's bothering you, son, let it go. You could have saved only yourself out there, but you didn't. You saved everyone by thinking on your feet. As a Hot Shot, that's what we do. It's the best we can hope for. Telling others could possibly save more lives."

"I didn't save everyone. Someone lost his nerve. Someone ran," Jackson admitted in a low voice, half hoping Sirus wouldn't hear. When Sirus didn't answer right away, Jackson looked up. The anguish in Sirus's eyes was almost too much to bear, and when he started talking, it became worse.

"Twenty-five years ago, I was fighting a fire in Montana. We weren't able to convince a civilian to stop trying to save his home." Sirus swallowed and looked out the tent door. Jackson realized this must be the fire that his mother had spoken of. "That kind of thing doesn't leave you easily. It can eat your insides. I should know. It ate away at me until there was nothing left of me to give. To the job or to my marriage."

Jackson had never even suspected Sirus had lost his nerve. When Jackson fought under the man's command, Sirus had always been brave and decisive. Yet, his words made Jackson more painfully aware of his own situation with Lexie. Sirus hadn't managed to make either of his marriages work. Why would Jackson believe he could save his own?

"We lost a lot of men back then through attrition," Sirus continued. "At the time, posttraumatic stress syndrome in the men who'd fought in Vietnam was just starting to hit the press. I read an article and it was as if they were writing about me. I sent in for a pamphlet. I talked to someone. I fought myself to gain control and live the life I wanted. And it was worth every bead of sweat, every agonizing bad dream, because I was able to get my life back."

Sirus brought his tormented gaze back to Jackson. "You can't save someone who's decided not to be saved, or even someone whose time has come. We're not superheroes who can walk across flames and not get burned. If you aren't afraid when you're out there, that's when you should worry—that's when you put lives in danger. We're just men in control of our fear.

"This could be the end...or just a bump in the road. You might want to think about that." Sirus tapped the box with the medal, then walked out of the tent. It didn't take long for Jackson to hear Sirus ordering people around with his usual confidence, as if he hadn't just bared his soul.

His mother, he realized, was in good hands with Sirus.

Slowly, Jackson picked up the small box and opened it. The polished brass glimmered in the fluorescent lights of the coordination center. He ran his thumb over the round medal, over the Russian characters proclaiming the honor of his deed, over the traditional relief of a fire helmet. For the first time since that fateful fire, Jackson allowed himself to begin to believe in the decisions he'd made, to begin to believe in himself again.

SOMEONE WAS IN LEXIE'S ROOM. Light footsteps crossed the carpet. From underneath the covers, Lexie couldn't bring herself to look. It wouldn't be Jackson. If it was Heidi, Lexie would have to put on a brave front she was far from feeling. Nope, it was better to hide and pretend she was asleep.

Something settled on the nightstand next to her. A glass, perhaps?

"Poor thing," Mary murmured.

Lexie rolled over and drew the comforter down to just below her eyes.

"Did I wake you?" Mary's features were drawn with concern.

"It's probably time for me to get up anyway." Lexie stayed beneath the covers, unable to bring herself to move.

Mary glanced over at the empty bassinet. "He'll come home soon."

She meant Henry.

In her mind's eye, Lexie saw the many tubes and wires

protruding from the tiny thing that was her baby, swollen from the drugs that might save his life.

Then she relived Jackson's departure. She was heart-broken over a different Garrett today.

"It's hard to imagine him coming home right now, but I don't think he'll make it if I don't keep the faith." Her words sounded hollow. What did Lexie have to show for all her bravado? Nothing. Instead of cuddling with her husband and baby, she was alone. "Jackson's given up on him." She didn't add that Jackson had given up on him-self.

"It's hard for a man to have a son that's sick. They expect so much from their boys." Mary rose gently to Jackson's defense as her fingers traced the edge of the bassinet. "Something happened to him in Russia. Some-thing that's made him more responsible to his family. But I'm afraid that same something left him aching inside."

Lexie reached for the glass of water Mary had brought her and took a sip to buy some time. But Jackson's mother deserved to know why her son was hurting. "Someone died in a fire he was on. He feels responsible."

"It's a step in the right direction, talking to you about it," Mary said. She didn't seem surprised by the news.

Lexie wondered if Sirus had told Mary about Jackson last night. Jackson's boss had to know what was going on with him. He'd talked with Jackson before they all left for the hospital.

Lexie drew the covers down to her chin. "He doesn't think he can fight fires anymore."

Mary's eyes instantly filled with tears. "I know."

"He didn't just give up on Henry. He left this morning. For good."

"Oh dear." Mary sank to the edge of the bed.

"He said he wasn't any use to us," Lexie admitted mis-erably, sitting up.

Mary considered Lexie's words carefully. "Perhaps he

just needs time to work this out on his own. He loves you something awful—"

"It's not enough." Lexie bit her lip, but she couldn't stop the worst from spilling out. "He broke down yesterday after discovering a little roadside fire. I've never seen him so lost. He refuses to bond with Henry in case…in case Henry doesn't make it."

"Give him a little time. If he can't go back to what he loves, he's got to find something else that makes him happy."

"I could make him happy," Lexie whispered. "If he worked nine to five."

Mary reached across the bed and patted her leg. "Have I ever told you how I came to own the Pony?"

Lexie shook her head.

"It was never my dream to own the local hangout—it was my husband's dream. That last year before he died, Jeremy worked there on weekends because we were short on money." Mary stared out the window, but Lexie knew she wasn't looking at the view. "He loved listening to the firemen talk, dishing out good food and advice. He always talked about buying the place. Not that it was possible with two kids and a wife to feed, and a mortgage to pay."

"But he bought it."

Mary smiled gently. "No, my dear. I bought it with the money from his life insurance settlement. Me?" She pointed to herself. "I was all for crawling into a hole and giving up on life when he died. But I needed a purpose and my kids needed me to have a steady income, so I went on to fulfill his dream."

"I can't imagine you not running the Pony." Mary was the heart of the restaurant.

"I can. That place has taken the better part of my life. I wanted to paint and travel. Can't do any of that when I'm living the life someone else dreamed of. I've painted one mural in eighteen years, the one on the wall of the Pony.''

"You're saying I'm going to make him miserable, aren't you? If he takes a regular job, he'll be living my dream and not his. But Mary, I don't think he can go back on the line. You should have seen him last night. I love him. What am I going to do?'' Lexie asked, flopping back on the bed and pulling the covers back up over her head.

She'd resigned herself to the fact that her starry dreams of owning a small business wouldn't get off the ground. Now Jackson was giving up on his dream of being a Hot Shot. One part of her wanted him to go back, to see the dark circles beneath his eyes gone forever. The smaller, more selfish part of her wanted him home for dinner every night and safe.

But the Jackson who would do the latter wasn't the Jackson she loved.

"Don't give up hope for either one of your Garrett men. As long as you hold on to that, you're sure to have your two men home to stay.''

# CHAPTER FOURTEEN

IN SEARCH OF COFFEE, Jackson went out to the chow line in mid-afternoon. Base camp was quieter at this time of day. Not that it was ever quiet, but now many crews were out fighting the fire.

A woman was restocking the snack bar with cookies, chips and soda. She set aside several bags of chips that were a dark-green color. Something about the shade caught Jackson's eye. He detoured closer and picked up a bag of vinegar chips.

"Better get one before they're gone," she said.

"Are these popular?"

"Only with Rob Hudson. He's addicted to these. No one else seems to like them."

Jackson smiled. That's where he'd seen them before. Rob couldn't work without at least two bags open on his desk.

"I'm a barbecue man, myself." Jackson continued on to the coffee table.

As he filled his cup, a strong gust of wind came up from the south, tossing several bags of potato chips out onto the ground.

Jackson swore as his coffee overflowed and burned his fingers. He tossed his cup into a trash can and hurried over to the sodas, then buried his hand in the ice. All the while, he tested the wind on his face.

Jackson pulled his hand out of the ice and rubbed it absently on his Nomex pants.

Movement to his left caught his eye.

"If it isn't the vinegar chip man," he muttered to himself. Grabbing a can of cola, he veered across camp to meet Rob as he climbed out of a Forest Service truck.

"Hey, Rob. Have you been out checking on crews?"

Rob reached back into the truck for a clipboard loaded with wrinkled papers. "Yeah, I didn't like the tally of workers on a water buffalo crew. I wanted to make sure they really had twenty people show up, you know?"

"Where were they working?"

Rob laughed and gave Jackson a look that said who was in command. "They're climbing up the slopes today in and around Falcon Ridge."

"I thought we were playing it conservatively on this one and staying off the ridges." Falcon Ridge was flanked by particularly steep slopes that created a wind funnel down to the river. Rob chuckled. "Not anymore. The brass at NIFC wants this fire out."

"Didn't anyone check the meteorologist reports? The winds are shifting from the south. If there's fire activity below, near the river, it could blow up just like we saw that first day in the helicopter." No one could outrun such a firestorm.

"The winds shifted?" Rob did a double take before flipping through the papers on his clipboard. "Naw. Look. It says winds from the west."

"I don't give a shit what the report says—look at the flagpole if you don't believe me."

Rob looked up at the flag, currently blowing on the north side of the pole. "I sure hope you're wrong, man."

The pair hurried back to the Command tent, where no one was sitting at the meteorologist's station.

"Vicki, where's the meteorologist on duty today?"

"She's out in the field adjusting some equipment."

Exchanging looks of frustration, Rob and Jackson bent

over the meteorologist's screen. They knew enough to read the basics.

"Damn." Rob pounded the desk. "Winds from the south. I didn't want you to be right."

The latest fire map was posted on the wall. Jackson went over and checked to see where fires had been reported, then he looked at the time it was updated. "Three hours ago," he said in disgust.

"Nothing new has come in through the radio. Maybe the wind is playing tricks with us down here," Rob said hopefully.

"Vicki." Jackson glanced around. "Have you seen Socrates?"

"He took some of the IC team out to evaluate the fire. He heard reports of fires starting back up and wanted to assess for himself what's been going wrong." Vicki turned her full attention back to her computer. "They should have been back already. Maybe that's them now."

Jackson heard a chopper in the distance. He went outside, shading his eyes as he searched for the helicopter in the smoke-blanketed sky. Unlike some of the refurbished troop carriers, this helicopter was small, not equipped to carry more than a few men.

Jackson ran across the compound to the small airstrip, Rob at his heels, as the chopper landed.

"Incident Command. Where've you been?" Jackson called over the decelerating blades.

The pilot wasn't anyone Jackson knew, and therefore Jackson wasn't someone the aviator might snap-to for. With personnel rotations starting, to reduce overtime, this could be the pilot's first day of work.

The aviator assessed him from behind mirrored sunglasses before answering. "I've been over by Deadwood Reservoir. I need to gas up and then I'm back out. I'm pulling water drops and flying rescue back up."

"Have you heard anything about Falcon Ridge?" Although there were fires around Falcon Ridge, nothing had come over the radio about any new fires in the area, but radio coverage was spotty throughout the mountainous region, so they could have missed something. Sometimes the quickest updates came from the pilots, who listened to the fire-crew radio frequency to know where to dump fire retardant and water, and when to make an emergency pickup.

The pilot looked at him funny. "Yeah, I think I did. Just as I was coming in. Something about the lower ridge starting to burn. How'd you know?"

Rob swore.

"Lucky guess. What about the Silver Bend Hot Shots or Socrates? Any location on them?"

The pilot shook his head. "Sorry, man."

Jackson jogged back to the Command tent and radio dispatch, Rob along with him.

"Where's Socrates?" Jackson demanded.

The radio operator on duty, a small, wiry young man, looked at Jackson with raised brows and rolled a toothpick to the corner of his mouth. "The Big Kahuna? He's out on some ridge with Jules and Amy."

"Which ridge?" Jackson asked tersely.

"I don't know, man. I want to say Falcon, but they've been moving. I lost contact about thirty minutes ago, which means they could be on any ridge on the far side of the range from us." He chewed on the toothpick.

"Have you heard any updates on the fire out that way?"

"There was some scuttle about fires on lower slopes, but no one's sent up the red flag. Hang on." He stopped chewing on the toothpick and pressed the headset against his ear.

Jackson waited impatiently, while the radio operator scribbled something illegible onto a sheet of paper.

"Well, chief, looks like you need to reassign forces to the southern slope of Falcon Ridge."

"Not the south," Rob lamented, rubbing a hand over his shaved head.

"Any word on Socrates and his team?" Jackson knew that Sirus could take care of himself in a fire, but if he had taken up anyone without fire experience, they'd be in trouble.

"That's the kicker. I have unconfirmed reports that there's a team trapped on top of the ridge. No telling which crew it is."

In the distance, Jackson heard the helicopter take off. "Rob—"

"I know, I know. Order the chopper that just left to dump water on the crews working the southern slope of Falcon Ridge."

Jackson nodded, pointing at the radio operator. "Find out who's on that ridge. And locate Socrates."

"Sure, I can try." The toothpick worked its way around the radio operator's mouth again.

Jackson leaned in until he was nose-to-nose with the smaller man. "Try. Try real hard. Or I'll have the next copter drop you off on the ridge to check it out personally."

Spinning away, Jackson called across the tent to Vicki. "Which crews are most likely on those ridges?"

"No." Rob strode across the room. "Which teams were working the south side of the ridge this morning?"

Vicki rummaged through sheets of paper on her desk, ran her mottled, manicured finger down a list. "I was afraid of that," she said, looking up at them apologetically. "Silver Bend."

The walls of the Command tent seemed to close in on Jackson. He struggled for breath. His team. His men. His friends.

He looked out the tent door, to the flag on the flagpole whipping in the wind. It could be nothing. He could be panicking for no reason.

Except, his team had almost died in a similar situation a few years ago, when Jackson's intuition and quick decisions had saved them, along with the rookie who was now selling shoes in Boise.

Jackson picked up the telephone and called Boise for the latest update on winds in the area. When the fire had started, the meteorologists had placed equipment at various points around the region. The camp meteorologist on duty was out somewhere, but the data would also be fed electronically back to the computers at Boise. When Jackson got the update, it didn't make him happy.

"The winds are coming right up the river from the south."

"Do you think they're all right?" Vicki asked.

"Of course they're all right." But Rob didn't sound very confident.

Jackson ignored the question. Every muscle in his body was tense. "Pull them out." Jackson turned to the radio operator. "I don't want anyone on a ridge on the south side. The winds are too dangerous."

"Jackson, think about what you're doing. You don't have the authority," Rob said. "If you overreact now—"

"Who does have the authority? You?" Jackson demanded. "Then, give the command—because I'm going on record as advising you to pull them out. Now!" Jackson could feel the doubt in the room. They'd all witnessed his breakdown this morning.

Still, Rob said nothing.

Jackson pointed at the radio operator. "Start relaying the information now."

"Okay, boss man. I'll see if I can't raise someone who knows where they are."

The sound of a helicopter approaching brought Jackson's head up, and he charged back out of the tent, grabbing a handheld radio and his hard hat on the way.

LEXIE DRAGGED HERSELF into the kitchen and noticed the item on the counter immediately—her high school track medal. After Jackson had driven off, she'd dropped it there without even looking at it or thinking about the medal's significance.

"He's giving up," she said, fingering her medal, unable to believe what the small, cool bit of metal meant. His words had broken her heart. The sight of her medal shattered what little hope she had for Jackson's return.

"What'd you say, Mom?"

"He's not coming back," Lexie repeated. She knew Jackson still loved her because he hadn't left his wedding ring. But the medal was another story. He'd listened to her and knew she'd been looking for signs. He'd left her a big one.

*Jackson isn't coming back.*

There was more at stake here than having the man she loved return to her. He was giving up on himself. Suddenly, Lexie realized she couldn't let Jackson become anything less than the man she'd loved when they were married, the man who had bravely worked his way to the top of the fire-fighting ranks because he loved it and had confidence in himself.

Lexie blinked back tears. Stripped of his self-worth, Jackson was in danger if he went out on the fire line. A desperate man with nothing to lose was a hazard to his safety and that of his team. How many times had she heard Jackson say that?

Frantically, Lexie searched through the bits of paper and cards next to the telephone until she found the number she was looking for, and punched it in.

"Incident Command, Garden Valley," a voice droned at the other end of the line.

"I'm trying to find Jackson Garrett. He works at IC with Sirus Socrath."

"Lexie, what's the matter?" Mary asked from the hallway.

Lexie held up a hand for silence.

There was a pause. "Who is this?"

"Lexie Garrett. His...his wife. Please, it's important that I speak with him right away."

There was the sound of the phone being covered, then muffled voices, then the phone was passed to someone else. Something had happened. Something too horrible to imagine.

"Mrs. Garrett?"

"Yes." Her reply was barely audible.

"This is Vicki at IC. Jackson went out to the line a few minutes ago."

Lexie covered her eyes with her hand. He went out to fight a fire? When she thought of the things he'd said to her last night and this morning, and added the things he'd left here at home, she was sure he had a death wish, that he believed she, Heidi and Henry were better off without him.

"I need to speak with him right away. Can't you patch me into a radio?"

"I'm sorry. No."

Lexie tried to remain calm. There had to be some way to know what was happening. "Did he go out with a crew?" He'd be safe if he was with Logan. She had to believe that.

"No."

"Please tell me why he went out." Maybe there was a valid reason he'd faced his fear. But her request was met with silence.

"Please." Lexie didn't filter any of the fear from her voice. "I'm not the kind of woman to panic without a reason. I have to speak with my husband."

Vicki sighed and lowered her voice. "I'll be in so much

trouble if they find out I told you. We're not supposed to reveal this information."

"Thank you." Lexie breathed a sigh of relief.

"We can't be sure at this point, but we think the Command Team and at least one Hot Shot crew might be in danger. Jackson seemed to think they were."

"The Command Team?" Lexie echoed, her eyes irresistibly drawn to Mary. Sirus was in danger, too. She knew Jackson would do anything to save people in trouble, particularly his friends, even if it meant risking his own life. "Was it...is the Silver Bend crew out there too?"

"We just don't know enough. I can't say any more."

Somehow, Lexie managed to thank Vicki and hang up the telephone. Mary sagged against the wall, looking pale and scared.

"Mom?" Heidi put her hand on Lexie's arm, her eyes wide with fear. "Is Dad going to be okay?"

Lexie couldn't reassure Heidi when her own heart couldn't shake the feeling that something was terribly wrong.

THE HELICOPTER LANDED at the small airstrip to his left. Jackson ran up to the bird while the rotors were still spinning, and recognized Wyatt Chappel, the pilot who had taken the Incident Command team up on Jackson's first day at base camp.

"What duty are you pulling today?" Jackson yelled over the whine of the slowing engine.

Wyatt pulled off his headset. "People mover, but I'm done for the day. Any more hours and it's overtime."

"Your wife is going to be happy, because I need you to take me up." Jackson climbed in the helicopter. "To Falcon Ridge."

Wyatt looked doubtful for a moment. "Do you have authorization?"

"Yes," Jackson lied. "If you've got enough gas, fire it back up and let's go."

"Okay, but just so you know, if you're not authorized, I'm billing you personally."

"Just go." That was the least of his worries.

They weren't in the air more than a few minutes when Wyatt glanced over at Jackson, his expression half hidden behind dark glasses and a headset. "Falcon Ridge, right?"

The knot in Jackson's stomach cinched. "Yeah."

"I've got a report of shelter deployment and a water drop. It's too hot to pick up. Might cool by the time we get there."

Jackson swore under his breath. The Hot Shots had fire shelters, but he had no idea where Socrates and the rest of the IC team were, or if they had fire shelters with them.

"I CAN'T TAKE NOT KNOWING. Heidi, get your things." Having made her decision, Lexie took Mary by the shoulders. "You can stay or you can come along, but I need you to be strong."

Mary nodded, holding back tears. She clutched her purse so tightly that her knuckles were white.

"Mom, where are we going?"

"To bring your father and Grandpa Sirus home." Lexie walked swiftly outside, clutching the keys to her SUV.

Heidi hopped into the front seat, while Mary climbed more slowly into the back. Before she could get the door closed, Rufus leaped across Mary and into the other rear seat.

"Mom, get him out."

"No time. He's coming along for the ride." Lexie backed the SUV out of the driveway, spewing gravel.

"THERE!" Jackson pointed at a spot to the south of the ridge. About twenty fire shelters had been deployed. From above, they looked like man-size baked potatoes wrapped in aluminum foil. Tools were scattered around the shelters, burned and melted into uselessness.

"Why aren't they coming out?" Wyatt yelled at him over the roar of the engine.

Jackson was wondering the same thing, trying to convince himself everyone was safe. Spot fires were retreating around the shelters. Just the sight of the islands of wavering fire at random points on the ground made Jackson's pulse race. If there had been a blowup and the wall of flames had stayed too long—

"Here they come." Wyatt interrupted Jackson's demoralizing train of thought.

Sure enough, one by one, the shake-and-bake shelters were opened, revealing the yellow shirts and gritty faces of Hot Shots. They stood slowly, as if dazed, taking in their surroundings, holding water bottles and backpacks. Then they looked up and waved, clearly more than ready to get off that ridge. Jackson watched closely. But there were still a few shelters where the occupant hadn't come out. As they flew nearer, Jackson could make out firefighters by their familiar stature.

The Silver Bend Hot Shots had been found.

Jackson hopped out of the chopper as soon as it was close enough to the ground and jogged up the ridge to the team's tree-chopping expert, who was crouching over a lump of twisted, melted metal—the charred remains of his chainsaw. "Chainsaw, what happened?"

Chainsaw stood up. "Somehow a fire started down below. The winds were pushing down the mountain. So Command decided to back-burn up on top, thinking that there'd be nothing up here left to burn when the two fires converged and that the wind would be on our side. Only, wouldn't you know—" Chainsaw's voice dripped with sarcasm "—the winds shifted."

Back-burning was a risky proposition. You started a fire, containing it on one side in the hopes that when the two fires met, they'd burn themselves out. But you had to gamble on the wind not changing its mind and blowing both fires back at you.

"Then we had one helluva fire racing up on us, and Tin Man radios that there's one coming up the next slope, torching trees like matches." Chainsaw shook his head.

Jackson knew the other side of the ridge had experienced a quick brushfire a few days ago, turning everything on the ground to ash, leaving trees primed to burn but little else as fuel. Fires had been known to race through treetops quickly, until the entire canopy was burning—a potential trap to anyone unlucky enough to be trapped on the ground.

The burly man sucked down some water. "Could have used you here."

Jackson nodded. The ground felt warm through his boots. Smoke irritated his nostrils. It was all so familiar. His stomach roiled and his palms felt sweaty, but if he concentrated on breathing steadily, he was okay. "Is Socrates with you?"

"Negative. He and his group were on the other side with Tin Man. Maybe they made it to safety before we were trapped."

Jackson walked past a dazed Rookie and slapped him on the back. "You all right, kid?"

"Yeah." Rookie gazed in awe at the smoldering landscape. "It was nothing like training. I could hear the fire roll right over me and I could barely breathe. It was like the fire sucked all the oxygen out of my shelter."

"Now you've got a story of your own to tell, don't you?"

Rookie's grin was priceless. "Hey, I guess I do."

Jackson continued trudging up the hill. He avoided looking directly at the spot fires still burning mere feet away and focused on finding Sirus and Logan.

"We missed that sixth sense of yours, Golden," Spider

said as he passed. "Any word where we should head for pickup?"

"Follow the chopper." Jackson gestured to Wyatt, hovering above in his helicopter, to land.

The helicopter moved over to a small plateau on the ridge above them.

"Thanks, Golden. Everybody up, let's move!" Spider called down the slope to the others.

"Wait, is everyone accounted for?"

Spider looked up and down the mountain. "I count nineteen. Tin Man would be twenty. Socrates had two more with him."

"Get as many as you can into the chopper, those most in need of medical attention first." Jackson knew from experience that the shelters couldn't always protect a firefighter from burns. If the wind whipped a shelter up even an inch, the flames would lick their way inside. "Have Wyatt call for another pickup, if he hasn't already. There's a third side to this ridge that hasn't burned yet and I'm not taking any chances."

"Where are you going?" Spider asked.

"To find Socrates and Tin Man."

"Wait for me, Golden." Spider hustled after him.

LEXIE WANTED TO CRY with frustration. Her gas gauge read empty, but there was no gas station in sight—just trees and mountainous slopes on either side of the two-lane highway. Her breasts were so swollen that they ached. She needed to pump. And the three of them still had a few steep miles to go.

"You don't think he's going to die out there, do you, Mom? I mean, he left you his good luck charm."

Lexie couldn't help but think about Alek running into the flame to end it all rather than face his fear. Had Jackson sunk to such depths that he'd choose to go out that way?

"I'm sure he's fine. I just want to make sure he knows we aren't letting him go." Lexie reached for Heidi's hand and gave it a quick squeeze. "You do want him to come home to stay, don't you?"

"Heck, yeah."

"He assured me they take every precaution when they go out. What do you suppose went wrong?" Mary asked.

"I don't know. I'm sure Jackson will find them all," Lexie replied, gritting her teeth as a car honked and passed them going uphill. She didn't dare push the gas pedal down any farther for fear she'd run out of gas and strand them all.

"There were others?" Mary clutched the back of Lexie's seat.

"Apparently so," Lexie said grimly.

In the distance, she saw a helicopter speeding off toward the fire. The sight gave her chills.

LEAVING CHAINSAW IN CHARGE of the half of the Hot Shot team still waiting for pickup, Jackson and Spider plodded up to the summit and down the other side, calling for Sirus and Logan.

"These trees were standing with needles this morning," Spider pointed out.

Now they were no more than charred spikes, some towering, some fallen. Occasionally, the singed trunk of thicker brush, no larger than baseball bats, stuck out of the ground. Rocks, some large enough to be called boulders, some no more than garden accents, had been scorched black.

Jackson gestured to a pair of petrified, blackened squirrels poised as if in flight, apparently unable to outrun the rolling march of the fire. "The fire must have come through fast."

"Quicker than I want to remember. We might not have

made it if that helicopter hadn't dumped water on us right as the blowup was beginning.

"You think there are roots burning underground?" Jackson asked. The land beneath his feet was still warm. Heat rose off the ash as if from a banked fire. Jackson was grateful for his helmet and Rookie's borrowed gloves—slim protection if he fell, but protection nonetheless.

The devastation called to mind other fires Jackson had fought, not just the ill-fated fire in Russia. Sometimes nature needed to clear away the growth to renew itself. Jackson wondered if he could somehow cleanse himself the same way.

As they rounded a bend, they heard shouting.

Pausing, Jackson wiped sweat from his forehead and scanned the steep incline above. Pine trees had toppled over the ridge and still burned, lying across a bed of rock. A patch of silver beneath the blazing, crossed giant trunks caught Jackson's eye. He ran over the hot, smoldering ash.

"Sirus? Logan?"

"Over here! Help!" The trapped fire shelter shook. Only the rocky overhang kept the crossed trees from direct contact with the aluminum shelter. But that didn't mean the aluminum wouldn't eventually melt from prolonged contact, trapping the group behind a wall of heat and choking smoke.

"Who's there? Is anybody injured?" Jackson called as he slid to a stop a few feet from the burning wood. The flame heated his exposed face as if he were being sunburned.

"Jackson?" Jackson barely recognized Sirus's voice.

"Yes. How many are back there?"

Cheers rose from behind the shelter.

"Four! All four of us," Sirus called.

"Spider, radio for help." Fear rippled through Jackson's bowels. He willed himself to ignore it.

"It's getting hot in here, Golden." There was no mistaking the urgency in Logan's voice. "Get us the hell outta here!"

"I've got no reception here, Golden. I need to move higher." Spider's face looked grim.

"All right, but hurry."

Spider jogged farther up the mountain.

Concentrating on the ground at his feet and nothing else, Jackson climbed around and above the flaming tree trunks until he stood on the overhang itself, nearly dwarfed beneath the roots of one tree. The pine tree had snapped out of the ground, roots and all. These had been mighty giants of the forest, perhaps eighty feet tall and five feet around. There was no way one man could budge them. Most of the treetop was gone, probably charred from the four-hundred-degree wall of fire that the blowup had created.

Forcing himself to lean out over the ledge, Jackson looked at the huge fiery trunks critically. The only thing he had going for him was the sharply dropping slope beneath the ledge. If he managed to shift the root tree out of the way, given the steepness of the bank, the tree under it might just roll free.

Jackson placed his gloved hands on two of the thick roots, still damp from being beneath the earth and not yet on fire. He had to turn his face away to breathe as the wind churned the smoke and flames at him. He pushed, trying not to think about the fire so near. The tree barely moved.

Why would it? It was huge.

Jackson squeezed his eyes shut. He would not leave them to burn alive down there. But there was no time to wait for Spider. If they were to be saved, they had only him.

*Hopeless.*

Jackson's knees gave out on him. He collapsed to the ground.

The voices of his trapped friends carried up to him. How

would he tell his mother that he couldn't save Sirus? How would he explain to Logan's family—to Tess and Hannah who were already about to lose their mother—that he hadn't been able to do anything to rescue him, that he'd been as helpless as a baby at the scene?

Opening his eyes, Jackson drew a shuddering breath.

The answer was, he couldn't. He had to try something.

He stood on shaky legs that felt as if he'd just run a marathon and peered once more over the edge of the overhang at the burning trees. The position of the two trees seemed precarious, as if it wouldn't take much to send them careening down the mountainside.

It was one heck of a sharp incline. Nothing was burning, thank you, God. There were, however, a couple of nasty-looking boulders that might get in the way.

He hadn't climbed a tree since he was ten, but Jackson mounted the rooted tree with the agility of a drunken monkey until he stood at its base and looked down the burning trunk, down the steep slope, wondering how his mother had managed to raise such a foolish man. With a final loving thought to his family—to Heidi who could bring sunshine to a cloudy day, to Lexie who loved him despite his lack of courage, to Henry who would need his mother's strength—Jackson launched himself straight up in the air, landing with a thud on the trunk.

The tree was stubborn and barely moved.

Balancing himself as he imagined surfers did, Jackson inched farther down the trunk toward the center of the tree-formed X, where the second trunk met the one he stood on. Closer to the fire.

*Don't look at the flames.*

Steadying his breathing, he jumped again. As soon as he'd regained his balance, the tree began to groan and crack, then it started rolling and sliding down the slope, picking up momentum—a burning surfboard. For several seconds, Jackson managed to stay on the wild ride, then he was pitched into the air.

As if in slow motion, Jackson saw the boulder. Knew he was going to smack into it. Made a weak attempt to roll away.

And then, nothing.

## CHAPTER FIFTEEN

A HELICOPTER LANDED at the small airstrip at the rear of base camp as Lexie pulled near the large tent she assumed housed Incident Command. When she put the vehicle in park, it coughed, sputtered and died with a loud backfire that had the entire camp jumping.

"Way to make an entrance, Mom."

"I only wish your Dad were here to see it." Lexie leaped out of the driver's seat. "Let me hold Rufus, Mary, so he won't get out when you do."

"Hey, isn't that Chainsaw? And Rookie?" Heidi pointed.

Indeed, the Silver Bend Hot Shot crew was pouring out of the helicopter. Their faces were streaked with soot and their yellow shirts dirty.

"They don't all have their packs," Mary noted.

Lexie knew enough about fire fighting to know that the crew only abandoned their packs if they deployed their fire shelters too quickly. The use of shelters was a last resort for safety, and if they couldn't get rid of the combustibles they carried, such as the flares they used to start controlled burns and the gas for the chainsaws, they tossed their packs as far away from themselves as they could.

"Jackson," she murmured, searching for him in the crowd of men, but she didn't see him. Or Logan.

"I don't see Sirus," Mary whispered.

The group—it was only about half the team, walked

slowly away from the airstrip, toward tables laden with food and drink.

"Chainsaw! Rookie! Have you seen my Dad?" Heidi shrieked, hopping out of the SUV and giving Rufus an opening to leap out after her.

Lexie forced her weak muscles into action and grabbed the dog by his collar as he hit the ground. "Oh, no you don't, fella. Back inside."

Mary climbed out while Lexie wrestled the dog back into the seat and rolled the windows down a bit for air.

Everyone in camp, including the Silver Bend Hot Shots, turned around. Heidi ran the short distance between them.

"That you, Runt?" Chainsaw asked.

"Yes." She leaped into his arms and repeated her question. "Have you seen my Dad?"


*"DAD! DAD!"*

*Jackson moaned and tried to open his eyes. The light was blinding. He squeezed them shut again.*

*"Dad, wake up!"*

*Jackson frowned. That wasn't Heidi's voice. It was the voice of a boy. A teenage boy.*

*"You've got to get up, Dad. They need you."*

*Jackson opened his eyes. He still lay on the ground, his shoulder half buried in ash, his head propped awkwardly against the boulder. A teenager knelt before him. A boy with bright green eyes and a shock of dark hair that tumbled over his right forehead in a wispy cowlick.*

*With a groan, Jackson pushed himself to a kneeling position, leaning on the boulder as the world spun crazily around him.*

*The teen had already stood. He glanced toward the burning trunk still blocking the overhang, then back to Jackson. "Dad. Hurry."*

*There was something familiar about the teen…something…* "Henry?"

*"Yeah."* Towering above Jackson, he smiled self-consciously. *"You're still needed, Dad. Can't give up now."*

"Come on, Golden! Wake up and tell me how you moved that gigantic tree out of the way." Spider helped Jackson to his feet.

Jackson pushed up on wobbly legs. "How...?" His head pounded relentlessly. It hurt like hell to breathe in more than shallow gasps. He looked around. Henry was gone.

"I don't know how you did it, but it would save a lot of time if you told me how you planned on moving that other granddaddy of a tree."

"Is he okay?" Sirus called.

"He's seen better days, but he's moving," Spider answered.

"Don't you give up, either, son," Jackson mumbled to himself, staggering back up the slope. Once he made it off this mountain, he was going straight to the hospital to see Henry.

"What's the ETA on that chopper, Spider?" Jackson paused at the ledge to catch his breath.

"Soon, sir." Spider squinted up at him. "Are you losing it? You're talking to yourself."

Jackson managed a weak laugh that sent shafts of pain across his rib cage. "Nope. I think I'm getting it back."

"IF IT ISN'T THE GARRETT WOMEN, come to call," Chainsaw said with a grunt as Heidi launched herself at him for the second time.

"My heroes. You each deserve a hug for whatever happened to you today." Mary went around the group and hugged them tight, followed by a grinning Heidi. "What fine young men you are."

"Where's Jackson?" Lexie asked Chainsaw, keeping her voice low.

"Golden brought a chopper to rescue us after we deployed shelters. Don't know how he knew we were in trouble." Chainsaw's expression turned grim. "He's still up on the ridge looking for Socrates and Tin Man. Spider's with him, and the rest of the team came on the previous ride. The chopper was going back as soon as he refueled."

The helicopter blades started up with a *whir*. Lexie took a step toward the airstrip, but Chainsaw held her arm.

"No civilians allowed on board, Mrs. G." He looked apologetic. "Why don't we head over to the chow line and get a drink while we wait? It won't take long."

"How do you know that?" Lexie wasn't so sure Jackson wanted to return.

Chainsaw shrugged. "He's Golden. It's like he's got this gift for reading the flame. I've never been scared when he's in charge."

One of the other Silver Bend Hot Shots laughed, and punched Chainsaw in the arm.

"Okay, I'll eat that. I've been plenty scared." Chainsaw rubbed his bulging biceps. "But seriously, when he's out there, you know you can handle whatever Mother Nature throws your way."

Lexie was too worried to derive much comfort from Chainsaw's praise. Jackson was still up there on a burning mountain. And he had nothing, not even his self-confidence, to save him.

JACKSON MANAGED TO CRAWL back up to the overhang, despite lungs he couldn't fill with air without stabbing pain, and vision that sometimes blurred with blood from his temple. His heart was racing and he was drenched in sweat.

"I don't know how you sent that first puppy tumbling down the hill, but you don't look so good," Spider commented.

"I surfed the first tree down the mountain." Jackson looked critically at the remaining burning tree.

"Damn, I'm sorry I missed that. What a ride that would have been."

"Yeah, but the landing sucked. I don't think surfing's going to work for this one. It's already splintered in too many places."

Bracing himself on the ground, Jackson waited for Spider to position himself a few feet away. At the count of three, they kicked at the remaining burning trunk. It only took a few good blows for the main trunk of the tree to give up and pitch down the slope.

Cries of joy filled the air as the now-blackened fire shelter was flung down the hillside after the trees.

Sirus came out first. The incline was so steep that he slid about ten feet, ankle-deep in the ash. He turned and squinted up at Jackson, holding his left arm close to his side.

"What happened to you?" Jackson asked.

"I fell down the mountain trying to help everybody get in."

Two women poked their heads out of the cave, then slid, one after the other, down the slope, just missing crashing into Sirus. Ash floated in the air as they passed.

"Can someone get me out of this coyote den? Now that the fire's gone, I'm no longer happy with the smell of coyote shit."

"Are there coyotes in there?" Spider joked, sliding down the slope for a peek.

"Are you hurt, Tin Man?" Careful of his pounding head and shaky balance, Jackson half slid, half climbed around the overhang to the small cave. He leaned over to look inside, and caught himself as the world spun. He opened his eyes slowly, peering into the shadowy, rank-smelling cave.

"Damn good to see you, too," Logan said with a grimace. He was sitting awkwardly on the ground.

"What happened to you?" Jackson asked.

"He cartwheeled down the mountain trying to reach me before the fire swept in," Sirus admitted. "Broke his leg."

"We were lucky this ridge had been burned before," Logan admitted gamely. "I never would have spotted this cave if it had been covered with brush."

"And we wouldn't have survived at all if you hadn't told me about your little Russian escapade this morning," Sirus added. "You still owe me that memo."

"You're making his head big," Logan teased. "He'll think he's golden when it comes to luck or something."

"No, I've got my own good luck charm, thanks," Jackson murmured, thinking of Henry. He believed in his son, all right, and the power of forgiveness. No matter how he'd come to the realization—vision, subconscious longing or a message from a higher power—Jackson wasn't leaving his family. And Henry was going to get tired of seeing Jackson's face standing vigil over his hospital bed.

"I had no doubt about making it once you showed up." Logan spoke low and earnestly. "No doubt, Golden."

The two friends exchanged knowing looks.

The whir of helicopter blades sounded enough like angel wings for Jackson.

"We're going to have to carry you up the hill." Jackson met Logan's gaze squarely. "Unless you want to wait for a stretcher."

"And risk that fire coming back over the other side for seconds? No, thank you."

With effort, Jackson scrambled back up to the overhang and weakly waved Wyatt over.

It didn't take long to get the women loaded into the bird. Jackson managed to hold himself together long enough to help Spider carry a white-faced Logan up the slope. Spider and Jackson carried Logan as gently as they could, each grasping the other's wrist behind Logan's back and under his knees. Logan seemed to hold his breath all the way. Jackson tried to breathe in shallow gasps that didn't send spikes of pain to his ribs.

"Hey, keep it clean, Spider," Logan warned at one point. "I'm not one of your girlfriends from Boise who likes to be groped."

"Tin Man, don't kiss and tell," Spider joked as he paused on the hill to give Jackson a chance to regain his equilibrium. "Besides, you're the one with a babe at every base camp."

"Right now, I'd settle for a beautiful, busty blonde with a name tag on her chest that reads Nurse Nadine."

Spider laughed. "Yeah, and make sure insurance gives you a private room for those intimate sponge baths."

"How long does it take a broken leg to heal?" Logan was dead serious now.

Jackson nodded to Spider that he was ready to tackle the last ten feet of the slope. "I think you've got at least three months of R and R."

Sirus helped Jackson up the last few feet of the incline.

"I'm indebted to you, Jackson," Sirus said solemnly, his injured arm held to his chest. "It was wrong for me to come out here as an observer to try and get a better read on the fire without the proper gear."

"Oh, yeah. Now Socrates admits he's human." Spider rolled his eyes. "Where was all that humbleness five years ago in training camp?"

Ignoring him, Sirus continued. "You have a lot of miles left in you for the line, Golden. I plan on telling them that in Boise. I'm strongly against them assigning you permanently to a desk. We need men like you out here."

Jackson didn't know what to say. Giving up the fire line meant getting Lexie back. But now that he'd proven he could control his fear, fire fighting was possible again. He'd be lying to himself if he said he didn't want back in the Hot Shots. What would Lexie think of that? He'd have to come up with a compromise.

As they lifted off, Logan leaned back against the chopper's wall and said weakly, "You can have your job back, Golden. I think I might be in rehab for a bit."

"I don't want your job."

"I know." Logan's voice was strained with pain but his smile was genuine. "But they'll give it to you anyway."

SURROUNDED BY THE NOISY Silver Bend Hot Shot crew, Lexie didn't hear the helicopter approach until it was almost to the helo pad.

"That's them," Chainsaw yelled over the noise. He started running toward the airstrip.

Lexie couldn't contain herself. She ran, nearly stumbling once because she couldn't take her eyes off the landing chopper. She only stopped at the edge of the helipad because one of the ground crew held her back.

The doors slid open, and Spider helped two women out. The women's faces were streaked with grime and their clothes looked as if they'd rolled in ash. They held on to each other as they bent and hurried away from the helicopter.

Two paramedics ran beneath the blades, carrying a stretcher between them. Lexie almost cried out with relief when she realized the man they loaded onto the stretcher was a blond, pale Logan. Logan was safe!

The rest of the Silver Bend Hot Shots were cocooned around her now. Heidi had slipped in front of her, pulling Lexie's arms over her shoulders. They stood silently as the paramedics wheeled Logan away from the helicopter.

Logan held up a hand when the stretcher reached the group. "Wait a sec."

"Uncle Logan," Heidi said in a small voice. "Are you going to be okay?"

"It's just a broken leg, Runt. I'll be back down at the Pony playing pool with you before you know it."

"Hang in there, Tin Man," Chainsaw said stonily.

Several of the others called similar words of encouragement, watching as they took Logan off to an ambulance. It just as easily could have been one of them being wheeled away.

Lexie looked back toward the helicopter and caught her breath.

*Jackson!*

Spider and Sirus stood just outside the helicopter on either side of Jackson, heedless of the slowing blades above. His arms were looped over their shoulders. All three were covered in soot from head to toe. Blood trickled down the side of Jackson's face, past a blood-soaked bandage wrapped around his head.

With a cry of anguish, Lexie broke through the crowd and ran to Jackson. Somehow, she managed to wrap her arms around him, holding him tight until she heard him gasp.

She gazed up at him. "Are you all right?"

"I think I might have cracked a rib or two, Lex." When she might have loosened her grip altogether, he added, "To hell with the ribs, baby, don't let go. I'm fine."

"Don't forget the possible concussion," Sirus added helpfully.

"Better be quiet, or I'll tell Mom about your broken arm," Jackson retorted between gasps for breath.

Lexie managed to laugh at the easy way the two men joked with each other. Then she took a step back and wiped the tears from her cheeks. "I was so worried. You left this at home." She offered him her track medal.

Jackson closed her hand over the medal, gently shaking his head.

Tears clogged her throat. "I won't let you quit," she said stubbornly. "You can't give up on any of us, either."

"You don't know what it means to me to hear you say that. I'm not giving up. It's just that I've got a new lucky charm." He pulled her back to him. "His name is Henry."

Lexie sobbed into his dirty shirt. "I love you so much. It almost killed me when you left this morning. I don't know what I'd do without you. Will you marry me?"

"We were always going to get married again, Lex," said Jackson. "I was just a stupider man ten hours ago. Because you were capable, I thought that you didn't need me around. It's family first, from now on. I promise. And those signs you've been looking for? They're right here in my eyes."

Sure enough, when Lexie looked into Jackson's eyes, they shone with an energy and hope that she hadn't seen since he'd come back from Russia.

Something rocketed into them. "Dad!"

Jackson grunted, his face pale beneath the grime. "Good to see you too, Runt."

Lexie eased her hold on Jackson and shifted until she stood beneath one of his arms and Heidi underneath the other.

"Let's take him over to the medic tent before he collapses here on the helipad," Sirus said.

"Come on, Pops. Admit it. You just want them to set that arm of yours," Jackson teased.

"What's wrong with his arm?"

They all turned to see Mary, her face as white as Lexie imagined her own had been a few minutes earlier.

"Just a break, love. Nothing that'll slow me down more than a day or two." In three steps, Sirus had his good arm around Mary.

"I was worried," Mary said, her body stiff and unyielding beneath Sirus's arm.

Sirus spoke out to the people surrounding him, Hot Shots and Garretts. "You know, as Spider reminded me earlier, I don't often do something stupid. I think I've just filled my stupidity quota for the next ten years or so."

Mary sucked in a shuddering breath but said nothing.

"It's all right, Mary. I'm back and more than ready for a good cup of coffee. What do you say we stop down the hill at that coffee place you like so much?"

"We'll do no such thing. You're going straight to the hospital." Mary put her arm around Sirus's waist. "I've already buried one husband. I just can't believe you can be so cavalier about this when you could have—"

"It wasn't his fault, Mom." Jackson spoke up. He was leaning on Lexie more heavily now and his breath came in ragged gasps. "The winds shifted unexpectedly."

"Shh," Lexie admonished him. "Don't talk if it hurts."

"It doesn't hurt to kiss you," Jackson whispered, leaning over to place his lips gently on her forehead.

Lexie couldn't resist pressing her body closer to Jackson's, until he drew in a sharp breath and she realized she'd hurt him. "No more kissing until the doctor checks you out."

"And the meteorologist was out fixing equipment in the field, so we didn't realize anything was wrong until Jackson noticed the shifting wind," Rob was saying. "You owe him your lives. He sent the chopper out for a water drop."

"Well, Rob did give me the authority," Jackson added. "I did?"

Jackson grinned. "You didn't stop me."

THE MEDICAL TENT hadn't seen as much action during the entire fire as it did that afternoon. In addition to the expected burns, bee stings and blisters, there were the more severe burns and cuts of those who'd been up on Falcon Ridge.

Rookie seemed to have picked up another burn, for which he apologized profusely to Jackson. "I've learned my lesson,'' the young man promised as he sat in the midst of the crowd that kept coming in to wish the survivors well. Rookie was in his element, sharing his perspective on the fire to anyone who asked.

Logan was the first one taken in the ambulance down the hill to Boise. Chainsaw and Spider had seen him off and then taken charge of Heidi, entertaining her somewhere in base camp while the medics examined Sirus and Jackson.

"Ours will be a November wedding," Sirus said to Jackson. Sirus had somehow managed to convince Mary to drive him to the hospital in Boise. "Are you okay with that?"

"I don't know when you had time to propose." Jackson took in his mother's beaming expression and added, "Besides, it's not up to me, is it, Mom."

"Our wedding will be in October." Mary only had eyes for Sirus.

"In that case, welcome to the family, Socrates." Then he teased, "Or should I say, Dad?"

"We'll talk about the specifics later," Sirus promised. "Over coffee."

Lexie held Jackson's hand while they wrapped his ribs for the trip down the hill. Even with the soot streaked across her face and her hair a wild halo around her deep blue eyes, she looked beautiful. Someone had brought her a spare denim shirt because her breasts had started leaking out on the helipad. The shirt was two sizes too big and hung nearly to her knees, but it covered most of the two large circles staining her T-shirt.

"Rufus is in the SUV. I ran out of gas and I have no idea how we're getting home," Lexie babbled.

"I'm glad you made it." There had been no sweeter sight to him than Lexie waiting for him when he climbed out of that helicopter. "We'll leave your SUV here and drive to the hospital in my truck."

"I'm sure we can get Chainsaw or Spider to take Rufus home," Lexie said.

Jackson squeezed Lexie's hand. "I'm sorry I lost it this morning. I guess I had to go over the edge in order to come back to myself."

"It's all right. We're okay now." Her eyes sparkled. "You're going back to the Hot Shots, aren't you?"

"If you'll let me."

"It was never my choice."

If only his ribs didn't hurt like hell, he'd wrap his arms around her. "We should sell the motor home. You're right, I've accumulated too much junk we'll never use. And I'll figure out some way to be home with the family more often. I won't let you down again."

"Back up to the motor home." She looked distressed. "We can't sell it now. The Silver Bend Hot Shots are family, too. How would we stay at base camp next summer without the motor home?"

"What about wanting a man who's home every day at five? Someone to fix the dishwasher and mow the lawn?"

"Well, those things are helpful, but I can always pay someone. You are not quitting. You're too good at it. Chainsaw says you're their good luck charm." She leaned in close so that only he could hear. "Besides, the sex would be dull if you came home every day at five."

"I wouldn't bet on that." God, he loved this woman. It was amazing that she still had faith in him. Jackson's grin must have stretched from ear to ear. The funny thing was, he now believed in himself. There was something to be said for being needed, even if it was only by a tiny, frail baby who'd never even cracked open his eyes and seen his father.

He held Lexie's hand as if he'd never let her go. "Hey, doc? I need you to bust me out of here. I've got another patient to visit down the hill."

THE EMERGENCY ROOM in Boise was filled with firefighters and Incident Command crew members who wanted to make sure Logan, Sirus and Jackson were all right. While Jackson waited for his turn in X-ray, he sat with Logan. His friend reclined on a bed partitioned off from the rest of the emergency ward by a five-foot screen.

"Is that painkiller kicking in yet?" Jackson asked between shallow breaths.

"It works when I don't move."

"I hope they don't play any dance music in here, then."

"A comedian you're not." Logan closed his eyes.

Imagining that his buddy was feeling sorry for himself, Jackson put a hand on his shoulder. "Three months isn't long to be out. I'll come over and hang out. We can start to train after the New Year. Come spring, we'll be stronger than ever."

"And what will I do with Tess and Hannah?" His tone was dull. "I can't leave them with Aunt Glen for more than an hour or so."

"We'll figure something out. At least you can stay with Deb while you recover."

"She doesn't want me there. Says it's too hard on her."

Jackson suspected it might remind her of dying. Logan didn't appear to be taking the news of his sister's death at all well.

"I think you should be with her."

"She doesn't want me there!" Logan repeated, gripping the bedsheet with one hand.

"So she says. I think you need to be strong for her. I've found recently that strong women still need our support."

Logan looked at his leg, wrapped in a brace until they could get him to Orthopedics. When he spoke, his voice was choked with pain. "I don't think I can do it."

"Do you think she said that when she found out there was no hope?" Jackson tossed back at his friend. "Because as long as you have Aunt Glen and those kids, you have to be strong.''

''I've been giving them money.''

''Come on. They need you more than money.''

''To do what? Sit around and wait for her to die?''

Jackson suddenly felt very old as he dispensed advice about death. ''No. To show Deb's kids that someone loves them and will be there even after their dad left and Deb is…gone. Or have you forgotten how much Aunt Glen meant to you?'' Logan's aunt Glen had taken Logan and Deb in when Logan's father committed the murder-suicide.

Logan wiped a shaky hand across his face. ''No, I haven't forgotten.''

''Up until today, I felt the same way you do,'' said Jackson. ''I was afraid of what would happen to me if Henry died. But it's not about me or you. It's about those that need us most.'' Jackson said these words harshly, berating himself for his callous behavior. He toned his next words down. ''I did everything I could to avoid seeing Henry because it made *me* feel guilty. I almost gave up Lexie because she needed me to be strong for her and I wasn't. I was only trying to take care of me.''

Jackson wasn't the man he'd thought he was. Somehow, he'd been given a handful of second chances—with his career, with his family, and with the only woman he'd ever loved.

An orderly came to wheel Logan down to Orthopedics for his cast.

''That was sweet,'' Lexie called from the other side of the curtain two cubicles down, where she sat with Sirus and Mary.

''You heard it all?'' Jackson felt himself flush and was glad they couldn't see.

''We heard it all,'' Lexie confirmed.

"You sounded real good, Dad." Heidi grinned as she peeked around the curtain. "You made Mom cry again."

LEXIE, HEIDI AND JACKSON scrubbed their hands and arms at the sink outside the NICU. It was late, past midnight. Mary was with Sirus in Orthopedics getting his arm set in a cast. Jackson had received stitches at the medical tent back at base camp, then X-rays in Emergency that identified two cracked ribs, which they taped up tightly again. It would be next season before any of them fought another fire.

The trio entered the bright room and headed straight for Henry's bed.

"I'm sorry, but only two family members at the bedside at a time," announced the sourpuss nurse who had been there the night Henry was born and again last night when Jackson visited. The nurse did a double take when she caught sight of Jackson's bandaged ribs and stitched forehead.

"Call Security, lady. This family isn't breaking up, no matter what you say." Jackson walked right past her as fast as he could, given his reduced breathing capacity.

"Don't think I won't," she replied tartly, sliding a tube down a baby's throat. "If you make any trouble."

Jackson grinned back at her. "Atta, girl."

"Jackson, look." Lexie was staring down at Henry. "They took off his respirator. He's breathing on his own."

"Dr. Kelly took it out this afternoon," the nurse said. "We were all a little surprised when he took right to it."

Jackson stood over Henry, his arm slung around his daughter and the woman who'd never stopped believing in him, remembering the calm voice and bright green eyes of his son on the mountain.

"I'm not surprised. He's an inspiration. He just needed to find the right way to do things, that's all."

## EPILOGUE

"...TWO HEARTS, DESTINED TO BE TOGETHER. I now pronounce you husband and wife. You may kiss the bride."

Cheers rang out as the double wedding inside the Painted Pony came to a close.

Sirus beamed down at his bride after enjoying a chaste kiss. "You owe me for that."

"No use announcing to the world that we won't be needing Viagra on our honeymoon." He'd agreed to a modest public display of affection during the ceremony, despite the fact that their nights were filled with a passion unexpected for a couple their age.

Mary reached up to stroke his cheek. Sirus looked better than Robert Redford in his black tuxedo and cowboy boots. His arm had been out of the cast for a few weeks now, but she'd noticed he still favored it every now and then.

Birdie and Marguerite rushed up to the couple.

"That was a beautiful ceremony." Birdie sniffed into her tissue. "I especially liked the part where Heidi read that poem about love growing stronger each day."

In deference to the occasion, Marguerite wore a low-cut peach dress and a necklace of small bells propped across her full bosom. "You look lovely, Mary."

Standing next·to Sirus in a robin's-egg blue taffeta gown, Mary felt like a princess at the end of a fairy tale. She couldn't remember the last time she'd worn a dress, much less one quite so grand.

"Did you say Lexie was serving her ribs today?" Smiley tottered up to the group. "I do so like her hot marinade. And someone told me she's going to sell them in jars."

"Hot Shot Sauces," Mary confirmed.

"Smiley Peterson," Birdie scolded. "Is that all you can say to the bride and groom?"

"No, it's not. Will you save me a dance?" Smiley winked at Mary.

"I hope you save one for Birdie and me," Marguerite huffed.

"I'm not one for that foolishness," Birdie said. "Let the young people dance."

Marguerite trembled, filling the air with the tinkle of bells. "You're only as young as you feel, Birdie. Maybe it's time you opened your eyes to love."

Birdie narrowed her eyes. "Love or lust?"

"What's come over the two of you? I'm headed for the buffet before you start making moon eyes at me. Weddings do the strangest things to some folk." Shaking his head, Smiley lumbered off.

Mary barely contained her laughter as Birdie and Marguerite continued to spar and Sirus drew her away to greet their other guests.


"HAPPY?" Jackson whispered in Lexie's ear in between greeting guests.

In answer, she kissed his cheek. She was practically bursting with joy that the day they were renewing their vows had finally arrived.

"I never thought I'd be your best man twice." Logan hobbled up on crutches. Rather than detracting from his good looks, the crutches were the pièce de résistance. He was a babe magnet. Every single woman in the room had her eye on him, including Marguerite.

"I never really considered us divorced." Jackson gazed

down at Lexie with such love in his eyes, she thought she might cry.

"Stubborn as mules, the both of you." Logan sighed. "Give me a kiss for luck, darlin'."

Lexie chuckled but obliged, careful of Logan's balance. "I thought you were supposed to kiss the bride and wish her luck."

"You've got all the luck you need in Golden. Trust me on this one." Only a few knew how brokenhearted Logan was, as his smile tended to fool all but those closest to him. Deb had passed away in September from the brain tumor. Deb's nine-year-old twin girls flanked him, looking subdued but precious in matching burgundy velvet dresses. His aunt Glen trailed behind him, her expression a little lost. Jackson and Lexie had been out to see them several times, bringing dinners and what they hoped was the welcome distraction of friends who cared.

"Dad, can I play with Hannah and Tess?" Heidi used her small bouquet to point at Logan's little blond nieces. Her own dress was yellow with blue flowers that matched the color of her grandmother's dress.

"Sure, Runt. Ask if you can spend the night, why don't you?" As Heidi skipped away, Jackson leaned over until his nose almost touched Lexie's, waggling his eyebrows suggestively. "How much longer do we have to stay before we can go home?"

Lexie smiled. "Only about two hours. We've still got to eat, toss the bouquet, snap the garter and cut the cake."

"Planning on cutting out early for some of the benefits of married life, Golden?" Spider stepped up to the couple in his black jeans and black button-down shirt, and elbowed Jackson.

"Restrain yourself, Spider. There are children present." Chainsaw looked over his friend's shoulder at the baby cradled in Lexie's arms.

Lexie gazed down at the little miracle she held. Henry

had been home for four weeks and she still couldn't get used to him. He was a little trouper who, like his father, had a smile for every occasion.

"It's funny how Henry just looks at you sometimes as if he knows exactly what you're thinking," Lexie observed when the Hot Shots had moved on to the buffet.

Jackson offered Henry his finger, which the little tyke quickly latched on to with a strong grip. "He's wise beyond his years, Lex."

Tears filled Lexie's eyes as she remembered how convinced Jackson was that Henry had appeared to him on that fateful day on the ridge. Trying to lighten the moment, she said, "Well, you just remember that when he's sixteen and he borrows your truck without asking."

"He'd never do that. Would you, Henry?"

Henry blew delicate little bubbles either in agreement or denial. Only he knew for sure.

LATER, AS THEY STOOD OUTSIDE waving goodbye to Sirus and Mary, who were departing for a two-month honeymoon in the newly restored motor home, Jackson cuddled his son on his shoulder. Lexie stood a few feet away, giving Rookie a hug and encouraging him to come to the Pony on Saturday night one last time before he moved on to fight fires in Arizona. Lexie and Jackson were running the Painted Pony until his mother and Sirus returned in December.

Lexie looked beautiful in a soft, yellow linen dress, with her thick brown hair pulled up. She'd wrapped her Russian shawl about her shoulders to chase off the chill of the late-October air. Jackson's eyes met hers, sharing the warmth of the moment. She was his wife again. His *love*.

On his shoulder, Henry squirmed under his blanket.

"I'm not going to let you down again," Jackson vowed under his breath. He and Henry shared a special bond. No matter what happened, they'd believe in each other. Jackson had spent almost every hour of every day for three weeks by Henry's bedside after the fire at Falcon Ridge. They'd even celebrated Heidi's twelfth birthday in the NICU. He'd sat next to Henry with Lexie, planning their wedding and her ideas to make her dream for Hot Shot Sauces come true. Every day, the little boy seemed to grow stronger, until he was finally big enough and hardy enough to come home.

Jackson stroked his son's soft cheek. "You've got more than luck on your side, Henry Alek Garrett. You have the faith of your family behind you. And with that, you can accomplish anything."

\*     \*     \*     \*     \*

*Watch for Logan's story, coming soon.*

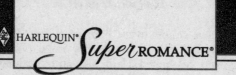

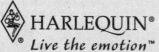

If you enjoyed what you just read,
then we've got an offer you can't resist!

# Take 2 bestselling love stories FREE!

# Plus get a FREE surprise gift!

# HARLEQUIN *Super*ROMANCE®

Sea View House in Pilgrim Cove offers
its residents the sea, the sun, the sound
of the surf and the call of the gulls.
But sometimes serenity is only an illusion...

# Pilgrim Cove

**Four heartwarming stories by popular author**

# Linda Barrett

### The House on the Beach

Laura McCloud's come back to Pilgrim Cove—the source of her fondest childhood memories—to pick up the pieces of her life. The tranquility of Sea View House is just what she needs. She moves in...and finds much more than she bargained for.

**Available in March 2004,
*The House on the Beach*
is the first title in this
charming series.**

*Available wherever
Harlequin books are sold.*

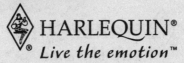

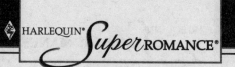

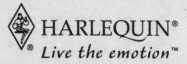